THE
ORDER OF THE
SCALES

Books by Stephen Deas

The Adamantine Palace
The King of the Crags
The Order of the Scales

THE
ORDER OF THE
SCALES

THE
MEMORY OF FLAMES,
BOOK III

STEPHEN DEAS

A ROC BOOK

ROC
Published by New American Library, a division of
Penguin Group (USA) Inc., 375 Hudson Street,
New York, New York 10014, USA
Penguin Group (Canada), 90 Eglinton Avenue East, Suite 700, Toronto,
Ontario M4P 2Y3, Canada (a division of Pearson Penguin Canada Inc.)
Penguin Books Ltd., 80 Strand, London WC2R 0RL, England
Penguin Ireland, 25 St. Stephen's Green, Dublin 2,
Ireland (a division of Penguin Books Ltd.)
Penguin Group (Australia), 250 Camberwell Road, Camberwell, Victoria 3124,
Australia (a division of Pearson Australia Group Pty. Ltd.)
Penguin Books India Pvt. Ltd., 11 Community Centre, Panchsheel Park,
New Delhi - 110 017, India
Penguin Group (NZ), 67 Apollo Drive, Rosedale, Auckland 0632,
New Zealand (a division of Pearson New Zealand Ltd.)
Penguin Books (South Africa) (Pty.) Ltd., 24 Sturdee Avenue,
Rosebank, Johannesburg 2196, South Africa

Penguin Books Ltd.. Registered Offices:
80 Strand, London WC2R 0RL, England

Published by Roc, an imprint of New American Library, a division of Penguin Group (USA) Inc.
Previously published in a Gollancz hardcover edition. For information contact Gollancz, an imprint
of the Orion Publishing Group, Orion House, 5 Upper St. Martin's Lane, London WC2H 9EA.

First Roc Hardcover Printing, February 2012
10   9   8   7   6   5   4   3   2   1

 REGISTERED TRADEMARK—MARCA REGISTRADA

Library of Congress Cataloging-in-Publication Data

Deas, Stephen, 1968–
    The order of the scales/Stephen Deas.
        p. cm.—(Memory of flames; 3)
"A Roc Book"
ISBN 978-0-451-46437-8 (hardback)
1. Dragons—Fiction.   I. Title.
PR6104.E25O73 2012
823'.92—dc23   2011046266

Set in Adobe Garamond
Designed by Ginger Legato

Printed in the United States of America

For Michaela. Wife, lover, friend, muse.

The Kings and Queens of Sand and Stone and Salt

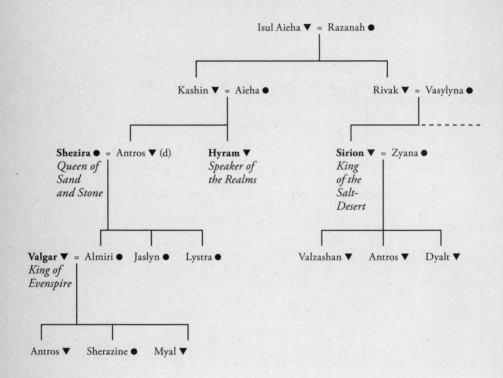

Isul Aieha ▼ = Razanah ●

Kashin ▼ = Aieha ●   Rivak ▼ = Vasylyna ●

Shezira ● = Antros ▼ (d)   **Hyram** ▼   **Sirion** ▼ = Zyana ●
Queen of   *Speaker of*   *King*
Sand   *the Realms*   *of the*
and Stone   *Salt-*
                                                        Desert

Valgar ▼ = Almiri ●   Jaslyn ●   Lystra ●   Valzashan ▼   Antros ▼   Dyalt ▼
King of
Evenspire

Antros ▼   Sherazine ●   Myal ▼

▼ Male

● Female

The Kings of the Endless Sea

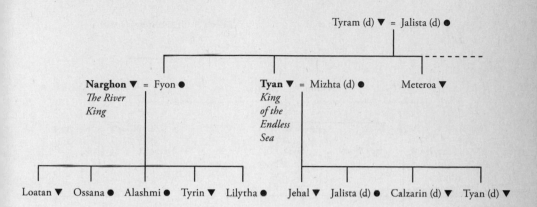

The Kings and Queens of the Plains

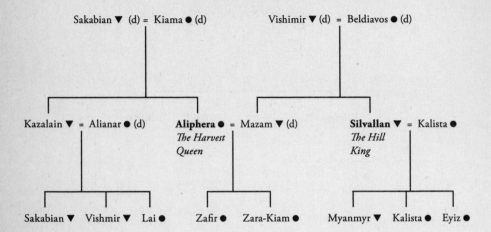

Sakabian ▼ (d) = Kiama ● (d)   Vishimir ▼ (d) = Beldiavos ● (d)

Kazalain ▼ = Alianar ● (d)   **Aliphera ●** = Mazam ▼ (d)   **Silvallan ▼** = Kalista ●
The Harvest Queen   *The Hill King*

Sakabian ▼   Vishmir ▼   Lai ●   Zafir ●   Zara-Kiam ●   Myanmyr ▼   Kalista ●   Eyiz ●

The King of the Worldspine

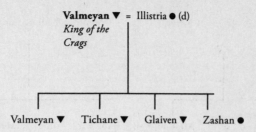

Valmeyan ▼ = Illistria ● (d)
*King of the
Crags*

Valmeyan ▼   Tichane ▼   Glaiven ▼   Zashan ●

THE
ORDER OF THE
SCALES

THE BLOOD-MAGE

They hate us.
They fear us.
They revile us.
They outlaw us.
And as they do these things, they forget what we truly are.
But we do not. We remember. For we are tamed dragons.

I

KITHYR

The blood-mage Kithyr slipped out of the Glass Cathedral and hurried across open ground to the Speaker's Tower. Speaker Zafir and her lover Jehal were gone to war at Evenspire. Tomorrow the battle would rage. Tomorrow Zafir would destroy Almiri and her eyries and then Jehal would turn on her and destroy her in her turn. That was what he had foreseen. That was what the blood-pool had told him.

None of that mattered. What mattered was today. Tonight. His heart was beating fast. A part of him was afraid that he would be caught. Another part urged him onward.

Nighttime shadows filled the Speaker's Yard. Men with lanterns walked the walls, but the walls were wide and far away and their eyes looked ever outward. Two men of the Adamantine Guard stood at the doors of the Speaker's Tower, but if anyone looked closely, they might have seen that something wasn't quite right. Even though the guards stood with their eyes staring open into the darkness, they were fast asleep. Kithyr had done that to them before he left the shelter of the Glass Cathedral, the black misshapen lump of stone that rose behind him. They were only ornamental anyway, those guards. He stepped past and forced the huge doors behind them open, just wide enough to slip inside. He closed them again and then stood in the pitch-darkness and waited to catch his breath. His heart was pounding even faster now.

He moved quietly, each step taken with care. If he was caught now, inside the tower, the Adamantine Men would kill him. He had enough magic to deal with them in twos and threes, but once the alarm was raised, they would come in tens and twenties. If they saw him, they'd catch him. If they caught him, they'd find out what he was. If they found out what he was, they'd kill him. They'd do it quickly too, no waiting for King Jehal or the speaker to come back from their war.

They'd find out what was waiting for him in Furymouth.

At the end of the Chamber of Audience, a huge open staircase rose toward the higher levels of the tower. Kithyr crept behind it to where a second staircase, hidden behind the first, sank into the vaults below. The blood-mage paused as he approached it and closed his eyes. He reached out his senses, searching for any guards that might be waiting for him, listening for their heartbeats, sniffing for the smell of their sweat. With the doors closed, with the speaker away and no torches lit, the huge emptiness of the Chamber of Audience was almost black. Moonlight filtered in through the high windows to cast dim and eerie shadows, and that was all.

The vault was empty too. Four legions of the Guard had marched to war. With the speaker away, the rest were far more concerned about being attacked from the air by dragons than they were about nasty people like Kithyr sneaking around in the palace at night.

He started down the stairs. They weren't a secret, merely hidden and not very well-known. At the bottom were a few small rooms. The place was a sanctuary, a place for the speaker to hide away, where he or she could mysteriously vanish for a few moments and then appear again. If Zafir had been here, there would always be soldiers at the bottom of these stairs. But she wasn't, and so the rooms were empty.

Almost empty. At the bottom, certain he was alone, the magician lit a candle. An entire wall of the first room was covered by bottles of wine racked on top of one another. Several cloaks and robes hung on another, each one meant for a different ceremony and with a different meaning. Unlike the bottles, they were covered in dust. Zafir hadn't worn any of them since she'd come to the throne. Kithyr spared them a glance, then ignored them and moved on to the second little room. This was where the guards should have been. This was what he'd come for. There were weapons here. Ornamental, ceremonial and deadly real. Vishmir's war-axe. If you looked hard enough you could still find flecks of blood, or so they said. The scorpion bolt that killed Prince Lai. Half a dozen other swords and knives that had killed or been carried by speakers over the ages. Kithyr wasn't interested in any of those; he barely even noticed them. What he wanted was hanging on the wall at the far end. Kithyr snuffed out the candle. He didn't need it now. The spear glowed with a very faint light that pushed away the utter darkness that filled the rest of the room.

The Adamantine Spear. The Speaker's Spear. The Spear of the Earth. As old as the world.

He stood in front of it, hardly daring to touch it. No one knew where it had come from. The dragon-priests said that the power of the dragons was bound into it. The alchemists claimed the Order had forged it. Others believed it had been made to tame dragons. All lies. Like the blood-mages, the spear came from a time before there were priests, before there were alchemists, before there were dragons even. The Silver King, the Isul Aieha, had brought it into the realms, but the spear was older than that, older than anything.

For a moment Kithyr couldn't move his hands. They simply refused. The spear was a glittering silver, glowing with a soft inner glory. The blood-mages had stories of other things crafted from silver. No, not stories; *stories* was wrong. Maybe legends. Myths. Yes, myths; that was it. Sorcerers forged of silver who had had the power to change the world on a whim; not just the one who'd come to the realms all those centuries ago, but hundreds, thousands who had once been. The spear came from that time. It had their power and more. In those myths, almost lost now, it could raise volcanoes from the ground, had once shattered the very earth. Trapped within lay something immeasurably potent, or so Kithyr had come to believe. And now that he was standing before it, he was paralyzed, as though the slightest touch of it would burn him to ash. Stupid, since every speaker since Narammed had touched it and none of *them* had been burned to ash.

None of them had been blood-mages, though. None of them had had the old power coursing through their veins.

In an instant of will, he closed his eyes and reached out with both hands to take the spear. His fingers brushed the cold metal of the shaft. He didn't burn to ash. Apart from the chill of the metal, he didn't feel anything at all. After all the anticipation, he felt almost . . . disappointed. There should have been *something*, shouldn't there? Or were all the old stories just that? Was it just a spear and nothing more?

He took the spear off the wall. Still not a flicker.

Perhaps that was for the best. Maybe it had had power once, but maybe that was long ago. Maybe the years had sucked it dry. Nothing lasted forever, after all. If the spear was dead, he'd still done his part of the bargain. Or maybe it wasn't the real spear at all. There had always been other stories. How the Silver King had taken the real spear away with him to his tomb. To the Black Mausoleum, if such a place even existed. Or maybe Vishmir . . .

No, that couldn't be right, could it? He'd know, wouldn't he?

The doubt nagged at him, tugging the corners of his mind. He brushed his fingers over the head of the spear. The tip was as sharp as a needle. Two flat-bladed edges ran down the shaft, as long as Kithyr's forearm. They were like razors. Kithyr ran a fingertip along one. He felt it cut him, felt the blood dribble out of him onto the spear. Instinct made his mind reach into the blood, and through the blood into the spear . . .

Kithyr staggered and gasped and almost dropped it. The snuffed-out candle fell to the floor. The light in the spear died, plunging him into darkness absolute. He hardly noticed. There was no mistake. The spear had a power to it all right. Something hard and bright and unbelievably immense, buried deep within it, so deep that Kithyr wasn't sure that anyone would ever get it out. Something that would surely consume whoever woke it. He was like a moth, drawn to the light of a lantern and suddenly gifted with a full understanding of the fire that lay at its heart. Fire and moths. He shivered and sucked his finger until it stopped bleeding. Cursed. That's what it was. That or it was the most powerful thing in the world.

Fire and moths. He could feel his hunger for it even so. Raw unthinking craving.

Quickly, before he could change his mind, he wrapped the spear in a blanket of black silk, smothering his hunger as he smothered the silver. He climbed softly back up the stairs and reached out his senses into the Speaker's Tower. The Chamber of Audience was still empty. The guards standing outside were still asleep. He slipped between them and pulled the darkness of the night around him like a cloak, hugging it to his chest. A faint light seemed to creep out of the spear again, out of its silk wrapping as if it knew his purpose and was trying to betray him. He felt his heart beating as he ran. He was exposed. A hundred guards walked the walls around him, above him, looking down on him. *They must see me. They must . . .*

They didn't. He slipped from the Speaker's Yard into the Fountain Court and then into the Gateyard. He stopped by the stables there to catch his breath, to tell himself his fear was foolish. The guards on the walls wouldn't see him. Their eyes were cast toward the City of Dragons and the black mass of the Purple Spur beyond, looking for dragons. On a night like this they'd be pressed to see even one of those. *I'm afraid of my own fear, jumping at shadows . . .* That wasn't right. He was a blood-mage. He had the power to literally rip men apart, to turn them inside out. He could barely even remember the last time he'd been afraid.

Was it the spear?

No. Whatever was inside it had been asleep for a long time and slumbered still. Awake, an edge of fear was the least it would bring.

He waited until his breathing eased. His heart still pounded, but that was good. That meant blood flowing fast, that his power was at its strongest.

In the stables he had a horse already saddled. He mounted and crossed the Gateyard. People would see him now, or if they didn't, they would hear him. That was to be expected. Under his skin, blood shifted, sculpted, arranged his features in subtle new ways. When he reached the gates, the Adamantine Men were already coming out of their guardhouse. They shone lanterns in his face and peered at him.

"Who's there?"

Kithyr threw back his hood. The face they saw now was that of alchemist Grand Master Jeiros. A fitting disguise, Kithyr thought. One that amused him, alchemists and blood-mages viewing each other as they did.

"Grand Master." The soldiers bowed. They looked a little confused.

"The gate, if you please," mumbled Kithyr. His face was that of the alchemist, but his voice was his own. He was counting on the soldiers not knowing the difference.

"We are at war. The gates are closed at night," said one of the soldiers. Presumably he was the one in charge. Kithyr pulled a flask out of his cloak and held it out to the man.

"Cold night, eh?" he muttered.

The man looked askance at the flask. Then he shrugged, accepted it and took a swig. "Still can't open the gates at night. Night Watchman's orders for as long as the speaker's away." The soldier wiped his lips on his sleeve and handed back the flask. Kithyr waited a few seconds. The liquid in the flask was mostly brandy, as strong and as vicious a spirit as he could find. What wasn't spirit was blood. His blood. He waited and then he felt the connection form, felt himself reaching inside the soldier.

"I am Jeiros," he said softly. Who he sounded like didn't matter anymore. "Even now, I may pass. That is my authority."

The soldier nodded. "Very well. Open the gate."

His men looked confused and didn't move. "Sir?"

"Come on, lads! This isn't just anyone. This is the grand master himself, and that makes him the man who gives the orders around here until the speaker returns. So if he wants to go out moonlighting into the city in the middle of the night, who are we to stop him?" The soldier leered. Annoying.

"I have business of the realms, man. If I wanted whores I'd have them sent." *There's no love lost between the Adamantine Men and the alchemists either,* he reminded himself. *Tolerate it. We'll soon be gone.*

The gates started to open. Kithyr feigned patience. One of the guards was missing. The soldier hadn't gone back into the gatehouse either. A silver to a copper he'd gone to wake up the Night Watchman. Kithyr offered his flask around to the other soldiers while he waited. A few of them took it, which would help if it came to a fight. Others looked at him with a deep suspicion and shook their heads. As soon as the gate was open enough, Kithyr kicked his horse into a canter. He was out of the palace in a flash, on his way down the hill to the City of Dragons. He didn't linger. The Night Watchman had a suspicious, devious and thorough sort of mind and wasn't the sort to let little things slide. He'd come down to the gate. It was entirely possible that he'd go and bang on the grand master alchemist's door even in the middle of the night just to make sure he was really gone. Kithyr might have hours or days or he might have a mere handful of minutes before his deception was unmasked. Once that happened, they'd know him for what he was. There was only one way for even a grand master alchemist to be in two places at once. The cry would rise up. *Blood-mage!* And the hunt would begin.

He had long enough, though. Long enough to get from the palace to the City of Dragons. Long enough to leave his horse in the stables of an inn. Long enough to hide the spear under the straw, change into some clothes that were hidden in the saddlebags of the next horse along and walk a street or two to the house of a wealthy grain merchant. Long enough to knock on the servants' entrance and be let inside by a man he'd enslaved months ago. Half the merchant's house was under his power now. The other half had no idea who or what he was. He was just another assayer, a man who occasionally weighed out their grain and checked their measures.

"Master weigher." A man stirred from where he'd been dozing by the kitchen fire. This one didn't move and bow like the servant, and his eyes cut the gloom like knives.

"Master Picker," murmured Kithyr. "It's done. Go, if you want to see it."

The Picker grumbled something and unfolded himself from his chair. He went outside without another word. In the morning Kithyr would find the spear again. He would take it, wrapped in its silk, and in King Jehal's city he would hand it over for what the Picker and the Taiytakei had promised him they would bring. The power of the Silver King himself. For the spear, they said, that power could be his. Years of planning. Years of learning. Years of preparation, and only one last chasm to cross.

Between here and Furymouth, there was the small matter of a dragon-war in the way.

THE EYRIE-MASTER

We are the masters of the dragons, no matter what the kings and queens of the realms might think. They sit in their palaces and wallow in their decadence and toss out their decrees and edicts, but without us they are nothing. We hold the keys to their power and they know it. We are their slaves and their puppets and their eyes are ever watching us, for they all, deep down, wonder the same thing: *Who does my eyrie-master truly serve? Is he bound to the alchemists as his position demands? Has he been bought by my enemies? Or is he mine, owned heart and soul? Have my bribes and threats been enough?*

Thus are our lives both rich and glorious, yet prone to unexpected interruptions and abrupt ends.

2

A BAD DAY AT THE ROCKS

Meteroa almost made it. He could actually see the bright morning sunlight streaming in through the doors that led out onto the eyrie rocks when the first flame strikes came in and a plume of fire erupted down the passage toward him. He had just enough time to slam shut the visor on his helm and spread out his arms, as if he could somehow catch the flames and stop them from reaching Queen Lystra behind him. *Whatever happens to her happens to you.* Jehal's words. Meteroa was quite sure that Jehal meant every one of them.

The fire swallowed him up, weak and at the end of its reach, not enough to even stagger him. His dragon-scale shrugged off the heat. He whipped around for Lystra, his heart in his mouth for an instant, but she was still there, reeling slightly, openmouthed, maybe a little red-faced and singed at the edges, but otherwise unhurt. The baby, wrapped in its blankets, started to cry again. Meteroa pushed her back down the hallway.

"Wait here out of sight! If I shout at you to come, then *run!*" *If we manage to get out of here, a red face and scorched hair will be a small price to pay.*

He reached the outside of the eyrie, cowering in the grand doorway, blinking in the sudden sunlight. The sky was bright blue, the air filled with fire and dragon-cries. Circling the Pinnacles were the dragons themselves. Hundreds of them. Hundreds and hundreds and hundreds.

Vishmir's cock! He ducked back inside as another dragon strafed the eyrie-top and then another.

So much for getting out.

Two riders cowered beside him. He cast his eyes about, looking for something—anything—that might inspire him. Low battlements surrounded the top of the fortress, carefully designed to give cover from dragon-fire. Tall spikes littered the place. They looked like decoration, but Meteroa knew better: under clay tiles were solid iron prongs embedded deep into the mountain, there to deter dragon-landings. Most of the rest of the flat top of the peak was taken up by the Reflecting Garden, a bizarre relic of the Silver King, with its fountain that conjured water from the air, its channels and pools where water flowed upwards and wouldn't lie flat. The handful of ornate little buildings between the garden and the tiny eyrie that made up the rest of the fortress was no more than a glorified entrance hall into the labyrinth beneath.

Or a place to hide when dragons were burning the shit out of everything. He crouched down and squinted, looking for a dragon he recognized, Prince Hyrkallan's B'thannan or King Sirion's Redemption. He didn't know what dragon Queen Jaslyn rode anymore. He didn't see either of those, though. What he did see was Prince Tichane's colossal Unmaker, heading straight toward the eyrie-top. The dragon was clutching a cage in his fore-claws, the sort of cage that the Mountain King used for carrying slaves. And soldiers. Meteroa ducked as another flight of dragons flew overhead, raking the top of the fortress with fire again. Clearing the ground for a landing.

The King of the Crags. Ancestors! If they knew how few men he had here . . .

He bolted back down the entrance stair and ran through the huge hall below. The High Hall, where Queen Zafir and Queen Aliphera before her had welcomed kings and queens and even speakers. One wall was open to the sky, letting the sun sweep in through a row of ornate carved columns while the rest lay in thick shadow, littered with paintings and statues, layered with exquisite rugs and tapestries—or at least that's the way it had been before Valmeyan's dragons had filled it with fire. All that was left now were blackened statues, a few charred shards and a haze of smoke. Meteroa hugged the far wall, away from the light in case one of the dragons came back for another go. His riders and his men-at-arms were waiting for him in a second hall lit by shafts of sunlight from above. Milling about, scared, uncertain. Useless.

"Down!" he shouted. He paused. Valmeyan could bring as many men as he wanted. The tunnels and halls of the Pinnacles were the perfect place for a small band of riders to hold off almost any number. They'd been built for exactly that. And as for dragons . . . The fortress had been carved out of the stone long before the coming of the Silver King, back when the dragons had flown free. He could seal himself inside and live off Queen Zafir's siege stocks and probably last almost forever. Question was, should he bother? There were rules to war. Written in *Principles*. His dragons were already lost, and to add to his problems there were men still loyal to Zafir lurking in the lower tunnels. If you believed the stories, there were ways out down there, catacombs and tunnels that led all the way down to a scattering of secret doors among the cellars of the Silver City a mile below. There were supposed to be tunnels that ran for a hundred miles and more, as far as the banks of the Fury. There was even supposed to be an underground river, fed by the waters of the Reflecting Garden, which tumbled and splashed through the heart of the mountain from its very top. If any of those rumors were true, Zafir's men would know them. Whereas he didn't.

Not a nice thought. Of course, if you believed *all* the stories, the tunnels were also filled with dark devices of the Silver King that would rip a man's soul from his flesh. So maybe not such a troublesome thought after all.

Meteroa slammed his fists together. Plenty of Princess Kiam's servants had chosen to stay and serve their new masters rather than flee into the tunnels. They weren't soldiers. To them, one dragon-lord was as good as another. Maybe one of them knew the way. If they did, they'd sell their knowledge. "Jubeyan, Gaizal, Xabian, you stay with me to welcome our guests. Hyaz, take Queen Lystra down past the Grand Stair. Hold there. If there are tunnels down to the Silver City, it'll be the servants who know them. Find a man who can show you the way. If I do not return ahead of Valmeyan's soldiers, do whatever you must to escape. Above all else, your duty is to preserve the life of your prince and your queen and bring them to King Jehal. Do you understand?" Outside, everything had fallen dangerously quiet. No shrieks of dragons, no roars of fire. Valmeyan must have landed. "Don't take any other servants with you. Lock them away if you can. I'm sure they'll all be just as keen to serve the King of the Crags as they were to serve us. They'll none of them mind the purse of gold that will doubtless be their reward if they help Valmeyan to catch you." *Best if you slaughtered them, but I suppose I'll not mention that.*

Hyaz nodded sharply and turned to go. You could see the eagerness in him, fluffing him up with his own importance.

"Hyaz!" The rider froze, mid-step. "If you *do* escape, whoever shows you the way will deserve a reward. A generous one, fit for the service he has done for us. Enough that he has no reason to help others follow you." *In other words, gut him as soon as you don't need him anymore; but since I can hardly say that with Lystra standing right in front of me, you'll just have to work it out for yourself.* Meteroa could hear shouting now, echoing down from the passages above. The King of the Crags was coming. He shooed Hyaz and Lystra and most of the rest away and strode back toward the little eyrie with the three riders he could best trust not to stab him in the back. *At least there isn't space up there for more than half a dozen dragons at once. It'll take time for Valmeyan to mass men for an assault.*

Hazy figures were moving in the smoke at the other end of the High Hall. They shouted, their words lost in the echoes of the hall. An arrow ricocheted off the wall beside him. He ducked back out of sight.

"You should know that you're shooting at Prince Meteroa," he shouted. "I hold the Pinnacles in the name of King Jehal, who, if you haven't heard by now, is in the Adamantine Palace, sitting on the Speaker's Throne." Unless Valmeyan had gone there first. That was always a possibility. *Oh well, if Valmeyan's men know any better, they'll tell me soon enough.* "Have you come to negotiate your surrender? Because if you have, I'm all ears."

The High Hall went very quiet. He risked a glance back out, but nothing was moving in the smoke.

"Show yourself," shouted a voice.

"So you can shoot at me again? I don't think so." There was always the chance that Valmeyan had simply sent in a couple of hundred of those slave-soldiers he was so fond of. They weren't known for their tenderness. "Perhaps you might tell me to whom you answer?" He toyed with acting all outraged and ranting about acts of war and terrible consequences, but that would have been a bit rich, all things considered.

"We fight for the King of the Crags," called a rousing voice. A few ragged cheers echoed after.

"Valmeyan himself is here? Well I certainly won't mind talking to *him* about which one of us is going to surrender." Time. The more time he gave Hyaz, the better.

There was a pause and then a different voice rang out. A woman's voice. "Lord Meteroa. Do you still have my sister, or have you murdered her like you murdered my uncle? Like Jehal would have murdered me?"

Zafir!

Meteroa's skin tingled. For a moment he couldn't move, couldn't even think. *Zafir? But she's dead. She fell at Evenspire. Jehal told me!* Yet there was no mistaking the voice. Zafir, very much alive. Which meant that maybe Jehal wasn't the speaker after all. Which meant that . . .

Which meant that he could piss all over whatever *Principles* had to say about the rules of war.

Shit!

Zafir was here for Lystra. Probably for her little sister Princess Kiam too. But mostly here for revenge and blood and plenty of it. Zafir alive! Zafir and her cages . . . He signaled to Jubeyan and the others behind him. *Back. Retreat. No quarter.* Then he waited as they slipped away. *So let's see how much time I can buy for you. Jehal, if I die here, I am going to come back and haunt you for a very long time. You were supposed to get rid of her.*

"Speaker Zafir! What a pleasant surprise. We'd heard you were dead."

"Well I am not, Meteroa. Is my sister alive or dead?"

"I am at a loss, Your Holiness, to know which you would prefer."

"You have one chance, Meteroa. Send out my sister and Queen Lystra. If you do that, I will give you a day to gather your riders and leave. I don't care where you go. I don't recommend Furymouth. You'll not find a friendly welcome in Three Rivers or Valin's Fields or Bazim Crag for that matter. The south is ours, Meteroa. You have lost. It is pointless to fight. I have no particular reason to kill you. Yet."

"Tell me, Zafir, is Valmeyan's hand up your skirt or is yours up his? I'll speak with the puppet master, if you please." *And now, time to run.*

He might have stayed to shout something else. Something defiant. A last few insults. Then dozens of soldiers would charge through the High Hall, crazed half with fear and half with bloodlust, ready to chop to bits anyone they found at the other end. Instead, he slipped away as quietly as he could. Once he thought he was far enough away that no one would hear his footsteps, he ran. Eventually they'd realize no one was there and they'd follow him anyway, but this way would take them longer. It wasn't exactly the honorable thing, and missing out on a good insult was always a disappointment, but at least this way skipped the part where he was chopped to bits, if only for a while. There were certain things he had to believe. That Jehal sat on the Speaker's Throne. That hundreds of dragons still filled the Adamantine Eyries: their own, Zafir's, Almiri's, Narghon's. That if he held out for long enough, Jehal would come. Yes, at times like these a man had to pick a thing, crush his doubts and believe in that thing as he believed in the rising of the sun. He *could* hold the Pinnacles forever. So that's what he would do.

Beyond the Grand Stair, where Meteroa would make his stand, lay Zafir's Enchanted Palace. Beyond that, the fortress spiraled down and down. Past the Hall of Mirages where every exit led you right back where you started. Now there was a thing. Before he'd seized the place, he'd assumed it was a child's fairy tale, but no. Real. Place made his skin crawl. And that was just the start of what the Silver King had left behind.

Yes, best not to delve too deep.

At the top of the Grand Stair Jubeyan was waiting for him. He looked flushed and out of breath and was holding a loaded crossbow. Gaizal and Xabian were with him.

"You weren't supposed to wait for me," snapped Meteroa. *Even if I'm glad that you did.* He didn't wait for an answer, but bounded down. The steps were huge, each one some twenty feet across. They must have spiraled down at least two hundred feet into the rock. No time to stop and admire the workmanship, though, not with Valmeyan's soldiers on his heels. He could hear them, if he stopped to listen. They weren't far behind. Not far at all . . .

Beyond the arch at the bottom of the stairs was a vast vaulted hall. There were no windows here, no sun and no sky, yet a warm yellow light filled the room from above, and it was just an atrium, the gateway to Zafir's Enchanted Palace. Beyond it lay the colossal Octagon, Zafir's throne room, the largest in the realms, where the Kings and Queens of the Harvest Realm held their court, where the blood-mages had held court before them, all the way back to the Silver King himself. A place of eerie beauty. Of walls that grew light and dark of their own will, mimicking the rise and fall of the sun and the moon outside. Of clean cool damp air, empty of any taint of woodsmoke. Sleeping in the halls of the Pinnacles was like sleeping out on a fresh and warm summer's night.

He shuddered. Everything about the Fortress of Watchfulness, right from the Reflecting Garden and its Endless Fountain at the top, down to whatever lurked a mile beneath his feet was all *wrong*. And it had him trapped.

Don't think about it. He ran through the arch and pointed up. "There." The ceiling here was different. Lower. A great stone slab was poised over his head. He'd known it was there before he'd even left Furymouth. What he hadn't believed until he saw it now with his own eyes, until he stopped to actually *look* at it, was the scale of it. A block of stone the size of a large barn and massive enough to crush a dragon flat. It was simply hanging in the air.

Pulleys. It has to be pulleys. He shivered. *Don't think about it!* However it worked, the principle was the same. *Stone comes down; no one gets in.* He'd made it his business to understand the fortress when he'd been planning his own attack, and now that knowledge would cut nicely the other way. Speed, that was the key. Valmeyan had already been too slow.

"Your Highness, there are men on the stairs. I hear voices."

Beyond the arch, hidden behind the hangings on the wall, there was a hole in the wall. He reached inside, felt something cold. His fingers closed around it . . .

And paused. He could see Princess Kiam, Zafir's sister, staring at him. They'd barely spoken since he'd taken her surrender and brought her back to the fortress, but they'd spoken that day, standing right here under the great hanging stone. He remembered the look in her eye, clear as a mountain lake, full of hate, blood oozing from a broken lip that she did nothing to wipe away. *No one built this place. It grew. On its own. It was always here. Mock me if you like, Prince, but this palace is alive and I am its mistress and I will have it eat you.* She'd spat out a gobbet of blood. Meteroa looked down. There was nothing on the floor, no trace of a stain. He didn't remember anyone cleaning it up.

There were other shapes carved in the wall behind the hanging. When he pushed the hanging aside, he saw that they were archways, sealed up and leading to nowhere. They were everywhere. The place was littered with them. Whispers said they opened sometimes, once in a lifetime, on to some inexplicable and unknown realm.

"My *Lord*! They *come*!"

You could argue all day about ghosts and old magics, but Valmeyan's men were real enough. Meteroa reached in again and pulled. His hand came out clutching a silver rod about as long as his forearm. The stone quivered. A grating noise filled the hall and then the stone came down, fast. It smashed into the floor and shook the room so hard that Meteroa fell to his knees. Dust filled the air. The archway was gone. Blocked completely. He stared at the piece of silver in his hand. His riders looked shocked. Understandable, but even if he felt the same, he couldn't let them see it.

"I appear to have the key." Then he smiled. "They won't be getting in that way then."

"My Lord, how do we get out?"

A good strategy for questions you couldn't answer, Meteroa had found, was to ignore them. Farther down, below the marvels of the Enchanted Palace, there were balconies and storerooms. Food and water for years. Beyond that . . . Meteroa gave half a shrug. He didn't know whether Jehal was dead or alive, but that really didn't matter anymore. Trapped was trapped. The fortress gave him nightmares, but still it was hard not to feel at least a little gleeful. They'd either find a way out or they wouldn't.

Until they did, there was always the other thing that had made the three peaks of the Pinnacles famous. Scorpions, giant crossbows big enough to hurt even a dragon. Hundreds of them. Buried in the walls of the most impregnable dragon-proof fortress in the world.

With a grin and a crack of his knuckles, he turned to face his waiting riders. If someone out there wanted a war, so be it.

THE DRAGON

There is an order to the world that you have perverted with your ways. It will not last; and when the natural shapes of things return, your pleas for mercy will not be heard.

3

FREEDOM

For all they were about to do, there was no joy to be had in it. Kemir lay at night beside Snow, eyes wide-open, the dragon keeping him warm. He saw Sollos, his cousin, faceup in the shallows of a river, lifeless, the water stained with his blood. He saw Nadira, the last time he'd seen her alive. And he saw Snow, rising from the lake of freezing blue glacier water. Sometimes he imagined he saw the rider who'd killed his cousin, Semian, head hacked off in a bed of bloody ice. It gave him no pleasure anymore.

He didn't see anything else.

During the day, when they were on the move, he still saw the same faces. Ghosts. Too many of them. He ate because his stomach told him he was hungry, drank because his throat was dry, pissed when his bladder demanded it. For the rest of the time he was numb, shifting aimlessly between emptiness and a rage of such intensity it seemed it must surely melt the stones beneath his boots. Those were the times when he traded insults with the dragons, told them they were useless, that they were cowards to be scared of a few scorpions. Always got a rise out of them, that one, particularly Snow. He didn't know why he taunted them. Because that was who he was. Because, perhaps, deep down he hoped they would tire of him. Would eat him and send him on his way.

They didn't, though.

Your drear is tiresome. The dragons had settled along a ridge of black rock, steep and sharp and speckled with snow. Either side and all around, white-capped mountains rose around them. A thick blanket of cloud lay across the eastern edge of the Worldspine and it was snowing. Not heavily, but enough to blur everything more than a valley away into a featureless white.

Around Kemir, steam rose from the scales of the dragons. The snow melted as soon as it touched them, water running in tiny little rivers and pooling in the hollows of their neck and shoulders. The ridge looked down over a typical mountain valley, steep and damp and lush and green, or it would have been if it hadn't vanished into a haze of gray and falling snow. Behind him, on another day when it wasn't smeared away, he would have seen the northern edge of the Raksheh, the great forest of the western realms.

Across the valley lay another mountain, dark blotches of stone barely visible through the thickness of the air. A mountain much taller than the ridge where they sat. The dragons had finally reached their destination. An eyrie.

"Bite me." They'd picked the northernmost eyrie of the Mountain King's realm. Something to do with the king moving his dragons to the south. Kemir had no idea how they knew what Valmeyan was up to, but they did. From what he could tell, they could sense the other dragons heading south. Sensed them from dozens of miles away. Maybe hundreds.

The temptation grows ever stronger, little one. Snow sat back on her hind legs and pointed a front claw into the whiteness across the valley. It had taken three weeks to meander their way this far without being seen and now they were where the dragons wanted to be, at the little mark on the map that Kemir carried and read for them, the map that was perhaps the only reason they tolerated him. They were waiting for twilight. Their impatience was a tangible thing, crackling the air between them. They endured it, though. They knew they would not have long to wait.

Three weeks in the company of four impatient and bloodthirsty dragons.

"What's stopping you?"

Your nest-mate who wanted to die.

Nadira. Yes, Kemir remembered her well enough. "That's what you said after you ate her. Convenient that she wasn't around to disagree, eh?" An old wound between them, that. One that would never go away. "What about her? Guilty conscience?" A dragon with a conscience? What was he saying?

I have eaten many of your kind, Kemir. Many have died between my teeth and in my claws. I am curious to know where you go. I try to follow your spirits as they flee, but I cannot. Your journey through the realms of the dead is more fleeting than ours, yet your destination is somewhere other, somewhere I cannot reach. Is it not unsettling to have such uncertainty before you? For our kind it is simple. Death, rebirth, death, rebirth, over and over and over again. But for you? You have such a mystery to face. Fear comes to your kind so easily, yet rather than fear this, you yearn for it. Why do you wish to die, Kemir?

The finality of Snow's question punctured Kemir's apathy. For a moment he did feel afraid. For a moment, until he realized that no, she didn't mean to eat him there and then. She was still pointing to the eyrie.

We go.

Kemir snorted. Smirked. Almost laughed. "Sun's not set yet. Got bored of waiting, did you?"

She sounded almost embarrassed now. *The snowfall will hide us. Kemir?*

"Dragon?"

If this is your time to die, what is it that awaits you?

"My ancestors, I suppose." He shrugged. "I have no idea."

And yet you go without fear. She spoke with wonder in her thoughts. *It is . . . surprising.*

"Disappointment is it, knowing you'll just come back and try again, eh? Not exciting enough for you? Think you're missing out, eh?"

If I die, my destiny is certain. I will return as a hatchling. I will be bound and I will have the choice to starve or take the potions your alchemists place into my food. There is no mystery to my fate. Yours, though, it is . . . It is a curiosity. Come. We are here. The beginning and the end. She lowered herself to let him climb onto her back. *I will not die today.*

"That's good to know, dragon, because I don't plan to either." Kemir paused for a moment before climbing onto the dragon's back. He could refuse. Just say no. Then maybe she'd eat him despite what she said and they'd be finished. Was that better or worse than flying into battle with her? He was her slave, when all was said and done.

But then, slavery was still life and life meant being not dead, and anyway, they were about to bring down a whole skyful of pain on some dragon-knights, and he hated dragon-knights. It was a dull hate, shorn of its old sharpness, but it was still there. He settled on Snow's back. For a moment he thought he caught a flash of some other thought from her, something far more laden with purpose than vague musings on what might happen if they failed. Only a flash, though; then Snow lunged forward and spread her wings, and the other dragons were moving beside her, kicking themselves off the mountainside, gliding across the open space of the valley, straight toward the eyrie with the setting sun somewhere behind the cloud. For a moment, suspended high over the valley, Kemir could see nothing at all. Nothing except whiteness, everywhere. Snow powered through the sky as fast as she could fly, the wind howling in Kemir's face. Then he caught a glimpse of a dark shape and then another. If anyone from the eyrie had seen them coming, Kemir wouldn't have known anything about it. He supposed they must have though, since he felt the familiar sharp spike of Snow's anger that came as a scorpion bolt found its mark. She'd taken enough of those with Kemir on her back that he knew the sensation exactly. The flash of fury, the desire to turn at once and lash toward whatever it was that had caused the pain.

He pressed himself down and clung on, gripping even tighter, turning his head away from the wind and closing his eyes as he felt the familiar tension in her shoulders. He was used to that now, a shudder just a moment before the flames would come. He hunched into himself and let the scorching air flood over him. At least this time he had proper dragon-scale armor and a helm to protect his face. Then Snow landed. She lurched and staggered and shrieked and spat fire over and over again. Pieces of something—loose stones—showered down around them.

Slowly Kemir opened his eyes. They were on the burning roof of some building. Beams cracked and split and stones crumbled with Snow's every move. She lunged forward, jumping down, lumbering across the ground.

Clouds of snow flew up from the wind of her wings while Kemir bounced up and down like a rag doll on a string. He caught a fleeting glimpse of panicked men before Snow lashed her tail and smashed one end of the building to bits. He wrapped his arms around his head and cringed as pieces of stone, burning wood and charred tiles rained around him. They bounced and thumped off his armor, stolen from knights Snow had killed weeks ago. That would be a thing to do when they were done here, he decided. Look for some better armor. Preferably a suit that fit properly. Preferably a suit that didn't have any parts missing. It would be nice too if it didn't have any gaping holes that were an exact match for Snow's teeth.

The dragon lunged forward into the guts of the building and doused its innards with fire. More stonework clattered around Kemir's head.

"Do you mind?"

You have metal and dragon-scale to protect you.

"Not much bloody good if the whole roof falls on top of me, is it? Even you might notice that. Some of these beams are bigger than I am." *Bugger this. I could be down in some valley somewhere, cozy and warm. Why did I stay with these monsters? Right now we could have been* . . . It was a ritual now, thinking these things. They both knew it. He flew with the dragons because he had nowhere else to go. Because everyone else was dead. Because of . . . Oh, what was the point? Nadira, Sollos, they were pricks on his conscience, faces to remind him of what happened to those who trusted themselves to him. He put his mind elsewhere. To the eyrie outside, to the mountain, covered in a thick coat of soft white snow, glowing gently in the fading light and about to be set on fire.

Snow backed out of the wreckage. The other three dragons had come in behind her, smashing their way into the buildings of the eyrie, shaking the mountain as they landed. As soon as they were down they began to move methodically apart, sweeping fire back and forth. Mist and steam swirled around them. Farther away, the snow was falling harder now. As Kemir watched, he saw one of the dragons rear up and use its tail to hurl a stone the size of a horse straight into a squat tower that bristled with scorpions. A second dragon raced across the ground, arriving only moments later, pouring fire into all its holes and then ripping it apart. Snow jogged around the ruins of what had apparently been a barracks. A group of men ran from it, screaming briefly before they burned. *Your kind are too fragile.*

"You're such a comfort."

Snow thrust her head into a door at the far end of the building and let loose another torrent of flame. Then she reared up into the air and landed her front half on the end of it. The building groaned and creaked and then collapsed.

Where are the alchemists?

"Try over there." Kemir pointed. In the flickering light of the burning barracks, looming out of the falling snow, a little cluster of buildings lay dimly outlined against the mountainside, half buried in white. Snow peered into the gloom. She stretched out her neck toward them and began to walk, slowly at first, then faster, shaking the mountain with every step.

They will not escape.

"I wouldn't hurry. It's not as though there's anywhere they can go."

They will have tunnels. They will hide under the ground.

Kemir shrugged. Probably would though, wouldn't they? He had no idea.

I have been looking forward to this day.

"Revenge, Snow?" Kemir sniggered. Snow claimed dragons didn't understand revenge. Didn't understand forgiveness either.

No, Kemir. Freedom.

"Right. Do you mind if I get off before you forget I'm here again?" Wind whipped at him, stinging his ears. The snow was easing as the day gave way to twilight.

If you must. Snow stopped and lowered her neck. Kemir could feel her impatience, her anger, her anticipation. And something else, something carefully hidden but not quite carefully enough. Pleasure? No, that wasn't it; that was too mild a word. Joy? Still not enough. *Ecstasy? A dragon-sized helping of vicious desire?*

I am losing patience, Kemir.

"You never had any in the first place." He shrugged. "Don't blame me if someone sneaks up and shoots you with a scorpion." He jumped off the dragon's back. On the ground, the snow was up to his knees. There'd be frozen feet and frostbite in the morning if he wasn't careful, but he'd had enough of being stuck to Snow's back. "Look after my stuff, dragon. I'll take it out of your hide if you don't. And try not to eat anyone you shouldn't."

One day, little one Kemir, you will test my restraint at the wrong time.

"And how would I do that, dragon? Can't test something that doesn't exist, now can I?"

Snow snarled, but she still couldn't quite hide her exhilaration. Kemir watched her go, bounding on toward the alchemists' houses, leaping up into the air with a great shriek and then landing on top of them, plumes of snow bursting like clouds around her, smashing left and right with her tail and burning everything into a thick haze of ash and steam. Kemir left her to it. Two of the other dragons had already made their way up the peak to the castle where the eyrie-master and his riders lived and were setting fire to it. He couldn't see much, but the bursts of orange light in the white sky told him enough. The last dragon had sought out the eyrie dragons and settled in their midst, standing guard. If Kemir strained his ears over the havoc and carnage that Snow had become, he thought he could hear them quietly calling to each other. He walked away, launching a vicious kick at a lump in the snow. That was another reason to be away from the dragons. He needed to think. Needed to think somewhere far enough away that they wouldn't be listening in. How far away that was, he had no idea.

Think. Yes. What was he doing here? That was the nub of it. What was he doing here? What was he doing flying with these dragons?

Killing dragon-knights. That was the obvious answer. *Putting an end to their tyranny.*

And then what? He had no answer to that.

He trudged on through the snow. The last rays of the dying sun were still doing a decent enough job of lighting up the mountainside, that and the eerie glowing fog that surrounded where the dragons were, a mist of steam lit up from within by the remnants of their fire. *In case anyone doesn't realize that we're here.*

What am I doing here? What I'm doing is staying alive, that's what I'm doing here.

Although frankly, he wasn't sure why.

4

THE STONE MAN

He didn't get very much farther before he had to stop. In front of him was a frozen lake, presumably the place where the eyrie dragons took their water. Kemir had never been to this particular eyrie, but he'd been to others and knew how they worked. The alchemists kept the dragons pliant and dull with their potions, which they gave to the beasts either in their food or in their water, usually both. So if this was where the dragons took their water, the lake was probably laced with dragon poison. Or dragon-make-stupid potion or whatever the alchemists happened to call it.

He thought about walking across it—keep on going, never come back—but you never knew with frozen lakes whether the ice was as thick as your leg or as thick as your fingernail, and there was really no reason to go and find out. Instead, he turned to follow the edge of the ice as it arced toward the valley below. A few run-down old buildings lay ahead of him that way, perched by the edge of the lake. Thick snowdrifts sat between them, more on the roofs. Half buried and half frozen. The sort of place to put unwanted sell-swords and the like. Not a part of the eyrie where dragon-knights would live, but still, they sometimes turned up in the most unusual places.

Almost as he thought it, he caught a glimpse of something moving. Some*one*. He tensed, nocked an arrow to his bow and dropped to a crouch. Whoever it was, they weren't likely to be friendly. He tried to remember what he'd seen from the air as Snow had approached the eyrie. Nothing useful. Most of the time his eyes had been screwed shut, and even when they weren't, he'd had a snowstorm blowing in his face. He drew the arrow back a way as warmth filled him. It would be good to kill a dragon-knight again.

Somewhere behind him one of the dragons let out a mighty shriek, loud enough to make him flinch. The sharp tang of smoke was starting to taint the air. By the end of the night you'd be able to smell what had happened here right across the mountain.

Whoever was there, they'd vanished among another collection of shacks toward the edge of the mountain. Kemir peered into the gloom. He shouldered his bow and let his hands drift to the knives in his belt as he crept a little closer. Knives were better for close work.

His feet were starting to hurt. The cold.

A scuff of leather on stone and a half-imagined glimpse of movement alerted him again. He peered into the fading twilight. The sun was behind the other peaks now, the sky still lit up in purples and orange on the horizon, nothing but the dark gray snow clouds above. The air was turning bitter. His toes were starting to go numb.

"Who's there?"

At the voice, Kemir leapt into the air and took a step back. He still couldn't see anyone. Not a dragon-knight though. The voice had a quiver in it. A dragon-knight wouldn't sound like that. A dragon-knight would come out with a roar and a drawn sword. An alchemist? *Now that would be precious, wouldn't it? What would I do with an alchemist, I wonder?*

"Who's there?" The voice called out again, louder. "What's going on? Do you know what's happening?" Still no movement. Kemir's ears thought they knew where the voice was coming from, but his eyes weren't pulling their weight.

All right. Let's pretend I'm one of you. Let's pretend I didn't come gliding in on the back of those monsters. Let's pretend I have nothing to do with this. Wouldn't that be nice? "My name's Kemir. I'm a scout. A tracker. I've been helping hunt bandits in the deep valleys." The sort of work he'd done with Sollos for a time, before they'd grown sick of it. "Ancestors! What *is* happening?"

33

Movement. He saw the man again now, closer, coming toward him. "I thought you might . . ." The man took a deep breath and blew it out. "Are we being attacked?"

They both glanced up to the castle. Two dragons were still up there, merrily setting it alight. You couldn't see them, but you could see the flames against the darkening sky. "Are we being *attacked*?" Kemir arched an eyebrow. How stupid, exactly, did you have to be?

"But that's . . . that's not possible." The man finished quietly, shaking his head. "Not possible."

Kemir let him come closer. He couldn't help glancing at the man's feet as he crunched through the snow. Good boots. *Warm* boots. He quietly slipped one of his long knives out of its sheath. "Yeah. Who'd do a thing like that?"

"The Red Riders, I suppose. They say they kill even alchemists and Scales."

"Never heard of them." Kemir held the knife so the man could see it now. "That's close enough, thanks. What's your name and what are you doing out here?"

"I . . . I was looking for some heavy rope. For the new hatchling. It needs rebinding."

Kemir lowered the knife. It was hard to feel particularly threatened by someone who seemed so completely unaware that he might have his throat cut at any moment. "All right. Come closer so I can see you." *Whatever rebinding is.*

The man came obediently closer. Kemir could see him more clearly now. The man's face was lumpy and hard, the skin cracked and weeping in places. A Scales.

"Look at you," grunted Kemir. "You're almost a statue." Ancestors! The world outside was ending and this idiot was out looking for a piece of rope? *Why aren't you running away?*

The Scales bowed awkwardly. "It's the new hatchling." He looked out across the flat shoulder of the mountain where the bulk of the eyrie was now ablaze. "Did you see them come?" He cringed as two huge gouts of fire lit up the night. The snow had stopped now, clearing the air so you might have been able to see properly, except that everything was now shrouded in warm mist instead. Everywhere buildings were burning. The Scales wrung his hands but he still seemed to be more confused than anything else. As if none of this actually *mattered*. "Whose riders are they? Are they from the speaker?"

Kemir licked his lips. By the look of things, the worst that this Scales was going to do to him was give him a dose of Statue Plague. And if he lived long enough to die of *that*, well then that would be a lot longer than he'd been expecting. "Do you really want to know?" He shrugged. "No one's riding them, Scales. There are no dragon-knights giving the orders here. The dragons are doing it themselves." It was hard to read the expression on the Scales' face. Hatchling Disease had him well enough in its grip that he almost didn't have one at all, just a hard mask of skin like stone. "I think after this they have some ambition to destroy the world or something like that." He shrugged and stepped closer so he could look the Scales in the eyes. "If you're wondering what you should do, I recommend running away. Not that it'll do you much good. Or you could wait until it's all over and then hope the dragons aren't hungry anymore. Which is pretty much just as futile, since, as far as I can make out, dragons are *always* hungry. So what's in all these huts, then?"

The Scales looked about. "Empty barrels. Rope. Crates. Bit of firewood. The alchemists use them to store all the things they don't need anymore."

Kemir pointed out into the gloom, away from the glowing mists and the fires and the shadows of the mountainside and toward the great empty space of the valley below. There was nothing there, no shape, no silhouette, just the edge of the mountain and then a big gray nothing. And the path around the lake. "Where's that go?"

The Scales shrugged. "The sluice at the end of the lake. Then I suppose it goes on down the mountainside. I never looked."

"That way then. I recommend you run that way."

He turned away, one knife drawn just in case. Past the huts was the place where the dragons came to take their water. The snow was thin, a light frost of white. The ground beneath had been torn into a great sea of mud, filled with huge craters now frozen hard, uneven, begging for a man to trip and twist his ankle. Beyond, an embankment rose up to the edge of the lake, while the path itself dropped below the level of the water. On the other side, Kemir could see the edge of the mountain, not far away and getting closer with every step. He twitched, uneasy. The sun was setting, the eyrie was already in shadow. The darker it got, the more chance he had of being ambushed.

Or of escaping.

The Scales was following him. He wondered briefly whether he should just put a knife between the man's shoulder blades and keep on walking. Be done with it. Get back to being on his own, wandering, wondering what in the name of all his ancestors he was doing here. Didn't seem fair really, though. The only other Scales he'd really come to know had been nice enough. Not that that had saved him from being eaten by his own dragon.

He reached another cluster of sheds, sandwiched between the slope up to the lake and a sheer drop into the valley far below. The snow between the huts came up past his knees. Kemir waded through it; the drop down to the valley was every bit as sharp as it had looked.

"It goes down there, Scales. Gets steep by the looks of it. Go easy on the running. Won't do you any good if you go over the edge." He stopped as he came to a bridge, so small he barely noticed it, half buried in the snow and covered in ice. "Did you say a sluice?"

There it was, right beneath his feet. A channel for the water to run off and down the rock. Little more than a ditch really, frozen and covered in snow, with a metal gate set into the base of the embankment, almost lost in the darkness and shadows of the twilight. A sluice. Which meant that . . . There. That was what he was looking for. A crank to lift the gate, tied in place by a very old and thick piece of rope, bound in a knot that probably hadn't been touched for years. He scrambled off the bridge, floundering through the snow. He didn't even bother trying to undo it, but set to work with a knife.

"What are you doing?" asked the Scales.

"Opening this. What does it look like?"

"No!" The Scales came at him, arms flailing, floundering in the snow. Kemir swatted him away, knocking him to the ground. The Scales sat where he fell, face full of shock and disbelief. "The dragons will have nothing to drink!"

Kemir burst out laughing. "The dragons will have nothing to drink? This is the Worldspine, you idiot! What isn't rocks is either trees or water. Close your eyes for a minute or two, walk in any direction and you'll wind up wet. And probably fall off a cliff. That's a little joke we used to have among ourselves, us outsiders."

"You're an outsider?" Even through the slabs of hard dead skin, the look of horror on the Scales' face was obvious. Kemir rolled his eyes.

"What? What is it they tell you about us? We're the ones your dragon-lord masters harvest for slaves to sell to their Taiytakei friends in Furymouth. Or else they burn us for the simple pleasure of it. I can believe that now. I always used to think they must have a reason, some cause I simply didn't understand, but I realize now that no, they do it simply because they can." The Scales was still looking at him aghast. Kemir stopped and then sneered. "What? Have I grown horns?"

"They'll die!"

"What?" It took a moment for Kemir to understand what on earth the Scales could possibly mean. "The dragons?"

"Yes!" The Scales was almost in tears.

Kemir stared at him in disbelief. "Die?" he burst out. He laughed again, then held up a finger. "Do you want to know how to kill a dragon? You kill a dragon the same way you kill a man. You take away all his freedom, and then if that's not good enough you can feed him full of poison. For dragons that means those lovely poisons that the alchemists have hidden away in their houses. For us outsiders it's a little easier. Dust and cheap spirits usually do the trick. Then you just stand back and watch us burn until everything inside is dead and all we are is a hollow shell. Kill a dragon?" He shrugged, laughing to himself. "I saw some soldiers shoot one with oversized crossbows once. I think that probably hurt it at least a little. Certainly annoyed it. Now get up!"

Without any protest, the Scales got to his feet. His movements were clumsy and difficult, as though he was an old man. Hatchling Disease did that. In the deep snow he was pathetic, almost comical.

Kemir finished cutting the rope that held the sluice handle. "You can still run off if you want. I won't try to stop you. Not sure where all this water's going to end up though. Probably worth thinking about that before you scarper down the mountain." He started to turn the crank. For a moment it wouldn't move. Ice cracked and groaned but nothing happened. Wood began to creak and metal moaned.

"Don't!" The Scales' voice was a whisper. "The dragons . . ."

"Yes. The dragons." Kemir smiled grimly as he turned the handle again. There were some more grinding sounds, a loud crack from down by the metal gate, and a trickle of water began to run past the Scales' feet, melting away the snow. Kemir's grin grew wider. He turned the crank some more. It moved freely now. The trickle of water turned into a surge; he gave it another few turns. Water sprayed out of the sluice in a torrent. There were more groaning noises from the gate.

"Right." Kemir danced away from the spraying water as a part of the bridge shook and then collapsed under the force of the rushing water. "I think now we'd better start running after all. It's going to get a bit wet."

When you had a big empty hole inside, there was nothing quite like smashing stuff up.

5

A REASON TO LIVE

He ran, slipping and sliding in the deep snow on the embankment, the Scales floundering in his wake. He heard a crash as the sluice and then the bridge finally gave way, the rush of the water tearing them both apart. The lake was emptying itself in its own way, sending everything that had held it cartwheeling down the mountainside in pieces. A part of Kemir still thought he should have sent the Scales down there too. Slit his throat and kicked the body into the torrent of water. Would probably have been kinder than taking him back to Snow. But the man was making his own choice. The Scales could run away any time he liked.

And then there was the dragon, who probably wouldn't manage to keep any of her precious alchemists alive for long enough to ask any interesting questions. A Scales was better than nothing. The dragon would be grateful . . . He laughed at himself for that. Grateful? Snow? No. Now he thought about it, he wasn't even sure why he'd emptied the lake. Because he could. Because alchemists did to dragons what riders did to outsiders. Because, even at their worst, he'd rather have dragons than dragon-riders . . .

Really? And if it had been a dragon without a rider who'd come to our little village, would the end really have been any different?

He was almost grateful for the errant piece of building that tripped him up and sent him sprawling in the mud. The twilight was fading now, the mist-shrouded blaze of the burning eyrie the only real light. Made it hard to see where a man was putting his feet, but then there was so much snow on everything out here that maybe that didn't make any difference either. Up above, the castle was burning properly now. Flames reached out of the windows to lick the night.

He picked himself up and hauled the Scales after him, back toward Snow and whatever was left of the alchemists she'd found. They passed the barracks where the dragon had landed, smashed to pieces now. Parts were still burning inside. Around it, the ground was bare and black and soaking wet, the snow all melted in the heat. The air stank of woodsmoke and burned flesh and damp. Farther on, where the alchemists had lived, Snow was where he'd left her, pacing up and down over the ruins of what had once been some stone building, raking the ground with her claws.

Tunnels. They have fled under the ground.

Behind Kemir the Scales let out a scream. It went on and on and on. For a few seconds Kemir thought it might never stop. Then the Scales took a deep breath. He looked as though he might be about to start again, so Kemir punched him in the stomach. The Scales went down. Kemir clutched his fist and swore. Either the Scales was wearing armor or he truly was well on his way to turning into stone.

"I brought you this one," he said to Snow.

He followed you, Kemir.

"He's a Scales. Which means he's stupid."

A Scales. Like the one who was with me when I awoke. Kailin. He was the only one of your kind I have found who was not afraid of me.

"Oh yes. Another one of the people who tried to help you and ended up eaten for their troubles." He'd forgotten the man's name. Almost forgotten he even existed. He shrugged. "I think the potions they take for the Hatchling Disease means they can't think properly." He hauled the Scales to his feet. "He might be useful; he might not. Hey! Scales!"

The Scales looked at him. He was white with fear.

"Well, *this* one isn't not afraid of you."

This one understands. Snow stamped on the ruins of the alchemist house and the whole mountain seemed to shake. *I feel them in there, Kemir. I will clear away one of their holes. You will go in and hunt them for me.*

"No, I bloody well won't, dragon. I'm not going in any dark holes full of soldiers, thank you." He sniffed and looked at the quivering Scales. "When it's daylight, maybe. After I've dealt with the riders up in the castle."

Why do you seek to anger me?

"I'm just not going to get killed for you. I don't give a stuff whether that angers you or not. Live with it."

She looked at him and he felt her wonder. *You fear me and so you defy me.*

"Don't be daft, dragon."

I see it in you. You fight your fear by defying me. It is a curious thing to do. It does not seem . . . wise.

He could almost feel her poking around inside his thoughts. The sensation was like having an itch in a place you couldn't scratch. "You know what? I think I'm going to lie down somewhere and get some sleep. Maybe I'll help you once it's light again."

Snow lowered her face toward him and bared her teeth. *Again you test me?*

Kemir cringed. "You have *bad* breath, dragon. Take that away!" He could see her tail begin to twitch. Not a good sign. With a quickness that belonged to a much smaller animal, Snow sprang across the stones. As she landed sideways, her tail lashed out into the darkness. There was a scream. When her tail emerged from the wreckage, something dangled from the tip. She tossed it up into the air. There was a limp flailing of limbs before the dragon caught it between her teeth and swallowed it down.

Shall I keep this one you have brought me alive? Shall I keep it as a means to persuade you, Kemir?

"Clutching at straws, dragon. You'll need a much better threat than that and you know it. Learn to wait. Your alchemists will still be cowering in their holes come the morning. They might be more interested in talking by then." He could feel the anger boiling inside her so he turned away, kept his steps slow and measured and didn't look back. The dragon was right. He fought his fear by refusing to be afraid, no matter how bad it got. It was what he'd always done.

Didn't need to have someone poke inside my head and point it out though. He kept walking. The eyrie was littered with places to hide and away from the fires it was dark now. He made his way to the barracks where Snow had first landed. The end she'd smashed was still burning nicely and looked like it would be going for some time. The other end wasn't much better, but not so shattered that it wouldn't offer some shelter. In the middle of the floor he almost trod on what turned out to be a jewelery box, half covered in ash. The outside was scorched and ruined, but inside he found a small stash of coin and a pouch filled with Souldust. He stared at it, wondering what to do. What use it was.

Six months ago I'd be jumping for joy. That's a month's pay and never mind the dust. But now what? Coins I can't spend and dust I don't want? He almost threw it away, but a lifetime of living from day to day got the better of him and he put the coins and the dust in his belt bag instead. Then he propped himself up against a piece of stone wall in the middle that looked like it wasn't going to fall down on top of him while he slept. He huddled down and tried to make himself comfortable, massaging his feet until he could feel his toes again. It was pleasantly warm from the fire and at least the ground here was dry. *Like a dead dragon, burning from the inside.*

The dragon had changed since they'd been on the island. Since she'd awoken three more of her kind, one had become four. Maybe that was it, maybe having company of her own kind was what had made her more remote. Or maybe she'd always been that way and he simply hadn't wanted to notice.

Or maybe it was something else. He caught a hint of something in the dragon's thoughts sometimes. Something to do with the ships they'd seen when they left the island. The Taiytakei they were called, but the dragon had spoken of something else. Silver men. She wouldn't talk to him about the silver men, whatever they were, but they were in the dragons' thoughts and made them uncomfortable.

Which led him nowhere. If the dragons weren't going to tell him then he wasn't going to find out. That was that. End of. Time to get some sleep. Amazing how easy that still was, falling asleep, with the world on fire around him.

* * *

HE WOKE UP FROZEN STIFF. A cold dawn was lighting up the peaks on the other side of the valley, making them shine like giant lanterns. Above, through the broken bones of the roof, he could see the sky, clear now, a deep violet blue, waiting for the sun to breach the mountaintops. The snow clouds had gone, off to bother someone else. Where he lay was still dark, wrapped in leftover shadows. The wall, so deliciously warm when he'd fallen asleep, was like ice, sucking the heat out of him, but what had woken him were screams. Long, piercing screams, over and over.

He tried to stand up. When that didn't work, he settled for climbing as far as all fours. Every muscle in his body seemed frozen solid. Eventually he managed to get to his feet. He could have kicked himself. Amazing how easily he fell asleep, and just as amazing how quickly he'd forgotten how cold these mountains were when you had a dragon to keep you warm every night.

The screaming was still there, fading in and out until it eventually stopped. There were embers glowing in the far parts of the barracks. Kemir went and sat by them until he felt warm again. That took long enough for the sun to creep over the summits, for it to light up the eyrie and let him see what the dragons had done. Every building had been smashed flat and then burned. Barracks, storehouses, stables, the houses of the alchemists, everything. Where the little lake had been there was nothing but mud and the fractured remains of a vast sheet of ice. Higher up, the castle seemed more intact, although a pall of smoke hung over it. Snow was still prowling around where the alchemists had been, picking at the wreckage, lifting out the occasional fragment of wall and tossing it aside. He couldn't see the other dragons.

Kemir sighed. Wearily, he walked over to her. All the snow was gone, melted by the heat of the dragons.

"Well, dragon? I heard screaming. Did you get one?"

Snow stopped. She regarded him with a steady glare. *Does it matter, Kemir? Another human. I would have spared her, but you were not here and I was annoyed and bored, so I toyed with her and then ate her. Is that what you wished to hear?* Nothing about her thoughts suggested she was joking.

Kemir shivered. *It is light. I require an alchemist. I feel them, deep beneath the earth, on the edge of my thoughts. You will get one for me now, yes?*

"How deep is deep, dragon?"

They are few, Kemir. They are weak. They will not be able to hurt you.

Kemir snorted. "You'd be amazed what even a weak man can do if you frighten him enough. So what's in it for me?"

If you cease to be useful, you become food.

"Bollocks to you." He picked up a stone and threw it at her as hard as he could. It bounced off her nose. "Without me, dragon, you and yours would be throwing yourselves against one of the vast eyries of the plains. You'd be riddled with poison and scorpion bolts and wondering what went wrong. Just maybe, as you were burning from the inside, you'd be thinking that you should have listened to me, but probably not, because you're all so blindly arrogant when it comes to that sort of thing. Without me, dragon, you wouldn't even know these mountain eyries existed, much less have found any of them. I thought *that's* why you tolerated me. Because without me your ignorance and your impatience make you so stupid that you might as well keep taking the alchemists' potions."

Snow lowered her face until she was inches from Kemir's nose. When she hissed, she smelled of warm blood. Her head seemed huge, even if she was small for a dragon. As large as a cart with a mouth big enough to swallow a horse and lined with a hundred dagger-like teeth as long as his forearm. Her eyes were as big as his head.

The little one you brought to me had knowledge in the ways of this world, Kemir, more than yours. He knew many things that you do not. Events have happened since I awoke. I require to know more. I require an alchemist.

Kemir took a step forward. He was nose to nose with the dragon now. "Maybe I just won't, dragon. Has that thought occurred to you?"

They have knowledge of the dragon-knight who killed your nest-brother. Shall I pluck it from their thoughts before I devour you, or do you prefer to die in ignorance? It matters little to me.

A silence hung between them. The silence of a wound ripped open. Time stopped. The mountain and the eyrie and the sky all vanished. There was only him and the dragon. "What?"

I require an alchemist, Kemir.

"The Scales. Where is he?" It had to be the Scales. He must have known something after all.

For an answer, Snow licked her lips.

"You ate him."

An alchemist, Kemir. You will bring me an alchemist.

THE ALCHEMY

"What is the secret? they always ask. What is the secret? It is
the Silver King, I sometimes say. The Isul Aieha, bound and
tied in the deepest caverns of the Worldspine, held forever in
torment with a hollow spike driven into his still-living brain,
from which drips an ichor of purest silver. That is the secret.
They stare at me with wide eyes, lapping up every word, and
then I laugh. Other times I say it is merely a plant, a common leaf, a happy chance of nature that renders our dragons
dull. What is the secret? It is a thing I will hold in my heart
like a lover and never let go. The secret is blood."

6

OUTWATCH

Isentine watched the four dragons circle his little oasis. The fact that three of them were hunters only made the fourth, the war-dragon B'thannan, seem even more immense than usual. They'd come from the south, over the hundred miles of empty burning dunes from Sand to the last outpost of the north. To his eyrie, built around the ancient tower of Outwatch and the fertile strip of land around it. The oasis he understood. A river ran underground, all the way from the Worldspine, right under his feet. It touched the surface here. Somehow, because of that water, Outwatch had grown to be the largest eyrie in the realms.

The tower was another matter. Someone had built it long ago. They'd never quite finished, and they hadn't been quite human, that much was clear to anyone who lived here.

The ground shuddered as the weight of the dragons hit the earth; he could feel the impacts through his feet, all the way up to the aches in his knees. He cast a nervous glance behind him at the tower. In his dreams things kept falling apart.

A tiny distant figure slid down from B'thannan's back and strode across the hard blasted earth of the eyrie. Lord Hyrkallan, hero of Evenspire, prince of the north and King of Sand in all but name. A big man, but out here he looked small and insignificant. Against the immensity of the sky and the vast empty sands and the dragons sprawled basking in the desert sun, most things did. Kings, queens, riders, alchemists, they were all little

49

more than oversized ants. At the head of his soldiers, standing stiffly erect, Isentine clenched his teeth. The pains in his knees and his back troubled him more every day. Age.

Hyrkallan ignored the soldiers. He walked straight to the eyrie-master and on, snapping his fingers at Isentine to follow him. Which was not something his rank entitled him to do, not until he was crowned. Isentine held his ground.

"Your victories are sweet, but you're not married to her yet, Your Highness," he said loudly.

Hyrkallan stopped dead. For a second he didn't move. He didn't turn. "Where is she?"

"Where she always is." Isentine hung his head. "Underground. With the abomination."

"It must stop, Isentine."

"Yes, but she is our queen. I can't force her. I need you to get her away from here." Now, finally, Isentine turned and walked side by side with Hyrkallan. "Or are you inclined to wonder, as I have heard others wonder, does it do such harm? The dragon is only a hatchling, after all." But no. An abomination was an abomination. Hyrkallan had the right of it.

Hyrkallan growled. "No, Eyrie-Master, I am not inclined to wonder. It must stop. She is a queen. She must behave as one."

"Shezira used to joke that you must have come out of your mother with that glare of disapproval on your face." Isentine tried to smile, but what came out was more of a wince. His hip this time.

"I disapprove of many things, Eyrie-Master. The last thing of which I disapproved was Speaker Zafir. Now that she's dead, I most strongly disapprove of her villainous lover Jehal sitting on her throne. I promised the Night Watchman that my dragons would not cross the Purple Spur and so they will not, but I will not watch from afar while the Viper triumphs. I have gone to war in the name of my queen and now I mean to marry her, just as she promised. I do not demand pomp and ceremony, old man, but I do demand that all do their duty. I have brought witnesses, from this realm and from King Sirion. You have priests here. We must strike while the ancestors favor us. Two weeks have passed since the rout at Evenspire and we have done nothing. Jaslyn must go to the Adamantine Palace. She must go in strength but in peace and she must do it soon. Unless I have judged matters awry, the Lesser Council will be glad to rid themselves of Jehal. The Speaker's Throne is hers for the taking. Jehal may even keep his life if his queen demands it, although the Veid Palace of Furymouth shall become his prison." He growled. "The most gilded of prisons. But time is not on our side. Our strength is fragile, Isentine. Jaslyn must understand this. She must act or I must act for her, and I cannot rule alone as a prince. Then there is the matter of heirs."

Isentine wiped his mouth. "I hope you brought a plentiful supply of Maiden's Regret."

"I have enough."

"Jaslyn is . . ." Isentine made a face. "I do not think she has ever had a lover, Your Highness."

A tinge of red touched Hyrkallan's face. "That is hard to believe, Eyrie-Master. Given her sisters . . ." Hyrkallan obviously hadn't looked where he was going before starting that sentence. Now he stopped, realizing far too late what he was about to say.

"Nevertheless," muttered Isentine when Hyrkallan had had enough time to feel suitably embarrassed. "I ask that you be gentle."

"She has to stop this foolishness, whatever it is that she's doing. I don't understand the nonsense that has possessed her."

No. You don't. The Order of the Scales had careful rules about which of their secrets they told to whom. Hard rules with harsh punishments for those who broke them. Princes learned more than dragon-lords. Kings and eyrie-masters more still.

"Then you will see it for yourself." Even after twenty years, Shezira had never quite believed. Isentine had always seen it as a compliment, really, a tacit nod to the meticulous care with which he ran his eyrie. Now Hyrkallan would see it all for himself. A dragon untouched by alchemy. Aware and awake. Alive. Intelligent. He would feel a dragon read his thoughts and plant its own straight into his head. All these things without a word being said. No rules broken. *Shezira never believed and left the dragons to me and to the alchemists. Antros? He simply didn't care. Almiri didn't need* to. *Lystra? I suppose I might never know whether she believed whatever she was told. Jaslyn saw half of it for herself before anyone told her anything. She was the only one. Did I even believe it myself, when I was first made into the master of Outwatch? I don't think I did.*

He frowned at himself. *No time for rambling, old man. Back to the present.* "The hatchling must be dulled," he said sharply, "and if that cannot be done, it must be killed."

That got Hyrkallan's attention. "You want to kill Jaslyn's hatchling?"

Too hard to explain until Hyrkallan saw the abomination for himself. Then he would understand. "We can agree, Lord Hyrkallan, that Queen Jaslyn's place is not here. She must be persuaded of this. If our reasons differ, the result does not. When she is gone, I will do what I have always done, what needs to be done, both for this realm and for others."

"Every dragon." Hyrkallan wagged a finger in Isentine's face. "You save every dragon and make it grow."

Isentine smiled. "You sound like her. Shezira." Would it help to tell Hyrkallan that one hatchling in every three refused to eat? Starved itself to death rather than take the alchemists' potions? Probably not. Hyrkallan could have that later, when he was ready for it. When he was ready to know that the problem was getting worse too.

"I know." They started to walk again, this time in silence, both of them lost in their memories of the dead queen they'd both admired and maybe loved. Isentine led them to the yawning shaft that formed the hub of the underground eyrie and started painfully on the stairs that circled downward.

"My legs aren't what they used to be."

"Shezira came to me before she was made speaker. She wanted to replace you. I told her she was mad. I think that was what she wanted to hear."

"She sent Jaslyn to me as my successor." Isentine sighed. "She would have made a good eyrie-mistress."

"Let her. Once her duty to me is done."

"She has to be a queen."

Hyrkallan shook his head. "No. I have to be a king. We both know that's why she offered to share her crown with me. That's a price I'll be happy to pay for this honor. Let Jaslyn live with her dragons if she wishes. I won't stop her. If anything it seems fitting for a dragon-queen. Perhaps others will see it that way."

"Perhaps." Half a year ago, the idea of Jaslyn becoming the heir to Outwatch had seemed perfect for both of them. Now he wasn't so sure. *She understands the dragons well enough, if anything too well. She has seen what monsters they are and what terrors they can become, and yet she has awoken another one. Would I sleep easy at night knowing the realms were at her mercy? I'm not at all sure I would.*

"Here." Isentine stepped off the stairs and into one of the endless tunnels that burrowed into the stone under Outwatch. "We keep the hatchling chained. Jaslyn is not quite herself either. I have to give her potions to hold the Hatchling Disease at bay every day, and that's another reason you should take her away. It's a battle that is always slowly lost and you wouldn't want her if she turned out looking like one of the Scales."

"I would do my duty, Eyrie-Master."

"Then let us say that *I* would not forgive myself if our queen could not retain the little beauty she has. I have given Jaslyn far more than the usual dose. It is starting to affect her thinking." He sighed again. "There is another thing you must know, Lord Hyrkallan. Queen Jaslyn does not like to be under the ground. She will ask you to force me to release the hatchling from its chains. You may say what you wish, Your Highness, but I will not do that. Not on your command or hers. You may bring dragon-knights and put us to the sword, but I will not give that monster its freedom and nor will any alchemist in my eyrie."

He hobbled along the tunnels that led toward the caves on the cliff, the bright places where the sun poured in from the south and the hatchlings took their first tentative breaths. A mercurial tension lingered among these caves, the hatchling caves. Men died here, and often. Isentine shook his head. "You never quite know what you're going to get with a hatchling. Some of them are dazed and confused and easily chained. Some of them seem not to mind at all. Many fight as though they know exactly what will happen to them. They come a spitting fury of teeth and claws and fire, right from the egg. I lose men, Hyrkallan, to try and save those. We fall on them, a dozen of us trying to pin one of the beasts down while others wrestle the chains around their wings and neck. Dressed up in the thickest dragon-scale. Always the biggest and strongest man gets the head. You have to press down with all your weight, wrap your arms around its mouth and squeeze. You would be a good choice, Your Highness. A good solid build and a smith's arms." He smiled. "I did it myself, many years ago. Look around any eyrie and you'll see it's the big men who are missing their arms or their hands. It's as though some dragons understand everything even before they hatch."

Now he shook his head. Those were usually the ones that starved themselves, the fighters. "And then Queen Jaslyn came and told us all that this one was her old dragon Silence and that we were to feed it with meat and water that had not been touched by any alchemist. When we wouldn't do that, she did it herself. And it ate and drank, but it will not touch anything that is put in front of it by anyone else. Her Holiness must hunt and kill for it. She must bring the food to the beast herself. I don't know how it knows, but it does. Her Holiness claims that the dragon speaks to her. That it remembers." He stopped at a door in the tunnel and shuddered. "I leave you to judge the truth of her claims." The door was heavy, bound in iron. Small too. Small enough that a large man like Hyrkallan would have some trouble getting through it in all his armor. Small enough to keep all but a newborn hatchling out. Or in, which was more to the point. "Here," he said, with a twinge of sadness in his voice. "Her Holiness is here. You will find her inside."

He let Hyrkallan go in first, since the prince was wearing armor and sometimes the hatchling was in a foul mood. When there were no shrieks or bursts of fire, he peered around the door himself. Jaslyn was sitting cross-legged in the middle of the floor. The dragon was curled up beside her, sleeping. She was stroking its scales.

"He likes this," she said distantly.

Isentine shook his head. "I'll leave you to it then. I'd rather be away from that thing. Watch it if it wakes, My Lord. The two of them seem to have an accommodation, but I wouldn't trust it not to bite your arm off. She says it reads your thoughts, so I advise you to guard them."

He slowly climbed back up to the surface and waited. Half an hour passed, and then Hyrkallan emerged. His face was dark with fury. Isentine knew exactly how things had gone. Whatever Hyrkallan had said, he'd already tried it all himself.

"I know, I know," he said, as Hyrkallan stormed toward him.

"She refused me! Will nothing sway her?"

"Nothing even reaches her, My Lord. I see little choice left but to drag her, kicking and screaming, out of there. A thing I cannot do."

"She is our queen, Isentine." Hyrkallan's expression didn't change. Lost in thought mixed with a heavy tinge of anger. "This is not how a queen should behave. Not at any time and especially not now." He sat down beside Isentine and scratched his nose. For the first time Isentine could remember, Hyrkallan looked lost. "Curse her. I need her. I need her with me at the Adamantine Palace."

Isentine pursed his lips. "Then force her. That would be your right as her husband. Get her away from that abomination and her mind will clear. Or give the word and I will do it. Let her blame me. It's time I took the dragon's fall." It cost him a lot to say such things. Jaslyn was the closest of Shezira's daughters to her mother and the one he loved the most. But they had to be said. He sighed. "I never thought to see days like these."

Hyrkallan took a deep breath and levered himself back to his feet. "If neither reason nor duty will persuade her, perhaps she will listen to her sister."

"To Queen Almiri?" Isentine chuckled. "After Evenspire, I don't think Almiri's cooperation is something you can rely on." No. Not Almiri. "Lystra?"

Hyrkallan nodded. "*Queen* Lystra." Then he laughed. "You spend too much time with your dragons, old man."

7

A SIEGE OF DRAGONS

They had half a day before Prince Tichane came back at them. When he did, he came with everything. Dragons, hundreds of them, wheeling and circling Meteroa's spire of stone, bathing it in flames until it must have seemed a column of fire, a bright shining thing seen across half the realms. Tichane came with riders, hundreds of them too, decked in dragon-scale. With scorpions that rained like hail on the unyielding stone. With barrels of lamp oil that turned the Reflecting Garden into an inferno and flowed in burning rivers down the sheer cliffs of the mountain. With endless hordes of slave-soldiers, carried in cages to mill in useless impotence on the wrong side of Meteroa's walls. Tichane could bury the Pinnacles in burned bodies and shattered scorpion bolts for all Meteroa cared. Impotent, all of them. All of them except the dragons. It was almost enough to make him laugh, even if he'd lost a dozen riders in that first hour and most of the scorpions in the upper caves had been ruined.

A learning experience. All because we didn't know how to work them. At least, not properly. But now . . . now we know better.

Three dragons flew straight at the cave. Meteroa gritted his teeth. *They can't reach me, they can't reach me.* Beside him, Gaizal calmly cranked the scorpion a little to the left and a little up. He fired. The recoil was vicious, rattling Meteroa's bones as he tried to watch the bolt to its target. The air tasted of iron.

Scorpions. Meteroa had hundreds and hundreds of them. Tichane had destroyed dozens, and it simply didn't matter. Meteroa was more likely to run out of people to shoot them.

"You missed."

"Hit the dragon," said Gaizal calmly. "Now he's an angry dragon. These scorpions are really hurting them. Bolt please."

Meteroa handed him another bolt. Together they put their weight behind the cocking mechanism and levered it open again. *In steady calm movements, the way we always trained. Paying as little attention as we can to the dragon that's about to kill us.*

The mechanism clacked into place and the new bolt dropped home. Gaizal spun wheels that turned the scorpion back to the right and up some more. The dragons were a few hundred yards away now and closing fast. *Any moment now.*

The bolt fired. One rider on the closest dragon lurched as a six-foot rod of sharpened steel struck him in the hip and speared him to his mount. Meteroa had just enough time to see a second rider have his head torn clean off by another bolt before the dragons opened their mouths. He must have sensed it coming, somehow, because he was already pulling the fire shield down over himself and the scorpion and cranking the lever that propelled them away from the light and toward the back of the cave. *It took us an hour of being slaughtered to realize how to do that.* He cringed and muttered a prayer to his ancestors.

Prince Lai built these scorpions. The realization reached him at much the same time as a wall of fire shook the cave, scouring its walls. Each cave had three scorpions. Each scorpion was on an iron rail that ran from the front of its cave to the back. At the front, it had an open field of view and a wide arc of fire. When a dragon came close, the scorpion withdrew to the back, out of reach of tooth and claw.

But not out of reach of fire. For that there was the shield. It hadn't taken long at all to discover *those*—hinged slabs of dragon-scale that wrapped the scorpion in a fireproof cocoon. Meteroa had never seen scorpions as big as these. Big enough to make a dragon scream.

The stifling scorched air drained away. Meteroa was vaguely surprised to find that he was still alive and in fact unhurt. Cautiously he lifted the fire shield up. The cave entrance was clear.

Prince Lai got it right. Meteroa couldn't help but smile. *You've got more dragons out there than I have riders. I'm really supposed to have lost already. Yet here I am in an impregnable fortress armed with the weapons designed by the Prince of War himself. Here I am, Tichane! Come and take me, if you can.* Vishmir and Prince Lai had fought the first Valmeyan here, around the Pinnacles, during the War of Thorns. The most famous battle in history, between the greatest dragon-knights the world had ever seen. *And here I am, with another Valmeyan outside, gifted these presents by my ancestors . . .*

"Bolt please." The scorpion was already riding forward on its rail. Meteroa lifted another bolt—they were surprisingly heavy—from the crate slung at the back of the weapon and started on the arming lever. That took both of them with all of their strength to crank back ready to fire again. Two dragons flashed across the mouth of the cave right in front of them. The scorpion shook as Gaizal fired. Missed. In the middle distance another dragon bucked and screamed and veered toward them. The other two scorpions in the cave fired in unison. The noise was like a thunderclap.

"Missed."

"Are you sure?" Meteroa felt his skin tingle. The dragon-fury was like lightning in the air.

Gaizal shrugged. "Bolt." Meteroa reached for another and then changed his mind. Another dragon was coming in, straight at them. *No time.* He pulled down the fire shield and sent the scorpion back along its rail instead. A moment later the whole cave shook. Fire filled the air again. Meteroa closed his eyes and clutched his hands to his head against the sheer noise as the dragon roared. It must have been right at the mouth of the cave when it let loose.

The cave shook again, so hard that it almost knocked the scorpion off its rail. Meteroa staggered, grabbing at the fire shield, almost falling out into the cave. He had his visor down and could barely see. Gaizal fell sideways off the scorpion and disappeared. There was another roar. Meteroa slipped into the firing seat simply to steady himself. He looked sideways for Gaizal but that was a waste of time. Through tiny slits lined with blurred glass, he'd be lucky to see a dragon standing right in front of him. The world wasn't bright though, which meant the flames were gone.

He lifted the visor. He could see Gaizal now, lying on the floor beside the scorpion. He was very still. His helmet had fallen off and he was staring wide-eyed at the mouth of the cave.

"Bolt," he mouthed. Mechanically, Meteroa loaded another bolt into the scorpion. He lifted the fire shield up by a few inches and peered out.

There was a dragon right in front of him, its head and one clawed limb jammed in through the mouth of the cave, blocking the entrance, thrashing for purchase. The other two scorpions that had been in the cave were gone. It took Meteroa a moment to realize, but a substantial chunk of the cave was gone too.

"Bolt," mouthed Gaizal again. The dragon wasn't really looking at them. Meteroa could feel its rage growing every second. *Is it stuck?* He started to chuckle at the absurdity of it.

The dragon's eye, the one that Meteroa could see, swiveled to look straight at him. Golden, the size of a man's head, with a long vertical slit of a pupil, a thin black window to the dragon's soul, it stared at him.

"You *are* stuck, aren't you?" Meteroa threw back the fire shield and cranked the scorpion around. The dragon's struggles grew more urgent. It lunged forward, trying to get at him. Stupid thing was still trying to get *in*, not out.

"See now, if you were a hunting-dragon, that would have worked. But you're not. You're a war-dragon. Of course, if you were a hunting-dragon, you probably wouldn't have got stuck in the first place." The scorpion was aimed straight at the dragon's eye. The one weak spot. Meteroa fired. The dragon's eye burst and a man's height of barbed wood and steel buried itself in the monster's head. All the struggles stopped. The dragon hung where it was, dangling by its head and claw for a moment. Meteroa tried to imagine how hard the dragon must have hit the cave to wedge itself in like that. Tried. Failed.

There was a cracking sound from the mouth of the cave and then a grinding, and then the dragon was gone, taking a chunk of the cave mouth with it. Meteroa couldn't help himself. He reached out a hand, helped

Gaizal to his feet and then walked to the edge and peered down, watching the dragon fall toward the ground.

"I reckon that's that for those scorpions," he said.

Gaizal stared beside him at the falling dragon. "You killed a dragon," he gasped, full of awe.

"Yes." Meteroa frowned. "I suppose I did." Wasn't this the sort of thing they made into stories? Although he wasn't sure it would be much of one. *What will it say? That the dragon walked up to within a dozen yards of my scorpion and then obligingly stood still for as long as it took for me to pick my spot and aim? Which is pretty much what happened. No, that won't do.*

The other thought which came along with the first was that he'd better keep Gaizal alive for long enough to start telling people a better one, otherwise no one would ever know.

"Your Highness!" The world suddenly lurched and spun. For a moment he had no idea what had happened, then he was lying flat on the cave floor. Not falling the several thousand feet to the Silver City far below. That was good.

Gaizal was lying on top of him.

"What the . . ." *What in the name of your unholy ancestors were you doing?* That's what he'd been going to say, right up until he saw a hunting-dragon's wing arc past the cave. "Tail?" he asked, shaken. Gaizal nodded. They both scrabbled away from the edge. At the back of the cave Meteroa stopped and looked over his shoulder. "There's still one scorpion working here," he said. He looked at the mangled ruins of the others. The riders who'd manned them lay about like broken dolls. He wasn't quite sure what had happened to them, except that they hadn't been quick enough to retreat from the cave mouth when the dragon crashed in.

Gaizal didn't say anything. Meteroa weighed up his options and then shrugged. Killing Tichane's riders and even his dragons was all well and good, but the *point*, he had to remind himself, was to defend the fortress. The only way in, as far as Meteroa could see, was either up through the tunnels or down from above. And if even Zafir didn't know the way in from below and the only way in from the Grand Stair was barred, then that left getting in through the scorpion caves. Meteroa couldn't quite see how they would do such a thing. Presumably on very long ropes, except most of the caves had overhanging roofs which would make attackers ridiculously easy to pick off one by one as they tried to swing inside. So far, no one had even tried.

I killed a dragon. The thought echoed in his head over and over, filling him with energy and purpose. He felt dangerously invincible. He turned back to the cave mouth in time to see another three dragons flying straight toward it. Two of them were carrying large cages in their back claws. The sky behind them was blue and clear and filled with sunlight. He suppressed a laugh. It was a nice day outside. Or would have been, if it wasn't filled with dragons,

"Bolt!" shouted Gaizal. Meteroa found himself jumping onto the scorpion in reflex. He had a bolt in his hands and Gaizal was already at the cocking crank. They weren't going to be able to move the scorpion up to the front of the cave anymore. He could see that now. The rail was buckled from the impact of the dragon. Not that it mattered, since the dragons were coming straight in again. He couldn't help but wonder what the cages were for. They looked like slave cages, but he couldn't fathom what Tichane might be doing with his slave-soldiers up here.

"Ready!" Gaizal sat down into the firing seat and started to turn the scorpion. They had a few seconds, Meteroa decided, before the first dragon was close enough to burn them. The reach of a dragon's fire—another thing you learned by not dying. Most people didn't understand what it took to be a dragon-knight. How many accidents there were. A careless flick of a tail and a lord's son was dead, just like that. And as for fire, well, there was simply no way to learn about dragon-fire except to feel it. It always amazed Meteroa how many knights didn't check that every part of their armor was locked together properly. Half the riders who came through his eyries were cripples before he was done training them.

The front dragon had several riders on its back. They weren't even trying to use the dragon to shield themselves. *Because they think we're all dead?* Meteroa permitted himself a vicious little grin as Gaizal fired the scorpion, neatly skewering the lead rider. He deserved it. *Yes. When you spend most of your life working around dragons, you learn not to take chances.*

He pulled the fire shield down and waited as the flames washed around him. When he lifted the shield and peeked past it, the first dragon was gone. The second, though, was heading right for the cave mouth. He slammed down the shield a second time, but instead of more fire, there was a pause and then a crashing splintering sound. Meteroa peered out from behind the shield again. There were *men* in his cave. About a dozen of them. Lightly armored soldiers, screaming and shouting amid a tangle of smashed wooden poles and ropes. Several of them looked quite badly hurt. In fact, now that he looked again, several of them weren't moving at all.

They threw a cage full of slaves at me? He couldn't help but stare, incredulous, as the last of the three dragons tossed another cage toward the cave and veered sharply away, so close its wings almost brushed the face of the stone outside.

To Meteroa, everything seemed to happen in slow motion. The cage turned slowly in the air. It clipped the roof of the cave entrance and immediately disintegrated. Parts of it, including several poorly armed soldiers, kept going, cartwheeling into the cave; most of it bounced against the bottom lip of the cave and spun away. A brief chorus of screams vanished into the void outside.

Several men managed to disentangle themselves from the wreckage. Meteroa screamed, jumped out from behind the shield of the scorpion and ran at them with his sword. They were so confused or injured or just plain stupid that he cut two of them down before they gathered their wits and realized they were under attack. A third managed to draw a short sword to defend himself, but all he was ever going to manage with that was to fend off Meteroa's own sword. *An axe, boy. You need an axe if you're up against dragon-scale. That or a scorpion or a really good bow.* Meteroa concentrated on putting down the half-alive soldiers who might have managed to make a nuisance of themselves if they ever managed to get up off the floor. After that, he slowly backed the last soldier into a corner. Here he paused.

"You can't possibly have volunteered for this," he shouted. "Look at you! Half crippled from being thrown in here by a dragon. You can barely fight and even if you could, look at what they gave you! What are you? One of Valmeyan's slave-soldiers? Did they promise you your freedom if you managed to open the doors for them? How were you going to do that?" Meteroa waited, watching. The soldier was clearly terrified—he knew that he was very close to death—but there was also an air of resignation about him, as though he'd been in this sort of position enough times before not to be overly bothered.

Meteroa slowly lowered his sword. "You *are* a slave, aren't you? And they did promise you your freedom." He laughed. "You can fight for me if you like. You'll probably die anyway, but I'll give you a better sword and some armor and some decent food." *And I could do with every man I can get. Where I get them doesn't really matter.* He laughed. "We all eat like kings in here. You can shoot scorpions at the riders who threw you in here. Bet you wouldn't mind that at all."

The soldier was clearly weighing up his options. Gaizal threw in another one.

"Dragon!"

Meteroa backed quickly away from the soldier and stole a glance toward the mouth of the cave. Another war-dragon was heading straight at them with yet another cage. The dragon opened its mouth. Meteroa leapt for the scorpion, dropping his sword, snapping down his visor and diving behind the fire shield as the cave exploded in flames. The dragon roared. Men screamed, wood and stone smashed, and then the dragon was gone again.

When Meteroa lifted his visor, the soldier was gone. Or rather, what was still there was a charred smoldering shape of something vaguely manlike. Behind the fire, the dragon had tossed in another cage filled with slave-soldiers. They were screaming. The cave floor, Meteroa realized, was still scorching hot.

"Gaizal!" Meteroa picked up his sword and then quickly dropped it again, clutching his hand. "Shit." The hilt was blistering. Dragon-scale was too tough and too thick for the inside of a pair of gauntlets. "Gaizal!" Slave-soldiers were pulling themselves out of the wreckage now, screaming and wild-eyed with terror. Back outside, in the blinding sky, Meteroa thought he could see more dragons clutching cages. Sheer weight of numbers would push him out of his cave eventually. Is that what they were doing everywhere? *Vishmir's cock—how many of these poor fools did Tichane have?*

He turned and ran. The slaves pulling themselves out of the cage shrieked and gave chase. They didn't even notice Gaizal still sat in the scorpion. They were faster than him, one of the drawbacks of dragon-scale armor. But there were men-at-arms waiting somewhere at the bottom of the tunnel. Somewhere.

A slave-soldier landed on his back. He spun, flinging him off, but that merely gave the others a chance to catch up with him. They threw themselves at him like a pack of wolves.

"Gaizal!" He punched one in the face, smashing the man's jaw, but toppled over backward under the sheer weight of bodies. He could feel them already stabbing at him with their short swords, trying to find a way through his armor. He writhed and thrashed, trying to throw them off. *Do you know who I am? Do you know what I did? I killed a dragon today! A fucking dragon!*

He roared and managed to free one of his arms to snap the neck of the man clawing at his helmet.

"I. Will. Not!"

But that was as far as he got before another one of the slaves grabbed hold of his head and bashed it into the stone floor over and over, and everything went black.

8

THE ALCHEMY OF FEAR

"I'm doing this for you, cousin," Kemir muttered to himself as he strung his bow. His bow or Sollos' bow? He wasn't sure anymore. They both looked the same. The realization hurt. He should know something like that. He cocked his head at Snow. "I want to know what the Scales told you."

After you bring me my alchemists, Kemir.

"After, after. You always have to get what you want first, don't you?" He didn't stop, though. His feet felt springy. If he didn't know better, he might have thought that Snow had put some kind of spell on him. Somehow he felt lighter. The rider who'd killed his cousin was still alive, could still be made to suffer. An arrow in the leg had been the start of it, but there would be more, so very much more. Yes, it was good to remember why he was here, after all this doubting. Good to have a simple answer again . . .

The alchemists, Kemir.

"You'd better leave a few of them alive after you're done." He looked at the hole in the ground that Snow had cleared. There were stairs underneath the dust and the rubble. Yesterday a large stone house had stood here but there was little sign of that now. No, house wasn't the right word. Something bigger, more like a castle but not.

They are far underground, said Snow in his head. *I taste their fear.*

"I don't suppose you can taste how many of them are down there?"

There are eight, Kemir.

Well, that's me told. He started down the stairs. One step at a time, his feet feeling their way through the scattered debris. The light from the sky faded quickly as he went deeper.

Can you not go quicker?

"Can you not shut up? It's dark down here."

I can light your way with fire, if you wish.

"Or you could go find something better to do for a while?"

No.

Kemir picked his way onwards. In parts he had to drop onto all fours, feeling at the floor with his hands. Either the alchemists were hiding in the pitch-black or else he was nowhere near them.

They are not in darkness. Your caution is unnecessary. You may go faster.

Kemir growled softly. "And how do you know that, dragon? Are you here?" Down near the bottom of the stairs he couldn't even see his hand in front of his face. The only light was the distant painful brightness of the sky, far behind him.

I can see the edges of their thoughts, Kemir, and they are not the thoughts of men hidden in darkness. They have light. I feel their minds and I feel yours. You are not yet close. Hasten!

Eventually the stairs stopped at a mound of rubble. Kemir felt at it and then crawled over the top, through a narrow gap beneath the ceiling. The earth smelled burned, felt powdery. When he reached the other side, though, the stones were different. It took him a moment to realize what it was. They were rough. They weren't warm. This was how far Snow's fire had reached.

The tunnel led farther, a lot farther. He could see that because he could see a light too, off in the distance, a flickering shadow hundreds of yards away.

"Are you still there, dragon?" he whispered.

Yes.

"I see light." He crept along the tunnel, one careful step at a time. There were still stones scattered on the ground. His feet felt for them. Not a place he wanted to sprain an ankle, and he needed to be quiet too. "Don't suppose you know if they're all together?" Gravel crunched under his boot. He winced.

They are close to each other.

"How close is close, exactly?" The dragon didn't answer. Kemir shuffled slowly along. The light wasn't flickering like a flame; it was moving as though someone was holding it, but otherwise it was steady. "Are there soldiers down here, or just alchemists?"

How will their minds feel different, Kemir?

"How would I know? Am I the one who reads them?"

You little ones all feel the same.

"Well now that's useful to know."

No. You are different. I have come to know your special taste. I will always know you. Always find you.

Kemir pulled out an arrow and nocked it loosely on the string of his bow. He passed a second passage, dark and lifeless, and then a third, more stairs leading back to the mountain slopes. As he came closer to the end of the tunnel, he could see that it opened out into a wider space. He started to hear voices.

". . . do you know?"

". . . outside . . ."

". . . Red Riders?"

Them again. Same as the Scales had said. *They kill even alchemists and Scales . . .* Kemir paused. "They're talking, dragon. Do you hear them?"

No. Their minds are unfamiliar. Which was worth knowing, Kemir decided, and he started trying to work out how far away he was from Snow. *How much farther before she can't feel me at all?*

Worlds could separate us, Kemir, and I would find you. Besides, I will know your intent before you know it yourself, and you do not have the desire to run from me. I do not understand why you expend such effort thinking about it when deep down you have already conceded that your life is tied to mine.

"You mean we have a shared destiny or some shit like that?" Kemir spat. "What makes you think any of that mystical crap is true?"

Dragons do not believe in destiny.

"You don't really believe in anything, do you."

I believe in what I see in your head, Kemir.

He took another few dozen steps forward and listened again. The air smelled of mold and earth and sweat. He could hear at least four different voices arguing in the tired labored way of men who'd argued about the same thing for far too long. Round and round. He crouched down with his back to the wall and listened. One of the voices wanted to go back outside. The others said no. On about those Red Riders again.

With a start, he realized he knew the legend. The rider who wore red and whose name was Justice. Who rode a white dragon called Vengeance. A mythical, never real, white dragon . . . *Well, one of us fits the part at least. With a bit more blood on me, who knows?*

Make them come out!

"I might have to explain why you tried so hard to kill them," breathed Kemir. Not a bad idea, if he could somehow convince the alchemists to come out of their own accord. He racked his memory for anything that might help. To be an alchemist probably meant you had to be clever, though. Cleverer than him. Certainly cleverer than a dragon . . . No, there were better ways. Tried and tested. He crept on a bit farther until he was right on the corner where the tunnel turned and widened out into an open space. The air here was warm and smelled bad, stale with the taste of too many men in too small a space for too long a time. *Sweat and piss. I know that smell well enough. Smells like home.*

He stepped around the corner and put an arrow in the chest of the first man he saw. *Think of them as dragon-knights.* They didn't even realize he was there, lurking in the shadows on the edge of their light. *Alchemists give dragon-knights their dragons.* He put an arrow through the throat of a second man. *They deserve the same.* Killing dragon-knights was as easy as breathing. He stepped forward with a third arrow at the ready, letting them see him just as they realized what was happening. There were six left in front of him. None of them was armed. *Alchemists, dragon-knights. Same difference, right?*

"Stay very still." *Same difference.* He had to keep telling himself that. Somehow it wasn't sticking.

It wasn't a big room. A few crude beds, a simple table, pots to piss in, that sort of thing. Food on the table. Leftover biscuits and dried meat. Alchemical lamps, several of them. And more tunnels leading out of the back of the room. Too many to be looking into. *Six men alive and two dead. You said there were eight. Are you sure?*

I cannot be certain, Kemir.

"Are there any more of you lurking back there?" he snapped and watched their faces carefully. There was no guile in these men; perhaps they were too shocked by the casual way he'd executed two of them. They didn't start to glance at the tunnels, just stared at him in slack-jawed horror.

"Well? Do I have to shoot a few more of you so the rest can find their tongues?" He took a step toward them and they cringed. *They could rush me if they wanted. I could only shoot one of them and the rest would be on top of me. With strength of numbers they would win, and yet they won't. They'll cower, too afraid, and then I'll herd them outside and they'll be slaughtered like cattle. All because every one of them would rather live for another few minutes more than win.*

Your kind are indeed curious, observed Snow. *What you are doing would not work on dragons.*

Kemir gritted his teeth. He muttered under his breath, "And how would you know that, Snow? Dragons find themselves on the wrong end of these situations often, do they?"

We are very old, Kemir. We remember much that your kind have forgotten. Powers far greater than us. Powers that made us. Snow went silent and there it was, the catch in her thoughts. The something that passed for a pause for breath, a mouth that opened to speak, and then closed and chose to be silent instead. One of those silver men moments. Even as he thought that, he sensed Snow bristle.

The alchemists, Kemir.

Yes. The alchemists. He'd given them far too much time to think about rushing him. They were exchanging glances and starting to fidget. Two bad signs. He switched his aim to the one who, in the dim glow of their lamps, looked the oldest. In Kemir's experience, the older men got, the keener they became on living. "You," he snapped, "are there any more or is it just you six?" He didn't dare take his eyes off them, but the room was far too shadowy for his liking. He couldn't even see the walls clearly, never mind their dark corners. A man with a bit of skill could sneak right up to him.

The man's jaw dropped. He made a squeaking noise that could have meant anything.

"On the count of five I'm going to shoot you. One."

"Uh . . . ah!"

"Two."

"We're all there are! Please! Oh, by all the gods, please don't kill me."

Kemir shot the man standing next to him instead. He had another arrow ready before they realized what he had done. Herding five was easier than herding six. Four would be even better . . . "Well done, old man. You're still alive. A bit quicker next time. Are you all alchemists?"

"Yes! Yes!" The old alchemist fell to his knees and lifted his hands to Kemir. "We are servants of the Order. We have no part in these battles. We serve the realms and tend to the dragons, all dragons, no matter who rides them."

He speaks of us as though we are no more than animals, snarled Snow in Kemir's head.

"You can eat him when I bring him out, dragon." Kemir hardly spoke, but his lips moved. The old alchemist looked at him in wild-eyed horror.

"Who . . . who are you?"

Kemir laughed. *Why not? They won't know what he looks like.* "I'm the Red Rider himself, old man. The real thing. Justice, with my white dragon Vengeance waiting up above. I used to have a different name but I don't use it anymore. We're above, taking what's left of this eyrie apart."

"But King Jehal destroyed you!"

Oh, so that one's a king now, is he? "Apparently not."

"What do you want from us, Rider?" The old man was almost crying, as if Kemir had confirmed his worst fears. "We serve all with equal dispassion. We do not take sides."

Rage flickered around the edges of Kemir's thoughts. The dragon's rage. "Get out." None of the alchemists moved. "Get outside or you'll all die where you stand. Go and I'll let you live. Take your lamps and make your way outside and you will not be killed. You have my word as a rider." *And we outsiders all know what that's worth, don't we? But you probably believe in that shit.*

He watched as they filed past him, heads hung low, broken men shuffling out to their doom. The oldest one went first. Kemir followed the last, careful to keep his distance. In the darkness all he could see were their lamps. If one of them decided to lag behind and hide with a knife somewhere, the first he'd know about it was when it was in his ribs. Tunnels, caves, dark closed places, he hated them all.

The alchemists got to the foot of the steps and the pile of rubble that blocked the way and stopped, milling uncertainly about. If they were going to think of stabbing him, it would be now.

There is another. You have left one behind. I sense it now.

"Too bloody late," snapped Kemir. "I'm not going back." He barked and prodded at the alchemists. "Clear it or climb over it. I don't care which you do, but you'd better do it quickly. My arm's getting tired." *Alchemists, dragon-knights. Same difference.* He thought about shooting another one to chivvy them along. It would be a mercy, after all, compared to what would happen when they went outside. Wouldn't it?

Murdering frightened old men in the dark. Was that what he'd come to?

Leave them for me. I wish to question them.

"You're welcome." Shooting unarmed men in the back, that was more the sort of thing that a rider would do. *Dragon-riders, alchemists, same difference. Right? RIGHT?* He could feel something building up inside him. It felt like Sollos, his dead cousin. The way he'd lurk in the background when Kemir was settling down to really have some fun with some crippled dragon-knight. Always there, telling him that what he was doing was wrong without ever saying a word.

"Piss off, cousin," he muttered to himself. "They deserve everything they're about to get." The words felt empty.

But they do, Kemir. They do.

The alchemists scrabbled over the stones, moaning and groaning and grunting all the way. The last one stopped and tried to plead with him, holding back from the rest to bargain his way to safety at their expense. Kemir ignored him—he wasn't interested—and pushed him through. *When you're dangling upside down in front of a row of drooling dragon fangs, then we'll see what you're made of.*

He wasn't that surprised when, as he started to crawl through himself, someone threw a stone at him. It missed, skipping a few inches past his face. He pushed himself back behind the rubble and shouted, "Go on then! Run! Go on, run! Run up the steps! See how far that gets you. Do you think I'm alone here?" He waited while that sank in. *If you were going to fight you should have done that much sooner.* "Run up the stairs and into the sunlight, where my comrades and I can see how sorry you are!"

"Why do you kill alchemists?" shouted one of them. "When word spreads of what you've done here, no one will follow you. Valmeyan will hunt you down and destroy you. Even Shezira's daughters will reject you. They'll declare you rogues. You'll get no more succor from them. Everything will stop until you're dead and your dragons are safely returned!"

"You have until I count to three this time!" Kemir aimed his bow through the gap. He had no idea what they were talking about. "One. Anyone I can see when I get to three doesn't get to the top. Two, three!" He fired an arrow, not bothering or caring to aim, snapped up another arrow and fired again and then again. By then, the alchemists were gone, their lamps left behind. He'd hit at least one, judging from the groans. As for the rest . . . well, chances were they got lucky.

You have killed another one of them. I felt his thoughts scream and fade. Three have escaped you. I am waiting for them. Three of eight. And you accuse me of waste, Kemir. I am displeased.

"Drink my piss, dragon." He pulled himself across the rubble. In the cold gleam of the alchemists' lamps, he could see the two he'd shot now, one of them with an arrow in his chest, the other one rocking back and forth, clutching the wound in his thigh. Kemir stood over him, shaking his head. He slung his bow over his shoulder and pulled out a knife.

"Please! No! I don't . . ."

Kemir!

He clenched a fist toward the light at the top of the stairs. "You're telling me not to kill someone?" He didn't get any further with that thought, as a roar filled the tunnel and orange light filled the stairs. A second later a sharp blast of hot wind almost knocked Kemir off his feet, and then someone was coming, uneven hurried footsteps stumbling back down toward the bottom of the stairs. In the dim light all Kemir could see was a vague shape. He readied his bow again. "Stop!"

The figure stopped. "It's a rogue. Oh dear ancestors! You *are* the Red Rider! You're not one of Shezira's riders, you're the Flamebringer. You're the herald of the end of the world!"

"I don't know what you're talking about, but you either go back up those steps or you die where you stand." He pointed his bow at the shadow on the steps.

Alive! Kemir, I want one of them alive! I have questions! Rage and fury filled his head, battering at him. Snow's, not his.

"The way you ask questions I should have kept all eight of them alive." He gritted his teeth.

Yes. You should.

"No." The alchemist was shaking his head. "I'm not going up there. Not with a rogue. I know what that means. Kill me then. Be quick. I'll not . . ."

Kemir sighed and shot the alchemist in the belly. "Maybe it comes from hanging around dragons for so long, but I don't have the patience anymore, I really don't." He put his bow away and then walked over to where the man had fallen. The arrow had been placed to pass through his stomach. Men always died from that, but it was slow. Painful and slow. "Four rogues actually," he said. "A whole eyrie of them in a few weeks, I dare say." He wrinkled his face. "You stink. You've soiled yourself, haven't you. Great. Now I'm going to have that smell on my clothes." He hefted the alchemist up over his back. His hand settled on something wet. "Ah. Is that blood? I hope that's blood." He let rip a deep-throated growl and started the long climb up the stairs and back into the light. "Dragon, this had better be worth it. You'd better give me the rider who murdered Sollos after this, you really better had."

Slung across his shoulders, the dying alchemist was sobbing.

"Hurts, does it?"

The alchemist didn't say anything, but Snow did. *Not pain, Kemir. Understanding. This one is wiser than you. This one knows what is coming.*

After he'd taken the first alchemist to the top, he went back down for the one with the arrow in his leg. With a bit of luck and care, a man with a wound like that could live. Recover, even. Ah well.

He brought out the bodies next, one at a time. Snow sat, patiently waiting, watching over the quivering alchemists, still as a statue, until he was done. Then, with slow and deliberate precision, she picked up a dead alchemist and ate him. Slowly, biting off one limb at a time, then ripping open the torso and shaking guts and organs down her throat. When she was done, she tossed what was left high into the air and caught it with a snap of her teeth. First one body, then another, with precise and deliberate care. When she was done, she turned to the two who were still alive.

You may stay or you may go, Kemir, she thought with such glee and anticipation that Kemir felt his own heart jump in sympathy.

"Well then, I reckon I'll stay." He sighed, found a place where he could make himself comfortable, sat back and settled down to watch. It wasn't as though he had anything else to do.

He was covered in blood. From the alchemist he'd carried, no doubt. He'd have to clean himself off before long, but for now it would have to wait.

The Red Rider. Justice and Vengeance.

9

LYSTRA

For some reason, Meteroa wasn't dead. He felt his consciousness begin to fade and his struggles lose their strength. There was a sharp stabbing pain in his shoulder, a bad, deep pain. He should have been dead, but he wasn't; the pack of slave-soldiers was suddenly flung aside and he was being dragged. Away from the light. Deeper into the tunnel. There were other men, other voices. His men, the ones he'd sent to wait at the end of the tunnel. A wave of relief washed through him and he must have passed out then, because the next thing he knew he was in one of the rooms with the softly glowing ceilings. There were a good few riders with him. He tried to sit up, but that turned out to be a mistake. His head spun so much that he almost fainted.

"Ancestors," he groaned. His shoulder hurt, a deep hard stabbing, aching pain. He couldn't move his left arm. At least, when he tried, his shoulder lit up as though someone had poured molten iron into the middle of it.

They'd stabbed him. The slave-soldiers. They'd stabbed him through the pit of his arm where there was no dragon-scale to protect him, only soft leather.

He groaned again and gave up on sitting. "Is it bad?" he whispered.

The rider beside him turned out not to be a rider at all, but Queen Lystra. "You killed a dragon," she said, breathing softly in his ear. The tenderness in her voice gave him the answer he didn't want. *Yes. It's bad then.*

"Rider Gaizal told us," she said. "They're all talking about it. No one's killed a dragon since . . . I don't think anyone knows. Since the first Night Watchman."

Balls. I'm going to die. "How much blood is there?" *If I can still think then it can't be too much. Not yet. Who dies of an arm wound?*

"A lot," she said with that irritating trace of sadness that said he wasn't going to be getting better. *And how does she know? What is she? How does a queen who's not much more than a girl and who's spent her life living in a library know when a wound is mortal? Eh? And if you don't know, then I'd appreciate you not being so bloody condescending about it.* He tried to sit up again, but that was clearly going to be beyond him for a while.

"Who's leading the defense?"

"Rider Jubeyan." She paused, and he could almost feel her fidgeting, trying to decide whether to tell him something. Then she sighed. "They took Princess Kiam. They were going to tie her to one of the scorpions, where every rider could see. There are soldiers in some of the caves now too. They were fighting in the tunnels."

"Right. So we're losing then." That didn't seem possible. Was Tichane really going to win by throwing cages full of barely trained slave-soldiers at him? That hardly seemed decent. *Not that I'm one to complain about a lack of decency. Too many bad habits of my own when it comes to that.*

"No, we cleared the scorpion caves, but it's getting hard. I don't know how long we're going to last."

"You know it's Zafir, out there, don't you? You should hide. Take Hyaz. Dress yourselves as servants. That sort of thing. Keep Zafir away from Jehal's heir. Hyaz was supposed to find the secret way out."

"No one knows a secret way out." Lystra mopped his brow. "And I don't think I would stay hidden for very long."

"No." *Although you don't seem all that bothered for someone who's best option is probably to take poison while you still can.* But the words stumbled over each other in his mouth, which somehow wasn't working again. *No. You sound like a little girl who's trying desperately hard to be brave. Well you're right to be scared.* And then he was fading again, perhaps for the last time . . .

No. I'm not having that. I'm not dying now. Especially not if that means my whole life has to flash before my eyes. I'm not ready for that. I need another few months or years before I can look you all in the eye, you ghosts, and tell you it was all worth it. Show you what I've done for us. Calzarin, you were so beautiful, too beautiful for me to resist. The sun to Jehal's moon. But don't pretend that you gave yourself to me unwillingly, or that you took me, as you did, under duress. Don't you dare blame me that your own father put you to death. He killed you because of what you did to him, not what you did with me. Do you say it was the sweet nothings I whispered in your ear that put such a bloody knife in your hand? Tell it to the gods, ghost. Maybe it was, but it was your hand that held the knife nonetheless, and I do not believe your heart was so frail.

Or Tyan? Do you have something to say to me, big brother? You point your wagging finger at me and accuse me of murder, do you? I would point out that it was Jehal who killed you in the end, not me, but we both know that would be splitting hairs. Do you think I somehow regret that I poisoned you? Do you think that I wish I had not watched you suffer for all those years, mad, useless and drooling. Do you think that it was not an endless pleasure to me to watch you like that, after what you did to me? Yes, I had your wife in my bed and I had your son there too. But you never knew it. Their loss pained me more than it pained you, and yet you were allowed to stand there, the grief-stricken king, while I stood beside you and held your hand and murmured "There there" in your ear while all the while my heart was bleeding. I fucked lots of other people as well until you denied me that pleasure forever. And you did what you did because of what? Whispers in your ear. Murmured half-truths and lies and conjecture. If you'd caught me with my prick stuck in Calzarin's arse or between Mizhta's legs then I would have understood, I really would. But on hearsay and rumor? To your own brother? You should have finished the job and had me killed with your son. No, I don't regret what I did to you, not one second of it. So bring it on, ghost. Let us spend the rest of eternity locked in our anguished embrace . . .

On and on, over and over it went, fading in and fading out. Mostly the ghost was Tyan. Sometimes it was Mizhta or Calzarin, sometimes even Jalista or the other Tyan, the little boy Calzarin had disemboweled through his arse. Once or twice it was Jehal, and then, perhaps, Meteroa felt a twinge of guilt for all the things the cleverest of the princes had never even begun to deduce. *I could tell you the truth. But why? What good would it do you?*

Mostly though it was Tyan, and Meteroa faced him down with salt and iron, as any good ghost-hunter would do. They fought and it seemed to be forever. In the distance sometimes he heard screams and wondered if they were his own. He felt pain too. Pain was good. Pain was life, even if the pain got worse and worse until he seemed to be bathing in fire.

And then someone was poking him, and the pain was blinding. He opened his eyes.

"He's alive, Your Holiness," said a voice. Not one that Meteroa recognized. He tried to open his eyes. The ghosts were gone but the fire wasn't. He felt sick. When he finally did manage to lift his eyelids, the effort almost broke him. The light was blinding.

"Are you sure?" There was no mistaking *that* scornful voice.

"Zafir." The word hissed between Meteroa's teeth. It probably sounded more like a sigh, a last dying gasp, than anything else, but someone understood him.

"Lord Meteroa." She was coming closer. "You're alive after all. You don't much look it and I'm not sure you're going to last much longer. But since you are . . ." She moved away again. "Get him up. Let him sit in my throne one last time." Hands hauled him up from wherever he was lying. The pain in his shoulder was like being stabbed with a thousand burning knives. Mercifully he fainted. When he woke up again he was soaking wet and a fierce skin-stripping smell was flaying his nose. He jerked away and opened his eyes. The first thing he saw was Zafir again. *So that wasn't a dream then. Or another ghost.*

"Where's my sister, you impotent little snake? Murdering Uncle Kazalain is something I could be persuaded to overlook, but not my sister. Where is she?"

You hate your sister. Why are you bothering me? Leave me alone. But the only speech he could manage was "Uh?"

"Is that all you have to say? Shall I tell you? I found her still alive, no thanks to you. She was stripped half naked and tied to the front of a scorpion. How Prince Tichane managed to find the competence not to burn her I shall never know. But she lived, you sick little gelding. And she told me *all* about you. About how you ordered your riders to rape her while you watched."

"What are you . . ." *Talking about? Your little sister is a liar, but that should hardly be a surprise. Shit! Come on, mouth, work!*

Zafir stepped away and raised her voice. "Yes. Ordered your riders to rape a royal princess so you could watch because you can't do it yourself? Was that it?" She shook her head theatrically. "The realms will be a lot better without you." *Ah, so that's it. Playing to the crowd. You want a reason to kill me? Do you really think you need one? That makes you seem all the weaker, you know. Better you just did the deed. Please go ahead, though. Anything to put an end to this pain. Although, if you can spare one, I'd prefer an alchemist or blood-mage, who might actually be able to heal me.* He laughed, a broken hacking sound. Zafir spun to face him, furious.

"You laugh?"

"Even when I could . . . I mostly preferred . . . boys . . . Or perhaps you didn't . . . know."

She came closer and a smile twisted her face. "I've been wondering which part of you I should cut off to send to Jehal. Your prick then. He'll recognize it, will he?"

Meteroa laughed some more. In the face of the agony in his arm, it was that or weep. "There's nothing . . . to cut. Tyan . . . saw to that . . . long time ago. You . . . know . . . nothing."

"Oh, I know quite enough." Zafir walked across to one of her riders and snatched his spear. Then she ran at him and jammed the spear into his belly with all the force she could muster. He gasped and groaned at the impact, but his armor held.

"Hold the spear," she barked. Two of Zafir's riders came and took hold of it. They seemed uncertain what to expect, until Zafir walked to the far end of the room and picked up a hammer. Meteroa felt himself almost vomit. *This isn't how I want to die.*

"Slow and painful?" Zafir snarled as she drew close again, as if reading his mind. "No more or less than you deserve, eh? You were behind all of this, weren't you? Jehal's puppet-master. Hyram called him the Viper, but that's you, isn't it? You're the venomous one."

"I think . . . you'll find . . . Jehal . . . has venom . . . enough . . . for us both."

Zafir cut him off. "Well if he does, you won't be here to see it." She swung the hammer. It was a good blow, slamming squarely into the butt end of the spear, and with quite enough force to finally split the dragon-scale that protected him. The impact knocked all the air out of his lungs. Strangely, he barely even felt the pain of the metal barbs ripping his guts apart. Zafir struck the hammer again. That one hurt more, as the point emerged from his back, grating against his spine on the way. The third blow pinned the spear solidly into the throne.

Meteroa closed his eyes. If he wasn't dying before, there was no escaping it now. Even a blood-mage couldn't help him. There was nothing left to do but slip away as quickly as he could and brace himself for some mightily angry spirits waiting in the halls of his ancestors. But Zafir wouldn't allow him even that much peace. The bitter acrid smell came again, slapping his senses, pummeling him awake until it was too much to bear even for a man with a spear through him. Until he opened his eyes.

"Mandras ammonium." Zafir laughed at him. "But you know that, don't you, master poisoner. Well here's some poison for you of a different sort." She snapped her fingers. Three riders hurried over to stand beside her. Two of them were dragging Queen Lystra. The third held a squalling bundle. "While we're having so much fun, before Prince Tichane stops blundering in circles outside and works out where the door is so he can run in to spoil it all, here's one last kingly decision for you. I need to keep one of these two alive in case I have to bargain with Prince Jehal. One. The other doesn't really matter to me, so I'd rather been thinking of getting rid of it. The question is which one. I thought Jehal might care more for his heir than his queen, but you decide. One of them gets to live and one of them gets to die. You get to watch."

She meant it. Every word. *Because she's mad.*

"And if you don't decide then I'll just kill both of them out of spite. I know what you're thinking. Jehal's little starling bride has proven herself fertile. There could be plenty more heirs in her yet. But are there any left in Jehal, eh? Do you know? Does even he? Or has Shezira gelded him like your brother gelded you?"

Meteroa barely heard her. The choice was obvious. *Play the odds.*

"So which one dies? Now!"

"Lystra." The sound that emerged from his lips was little more than a hiss. Zafir smirked.

"Really? Are you sure? I suppose I should have known, but . . ." She cocked her head and gave him a knowing smile. "Are you trying to curry favor with me, Meteroa?" She glanced down at the spear stuck through him. "It's a bit late for that, don't you think?"

"Sword . . . and . . . axe . . ." What came out of his mouth weren't so much words as the bastard child of a hiss and a groan. Zafir's smile grew even sweeter.

"Pardon, My Lord?"

"Sword. And. Axe." There. She must have heard this time.

"Sword and axe?" Zafir threw back her head and laughed, rich and throaty. She seemed to be truly amused. "Sword and axe?" she asked again. "Lystra's a girl, Meteroa. What do you think she can do? Do you think she's even learned to fight? And how long ago did she give birth? She's still milking her brat. She's in no state to fight." She shook her head.

"Scared, Zafir?" If she didn't bite soon then the pain was going to get too much. He could barely speak.

Her smiled faded and her face fell to stone. "You think *that's* going to work?"

Meteroa mustered the last of his strength. He managed a weak shrug. "I just want to see a little sport while I die."

The smile came back. She gave him one last long look, then nodded her head. "Then yes. Sword and axe. Just for you." She tapped hard on the shaft of the spear, which sent such a shock of pain through Meteroa that he nearly passed out.

When the ammonium forced him back to his senses, Zafir had turned away and raised her voice to her riders. "Get me an axe. Give Queen Lystra an axe too. A sword as well if she knows how to hold one." Zafir sauntered away from Meteroa into the center of the throne room and drew her sword. She was already armored and she began to prowl up and down, swishing it back and forth. She could handle a blade, he could see that much. Whether she could handle it well was another matter. *I'm the last person to ask.*

It hit him then that he really was dying. Never mind the pain and the confusion and drifting, he was coming to an end. This wasn't a dream. No more Meteroa. The end of his line. Unless Jehal was his, which was a distinct possibility. *But even then it's not looking very promising, is it?*

He watched as Lystra was pushed out toward Zafir. *You. Your fault. If Jehal hadn't decided that he wanted to keep you, this would never have happened. I would never have come here. There wouldn't have been a Battle of Evenspire. Valmeyan would never have left his mountains. I wouldn't be dead.* Suddenly he didn't much care which one of them lived and which one died.

Someone tossed Lystra a sword. Someone else tossed her an axe. They landed by her feet. Zafir was still prowling back and forth in front of her. For a second Meteroa thought that Lystra was going to fold. *She'll stare at the weapons.* He sighed. *A little quiver of the bottom lip. A faltering step away and then she'll fall to her knees and weep and beg, and Zafir will watch and laugh for as long as it suits her. Then she'll give me a little glance because she'll need to know that I'm still here to see, and then she'll end it with an axe in Lystra's skull. Why did I even bother . . . Oh.*

The other thing Lystra might have done was scoop up the sword and the axe and charge at Zafir with both arms flailing like windmills. It wasn't a bad strategy for a novice, especially if Zafir was a novice too. What he certainly didn't expect was for Lystra to pick up the sword and the axe, give them a couple of experimental swings and throw them both back to the riders lining the walls of the throne room. Then she walked over to them and eventually selected another sword and a different axe. A short stabbing sword and a hatchet. Quick weapons instead of the broadsword and the war-axe she'd been given. Meteroa tried to sit higher in

Zafir's throne and immediately regretted it. Pain hit him like the swing of a dragon's tail. He grimaced. *But I'm going to stay awake for this. I'm not going to die. Not yet. I'll have my sport.*

Lystra weighed both weapons carefully in her hands. She tested their edges. Content, she walked back to the center of the room, the great Octagon that had all but ruled the realms for two hundred years before Vishmir and the War of Thorns. She didn't pause, but sprang straight at Zafir, swinging the axe at her head. Zafir ducked, obviously taken by surprise. She parried the sword aimed at her face but missed the return swing of the hatchet, which caught her a solid blow on the hip. She staggered back, covering her retreat with a wild swing of her broadsword.

Meteroa sniggered, and never mind how much it hurt. Zafir's armor had taken most of the blow, but she wasn't quite standing straight. The shock on her face was priceless. Despite the pain it gave him, Meteroa cackled. *Priceless. Lystra was Shezira's daughter. Raised by the Queen of Flint in the deserts of sand and stone, where there really isn't much else to do. You really shouldn't be surprised, Zafir, you really shouldn't. Although I admit, to look at her, who would have thought, eh?*

"Good you've got all that armor on. Reckon you'd already have lost otherwise," he croaked.

Zafir didn't turn her head, but she must have glanced at him, because Lystra launched herself at Zafir again. She feinted at her head, parried Zafir's backswing and then rolled underneath her axe, lashing out with her hatchet at Zafir's ankle. Zafir saw it coming and tried to jump out of the way but wasn't quick enough. Meteroa heard Zafir gasp. She staggered and hopped a few paces. The armor had saved her again in that her foot was still attached to her leg, but she was limping. With a bit of luck, Lystra had hit hard enough to crack a bone or two.

You're taller, you have longer arms, you have longer blades, you have armor, and yet look at you, Zafir. She's quicker than you and better than you too. Who'd have thought, eh? "Who'd have thought?" He forced a grin. *If I have to die, I might as well die laughing.*

Zafir changed her guard. With one foot crippled, there wasn't much she could do, and Lystra plainly knew it. She took her time now.

"You can concede now if you want," she said in a matter-of-fact voice. "You might as well."

Zafir spat. "I'm going to have your head, girl."

"Jehal will destroy you."

The speaker laughed. "Do you think so? When you're dead, Jehal will climb back into my bed so fast you won't even be cold. You were never anything but a nuisance. Did you know he tried to have you murdered? He wrote a letter." She glanced at Meteroa. "On the morning I had your mother killed, before the sword fell on her treacherous neck, your dear husband wrote a letter to have you killed. Did you know that? Little *girl*?"

Lystra threw Meteroa a glance. Meteroa closed his eyes. *Don't fall for it . . .* But he could see in her face that something had crumbled, as if, deep down, she'd always known she was second-best for Jehal. *Don't believe it. Not now! Evenspire . . .*

Evenspire. They'd only ever had Jehal's word for what had happened at Evenspire.

Lystra's jaw set. She advanced on Zafir a third time, now with measured purpose. "Is that why he snubbed you at your own councils?" She swatted at the tip of Zafir's sword, batting it away. Zafir was barely moving, her injured foot almost useless. "Is that why he left you and came back home? He told us that he was bored. If he was sharing your bed then I suppose that must have been why."

Zafir's jaw tightened. Meteroa coughed a hacking laugh. "She's got you there, Zafir." He was starting to have trouble keeping his eyes open.

"If you lose, I will take your life. If you win then I have to spare it. So you'll just have to watch while I strangle your baby and then hang Jehal in a cage. I suppose your sisters can wait. I had your mother put down for the murderous bitch that she was and neither of them seemed to mind all that much."

Lystra sprang. This time Zafir was ready. Sword met sword. Lystra swung her axe at Zafir's chest; Zafir didn't even bother to try and block it. She jumped away on a foot that wasn't nearly as hurt as she'd let it seem. Lystra's axe hit her in the ribs, hard enough to hurt but not hard enough to trouble her armor, and then Zafir's axe was coming straight back, ready to cut Lystra in two and there was nowhere for Lystra to go.

Meteroa closed his eyes and sighed, but the sound of Lystra being cut in half didn't come. His eyes snapped open again.

She'd twisted inside the blow. The swinging shaft caught her in the midriff and knocked her sideways. Zafir dropped her sword and took the axe in a double grip, hop-stepped after Lystra and caught her a blow around the head with the pommel. Lystra staggered away, dazed, and dropped her weapons. Zafir leapt after her, pressing her advantage, swinging the axe in both hands. The fight was hers. But Lystra kicked, smashing Zafir's injured foot. Her ankle collapsed under her and she sprawled to the floor, cursing.

"Oops," murmured Meteroa as loudly as he could. The pain was going away. He didn't feel much of anything anymore, except a strong urge to fall asleep. Even the Mandras still held under his nose had lost its sting. His eyes were blurred, but he could see well enough to watch Lystra snatch up her sword and jump, blade first, onto Zafir. Zafir rolled and the sword missed and then Zafir kicked Lystra's legs out from under her and Lystra was down too, sprawled atop Zafir. He saw Lystra's fist rise and punch Zafir in the face and then watched her fly back from a foot in the belly. Zafir struggled to her one good foot. Her face was bloody. Lystra had broken her nose as well as her ankle. Zafir picked up her axe and hopped toward Lystra, slow and heavy in her dragon-scale. The room was wobbling up and down. It took an age for Meteroa to realize that that was because he was laughing.

"She's a girl," he groaned. *How long ago did she give birth? She's still milking her brat. She's in no state to fight. What do you think she can do?* He couldn't stop himself from shaking. The whole sorry business was too absurdly funny.

Zafir tried to lift her axe with both hands, staggered, dropped it and nearly fell over. Meteroa made strange sounds, thin merry hoots. He was weeping now. "She's a girl," he gasped. "A nothing."

Zafir hobbled away. "Enough. Someone give me a crossbow."

No one moved. Lystra was still bent double on the floor, but Meteroa's laughter grew. *You can't do that. Everyone will know. Sword and axe. That's what you agreed to. You lose. Look at you.*

"Crossbow." Zafir didn't ask a third time. She hobbled over to one of her riders who held one and snatched it. She took her time to load it.

"Are you . . . so outclassed . . . that . . . you have . . . to cheat?" That took all the breath he had. He wasn't sure he was going to have any more. Lystra was on her hands and knees now, but Zafir wasn't watching her anymore. She was looking at him.

"Enough. Of you."

Come on, you fickle northern shit. Get up, get up! Get up and stab her in the back! I can't keep— Meteroa never finished the thought. Zafir brought up the crossbow and fired. Meteroa's head snapped back as the bolt hit him between the eyes and nailed him a second time to Zafir's throne.

"Go piss with your ancestors," she hissed; and that was all he heard before they came rushing to meet him, to haul him kicking and screaming into the realms of the beyond.

10

POTIONS AND FOOD

Once you got past the horror of it, watching Snow torment the last two alchemists turned out to be almost boring. Once you got past the reek of blood and offal and the screaming that went on and on in Kemir's head even when the alchemists themselves fell silent. They didn't actually say anything very much except for a lot of squeaks and squeals, a few *Please-don't-kill-me*'s and, when Snow picked one up in her claws and dangled him over her mouth, a great deal of terrified shrieking. But they didn't *say* anything. Snow was battering her thoughts into their heads and then picking over whatever bubbled to the surface.

Kemir caught snippets, when he tried. Mostly Snow seemed to be demanding to know where the other alchemists could be found, where other eyries were, where there were dragons and, above all, where and how the alchemists made their potions. She certainly wasn't asking about Rider Semian.

They're no better than dragon-riders. They're no better than dragon-riders. He ran the mantra over and over in his head, trying to believe it. Trying to think of them as something other than scared old men. Eventually, when he'd finished picking his fingernails clean and was on to scraping at the little flecks of blood that still stained his dragon-scale, he got up. Enough. There was only so much of this he could watch.

"Bored now." Snow ignored him. Judging from the way she was acting, the answers weren't much to her liking. Which meant the alchemists probably wouldn't survive for long enough to tell Kemir anything that *he* wanted to hear.

"Oi, dragon." He got up and kicked her foot. She slowly turned to look at him.

You become ever more wearying, little one. What?

"What do you want me to do? Sit on my arse and scratch myself while you eat this lot?"

If it comforts you. Now be silent.

Kemir's face darkened. "Look, I winkled them out for you. Me. So this is where you take a break from mangling them and you tell me about the man who killed my cousin. You tell me what the Scales knew."

He knew nothing.

"What?"

He knew nothing. These know nothing.

"*What?* You said they *knew!*"

In a sudden flash of motion, Snow's tailed flicked out. The tip wrapped around Kemir's waist and he found himself being lifted up into the air. The dragon lunged and snatched up the two alchemists in her front talons. Their wailing beat at the emptiness of the mountain air. Then she launched herself into a run on her massive hind legs, claws shredding the earth, shaking the mountainside, wings beating like thunder until she lifted up into the air and powered up toward the remains of the castle. *You wanted dragon-knights, Kemir, did you not? Perhaps you thought there might be a fight? You thought they might resist? Look, Kemir! Look, all of you, at how your mighty fortresses will fall.* By now she'd almost reached it, a climb that would take Kemir more than an hour on foot. *Look at it!*

There wasn't much left but a big pile of broken stone. Charred pieces of wood smoldered in tumbled heaps, the last glowing embers slowly fading out. Here and there, pieces of stone carried some feature that marked them. A crenellation here, half a window there, broken pieces of archways, maybe a part of a door, sticking out from under the rubble. If Kemir tried, he could picture the castle as it had been before the dragons arrived, and then, just maybe, he could see how one pile of stones had once been a tower, how another had been the keep, another the gatehouse.

Just about.

"It wasn't exactly a very big castle, was it?" he muttered, and then gasped as Snow's tail drew a fraction tighter. She landed amid the stone.

Look, Kemir! Look, you alchemists, you who would enslave my kind. This is what will come. She set Kemir down in front of her and then lowered her face so they were almost eye to eye. *I have told you, little one, that dragons do not act out of spite or revenge, but as you have seen, we have little patience, we are prone to anger, and if we do not avenge, nor do we forgive. I will not forget your Rider Semian, Kemir. In time he will cross our paths and burn like all the rest, and I will hardly notice his passing, but as I do, I will think of you and consider any last debt between us paid.* She set him down and turned to look at him. *And now you have served your purpose. You have given me these alchemists. You are no longer useful.*

Kemir took a step away. "You need me." He tried to sound convincing but didn't really manage it. Belatedly he remembered that the dragon could see into his thoughts.

Yes, Kemir. I see how riven with fear you are. You may hide it from your own kind, but not from me. And fear me you might. She reached out a front claw, still with a wriggling, screaming alchemist held tight within. Kemir could see his face, white with terror and lost blood, only a few feet from his own. He could see the hopeless plea, the tears, the sheer utter despair, the mad idea of mercy . . .

Mercy? Snow snarled. *Why? What mercy have you shown to me?* Very slowly, she squeezed. The screaming became frenzied. Then something cracked, and the screaming stopped. Kemir closed his eyes. *No matter, Kemir. Do not forget the one you left behind, the one still under the ground. That is the greatest achievement of your kind. No matter what we do, there are always more of you. So you will always have ears to bleed with your questions.*

For a moment he thought of running, of how quickly he might reach the nearest pile of rubble. Maybe there would be a tunnel. Could he move fast enough?

I see it in you, Kemir, the empty hole where your purpose used to be. You think, somehow, that striking those who have wronged you will make this change, but it never does and never will. The wrong is never undone. Your hole remains. So you tempt me, over and over, to put an end to your meaningless life. Very well. This time I shall oblige. You may have your wish.

No. That was the very obvious answer. No, he couldn't run fast enough. Nowhere near fast enough.

Stay very still, Kemir. Watch and listen. Snow kept squeezing. More bones cracked, and then there was a soft popping noise. A thick reddish brown ooze began to leak between her claws. Abruptly, Snow opened them. What was left of the alchemist landed by Kemir's feet. He'd been crushed to a pulp.

Tail, claw, tooth or fire? Or do you wish to die in battle? There may still be some dragon-riders that are still alive. I sense their thoughts. They are some-where underneath us. You may look for them if you wish.

Kemir didn't move. Absolutely nothing was left intact.

Yes. Alive but buried. You may dig if you wish. Do you know how many dragons we have found here?

Kemir shrugged.

Seventeen. Twelve are young, five are full grown. There were more here not long ago.

He was shaking. She didn't mean it. Did she? Dragons lied. He knew that now. "You still need me, dragon."

Why, Kemir?

A brief flash of anger pushed past the sight of Snow's jaws, right in front of him. "Because you're so bloody impatiently stupid . . ."

We fly, Kemir. Sooner or later we would have found this place without your map.

"Well you still—"

Scorpions? Would have hurt us, but they would not have stopped us. She set the other alchemist onto the ground next to Kemir and gently pinned him there with the tip of one claw resting on his chest. *Look around you, Kemir. This is what I bring. We will destroy every place like this. We will an-nihilate every dragon-rider and every alchemist and every man who calls him-self a king or a queen or a prince, but this is only the beginning. What of the little people whose life is nothing but toil and graft, whose wants are simply a full belly and strong sons? We will feed on them as we feed on kings and princes, for to our kind you are all the same. Ants. You see the future, I know you do, for I have plucked these questions from your thoughts. We have begun and we cannot stop and there can only be one end. Some of you will try to fight us, some will hide, others will simply stand and do nothing as they die. You are one of those who will fight. I see it in you. You will turn on us. You will die.*

The alchemist on the ground put up a feeble struggle and then gave up.

Yes. Like that, and every bit as futile. Sometimes we will play with you before we eat you. We will not be able to resist. We are, as you once told me, like children. It is true.

She tapped her claw on the last alchemist, very softly but still enough to make him squeal. *This one knows. Your kind war upon one another. Realms here have seized power and prepare to make war against realms there. And all the while your king in the mountains watches and bides his time to strike, but it matters not to us which realm is which. Your kind has fallen to chaos. You will not even see us coming until it is far, far too late.* She tapped the alchemist again. *Tell him, alchemist. Tell him what you have told me.* The claw pressed harder into the alchemist's chest. He screamed.

"Potions!"

Tell him, alchemist.

"The potions! They're running out!"

Yes. The potions are running out. At last Kemir sensed a color to Snow's thoughts. Anticipation. Glee. Joy. Lots of all of them. *Our first fight was not so wasted after all. They are running out of potions. They can no longer make them quickly enough to contain us. The man this alchemist calls master speaks of a cull to conserve their supplies. So that is where we will start. With potions.* Her thoughts grew black and savage. *A cull, Kemir. A cull of dragons. Your kind mean to poison us. Every one of us.*

Abruptly she lifted her claw, balled it into a fist and brought it down on the alchemist with enough force to make the earth quiver. She completely crushed everything between his neck and his knees. A fine spray of blood spattered Kemir's face.

"You going to eat me now after all that, or not?" He managed to keep his voice steady, at least. Would it be so bad to be dead? To join his ancestors? To find Sollos again?

Your nest-mate Nadira wanted to die and you would not believe me. Now do you see? Your emptiness is the same.

"Bones and piss, dragon." His bow wasn't strung, so he went for his knives, one in each hand, and hurled himself at Snow's head. Completely futile, but maybe, just maybe, he could grab a hold of her and stick a knife in one eye far enough to do some real damage. He was quick, very quick . . .

Somehow her head wasn't there. Instead, the end of her tail whipped in from one side and snatched him out of the air with such speed it almost wrenched his spine apart. So fast . . . how could something so big be so blindingly fast?

I see you move in your head, Kemir, that is how. I know what you will do before even your feet understand. She sat back, lifted her head in the air and dangled him high up in front of her. *I have thought about this often, what I will do with you when I no longer have a use for you. I had thought I would simply eat you, but now in this moment I am not hungry. So I will let you go. For what little service you have rendered, you are free to leave us. Run, Kemir. Long and far. When I am hungry again, I will come for you.*

"And how long and far will be enough, dragon?"

Snow seemed to laugh. *There is never an enough, Kemir.*

"Then perhaps I'll stay here and see if I can put your eye out after all. Or perhaps you'd better just get on with it and eat me."

If that is what you would prefer, I will ask the other dragons. We have eaten well, but perhaps one of them still has an appetite.

"And then? What about you, Snow. What do you do?"

I will take my sleeping brothers and sisters far away where we will not be found until they awake. And then we will come, and our hunger will be endless. I am surprised at you, little one Kemir. Most of your kind have not been given such a generous choice, and yet I do sense that you are . . . ungrateful.

"You sound a lot like a rider."

Arrogant? Cruel? Heartless? Without mercy? Look at me, Kemir. Look at what I am. Your riders are nothing more than men draped with an illusion of power. You have fought and killed such men. They are as small and fragile as the rest of you. Look at me, Kemir. Your arrows will not even punch through my scales. Your scorpions are to me as an insect's bite is to you. LOOK AT ME! The thought thundered into Kemir's head. His arms fell limp, almost dropping his knives. He stared at the dragon, helpless. *Arrogant? This is not arrogance, Kemir. This is the natural order our creators intended, that is all. Arrogance is built on hubris. We do not imagine the magnitude of our strength, Kemir. We see it around us, in the ruins of this castle. Do not talk to me of arrogance, little one. Arrogance is thinking your kind have any say in your destiny. Arrogance is thinking you could do anything more than amuse us.*

She lowered him back to the ground. He was shaking, still rooted to the spot, his feet refusing to move as Snow very slowly wrapped her foreclaw around him. "What about cruel? What about heartless? What about mercy?" The words stuttered out of his mouth, kicked out between reluctant lips by the part of him that refused to crumble. Ever.

What of them? She picked him up and lifted him into the air, peering at him as she rose onto her back legs and towered fifty feet above the ground. *We play when we are playful. We rage when we are angry. We eat when we are hungry. We pay as little attention to what our food is called as your kind do, Kemir. If that is cruel and without heart or mercy then that is what we are. I might wonder if we even understand the meanings you give to these words.* With a languid, almost careless motion she dropped him and then caught him again, this time between her teeth. He could feel her breath blowing past him in heavy slow gusts. He'd once, before he'd learned better, imagined that dragons' breath always reeked of rotten meat, but in fact there was usually almost no scent to it at all. Snow smelt warm and slightly acrid, with a whiff of fresh blood.

Tell me what you want, Kemir. Shall I let you go? If I do, one of us, one day, will find you.

For a moment he twitched and wriggled, unable to stop the animal instinct that screamed at him to tear himself free, even if he had to rip himself half to pieces to escape. Snow held him fast.

It is hard to be so gentle, Kemir. If I am distracted I might forget you are there for a moment. That is how little you mean to me.

Most of her teeth were like sword edges, long and hard and sharp as razors, built for shearing flesh and bone and nothing else. Her larger fangs were the size of his thigh. He couldn't imagine what prey they were meant to pin.

Oh, the world was once full of many creatures that are now lost. A few were made like us. Others came when the world was first made. They are all gone now. We ate them. We are what is left.

With a soft gasp, Kemir pissed himself. He started to sob. Fear. That's all it took. Enough of it would break anything, and he'd finally found what was enough to break him. The last little part, the part that had always held out no matter what the world did to him, cracked and fell to pieces.

There. Finally you understand what I am. With that, she took him back in her claws and casually tossed him away over the edge of the mountain.

11

A NEST OF SNAKES

Jehal slid languidly out of bed and hobbled to his dresser. Discarded silks littered the floor. Bright yellows and greens and blues. The best colors, the best dyes, the finest silk. It all came from the silk farms on Tyan's Peninsula, close to his home in Furymouth.

"Does it hurt?" The voice came from somewhere under the tangle of soft furs piled up on the bed.

"No," he lied. "Not at all." Three months had passed since Shezira had tried to neuter him. He threw on a robe and went to stand in one of the windows. Vale was out there somewhere, the Night Watchman who'd placed the crossbow in Shezira's hands the day before he'd cut off her head. He'd be down below, stomping up and down and shouting at his men most likely. At any other time, Jehal would simply have had Vale hanged, drawn and left to die in a cage outside the gates, that old ritual that Zafir had so gleefully revived. *But I need him, and he needs me, and however much we'd love to slit each other's throats, neither of us can stand alone. Put him away for later. When the war peters out, they'll either make me speaker or they won't. If they do, I can do what I like with him. If they don't, well then does it really matter? I should savor the view while I've got it.*

He was back in his favorite room in the palace, in the bedroom at the very top of the slender Tower of Air, looking out over the Speaker's Yard, the Glass Cathedral, the City of Dragons, the Mirror Lakes, the Purple Spur and the Diamond Cascade beyond, except today it was raining buckets and there wasn't much to see of any of those. He'd tried Hyram's rooms for a while, but they made him restless. Too gloomy for his taste. The air was too heavy. Too many ghosts and too much taint of failure and sickness and decrepitude. So he'd come back to the place that had been Zafir's favorite as well as his own, the place that held all his best memories. It was hard. Strange. Ever since Evenspire, he'd missed her almost constantly. Far more than he'd ever missed her when she was alive.

What I mean, if I'm honest with myself, is that this is the place where I had all the best sex. Speaking of which . . .

He'd picked her carefully. She had lips and a tongue that worked miracles, they said, and so they had. The pain had been something like having a white hot and very long needle stabbed between his legs and pushed very slowly but surely deeper and deeper, but there had been more to it than that. *Something* had happened, at least. When she'd stopped and he was gasping, blind with something between ecstasy and agony, her tongue had brushed his lips. There'd been salt. He'd tasted himself on her. She was letting him know.

He still throbbed with the aftermath, pulses of pain enough to make him wince and that wouldn't go away. Through it, he could hardly stop himself from grinning. *I'm still a man. At last I know the answer. Shezira didn't neuter me after all.*

It was a good thing. Not least because it meant he didn't have to throw the woman in his bed out of a window in order to keep his secret. On the contrary. Now they both knew, he could let her go to spread the word that the speaker was whole. He chuckled to himself and set about dressing. The sun had come up hours ago. There were probably things he ought to be doing.

Yes. All the trivial little palace things that Jeiros and Tassan haven't dealt with because they're too busy saving the realms. I'm hardly in a hurry, am I?

By the time he was thinking of putting his boots on, the waves of pain had faded into something that was more a reminder of something sharp than anything truly unpleasant. Gentle snores came from under the furs. Jehal pulled them back and let his eyes wander over the curves underneath. *We could try again. Maybe the second time won't hurt so much?*

He was still pondering when someone started hammering at his door and a dragon shot through the air right past his windows, the wind of its wings ripping through the open balconies, staggering him. One silk curtain tore free and dived away into the void, sucked into the dragon's wake. The woman in his bed was suddenly forgotten. Jehal was out and down the stairs before he could even begin to think. *Are we under attack?*

Vale was waiting for him at the bottom. Of course he was. He bowed, just a fraction late, just a tad too high and an instant too abrupt. "Your Holiness." He smiled thinly, reading Jehal's face. "No, we are not being attacked. If we were, I would be on the walls, supervising our defense." He glanced at Jehal's bare feet. "Shall I find you some shoes?"

"Only if you have nothing better to do," Jehal snapped. "Why is a dragon flying so close to my bed? Whoever was guiding it should be hanged."

Vale gave the faintest of shrugs. "As you wish. They are your riders, Your Holiness. I have asked them before to avoid the palace. There is always the risk that my scorpioneers will not recognize them. I'd be disappointed if we had some sort of an accident. My men have been practicing, Your Holiness, and they are really quite good." Which was certainly true. Day in, day out, Vale had men on horseback charging around the palace flying target kites from their saddles. The parts of the Hungry Mountain Plain that were in range had become so littered with scorpion bolts that when they'd stopped for a day and offered a penny for each bolt returned to the palace, they'd come in by the cartload.

"The dragon was a messenger, Your Holiness. There are dragons massing north of the Purple Spur," said Vale, when Jehal didn't speak. "I will be glad to make an example of the rider, nonetheless, if that is your command."

A spike of dread momentarily nailed Jehal's feet to the earth. "Hyrkallan or Sirion? Or both?"

"Both." Vale's face didn't betray him at all, but Jehal was sure he heard the faintest twitch of glee in the Night Watchman's voice.

Yes, we both know you'd be rid of me in a flash if you could have either of them as speaker. But you can't. Sirion is Hyram's cousin and Hyrkallan is just some jumped-up dragon-knight. He might be the jumped-up dragon-knight who kicked me out of the sky over Evenspire, but that doesn't mean you can make him speaker.

Jehal allowed himself a slight smirking smile, the sort calculated to get under Vale's skin. *If anything can.* "Well, so? What do they want? Come to pay their respects? Come to pay homage to the dead? If that's the case, I hope your men have been keeping themselves busy in the eyries, raking through dragon-shit for any sign of Zafir. If there's anything left, it should have come out by now, after all." What did come out of the wrong end of a dragon? Something, Jehal knew that much. Did anything survive of the bones and armor of a dragon-rider unfortunate enough to become a dragon-snack? He had no idea. Maybe it all burned to ash on the way through. Meteroa. Meteroa would know about that. When it came to dragons, Meteroa knew most things.

Vale bowed another one of his insolent little bows. "Grand Master Jeiros is having a new ring forged. I am not hopeful that we will find the one Zafir wore."

"Perhaps finding the spear will be a little easier?" But the spear had gone somewhere else. *And Jeiros must do something about that.*

"Lord Hyrkallan and King Sirion, it seems, wish to parley. With you."

"And why am I hearing this from you, Vale Tassan? Where is Hyrkallan's messenger?"

"Hyrkallan's messenger, as you call him, is a rider from your own guard, seized over the Purple Spur. He is in the Gateyard, Your Holiness. The message he bore was sealed and for me. I can't imagine why or whether he has others. Hyrkallan also says you may keep the dragon, as a token of his good faith."

"I can keep my own dragon. How very kind." Jehal stared at Vale. *Why? Why don't they simply swarm across the mountains and fall on us?* "Tell me, Night Watchman, if the full force of the north came at us, would we hold?"

Vale smiled and shook his head. "No, Your Holiness. Not even if the Adamantine Men fought to the very last. There would be very little to fight over by the time they were done, however. Perhaps that is what concerns them." He half let out a derisive snigger, and for a moment Jehal wasn't sure at whom it was aimed.

Me. It's aimed at me. Who else, after all? He sighed, waved a bored hand and turned away. "Very well, very well, let them come. Twenty dragons each and a hundred men between them, including servants. The usual promises of hospitality if anyone feels they're necessary, but really it's not as if we're at war with each other." *Ha! Try making Hyrkallan see it that way!*

Vale blinked. "Your Holiness, they have requested that you and the Lesser Council come to meet them at Narammed's Bridge." He raised an eyebrow. "I have informed you ahead of the council, but I imagine they will be eager to agree."

Jehal turned back and beamed at Vale. "Marvelous." *Yes. So absolutely marvelous I'd better be careful I don't faint with delight. So I can either sit here and do nothing while the Lesser Council and Shezira's bloody avatars quietly settle on a new Speaker of the Realms that will clearly not be me, or else I can go with some vague hope of putting a stop to whatever they're planning and conveniently put myself within easy reach.* He gave a short sigh. *Right then. As long as I keep out of reach of Hyrkallan's arm plus the length of one sword, I suppose we'll get on just fine.* He forced the smile a little wider. "Whenever they propose, Night Watchman. The sooner the better. Won't it be nice to put all this behind us?"

Vale bowed deeply. "I would like almost nothing more, Your Holiness."

Jehal shooed him away and then watched him go. *As long as you get to watch me dangle in one of Zafir's cages, eh? Pity I had them all cut down after Evenspire.* Jeiros was no use either. The alchemist had the power to pull Vale's strings if he really tried, but the poor man was too busy watching potion supplies across the realms slowly run dry. In the Palace of Alchemy they were talking about a cull, about sending orders to every eyrie-master to poison their dragons. No one had bothered to mention this to Jehal—he was only the speaker, after all—but it was hard to get particularly worked up about something so inane. At a time like this not one single eyrie-master would heed such an order. The fact that Jeiros was thinking of it merely served to show how distracted he was. At some point, he supposed, he would have to have the master alchemist explain why they couldn't just make more of the stuff.

We can agree on one thing: we need this phony war to end. The way I want it to.

He took his time while Vale prepared the palace for battle, just in case—picking his best clothes, then picking his nails, idling away his time while his servants and soldiers rushed around. When they were finally done, he hobbled out of the Tower of Air, the wound in his leg still aching from the morning. Riding a horse was a pleasure Vale and Shezira's crossbow had taken from him probably forever; instead he allowed himself to be carried in a covered chair down the hill from the Adamantine Palace. He was surprised by how peaceful it was. They didn't hurry—no need for that—and he was left with little to do but stare at the glory of the City of Dragons, with all its little square towers, the ornate palaces around the edge or the nearest Mirror Lake. The cliffs of the Purple Spur behind the city seemed larger and darker than usual, while the water of the Diamond Cascade glittered and shimmered in the morning sun. Now and then, as the wind changed, little rainbows came and went, chasing each other up and down the cliff amid the falling spray. All very pretty.

Or at least it would have been if the rain wasn't still tipping out of the skies. You didn't notice these things, he thought. Not when you were forever riding around here and there, this way and that, getting to some place as fast as you could on the back of a horse or better yet a dragon. He'd never been one for stopping to admire the scenery back when he'd been a prince. Then he'd become a king, and now he was Speaker of the Realms. He was where he'd always wanted to be, and there was nowhere else to go. There was nowhere to race to anymore. Nothing to do but stop and take a look at what was around him.

The impatience came back quickly enough, though. Once he was on Wraithwing's back in a cloud of warm steam, getting slowly wetter and wetter while he waited for Jeiros and Aruch and the Night Watchman to follow him. Cursed dragons kept you warm in the cold, but ancestors help you if it rained after you'd flown them hard. He'd seen whole eyries vanish in a cloud of tepid fog so thick that a man couldn't see his hand in front of his face. You didn't go out in an eyrie fog, not unless you wanted to get stepped on.

Suddenly there was Jeiros, and the Grand Master Alchemist of the Nine Realms was climbing up onto Wraithwing's back as well. The alchemist slid in behind Jehal and began strapping himself into his harness.

"Well this is unexpected," said Jehal as Jeiros settled himself. "Comfortable there? I thought we were all obliged to fly on different dragons."

"Is it always like this when it rains? I don't remember. I did most of my eyrie time in Bloodsalt. If it rained *there* we thought the end of the world was coming." Jeiros flapped at the mist. "The Lesser Council must not fly together. Any of us can fly with you. I got here first." He sounded uncomfortable.

"Ah." *Yes, remind me again that I'm merely some near-worthless figurehead.*

"I imagine that Wraithwing's back will be the safest place to be, will it not?"

"That depends very much on whom you fear, master alchemist." *How easy it would be for one of our passengers to suffer some terrible misfortune. Let's not pretend that I wasn't tempted to have the Night Watchman fall out of his harness once he was a few thousand feet up in the air.* Jehal gave a bitter laugh. "No, since you're the one who makes sure I don't wake up in the middle of the night being dragged out of my bed by a gang of Adamantine Men. I suppose I should be happy to have *you* close."

Jeiros smiled and gently shook his head. "Vale understands your worth."

"Yes." *But is that enough?* "If this is a trap, Wraithwing will be a prize target for Hyrkallan's riders."

"Yes, and that's why I'm here, to deter such treachery, although I think it unlikely. I thought *you* might pick another."

He'd had the same thought, but what was a speaker to do? Hide all the time? Show how weak and fearful he was? No. Enough of hiding and skulking. Enough of poisons and knives in the dark. "I've never been to Narammed's Bridge."

"There wasn't much to see even before the Red Riders burned it down.

Only a few fields and some farms, some huts and a stone house. Hyram used to keep a good stable there with some very fine horses, but Sirion took them after Hyram fell."

"Is there actually a bridge?" *What did you say? After Hyram* fell?

"There was, once. I don't know if it survived the fire."

"You don't know?" *After Hyram fell? Not after Hyram was pushed?*

"For a time it was the only bridge across the Sapphire River. Before Narammed became the first speaker. Afterwards it used to mark the end of the speaker's realm and the start of the Evenspire Road." The alchemist shrugged. "Vishmir built a bigger bridge at Samir's Crossing. There are probably dozens of other places with Narammed's name on them and I don't doubt that a few more of them happen to be bridges. This one just happens to have an eyrie built beside it." He frowned. "Had, at least, before the Red Riders burned it. It was where Narammed hammered out his peace with the northern eyries. It has a symbolism for them, I suppose."

"Do you think Shezira killed Hyram?" Jehal didn't change his tone at all. *Just dropped casually into the conversation as if it hardly mattered at all.*

Behind him, Jeiros stiffened. "It's a bit late for that, isn't it, Your Holiness?"

"I suppose it is. But still relevant, don't you think? Given who we're going to see?"

"The Speaker's Council declared her guilty . . ."

"*Zafir* declared her guilty." Jehal twisted to show off his teeth. "You said fell, not pushed, just now. You think it was an accident. You think Shezira was innocent."

"Vale—"

"Vale knows. I know. Now it turns out you know too. We all know. Shezira never touched Hyram." He twisted himself further toward the alchemist. "*I* tried to stop her. You let Zafir murder her, you and Vale."

The alchemist's face hardened. "You were the one who put her on the throne, Your Holiness."

"Yes. You've got me there."

Jeiros' expression remained stony. Jehal turned away. *I suppose of all of us you're the least to blame. If you knew how much I miss her, you'd have to wonder at my sanity, master alchemist. Mine and hers. If I could bring her back, I just might.* The pain of losing her, now she was gone, was almost a physical thing. He had to pinch himself to remember that Zafir would have murdered Lystra and probably, eventually, all of them.

He closed his eyes and tried to forget the smell of her, the taste of her, the touch of her, until at last the rest of the dragons were finally ready, until Wraithwing powered into the air and set off to fly the few short hours around the edge of the Purple Spur to Narammed's Bridge.

That was, until the grand master alchemist signaled him to land high in the empty peaks and told him that Zafir wasn't dead after all. As Jehal's dragons circled uncertainly overhead, Jeiros whispered it in his ear where no one else would hear, and when Jehal shook his head and wouldn't believe a word of it, the alchemist showed him what had come from the Pinnacles.

His uncle Meteroa's ring, still wrapped around his finger.

THE OUTSIDER

Your ways are not our ways. When your world crumbles, you may expect nothing from me but laughter.

12

✦

CROSSING OVER

The first thing that broke his fall was the top of a tree and an explosion of soft snow. Kemir tumbled down, twisting and crashing off sloping branches, clutching at them with his gauntleted hands, ripping out fingerfuls of twigs and spines and more snow. Something punched his face, twisting his helm sideways so he couldn't see. He clattered off a branch hard enough to wind him even though the dragon-scale armor took the worst of it. His shoulder ricocheted off another branch. Pain burst through the length of his arm. He screamed and then the freezing white ground slammed into him and knocked his breath away.

He wasn't dead. It took him a moment to realize that, another moment to realize that he was freezing cold. That was something to be grateful for. Cold numbed the pain.

Also he couldn't breathe. His helm was gone and his face was pressed into the crushed snow.

He tried to move. Had to. Managed to lift his face and gasped a deep breath. Cold or not, his arm shrieked every time he so much as touched it. Broken. Definitely broken.

He managed to roll onto his back. The other arm seemed to work and so did his legs. His ribs and his spine snarled with a hundred stabbing pains, but nothing was actually refusing to move. He wasn't hacking up blood, so that was good.

He'd been thrown down a mountain by a dragon. For a few seconds panic overtook him. He scrambled to his feet, clawing and kicking his way out of the snowdrift, and never mind how much everything hurt. The snow was deep on the slope here, held in place by the press of trees. He clutched at a trunk, eyes screwed shut, weeping at the pain. Another part of him wanted to laugh. He was alive. Thrown down a mountain by a dragon and he was alive. The tree branches had broken his fall as well as his bones; the snow and the dragon-armor had done the rest. *Ancestors!* It was enough to make a man want to climb right back up, kick the dragon in the face and shout, *Missed me!*

Yes. If he could move at all. The pain was crushing now, coming at him from everywhere. He sagged. Climbing anything was out of the question. If he hadn't been afraid of how much it would hurt, he might have curled up into a ball and simply rolled the rest of the way down the slope.

No, no, no. Stop. Think. You're an outsider. You survive. The pain will go, but now you need to move.

Shelter first. A place the dragons couldn't reach him. He had no idea whether Snow had meant to kill him or simply hadn't thought before tossing him away. *Our kind. So fucking fragile, eh? Well here I am, dragon. Still breathing.*

Shelter. Food. Then water, although it was the Worldspine, so water was easy. And so were the food and the shelter, come to think about it. Back where the alchemists had been hiding. Made him want to laugh.

He started to make his way down the slope among the trees, wading down through snow that reached well past his knees, stumbling and staggering his way from one tree to the next, stopping at each to catch his breath. Every few steps he lost his balance and tipped over, falling as best he could to protect his broken arm. And then he had to get up again. By the time he got to the bottom of the slope, he was exhausted, gasping for breath. He had no idea how long it had taken. There weren't any dragons, though. Snow hadn't come for him.

He was near the lake, or what was left of it. The bridge he'd found last night was gone, the nice neat little channel that had been dug beneath it had vanished too, both washed away without a trace. Where the sluice had been was now surrounded by a wide expanse of mud and slime. Here and there rivulets ran through a dozen and more new channels gouged out of the earth. The last trickles, rushing to find a way down the mountain. There was nothing left except one pole driven deep into the ground, the post that had once held up one end of the sluice itself. That and the huge sheet of ice, sprinkled with a fine dusting of snow, shattered into giant shards as thick as his wrist.

Kemir stared at it. He'd done this. Done it for Snow. Joined in the spirit of smashing and burning.

Ungrateful . . .

He looked back, up through the steep stand of conifers toward the castle. He'd been struggling through the trees and the snow for what felt like hours, but the castle wasn't that far away, now that he looked back. The dragons were still up there, all four of them. As he looked, one of them pushed the remains of half a tower over the edge of the slope. Stones as big as horses tumbled down into the darkness under the trees. The forest shuddered. Pieces of masonry big enough to crush a house toppled over and chased each other, driving a miniature avalanche before them. A tree cracked and toppled sideways, shaking loose a cloud of snow.

Kemir ran, limped, jogged and staggered toward the ruin where the alchemists had been. There were still patches of snow and ice, but most of it here had melted to slush. He tried not to think about how he must look. More lurching than running, cradling his broken arm. When he reached the stair, he went down on his backside, sliding from one step to the next. There wasn't much grace or dignity to it, but at least he wouldn't trip over and kill himself.

He reached the bottom. Knew he was there by the change in the smell of the air, the whiff of charred earth. With his one good hand held out in front of him, he shuffled back and forth in the darkness until he found a wall, then another, and then the pile of debris that half-blocked the passage onwards. Hauled himself over it, whimpering with every movement. Snow had said there was someone else down here. Probably another alchemist. He'd been putting that out of his mind, concentrating on one thing at a time—getting to shelter—but he was going to have to think about it now, down here in the gloom. Didn't have his bow—that was somewhere up the slope by the castle where the dragons were. Didn't have any arrows with him anymore, what with being thrown down a mountain. Nor two working arms. Knives then. Softly creeping closer, a quick stab in the neck and he'd be done. And then just lie here until the dragons went away and his arm got better or else the food ran out. Whatever happened first.

One of his knives was missing too. Just gone. Probably buried in the snow under the trees somewhere. Still had the other one, though. One was enough. Only had one good hand anyway.

At least the light was still there, off in the distance, the same shadow hundreds of yards away. Steady this time. He shuffled along the tunnel, propping himself up against the wall, trying to be quiet. There was still plenty to trip on. He passed passages, dark and lifeless, one, two, then the third, the other stairs leading back to gods knew where. As he reached the light, he heard a noise, a sort of rasping, gasping noise. He gripped the knife in his good hand. His left hand, which wasn't his better hand. Then he peered around the corner.

The refuge was as he remembered it. Beds, table, pots to piss in. The food was still there, and the lamps too. Three dead bodies on the floor with Kemir's arrows in them. And a woman. Sitting at the table with her head in her hands and her back to him. She had no idea he was there.

He held the knife tighter still. The easy thing, the wise thing, would be to creep around behind her and send her the way of the rest of them. He didn't know how he'd missed her when he'd come down before. Must have been lurking in the shadows at the back, invisible in the dark. Chances were she'd seen him. Would remember him. Couldn't be many folk came creeping down these tunnels, after all . . .

Dragon-riders, alchemists, same difference. He was about to take a step, but then hesitated. He'd never cut a throat with his off-hand before. Never done it with one hand. Wasn't sure he knew how. Best to bury the knife in her back then. Or into her neck. His hands and feet wouldn't move, though. Stabbing a weeping woman in the back was enough to make him at least pause.

So what if she's a woman? Makes no odds. Why should it?

Maybe she wasn't an alchemist. Maybe she was just some serving girl they'd dragged down here to amuse them while they waited for the dragons to go.

Or maybe she is an alchemist. *Get on with it!*

His feet still weren't moving. If he made a noise, he didn't hear it, yet the woman suddenly looked up, right at him. She blinked, saw the knife and then jumped up, skittering away to the other side of the table. Scared witless. He searched her eyes. No sign of anything except what you'd expect when you'd just spotted someone creeping up on you with a knife.

He was so gods-damned tired. The knife quivered in his hand. He slumped against the wall and let out a low moan of pain. "I thought . . ." *Thought what, Kemir? Go on, talk your way out of this one.* He closed his eyes for a moment and found it hard to open them again. Gods, but it was dark. "Can you help me?"

"Who are you?" Her eyes were wide and wild.

"Are you an alchemist?" She was young, when he finally forced his eyes open again. Alchemists were always old, weren't they? But it was hard to say in the strange half-light of the shelter, in the dim white glow of the alchemical lamps that lit it.

She shook her head.

There was food on the table. A bit old and a bit stale, but it was still food. Kemir lurched to the table, crashed down into a chair and slumped across the table. He was ravenous. "You're the only person I've seen alive. Dragons have destroyed everything." He coughed, which still sent pains ripping through his chest. Not good. Maybe Snow had done more than break his arm.

"You . . ." She was looking at the knife. Kemir glanced at it, still in his hand. A good killing blade. Snuffed a few in its time. She wouldn't be much of a problem. Small and scared and fragile. Even as broken as he was. For the second time he stepped through in his head exactly how he'd kill her.

Dragon-riders, alchemists, same difference.

No. He was sick of killing.

The dead men on the floor with the arrows sticking out of them told him he was a liar, that he wasn't sick of killing at all. He was afraid, that's what it was. Afraid of being alone. Afraid of dying with no one to hold his hand. That was more like it.

"No," he said. He let go of the knife and pushed it across the table. "I don't want to hurt you." And then he watched, willing her to believe him. She didn't say anything. Just stared. Kemir shrugged. The less said the better. "First I knew about anything was the roof coming down. Spent the night buried in rubble. Couldn't see a thing. Managed to get out in the end. There's dragons up at the castle, tearing it to pieces. Lake's gone. Empty. Everything else smashed to bits and burning." He narrowed his eyes. Looked down at the three dead men with arrows in them. "Did you see them, the ones who did this?" The knife was still there, still in reach if he needed it.

She shook her head.

"I didn't see anything except a roof fall on my head. By the time I got out they were on up the mountain. Just as well. I've got no strength for a fight." Kemir closed his eyes. Mostly he wanted to lie down. He needed rest, and lots of it. Then maybe he'd get to find out whether Snow had broken anything that wouldn't get better. Broken bones he'd had before. He sighed and stood up. "Can you help me?"

She looked at him like a frightened rabbit.

"My arm's broken. I need to set it straight. It would be a lot easier if you helped." He wrinkled his nose. "Don't you alchemists learn about that sort of thing?"

"I'm not an alchemist." There. Words. Not screaming spitting hatred. Words.

"You know how to set a splint?"

Eventually he got a reluctant nod. He started plucking the arrows out of the dead men on the floor. Good strong shafts. Good for splinting a break. Shame to have to snap them in half, but needs must as the Silver King drives . . . He frowned, hearing himself think that old saying. Silver King, silver ones. What did they have to do with all this? Could they be the same? Had to be, didn't they? Did that mean the Silver King was coming back? Not that he had much of an idea of who the Silver King even was. A demon? Outsiders knew nothing when it came to things like that.

He put the thought aside. For now he had other worries.

She watched him. Didn't help, just watched, even as he got to taking off the shirts from the dead men, cutting them into ribbons then tying them back together. One-handed it was hard, and he had to hold his knife between his teeth, but she still didn't help. Finally he was done.

"Come here." He held out the arrow shafts and the strips of cloth. The woman shook her head. Didn't move. He clenched his fist, but she just backed farther away. Staring, watching. For a moment Kemir wondered whether she was as much a liar as him, whether she knew exactly who he was and was just waiting for the chance to kill him.

Well fine. If that's what it is, let's get on with it. I've gambled worse in my time. He started to bind his right hand to the top of a table leg, wincing and groaning. Every movement made his arm worse. When he was done, he looked at her. One last chance.

"Please?"

Another shake of the head. Another step away.

Right then. He put a wad of cloth in his mouth. Then he braced his feet and his good arm against the table and pushed, separating the two broken halves of his arm. And screamed. Lots of screaming. Vaguely, through the walls of pain, it looked like his one good arm was doing something vaguely right. Splinting the break. Wrapping strip after strip of cloth around as tightly as he could. Strip after strip . . .

Screaming felt good. At some point he either finished or gave up. He didn't remember untying his hand. The screams faltered to weeping and whimpering. He forgot about the woman then. She was a vague thing across the room, as significant as the food on the table and the dead bodies on the floor. He stumbled and crawled to one of the cots and fell into it, sobbing. The pain overwhelmed him. Turned out he had a lot more than a broken arm to scream about.

Eventually he fell asleep.

13

THE SCALES

Kemir.

He had no idea how far he'd gone or for how long. Long and far, though, and still the dragon had found him.

Kemir.

"You tried to kill me."

If I had tried, you would be dead.

"Why didn't you finish me, dragon?"

Can it not be generosity? she asked him. Which made him laugh. She was laughing too.

Generosity? I don't think so. Laughter was good. Laughter helped him clean up the mess that a tidal wave of fear and sorrow and regret had left behind.

Then I had some other purpose. It matters not. Goodbye, Kemir.

"You're an ungrateful shit," he shouted at her in his dream.

You are still alive, Kemir. Remember, while I tear these kingdoms down, that this is what you wanted.

He felt the dragon lever her way back into the air and glide away from the ruined eyrie, her thoughts fading as she flew. He didn't have much of an answer to that. Didn't have much of an answer to anything anymore. *No family, no friends, no Sollos, no Nadira, no reason for doing anything much anymore except looking for Rider Rod so I can kill him, and then what? No hate, no revenge, no nothing.*

No, that wasn't right. He had pain, plenty of pain. In his arm. He sat up and wished he hadn't. He could walk. That was something. He was breathing hard, not getting enough air. His chest hurt. *Everything* hurt. Down here smelled bad too. He got up. He needed to be out. He wasn't sure whether Snow's voice in his head had been real or a dream, but she was gone, he was sure. Gone into the deep mountains with her kin.

Why is it so dark? The alchemical lamps seemed dimmer than he remembered. He couldn't see across the room anymore. They were fading. Going out. Leaving him trapped down here in blank nothing.

The woman was awake, backing away from him. He ignored her, heading for the surface as fast as he dared, gasping for breath. Back to fresh air and the sky over his head. When she saw where he was going, her face changed. Scared. Afraid he was going to abandon her. Afraid of being alone.

I was going to kill you. The thought horrified him.

"The dragons are gone." He stumbled down the passage as fast as he dared, over the mound of rubble, up the stairs and into the glorious freezing air, and never mind how much it all hurt to get there. Outside, the early morning sun had crept high enough to light up the eyrie. Most of the valley below was still in shadow. He stood amid the ruins, taking deep breaths, staring up at the sky. Better. Better to be outside. The cold took away the worst of the pain. Took the edge off it at least. He was right. The dragons had gone. He squatted among the broken stones, rocking back on his heels, wondering what to do. He'd lost his sword, lost his bow. When he looked, he didn't even have a knife with him anymore. Must have left it down with the woman. Didn't matter. There'd be more lying about, if he looked hard enough.

I will take my sleeping brothers and sisters far away, where we will not be found until they awake. That is how long you have to run before I will come. And how long was that? Weeks? Maybe a month? Never mind swords and bows. He had a purse full of coin and a pouch full of Souldust. Should be able to have a lot of fun with that in a month. He could at least die with a smile on his face. Had a lot more appeal than spending his last days trying to dodge swords and arrows. Especially with a broken arm.

And then what? Roll over and burn just like everyone else?

A boat down the river to Furymouth then. Away on a Taiytakei ship by whatever bargain it took, to whatever lands lay beyond the Sea of Storms. The Taiytakei had to come from somewhere, right? They couldn't just live on their ships. And Snow had found those islands. And even if they *did* live on their ships, that had to be better than being burned and eaten, right? What did the Taiytakei want? He had money and Souldust, but somehow that didn't seem enough. They traded in slaves, but that was too much like being a dragon-knight. Dragons. The Taiytakei wanted dragons. Everyone knew that. Or failing that, they wanted the secrets of the alchemists . . .

Alchemists. He couldn't help but laugh. With one hand, the fates pissed on him, with the next they showered him with gold. The woman. He could make her up as an alchemist, even if she wasn't. She had to know something to have been in those tunnels with the rest, right? He could trade her for passage. Or maybe there were other bits and pieces hidden under the ground. Potions. Recipes. Anything.

Dragon-riders, alchemists, same difference. There was that mantra again. Wasn't really working.

Most likely he'd wind up a slave. But slavery was better than dead, wasn't it? Slaves could always dream of breaking free.

He glanced up at the sky. The dragon was gone but she was up there somewhere, off into the lifeless glaciers at the heart of the Worldspine or the arid peaks of the Purple Spur. *If I was a dragon, that's where I'd go. Nothing there.*

The start of the long road up to the ruins of the castle wasn't much more than a track, a path wide enough for a man on a horse maybe but no bigger, certainly not wide enough for a wagon. It wound up the slope down which Snow had thrown him the day before, cutting though the black trees, gloomy and overhung. The snow was clean, unmarked. No one had come down here for days. There was probably a stair, somewhere underground. Or a shaft and a cage on pulleys for lifting loads up from the eyrie. No need for a road at all really. At least not until some passing dragon smashed your stairs and ate your slaves.

He sighed. On the one hand, he didn't have the energy for climbing mountains. On the other, his arm wouldn't stay that way forever. Sooner or later he was going to need a sword and a bow again. Chances were he'd be good for that around about the same time that Snow came back to set fire to the world. Perfect. Still, he could always take his mind off how much his arm hurt by thinking about how much his ribs and spine hurt instead. Or his legs, or his knees, or the windburn on his neck or the creeping numbness in his toes. Plenty to choose from there.

By the time he reached the first bend in the road, he felt as though he'd spent the whole day running. He leaned against a tree, caught his breath and listened. Nothing. Not a sound. Not even a bird. Not even the rustle of the wind in the trees. Just a stillness. Silence, muffled up in a blanket of snow.

It really shouldn't have taken him more than an hour to get to the castle, but instead it took half a day, wading through the snow and the scattered lumps of stonework that littered the road and the forest, tossed aside in the destruction of the castle. When he got to the top, his bow was right there where he'd dropped it, still in one piece. He gave a murmur of thanks to his ancestors for that. It was a nice bow, carved from the wing bone of some long-dead dragon. It was the kind of bow that a dragon-knight would have, and in fact *had* had, right up until Kemir had slit his throat. They'd had one each, him and his cousin Sollos. The second one was carefully wrapped and padded and, for all Kemir knew, still tied to Snow's back. The bow that he'd taken from his dead cousin's still-warm body on the same day that he'd first met Snow. The bow he'd sworn he'd use to kill the dragon-knight who murdered him. Or was that the one he was holding in his hand, and was it his own bow left on the back of the dragon?

Yeah. That was something else he could do. He could spend his last few months hunting down one last dragon-rider while around them the world burned.

He shook his head. He needed to rest, to lie down, to go back to sleep, preferably for days, but up here there was nowhere. Bright brilliant mountain sun, gleaming off the slopes around the ruins. Smashed blackened stone. Churned-up earth, ripped and torn by dragon claws. The charred skeletons of a few trees, caught in Snow's fire. All the snow for hundreds of yards had melted and then frozen again in the night. Everywhere hard and cold and bright and glistening and unforgiving. He sat down on a flat rock for a while and slumped into a doze, soaking up the feeble warmth of the sun until the shadows of the broken trees and stones started to grow long again. Then he forced himself up, forced himself to look through the ruins, even though all he wanted was to lie down and sleep. Didn't find anything more either, so that was all a waste and in the end he trudged away, back down the road between the trees with just the bow. A sword could wait. Arrows he could find on the way. Make, if he had to. A knife, though. Couldn't do without a good knife. Best get his old one back from the underground refuge. Best get as much food and whatever else they had down there too, since he wasn't going to be doing much hunting for a while. Couldn't stay up here forever. Sooner or later, people would come. Wasn't sure which was worse, people or dragons.

The sun was behind the mountain by the time he got back, the whole eyrie cast in freezing shadow even while the mountains across the valley gleamed a pinky-white. The woman was waiting for him. Or she was waiting, at least. Sitting on the stones just as he'd done before her, staring at the devastation. She was shivering. He sat down beside her, close enough that he could feel the warmth of her on his skin through the biting air. She didn't seem to even notice him, but even so the feeling of being close to someone almost made him cry. Strange way to feel about someone you'd planned to murder, were planning even now to sell into slavery, but that was how it was. He would take them both to Furymouth. He would get them both away before the dragons came out of the mountains, and he'd do whatever it took. That was the way to look at it. Never mind what happened at the end.

A light dusting of snow covered the eyrie now. Not enough to hide anything. Must have come in the night. The sky had been clear all day. Clear and cold.

"We should go," he said after they'd sat together for some time. The woman didn't move. Eventually, Kemir left her there and made his way slowly and painfully back down into the refuge. At least she'd found some more lamps. With a bit of light, the place wasn't quite as bad. Didn't make him constantly feel like the air was being crushed out of his lungs. At some point, when his arm was throbbing so much he could hardly think, he lay down for a rest and fell asleep. When he woke up, the woman was back. She'd made a bed for herself in one of the storerooms, as far away from him as she could be, all mounded up in blankets and furs. If it hadn't been for the snoring, he'd never have known she was there.

He went back up to the surface but it was the middle of the night, snowing again, the air so cold it seemed to freeze the breath in his lungs. Down under the ground, he had no idea what time of day it was. He tried going back, tried going to sleep again, but for some reason he wasn't tired anymore. Arm hurt like someone was taking a hammer to it, but that was just pain. Cold, now that was a killer.

Later he went out again. The sun was up and he found himself a hand-cart over by the frozen mud of the lake. Loaded it with as many blankets and furs as he could find. Food too. Then he walked a little way down the path beneath the frozen lake to see where it went. Down toward the valley, that was as much as he could tell. The torrent of water hadn't washed it away, which was something. It was a good path. Uneven, but laid in heavy chunks of stone, one of the old paths that littered the mountains. Farther away, he thought he could see the line of it etched into the sheer gray sides of another mountain. No idea where it went. There were paths like this all over the Worldspine, and most of them didn't seem to go anywhere at all. Just meandered about the place, all so old that no one could remember what they were for or who made them or why. So old there were barely even any stories.

Any kind of down was good enough. After that, he went back to the refuge and slept for the rest of the day. When he couldn't sleep anymore, he went back to the surface and waited as the sun went down, as another night fell and the freezing air pricked at his skin. The sky was clear. Thousands of stars shone bright and half a silver moon lit the corpse of the eyrie. The sort of night Kemir remembered from a long time ago, from before he'd ever seen a dragon. Crisp and brilliant and beautiful and deadly cold.

Once it was about as cold as it was going to get, he got ready to leave.

"Get dressed." He found the woman and shook her awake. She cringed and whimpered until he backed away and tossed her a pile of blankets and furs. When the fear ebbed away, the expression on her face was blank and vacant. "Time to go." He pointed to a pair of bags filled with food. "You carry those. Put the furs on. It's cold."

She followed him, mute and compliant. From her face, she didn't understand what or why or how, and cared even less. Kemir frowned. "It's a long way to the bottom," he said. "We start walking at night and take our warmth with us. If we don't get to shelter before the end of the day, we walk on. That's the way of the mountains." He reached out and tapped her gently on the shoulder, looking for some sort of response. "Better to die on your feet than in your sleep, eh?"

She didn't even blink. He shrugged and left. At least she followed.

His toes went numb first. That was always the way. No matter how many strips of fur he wrapped around his boots, the cold always found a way in. His fingers went next, then the rest of his feet, then his face. He was still walking, though, when the sun slowly crept up from the east to set fire to the mountain tops. His legs grumbled bitterly. The broken arm was the worst, even though he had that hand stuffed under his furs to try and save it. The woman was still following in his wake, wordless.

The path was no help. Lumpy stones, and steps, everywhere steps. Up, down, whichever way you went. Steps made for agile men with strong legs, not for cripples and whimpering women. The paths he'd known before had been down in the valleys, where it was flat. Hadn't been ready for steps. The handcart had been dumped long ago and most of the blankets with it. On the other hand, the alternative was mostly a sharp black tumble of rocks, scree and scraggy trees that propped up mounds of snow. You could see how old the stones of the path were from how they'd been smoothed around the edges. Where there were steps, they'd been worn by passing footsteps. But then the moss and the grass that grew between the cracks said that whoever those many feet had belonged to had passed this way long ago. Not many came here now.

When the sun was finally high enough to feel warm, he stopped on a cluster of rocks and cleared away the snow. They made a little fire and boiled some water. With only one hand, with fingers that could barely move, everything took ten times longer than it should. He spent most of his time on his knees, fumbling in the snow for things that he'd dropped.

The woman watched him, staring with empty eyes.

"You could help, you know," he growled, but she didn't seem to hear. His arm was hurting so much that as soon as he'd got a pot of snow melting over the fire, he collapsed, panting and gasping, lying on his back and staring at the sky. The world started to spin.

The next thing he knew, the woman was squatting beside him. She was lifting his head, trying to pour something scalding hot between his lips. Bewildered, he shook her away; she jumped back. As he sat up, she held out a wooden cup.

"Awake now, are you?" he asked tersely, staring at the cup. What had she been trying to do? Poison him?

She shivered.

"Cold? No shit." He was swaying. He felt as though he was light enough to float up into the air and at the same time heavy enough to sink into the ground.

The wooden cup waved itself at him again.

"What is it?"

She didn't answer. After a moment's thought, he took it from her and drank. If she had wanted to kill him, she'd had chances enough by now.

"I'm Kemir," he said, handing back the cup. She nodded, wary, and didn't answer. Wary was good, though. Better than vacant. "Where are we? Any idea?" He finally managed to get back to his feet. Whatever she'd given him, he was feeling it straightaway. A warmth and an energy. If she'd poisoned him, at least he was going to die comfortable.

She shrugged.

"The end of this road has to be a place we can sit down and get some food and fall asleep without freezing to death. Has to." *Fall asleep, yes, that would be good.* Even thinking about it was dangerous. His legs had heard and were already getting started without the rest of him, and it was only the middle of the morning. His hips were aching, as if to beg him to lie down and take the weight off them. He was in worse condition than he'd realized. There *had* to be some sort of shelter at the bottom, didn't there? Although the farther he followed the path, the less promising it seemed. There had been ruts under the snow at the top of the eyrie, handcart tracks, but they'd led only as far as a collection of little houses, all smashed and burned by the meticulous dragons. After that the path had run past the lake and turned into this narrow stony thing that wound along the side of the mountain, not going up much, not going down. All around were snow, outcrops of black rock and a vast silent emptiness.

"No one comes this way much, do they." He looked at the woman, but she'd withdrawn again. "Bring everything up by dragon? But where are the farms? Where's the food for the dragons themselves?" He walked off a little way to peer down the slope. There wasn't much sign of life down in the bottom of the valley. Not civilized life, anyway. Trees and trees and more trees. Probably a lot of rocks and little rivers too. For a moment he wondered if they should go back, but when he looked that way, he could see that they had in fact come down, and quite a way, and the thought of trying to climb back up again made him want to sink to his knees and cry.

On then. Like it or not. He'd lived half his life in valleys like these, survived and prospered in them. Could even carry the weight of a useless woman if he had to. But not with a broken arm. Dragging what he'd saved from the handcart down was wearing him out, but if he left it, they'd have no food, no firewood, no shelter and no means to get any.

The path was still a path, even if no one used it anymore. It had to go *somewhere.*

"Want to go back?" he muttered, glancing at the woman, as much to see what she'd say as anything. Go back to what? To wait for another dragon to come and hope it was one with a rider on its back? They'd kill him anyway. Certainly if they knew who he was.

"No!"

Speech. That was good. "What?"

She was staring at him. "No! Not back!"

He nodded slowly, wondering. "I don't want to die down there. If there's no shelter and no help, that's what's going to happen." He looked meaningfully at his arm.

"Give me your knife!"

"What?"

"Give me your knife!" She thrust out her hand as though punching someone. Slowly and carefully, Kemir gave her his knife. He watched as she mixed herbs and mushrooms and bits of what looked like dried black flesh in boiling water. The last thing she did was cut her hand and bleed into the infusion. She put the bowl on the ground and pushed it toward him.

Kemir wrinkled his nose. "What is it?"

"Drink!"

"I've seen your sort do blood-magic before, to make a dead man talk. Well, I'm not dead and I can already talk, so what is it, alchemist?"

"I'm not an alchemist," she hissed.

Kemir looked at the bowl. "Could have fooled me."

"For your arm. It will heal much quicker with this." She looked ready to run away. When Kemir still didn't move, she took another step away from him. "There are people. In the woods. There is shelter along this path. Old places. You mustn't tell them we come from the mountain. Say nothing."

In a flash Kemir understood. Her fear gave her away. Her fear of him. "Outsiders, are they?"

Her face was answer enough. Yes.

"Your dragons feed on them. You hunt them."

She held the knife out, pointing it at him. Even with a broken arm, it was hard to be scared of someone who was shaking so much. For a second or two he thought about killing her again, but he needed her to sell to the Taiytakei. Which wasn't really even the start of why he couldn't kill her, but it would do for now.

In the end, he reached out, took the bowl and drank the potion that she'd made for him. It tasted foul. He sat down and regarded her.

"If that was poison, how long do I have to wait?"

She watched him, torn between staying and running away. Eventually he'd had enough.

"If you're not staying with me, I'd like my knife back, please. If you are, then we need to keep going. This cold will suck the life out of you if you stay still. So let's try this again. My name's Kemir." He gave her a close look. Her eyes were bleary and fogged with fatigue. But she wasn't slack-jawed and empty. When she still didn't move, he shrugged and got up and started down the mountain on his own. It wasn't long before he heard her behind him.

"Kataros," she said. "My name is Kataros."

Kataros. Carefully making sure he was looking ahead so she couldn't see, Kemir smiled. *Kataros. Pleased to meet you, Kataros.*

"Kataros. Isn't that an alchemist name?"

14

❖

JUSTICE AND VENGEANCE

They stopped one more time, late in the afternoon and still a long way from the bottom. They were among the trees now but still above the snow line. There was an old ruin. Not much, just a few walls about as high as a man and a place where the path widened into a carefully laid circle of stones. Kemir watched this almost-alchemist search around, almost frantic, looking for something. Caves, probably. Shelter.

"There aren't any," he said. Every ruin in the realms had caves. Except in the mountains and the buildings put up before there were dragons. That's what the old folk in the mountain villages said. Made before there were dragons, so there weren't any caves. No need, you see. He said that to the woman. She looked at him for a moment as though he was mad and went back to searching. When you thought about it, probably he *was* mad. Before there were dragons? There had always been dragons.

Night was coming, came quickly down in the valleys. The deep cold would come with it. Kemir made a fire. Kataros brewed another potion and then they walked on. The potion and outsider bloody-mindedness kept him on his feet. Those and the certain knowledge that if he fell, even once, he'd never get up again, and the cold would kill him.

He had no memory of the night. Afterward, all he could remember was the sunlight seeping lower into the valley again, down where a wide and shallow river ran through the trees. The snow was gone, the air almost warm and the path was still there, barely visible, overgrown and almost buried in grass and ferns and moss and vines. He remembered the sunlight because that was when his legs finally gave out. He collapsed by the river, dead on his feet, too tired to even light a fire. The burning from his arm was pushing through the woman's potions. Steps. There had been steps too. Endless steps, steps, steps coming down the mountain, big and uneven and steep and filled with a malice that wanted to pitch him over and into the void below. Steps.

"Make a fire," he groaned, but Kataros only stood and looked helpless. *What does an alchemist know about starting a fire in the wilds?* He just about managed to get one going, almost weeping with fatigue; that done, he wrapped himself up in a heap of furs and fell asleep. Warm.

He woke up again in the afternoon feeling almost as bad as when he'd fallen asleep, but they walked on anyway, through the evening, and gave up again when the sun set and darkness came. The moon and the stars were up, but the trees were thick now and little light reached through the leaves and branches. The path was too rough to follow blind, the stones too uneven, lifted up by tree roots, washed loose by water or simply gone. A broken arm was one thing; a turned ankle could be the death of them. Down here they had enough furs to keep warm. As long as it didn't rain, which, this being the Worldspine it usually did.

As long as they kept going.

When he woke up again, he was shivering. Kataros was huddled next to him for warmth. She still wouldn't speak, still seemed terrified of him, but at least she seemed to understand that he wasn't about to rape and murder her. That day they passed a place where a slurry of mud had washed down from the mountain. The sluice and the lake? he wondered later. Or maybe something else. Were they anywhere near the eyrie still? He was having trouble thinking. Fatigue, that was it. He was simply too exhausted. They had food from the eyrie for a week or two. Water from the river. Shelter and furs enough that the cold wouldn't kill them down here. Maybe they should rest. Build a shelter to keep the rain off and just rest.

He had strange dreams that night. Dreams of dragons. As though, fleetingly, he was slipping in and out of Snow's thoughts again.

Why are you here? The dragon was flying high. Snow fields shone below in the moonlight. A dozen dragons flew around her. They were angry. No, annoyed. They didn't like flying in the night.

You are dying.

He slipped away from them. A bit later, he slipped back. Now the dragons were settled in a valley somewhere. Could have been any mountain valley—they all looked the same. For no better reason than that, Kemir decided it must be the valley where all of this had begun. Where riders from some mad dragon-lord had attacked Queen Shezira's party while the queen herself had been at the Adamantine Palace. Where he'd run from dragon-fire and Snow had first flown free. That was a Scales who'd done that. The Scales who'd raised Snow from an egg had urged her away and she'd taken him with her.

Daylight. Potions. He didn't remember making a fire or breaking his fast, but he must have done both, since there was a fire and his belly was full. Then more walking. All blurred together. The next night Kataros might have tried talking to him, but if she did, he didn't hear her. Too full of dragon-dreams. They came again, stronger this time. Snow and Ash and the others. All flying. Their joy of freedom and the simmering rage filled him. Made him smile.

There might have been another day. Another night. Kataros shaking him, he remembered that. No fire. Didn't matter. Dragon-dreams were more real anyway.

They flew across the sea, Kemir and Snow and the dragons she'd freed. They flew across the sea and buried themselves in the high mountains by the coast, where titanic waves crashed against towering cliffs, and the cliffs vanished into the clouds. In the ice-bound high places where no dragon-rider ever flew, he pored over a map . . .

Snow flew in the dark . . .

. . . as close as she dared, Kemir on her back . . .

. . . eyries buried deep in the stone, guarded by hundreds of scorpions . . .

Frustration and rage.

A dozen horsemen, riding through the high valleys. The horsemen were unexpected and the dragons were hungry. They were always hungry. Kemir watched the slaughter, watched the dragons play with the horsemen. When they came back, they were gleeful. He thought it was the joy of the hunt, the taste of human fear, but no. The Mountain King was moving his dragons south, Snow told him. His eyries farthest from the sea were almost empty. Kemir hardly cared. He looked at the riders. The sight of them brought back every reason he'd ever had for everything he'd ever done. Pain, hate, rage. Watching, helpless, as his cousin was killed. Watching, helpless, as his home had burned.

You are one of us, Snow said to him, and they were flying again up to the bleak icy heart of the Worldspine.

Memories?

"What are you saying?"

He blinked. He was in a valley surrounded by trees, next to a river, walking along a trail. He had no idea how he'd got where he was but, for a moment, everything was clear. Kataros was standing in front of him, shaking him.

"What's wrong with you? You're raving."

"What am I doing here? This isn't right?"

And then that moment of clarity slipped beneath the waves. Pain. He was in pain.

Still dying.

Night again. More dragons.

I see you, Kemir.

Come and get me then.

Night changed to day. Kataros drifted through his dreams, dragging him by the arm. Trees. Lots of trees. And mud. The path changed under his feet. No more uneven stones. Slick and smooth now. Mud. Something warm and bitter in his mouth. None of that seemed real anymore. Snow, that was what felt real.

I have something. A gift. Ride with me.

He seemed to fly. Fast, impossibly fast, flitting from one place to another. Leaping and dancing through the dragon's memories. He roamed the emptiness between the Worldspine and the Maze and the Purple Spur. Dry dead stone peaks drifting below or else furious torrents of water between a cage of dark sheer walls. Nothing lived here, nothing at all; there were only titanic spires and curtains of ruddy stone where even dragon-riders had no reason to fly.

Come! See!

Between flashing peaks, away into the Worldspine, where the mountains were capped with snow again. Faraway words echoed through the cold air and the untouched peaks. They came, carried on the silence, flecked with a fusion of anger and despair.

"Kemir!"

Rider Semian. He knew, not from the voice but from the way the thoughts tasted inside his head. The cold was so bitter that he was surprised it didn't freeze Semian's call to his lips. There wasn't even a breath of wind. Semian had bawled out his challenge and it had rung clear. The mountains and the Worldspine scorned him with their silence.

"I have a destiny!" he screamed again, and Kemir heard him clearly.

He jumped off the mountainside from where he sat and slid out into the void, gliding silently, searching for the rising air that would carry him upwards. He felt the call to war. Saw men and dragons, eyries and castles and cities and palaces, all aflame. It would not be long. He gave a few lazy flaps of his wings and then stretched them out and soared up toward the mountain peak. He could see Rider Semian clearly now. He was standing, arms outstretched. He must have been looking the other way. *He will have nothing. Be nothing. Kill! Burn!*

"Kemir!"

He seemed to float toward Semian, drifting with easy deadly purpose. The sun shone behind him, brilliant and cleansing. Perhaps it was his shadow falling over Semian that made the dragon-rider turn as Kemir rose up the side of the mountain to meet him. Huge, wings outstretched, filling the sky. The sun cast a halo of fire around him. Semian didn't move, but Kemir heard his thoughts, over and over, the same. *Out of the sun there shall come a white dragon.*

He swooped closer, grinned wide. His jaws opened, a hundred bone-swords sharp and gleaming to carry Semian to his destiny. *And the dragon shall be Vengeance.*

"Kemir! Kemir!"

Kill! Kill! He bit down. Thoughts fluttered and died and the glorious taste of salt and iron took their place.

And yet there, in his moment of ecstasy, in his final triumph, something was pulling him away, away from death and the clear blue sky. Away to somewhere dirty and blurred that tasted foul. He suddenly couldn't breathe.

Kill! Snow! Kill him!

Be at peace, little one.

His own voice sounded faint. Weak. Distant.

"Kemir!"

The red rider and the white dragon. Justice and Vengeance.

"Kemir!"

Hands were shaking him. Hard. His mouth tasted of earth and blood. The air smelled of fire. He was lying on his back. Kataros was crouched over him. The hands doing the shaking were hers.

"Kemir!" Hers was the voice he'd heard on the wind. The voice that had pulled him back. Gentler now, but the same nonetheless. "Thank the ancestors."

He sat up, dazed, bemused. Horrified to see they were somewhere far away from the last place he remembered. Lower. The eyrie mountain was somewhere far behind them, lost to sight.

They were beside a road. Not some never-used valley trail, but a proper road made of mud and hoof-prints and the ruts of cartwheels.

"Where . . . where are we?"

The woman shrugged.

"How long . . . How long have I been here?"

She sat back. "You've had a fever for days. Then you were walking and you just fell over. I thought you were going to die."

Would probably have been best for both of us. He rubbed his head. He felt woolly inside but otherwise strangely well. His arm barely hurt at all. It was in a sling. When did that happen?

"I was with the dragons. The dragons from the eyrie."

Kataros looked at him askance. "How do you know they were from my eyrie?"

"The dragon was white. One of the dragons from the eyrie was white." He shrugged.

"And did you see who rode them?"

"They didn't have any riders."

"When you were at the eyrie, you drank water from the lake." She shrugged as if that was the end of the matter. "You can fly with the dragons if you do that."

"No, I didn't."

"Then you've become feverish from your injuries. You've been having visions. I'm not surprised. I barely brought you back."

She looked different. Sounded different. She was talking to him for a start. Not staring into space. Not vacant and empty or wide-eyed and frightened.

"How long since we left the eyrie."

She shrugged. "A week. More. I've lost count."

"A *week*!"

"We followed the path. We found a road. You made fire and shelter. But now our food is nearly gone. People use this road. Outsiders. You have to talk to them. I'm sorry."

"You're sorry?" His eyes narrowed. "What did you do to me, alchemist?"

"I kept you alive. I kept the cold at bay and I broke your fever. What caused it I can't say." She shrugged. "Since you say you didn't drink dragon-water."

There wasn't much to be said to that. They'd kept each other alive. As for Semian, Kemir wasn't sure whether what he'd seen had been real or a dream.

Let Semian be dead, he decided. That was for the best.

15

THE PICKER

The morning after he'd stolen the Speaker's Spear, the blood-mage Kithyr was gone again from the City of Dragons, this time riding out into the Hungry Mountain Plains with a dozen carts and twice as many men from the merchant's house. As an assayer, Kithyr was good at what he did: precise, shrewd enough to see when he was being cheated, honest enough not to be bought, flexible enough to make an exception when he saw a farmer in real need. The Adamantine Spear lay wrapped in its black silk at the bottom of a wagon full of grain. The Picker came too, driving that very same cart after the regular carter had fallen conveniently ill. As best he could, Kithyr forgot that the spear was there and lost himself in his work. The grain, when they had enough of it, would be carried to the Fury River gorge. It would make its precipitous way down from Watersgate to the river and the waiting barges at Plag's Bay. He didn't know where it would go after that, probably up the river rather than down it, but he knew where the spear went. It went with the river, to Furymouth, to the Taiytakei and the half-gods they had brought with them.

In all of Kithyr's calculations the one thing he'd never contemplated was that no one would even notice what he'd done. In the eye of his mind he'd seen the soldiers on the gate rush to the Night Watchman almost as he was riding through the gates. He'd seen the Night Watchman run to the alchemists and the grand master roused. He'd seen his deception exposed. They'd know him for what he was. *Blood-mage!* The cry would echo around the palace. Everyone would be torn from their beds. The Night Watchman himself would lead the pursuit, racing into the City of Dragons only a moment too late, tearing the doors off every inn and dosshouse. And then, with a great moaning cry of despair, the grand master alchemist would find that the spear was gone and they'd all know what he'd done.

It was what he'd feared and so he'd planned to meet that fear. A lesser man would have bolted for the river, but no. Kithyr and the Picker and their wagons of grain meandered the Hungry Mountain Plains, wandering among the golden fields south of the Sapphire River valley and the rain shadow cast by the western edge of the Purple Spur. Every day they bought another wagon of grain, sometimes two, sometimes three. At every stop the wagon train grew bigger, picked up more men. In the evenings, when they stopped for the night to set their camp in the balmy twilight air, Kithyr looked south. Out toward the deep purple blotches of cloud that littered the southern sky. Toward the hidden scar of Gliding Dragon Gorge only a few days away. Toward Plag's Bay, the gateway to the Fury, the start of the long road to Furymouth, the south, the Taiytakei, the realization of all the power he'd ever dreamt of. He could run toward it at any moment, but no. He would stay close to the palace and the City of Dragons while the Adamantine Men and their dragons scattered to the four corners of the realms on their search for their precious stolen spear. He would wait for them to be gone. Only then would the journey south begin.

Except it was beginning to look, if he waited for that, like he'd be wandering the plains for a very long time indeed. No hue and cry had been raised. As far as he could tell, no one even knew that the spear was missing. At the very least he'd expected to see soldiers on the roads, riding swiftly to carry the news: *Blood-mage abroad.* Nothing at all was almost an insult. Now as he watched the setting sun, his feet began to twitch, eager to be gone. Eager to put an end to this.

"The best thievery is when a man doesn't even know he's been robbed," mused the Picker. He was wearing a sly smile, watching Kithyr staring at the southern sky.

"Is it that obvious what I'm thinking?"

The Picker nodded. "About as obvious as having it writ all over your face in ink, I should say. Course, I know a few things the rest of these fellows don't. It might behoove you to look a little less troubled, if I may say." By "the rest of these fellows" he meant the other carters and teamsters driving their wagons toward the river.

Kithyr nodded. The Picker looked like any other man, but Kithyr knew better. The Picker, although his skin was light, had come from the Taiytakei. If he had powers of his own then Kithyr had never seen them used, but the sense was always there that the Picker could *do* things. In equal parts, the Picker was here to help him and to keep him honest. He certainly wasn't averse to the odd murder or two with those strange knives he carried with their invisible blades.

The magician stretched and forced out a smile to briefly smother the frown that lived on his face. "If only we knew that was the case."

"Careful, was you?" You could tell he was Taiytakei from the way he spoke. Most men didn't see past the pale skin and just thought he had a funny accent and a weird way with putting words together, but if you stopped and listened hard enough, it was clear that he came from across the sea.

Kithyr snorted and his smile faded. "If you have to ask then my only answer is scorn and disdain."

"Got what you went for, maybe. Not the same as careful." The Picker picked up a stem of straw off the back of one of the carts and sucked on it. "Could be you left a trail wide enough even a dragon-rider fellow could follow."

"No."

"Well then, stop your worrying."

The blood-mage stood up and went to the Picker's cart. The cart where the spear was hidden. He stood by it, frozen.

"Don't be messing with my cart." The Picker's voice hardly changed, but now there was a flash of steel lurking inside it. *I can do things when I has to . . .* One of the first things the Picker had said, years ago when they'd first come together.

Years. It really was that long. When he, Kithyr, had been little more than a dabbler, and the Picker had casually walked into his life and made him an offer he couldn't refuse. *A few things you and I have to do to keep our masters from over the seas happy, and they'll be letting you into a few secrets as the time goes by.* They'd lived up to that promise too, and now here he was, perhaps the strongest blood-mage since the Edict of Vishmir and the purges that had followed.

Being ordered about by a thief.

"Why do they want it?" he asked suddenly. The Picker had never actually said so, but the spear was quite obviously meant to end up in the hands of the Taiytakei.

"Why'd you think?"

"Because it has power."

"I expect lots of things has power. I'd say it's because it commands the dragons."

"Old stories aren't necessarily true ones."

The Picker shrugged and chewed on his stick of straw. "Best kind though, old stories. You have to admire them. It's like an old soldier. It might not be pretty but it's got something, something lots of other stories didn't when they fell by the wayside and got forgotten. It's got the urge to keep on, to keep going, to keep being said. Gutsy like. And there's nothing as good as a kernel of truth at the heart to keep a story alive."

"Does *your* blood run with magic too?" All those years together and he'd never actually asked. *I could find out now. When you came to me, you were the dangerous one. But I've learned so much more than what you showed me . . .*

"Make a difference, would it?"

"Not really."

"No reason to spoil a mystery then, is there." The Picker didn't move. "That's another thing a good story likes, that is. A mystery."

Kithyr suddenly found his insouciance immensely annoying. He stepped away from the cart, though. The Picker was right about that. No need to draw any attention where it wasn't needed. Instead he moved among the roadside camp, helping with the fires, chatting idly to the grain merchant's sons and the few drivers he'd come to know. It was a mask of amiable obscurity and one he wore well.

The voices came later. At night and only at night, after all but a few watchmen had gone to sleep and the air was filled with snoring, that's when they came. Every night the spear spoke to him. The first time he'd been dreaming, but now it spoke when he was awake. To him and only to him.

Earth-mage.

Earth-spear.

Become as one.

We tasted your blood.

We will serve you.

If you free us.

Sometimes, if he closed his eyes, he saw himself in another land, or another time, or perhaps both. Armies that filled the landscape crashed together like the sea breaking against the land. Dragons fought dragons, and on their backs they carried men of glittering silver. He saw even bigger monsters, creatures the size of cities. And he saw the sorcerers of the Dark Moon, clad in their black steel and calling down the powers of night and day, of darkness and light. He saw it all, from far above, circled it, and then fell, diving toward its midst.

. . . he was the Black Sorcerer, the dark wizard carrying the Adamantine Spear and with it all the power of the earth. He strode through the armies like a colossus, flinging aside all who stood in his way. When the dragons came he raised the spear and they melted before his will. The silver magicians fell helpless before the spear as it drew their power and added their strength to its own.

And there, in the middle of it all, he found the Ice King. The two charged at one another and their shared scream of glee shattered the world.

He woke up. Always at that moment of coming together, and then the voices would start again, whispering and pleading. *Free us. We will serve you . . .*

The watchmen were at their posts, sitting around their fires at either end of the camp, talking idly, making jokes. Not paying much attention, because out here in the middle of the plains there simply weren't the bands of roaming thieves that lurked in other parts of the realms. Now and then bursts of laughter broke the quiet and the rhythm of snores. Every night Kithyr left the watchmen a bottle of spirits to keep them warm. Every night they drank, and with it they drank a drop of his blood. Every night they became more his. He had nothing to fear from them. *Look away.* That was all he needed to think and they would obey, casting their eyes into the gloom around them. The Picker was the one who troubled him. The Picker drank nothing except fresh water, taken straight from a stream or a well if he could. Sometimes, when they were in a city, he would settle for a trough or a fountain. Kithyr had even seen him bend down and drink from a puddle. He was the same with his food. Never anything where another man's hands could have touched it. And so, for all Kithyr's trying, the Picker had never drunk his blood.

But now the Picker was asleep. Kithyr got up and walked to the cart. Sometimes, when he slipped his hand into the grain until he touched the spear, the voices fell silent, as if soothed by his touch. Then he felt something else, another power, a thing for which he had no name but that was as large as the sky. Something deep asleep but slowly waking. A power that terrified him with its sheer immensity.

We are yours for the taking. We will show you. Let us free.

This time, when his hand touched the spear, it reached farther. This time his fingers wrapped themselves around the shaft.

Why would you let this go? Why would you give us to mere sailors? Men?

Because they have promised the power of the silver kings to me, that's why.

But that is who we are, blood-mage. Killed by the spear in the madness at the end of the world. We can give you the power we once knew if you choose it. Why would you give us away?

Why? His head swam. Why indeed.

"I wouldn't be listening to them if I were you," said the Picker. His eyes were open now, staring at Kithyr. Apart from that he hadn't moved.

"Listening to what?" Kithyr let go of the spear. The voices hissed their disappointment.

"Them voices from the spear. Them."

"You hear them too?"

"No, but now I knows that you does. Watch out for voices, so I was told. Voices always gets you in the end. All that whispering of power and such. Best you pay them no heed. Best you go back to sleep."

So he can cut your throat while you dream. He knows. He wants us. He hears us. He speaks with us.

He will take us.

Leave you with nothing.

Kithyr didn't move. His fingers stretched and touched the spear again. He glanced at the watchmen, but they were still obediently paying no attention at all to anything happening in the middle of the camp. "Who are you?"

"The Picker. That's all I am. I makes sure that all sides keeps their promises."

Kithyr's fingers tightened on the spear again. *If I was a true sorcerer, I could destroy you in a blink. That's what this spear would give me.* He reached out with his mind to the men around the fires. Touched them where only he could thanks to the blood they'd drunk. *Picker. He's a thief. He needs to be taught a lesson. He needs to be an example to others. He needs to feed the crows.*

Yes! He felt the spear-voices and their glee. As one, the watchmen stopped what they were doing. Their mouths hung open, midword. They scratched their heads and looked among the wagons.

"What have you done?" asked the Picker, still not moving. "Not something stupid, I hope."

"Stay very still," whispered Kithyr. "It'll go better for you. I'm thinking I might not be taking the spear to Furymouth after all."

"That so, is it?" The Picker sat up, very slowly, and adjusted his cloak. "Well if you changes your mind sharply, I might scratch my ear and wonder if I'd heard right. You might want to do your reconsidering quick-like though."

"No."

"Shame. You're a wise and educated fellow, full of books and learning, so you've maybe heard a thing or two about the Elemental Men?"

"Killers. Lots of mystic claptrap."

"About melding with the earth and turning into air and water and so forth. That sort of thing, aye?"

"Yes." Kithyr felt his throat tighten. The watchmen were moving much too slowly, still not quite grasping the compulsion he'd placed into them. *Too many at once. I should have picked on one and then the next and then the next.* He concentrated his mind on the nearest, let the compulsion change and morph into something new. Into an order. *Kill him. Now.*

"Aye. Mystic claptrap." Abruptly the Picker sank into the ground and vanished. All that was left was his blanket, collapsing slowly to the ground. Kithyr felt a sudden shock of wind behind him, a presence right beside him and then something that burned gave his throat a fleeting touch. "Not as mystic as you thought." He felt movement, but he couldn't move. His feet were stuck to the ground. He didn't dare turn his head. The voice shifted to under the cart. "They tells us that every time we do it is a year off our life. A year, blood-mage. Take that on your soul." He could feel the blood running down his neck now, running down his throat. He coughed, only the slightest shake, but that was enough. The trickle turned into a flood.

"Our blades are so thin the sun shines right through them. Cast no shadow. But one thing we can't do is carry that wretched spear with us. Tried that already. Didn't go well. No, so that were your purpose and well you served it, wizard. Annoying we got no further, but hidden in a wagon full of grain will do."

Kithyr collapsed, all the strength rushing out of him in a red torrent. *No.*

He was a blood-mage. Blood obeyed his commands, and so he commanded it now not to leave him. The flood stopped. Reversed. He turned his head. The Picker was there, crouched under the wagon that held the spear.

"Strong you've got," he hissed.

"Dead you've got," snapped Kithyr. He ran his hand across his throat, catching drops of the blood that still covered his skin and hurling them at the Picker. They would eat into him like acid. They'd consume him in seconds! They'd . . .

Kithyr blinked. The Picker was gone. Vanished. He looked frantically behind him, but the Picker wasn't anywhere to be seen.

Gone. And good riddance. He felt a coldness inside, though. *Surely the blood had touched him before he could vanish himself a second time. It must have . . .* Eyes somewhere nearby were watching him. Hairs prickled where their gaze lingered on his skin. He was out there, in the darkness. Not dead. Maybe crippled, but not dead. *The Elemental Men. There can only ever be ten. When one dies, the next five in line fight to the death to see who will take his place.* But those were Taiytakei stories, and Kithyr had no idea whether to believe them. Most likely he'd heard them from the Picker himself. Made them questionable, to say the least, but the Picker was clearly *some* sort of magician. A blood-mage then, or something else? From what little he knew, the Elemental Men were mostly a myth, but in those myths they were the most deadly hunters in the world. Only one man had ever survived them. A sorcerer who was also a sailor, who'd fled to sea and was never seen again. Because the Elemental Men, for some reason, couldn't cross water . . .

The river. He can't reach me if I'm on the river.

The river then. Right now. Never mind the wagons and the grain; they could sit and rot. He'd hold the spear in his hand if he had to . . .

He fought back the urge to run, right now. Running wouldn't do him any good. The Picker had always found him before. But here . . . He looked around him at the watchmen moving uncertainly toward him. They had his blood in them, all of them, waiting for his call to serve. Well now they would. Not that they'd stop an assassin like that, but they might get in the way. They might die usefully. And if there were only so many times the Picker could use his power . . .

By the time the men reached Kithyr, scratching their heads in confusion with a vague memory of something they were supposed to do, they were his.

16

DUST AND THE CITY OF DRAGONS

After half a day on the road, they met a cart and hitched a ride. Outsiders. Old traders. Old was good. Sometimes young men would fight just because there was a fight to be had. Old men, on the other hand, usually wanted to grow older. Like the alchemists, for all the good it had done them. Kemir handed over some of the coin he'd taken from the eyrie. They eyed him up, eyed his clothes, his bow, his arm, his knife. Then they eyed his coin and the woman and decided they'd take his coin the easy way. They were headed for a camp by a river. Kemir had no idea what river or what camp they meant and didn't bother to ask. Didn't matter. All rivers went to the same place in the end. Furymouth. The sea.

"Three days 'less there be storms. Ye can share our fire. Water's for free. Eats I don't have to spare. Eats old Hanzen will have for ye at the river if ye have a gift for him. Ye live with a bit of hungry?"

Kemir nodded.

"We get to the river, we go our own ways. Ye'll be on ye's own. Trail between here and there, that's quiet enough. Empty mostly. River camp, though . . ." The old man tutted and shook his head. "Two of ye looking like ye do, ye'll find trouble, whether ye look for it or no."

And that was that. As much as the men ever spoke.

The wagons rolled from one valley to the next, following the passage of the mountain rivers, which became ever more broad and swift, sometimes swelling out into great lakes. Now and then Kemir saw little boats out, fishing. Rafts really, nothing more. On either side, sheer walls of stone rose up toward the sky. They showed no sign of fading into hills, but the farther they went, the denser the forests became, a heavy deep green, thick with scent, pines all packed so close together they could barely breathe and hardly ever saw the snowcapped peaks towering above.

When they camped, Kemir made a token effort at staying awake. Outsiders were a fickle lot. Chances were as good as anything they'd decide to murder him in his sleep. But really he couldn't be bothered. He had a splitting headache. He gave Kataros the last of their food. Let them kill him. There was something to be said for being dead.

No. That wouldn't do. He had to stay awake. Had to live.

He must have fallen asleep anyway, though, because the next thing he heard was Snow laughing at him.

Why do you want to live, Kemir?

Because that's what outsiders do, and that's what I am. We live. We do whatever it takes. Sometimes we do horrible, terrible things, but we fight so we can live. We fight so we can be free.

So do we, Kemir.

He tried to turn his back on her, tried to make her go away. Eventually she did. He felt her mirth ringing in his mind long after she was gone. When he woke up and discovered no one had murdered him after all, he wondered if he'd have been so generous.

For the rest of that day and all of the next it rained. Worldspine rain. No drama but steady and relentless. The carter sat impassively and watched the road roll toward them. Kemir sat at the back and watched it roll away again and with it the mountains. Rain trickled through the cracks in his stolen armor and glued itself cold to his skin. The road started to descend, a slight slope that grew steeper as the last day passed and they sank into a sharp-sided canyon gouged out from the heart of the Worldspine, a scar of mud, crisscrossed by a hundred rivulets jumping and dashing down the broken boulder slopes. The sun dipped toward the horizon, and this time the carter kept on going right into the night, until at last they reached the bottom of this gouge between the mountains. When he looked at the river in front of him, past the throng of tents and animals and people and campfires to the almost endless black wall of rock on the other side, Kemir knew where he was. The Fury.

The old carter drew his wagon to a halt. "Here ye be. Hanzen's Camp. Be going no farther, me. Boats be going from the water's edge." He stared at Kemir, unblinking, as if he didn't quite understand why Kemir was still there.

Kemir shrugged. He slid off the back of the wagon. He didn't pull the woman with him. *You choose,* he thought. *Them or me. They're a better choice. They'll look after you. At least until the dragons come.* But by the time he'd finished thinking that, she'd climbed down and was standing beside him. The old man turned away, barked his animals back into motion and slowly vanished into the throng.

"I knew this place existed," he said quietly. He was talking to his dead cousin, he realized, not to Kataros at all. Sollos would have liked it here. To him, it would have felt like home. Open fires everywhere. Noise, tents, huts. Enough people to fill up a town and, as best Kemir could tell, every one of them was busy getting drunk or singing songs. Quite a few were doing both.

He walked farther into the chaos, weaving between the fires. In one place there were snappers, tame ones. That was a thing he'd never seen. They yawned and growled and stretched their necks. They had bloody claws and bloody muzzles, and around each one was a little cluster of men, fussing and cooing over them. Strange-looking men with painted faces and feathers wandered to and fro among them, receiving little nods of deference as they passed. They carried bags of powder on their belt. Now and then they stopped to sprinkle some on the slabs of rancid meat that the men fed to the snappers.

Alchemists. They're like alchemists. The snappers are their dragons and the powder is the potion to keep them docile. He had no idea if it was true, but it seemed to fit. Idly he tried to imagine the same scene without the feathered men, with the snappers freed from whatever dulled their urge to hunt. All the men he could see, all gone. He'd killed a couple of snappers in his time, when the ground had favored him and his arrows had flown true. He had no illusions about how lucky he'd been.

Now give them wings and fire and make them a hundred times bigger. He shook his head. It was hard, even thinking about it, not to be afraid. He tried looking at the men camped around him. Bandits, vagabonds, dust traders. *What will you do when the dragons awake? What will you do when Snow comes out of the mountains? Will you fare any better than the rest? No. You'll be food, just like everyone else.* He tried imagining them as dragon-knights when Snow came. The carnage in his mind's eye looked much better that way. Then he went and found himself a good place to sleep. The woman followed him, mute, like a lost dog. That would end soon enough. They'd get a boat and it would take him into the heart of the realms and she'd abandon him the first chance she got. For some reason the thought made him sad. Alone again.

Never that, Kemir.

The dragon, still there now and then. Neither of them, it seemed, knew why. She mostly left him alone now, ever since Kataros had fed him whatever potion had pulled him out of his fever. But he could feel her, always, still there, a tiny feather-tickle against his skull.

As soon as the sun rose, Kemir shook the woman. They picked their way through the confusion on the banks of the river to where a cluster of boats had appeared, waiting to take anyone who could pay in gold to the City of Dragons. He held Kataros' hand without thinking much about it, almost dragging her through the mass of men and crates. Picked a boat on a whim, haggled without any real enthusiasm. Then sat and stared at nothing very much until the river sped them on their way. The Fury was riding fast and high, swollen with snowmelt. *The river knows what's coming,* he thought. *Even the water wants to get away.* Now and then he opened his mouth to speak, but he couldn't find any words. What was he going to say? That in a few weeks the world would end? That they were all going to die? Beg her to stay with him so he could sell her as a slave to the Taiytakei?

Eventually she got bored and wandered off among the other passengers. She always came back, though, never strayed far, always sheltered close as the sun began to set. He even saw her smile when she thought he wasn't looking. It had been a long time since he'd seen anyone happy, if that was what it was. No, he didn't have the heart to tell her what was waiting for them both.

"Are we going to the City of Dragons?" she asked as she sat beside him on their first night afloat. "I grew up in the City of Dragons. In the Palace of Alchemy. I never saw much of the city. Then they took me away to the mountains."

He could smell her, and that made him want her. He tried not to think about that. "You can go wherever you want. I'm going to Furymouth."

"Oh." She sounded disappointed.

"I'm going to see the sea." He laughed, in spite of himself. "If you've got any sense, you'll come with me. We can find a great ship to take us to another land where there aren't any dragons. Or any dragon-knights. I've been to the City of Dragons too. It's not for me."

She was looking at him. Asking him with her eyes to say more.

"What's to say? It's a city filled with rich men who despise anyone who is beneath them and grovel at the feet of any lords or princes that happen to pass them by. And there are a lot of those." *Far too many.* He could remember the first time he'd been there as though it was yesterday. The first time he'd flown on the back of a dragon. "Well, that's how I saw it."

She didn't reply. In her face he saw how bitter he sounded.

"I went there with Sollos," he added quietly. "My cousin." It felt as though half a lifetime had passed since he'd died. "We had an errand to run. A bloody one that ended badly and gave me one of my prettier scars." Without thinking, he touched his chest. "No, nothing much I want to remember about the City of Dragons. It's pretty, I'll give it that." Hard to forget, though, that first sight of it. Sitting on the back of some war-dragon, finally seeing the mountains of the Purple Spur fall away into the empty space that was the Hungry Mountain Plain. At the far tip of the Spur, water, glittering on the ground. The fabled Mirror Lakes. Kemir's voice dropped low. "I'd never been to the City of Dragons before, never seen the Adamantine Palace, but we'd sold our swords around dragon-knights for long enough to know all the stories of how beautiful the city was from the air. And it was." Nestled against the southernmost foot of the mountains, backed into a sheer wall of rock that must have been at least half a mile high, it had still gleamed in the sun. High above, the waterfalls of the Diamond Cascade pitched over the edge of the cliff. A fine spray of water kept the city permanently fresh and cool, and if you looked for it, you could always find a rainbow on any sunny day, hovering somewhere among the low towers. He smiled thinly. "Yes, from a distance, it's probably the most beautiful place in the world. But under its pretty skin, it's ugly." The towers of the city had shimmered and shone their best that day, snatches of rainbow colors floating in between them. Yet the silvery jewel of the Speaker's Palace had put them all into shade.

But that's her world, he reminded himself. *Not yours.* He tried to remember that he was supposed to be dragging her to Furymouth with him. Making her a slave in exchange for passage away.

Sounds like the sort of thing a dragon-knight would do.

Oh shut up.

He stood up, pushing Kataros away. Seeking out his own space to clear the memories from his head. "Beautiful on the outside, rotten on the inside. After the arrow I took out in the swamps the year before, I suppose I should have known better." He shivered. "We went there to kill a man. Turned out he was bonded to a blood-mage. We were lucky to live. And you know what? After we'd failed to get rid of him, after we winkled out a blood-mage in the middle of the city, what does Queen Shezira's knight-marshal do? Does she expose him? Does she have the mage hunted down and hanged? No, she pays him the queen's gold instead." He sat down and raised a hand in mute apology. "I saw him, a year later, at Outwatch. Both of them, in the queen's eyrie, the blood-mage masquerading as an alchemist. The Picker. That's what they called him." He sighed. "Creepy bastard."

"I don't want to be a Scales," she said, but he didn't really hear.

EARLY THE NEXT MORNING, THE boat stopped at another riverside shanty town. Kemir and Kataros got off while the boatman busied himself getting ready for the long haul through Gliding Dragon Gorge to Plag's Bay, where the only road for hundreds of miles wound its way up and out of the gorge and eventually to the City of Dragons. Kataros would get off there. Kemir didn't think he'd be stopping her.

Oh well. Just have to sell myself into slavery then.

He looked back up the river. The valley was already deep and steep here, but you could still see the peaks of the Worldspine in the distance. Back there they were mountains. Here they were more craggy hills. Ahead lay the Maze. A dozen or more rivers, each carving their own way down from the heights of the Purple Spur. The mountains stole all the clouds, and so the Maze was a barren hard mess of hard rock, sand and dusty earth where it never, ever rained. Of towering mesas and stone pinnacles, of canyons, rivers, rapids, waterfalls and flash floods. No one lived here. No one except bandits.

Absently he looked at his fingers. No rings. That was good. The Order of the Finger hid away in the Maze. They had a liking for rings, or so he'd heard.

The dragon was out there too. Snow. Didn't know how he knew, but he did. Even thinking about her, he could feel his connection to her stir. Maybe she'd fly out of wherever she was hiding, burn them all and be gone again. And no one would ever know.

Well bring it on, dragon, you know I'll be waiting.

As the boat pulled out from the bank once more and the current took hold and dragged it away, he found it hard not to look back. With a force of will, he pulled himself away and marched to the bows, staring ahead at the wide expanse of water ahead. Kataros came to stand beside him.

"It's all there behind me," he said quietly. The woman surely couldn't care less, but some things needed to be said, if only to the wind. "Everything I was is gone. All that matters is whether I can run fast enough to get away. Nothing else." Nothing else at all.

To his surprise, she took his hand in hers. He wondered what that meant. "I know," she said, and squeezed.

"Do you think there's much to see between here and the sea? I've never been south."

"I think there'll be a war," she said.

17

❧

NARAMMED'S BRIDGE

Jehal peered over the dragon's shoulder as Wraithwing circled what was left of the landing fields. Jeiros had described the place well. Most of it was blackened soil, the grass just beginning to regrow. There had been buildings once, but they'd been smashed and weeds were growing up among them. A mile to the west and a mile high, the cliffs of the Purple Spur threw long afternoon shadows out across the northern edge of the Hungry Mountain Plain. A thousand trickles of meltwater ran down from the sheer stone walls and merged into a maze of creeks and streams, everything converging into the steep-sided scar that ran across the land. The valley of the Sapphire River. The last water before the deserts of the north.

The bridge itself was still in one piece. You could see why Vishmir had built another one farther to the east where the Sapphire valley flattened out. Narammed's was nothing more than a lot of planks suspended high above the rushing waters by some ropes, all swaying gently in the wind. Jehal felt somehow let down. He'd expected something grand. This was where Narammed had forged the Speaker's Peace?

Let down by the bridge, perhaps, but not by the dragons waiting beside it. Hyrkallan's outriders had seen him coming from miles away. Counted his dragons and then flown back to their master to say that the speaker and the Lesser Council had come to honor their truce. Waiting on the ground on the north side of the bridge were two of the biggest dragons in the realms. Hyrkallan's B'thannan and Sirion's Valediction. *Almost as big as the monster that Prince Tichane brought to Zafir's council when she condemned Shezira. Almost.* Beside them were a motley collection of hunters and war-dragons, all of them made small by the two monsters. He spared a lingering glance for the hunters, but none of them had any colors that he hadn't seen before. Nothing here to add to his eyries.

Meteroa's eyries. His uncle had been the one with the passion for breeds.

He landed Wraithwing on the south side, walked him up close to the bridge. The dragon stared out across the chasm. His muscles were tense. He tossed his head and snarled. That was dragons for you. Always looking for a fight.

You had to wonder who'd gone to the trouble of building a bridge out here and why they'd bothered. Most likely some nameless company of Adamantine Men had done it simply because they could. All he knew was what Jeiros had told him, that Narammed had come here in his later years, when his power was almost secure, to broker a final peace with the northern kings after he'd betrayed their trust and made a peace with the south. *Rather like this. Except when Narammed met them in the middle of the bridge, he'd had the strength to force them to their knees. Can't see Hyrkallan bending much of anything this time. My neck, maybe, if he can get his hands on it.*

The sight of Meteroa's severed finger haunted him.

"No one else knows," Jeiros had said up in the Spur where no one could possibly overhear. "Valmeyan has come out of the mountains. Zafir lives. They have taken the Pinnacles and doubtless Furymouth as well. They send you this gift." Valmeyan had sent his message with one of Meteroa's riders on one of Meteroa's dragons, and yet somehow the alchemist had intercepted both before they could reach Jehal. Just as the Night Watchman had intercepted the message from the north. They might as well have told him to his face that he was superfluous.

Jehal dismounted. His bad leg was playing up again, making it difficult to keep his footing on the soft blackened earth. Armored figures were already standing on the far side of the bridge, waiting for him. *Or waiting for someone.* He limped toward them.

Zafir. Never mind his uncle—he'd be the first to say there were far worse things than losing a finger. Valmeyan was a dragon-king. He'd treat his prisoners well enough. Jehal might have to part with a small fortune to get his eyrie-master back, but he'd come back fat and well fed. No, that wasn't the fear that gnawed at him. What mattered was that Valmeyan had Lystra and Zafir. Were they both his prisoners now? Jeiros seemed to think not. Zafir alive. Was that a feeling of hope or dread? He'd gone to Evenspire to murder her and then wept when someone else had beaten him to it.

Lystra, Zafir. Zafir, Lystra. He reached the middle of the bridge. Cursed thing swayed so much he felt like he was trying to balance on the back of a horse. Hyrkallan and two other riders were coming out to meet him. When he looked down, the empty space and the churning water below made his head spin, but if he didn't look down, he was quite sure he'd fall. *Damn stupid place to make a peace. One good gust of wind and we'll all be tossed in the river and half the realms will be looking for new kings.* Maybe Hyrkallan had had the same thought. Maybe he and Sirion would simply push him into the river and get on with the serious business of talking to men whose opinions actually mattered. Ironic, really, after what had happened to Hyram.

The clever thing would be to step aside right now. Let Hyrkallan and Valmeyan destroy each other and then swoop back to pick up the pieces when they were done.

And then King Sirion was in front of him, with Hyrkallan at his side almost spitting in Jehal's face. Ancestors, but the man was big!

"Viper!" Hyrkallan spat from where he stood on Sirion's right; Queen Almiri was on Sirion's left. She looked twice as old as he remembered, the paleness of her skin setting off the dark rings under her eyes. *Hard to get a good night's sleep when your realm's been burned to ash, eh?*

She hissed at him as though she'd read his mind. "Son of a whore." She turned to Sirion. "What's *he* doing here?"

Jehal met her gaze. All the contempt she threw in his face, well, he'd just throw it right back. "I am the speaker, Your Holiness." Jeiros and the Night Watchman were behind him. The old priest, Aruch, sat on the blasted earth among the dragons, too old and unsteady to come out onto the bridge.

Almiri took a quick step forward and shouted in his face. "You are a traitor and a murderer! Evenspire burned because of you!"

"Really?" He didn't let himself flinch but met her assault with a faint smile. "Because I thought it was Zafir who burned your castle. I seem to remember fighting *against* her on that particular occasion. Perhaps I am mistaken, or perhaps you and yours had already fled the skies by then and were too far away to see."

If Sirion hadn't gripped her shoulder, Jehal thought she might have flung herself at him to rip him to pieces with her bare hands while they tumbled into the rushing waters below. "You lying, cess-born stain on the floor of a—"

"Enough." Sirion didn't even raise his voice and Almiri stopped at once. *Fascinating. Good to know who pulls her strings. Not her sister, then. And speaking of sisters, I wonder where little Jaslyn might be. Not here, it seems.*

Sirion's voice was cold. "We are here to request a council of kings and queens so that a new speaker may be chosen." He gave Jehal a hard look. "It's a pity there are only four of us. Five and we could have held it here and now."

Jehal smirked in his face. "Four? Lord Hyrkallan has helped himself to the last of Shezira's daughters, has he?" *Well that answers that, then.* He turned to Hyrkallan. "Congratulations, *brother*. Although I still think I got the best of them."

Hyrkallan growled through his teeth. "Queen Jaslyn is a true queen of the north."

Jehal cocked his head. "Really? The impression I got was of a woman who hadn't quite grown up yet, cold and hard and far more interested in her dragons than her people." His brow furrowed. "Although now I think about it, maybe you are right and she *is* her mother's daughter." He forced a smile. "Your Holiness. I'm sure the alchemists will post a notice in the Glass Cathedral shortly. Did you bring the sealed bands with you? I'm sure the other realms will be aching to know that the north has a new king."

"We are betrothed, King Viper, not yet wed."

"Oh. Then we are three kings, not four." Jehal put on his disappointed face. "And I had so looked forward to comparing sisters with you, Lord Hyrkallan. Lystra turned out to be quite a surprise when it came to our conjugal duties. Quite enthusiastic, if a little crude. I wondered whether her big sister had similar appetites. Or perhaps some different hidden desires. She strikes me as the sort, after all." He watched as Hyrkallan's face turned storm-cloud purple. *It's always so easy with your type.* "Queen Lystra and Queen Jaslyn are very close, after all. I heard a rumor from my eyrie-master that they might be"—he pursed his lips—"very close indeed. Perhaps, if an alliance is to be agreed between our realms, we might seal it in a very particular way." He glanced at Sirion. "Hyram acquired some very large beds in his time as speaker. I'd been wondering what to do with them."

He didn't get any further. Hyrkallan let out a roar and lunged. Jehal tried to dance out of reach but his injured leg betrayed him and buckled. He staggered and then fell back. The bridge twisted, rolling him to one edge until it caught him with its ropes. Hyrkallan had his sword out by now, every intention of using it, and neither Sirion nor Queen Almiri showed any sign of stopping him. In fact, if anything, they looked positively pleased. *A cripple baiting an armored knight? I really need to have words with my mouth.* Jehal closed his eyes, but the blow never came. Instead, he heard steel clash on steel. When he opened his eyes again, Vale was standing over him. He had Hyrkallan's blade caught on his own. The Night Watchman was shaking his head.

"I cannot allow that, My Lord."

"You cannot deny the realms would be better for it," growled Hyrkallan through gritted teeth.

Vale didn't move. "I cannot allow that, My Lord," he said again. He spoke slowly and carefully. Jehal took a deep breath and muttered a prayer to thank whatever ancestors had made the Night Watchman so blindly committed to his duty.

"Night Watchman, Lord Hyrkallan has raised a blade against the speaker," he gasped when he'd recovered enough composure to speak. "I believe that makes his life forfeit, does it not?"

"No injury has been done," snapped Vale.

Jehal snorted. "I am flat on my back. I have bruises from my fall." *Ah well. Not as blindly committed as you could be then.*

"You fell because you are a cripple."

And whose fault is that? Fury helped Jehal find the strength to get back to his feet. "His intent was clear, Night Watchman." He could see Hyrkallan's blood was up. The fool actually *wanted* to fight. With a bit of luck Vale would have to kill him if it came to blows. "See his face. He thinks he can beat you."

"No." Jeiros. "There will be no fighting here."

Hyrkallan sneered. "Hyram named you Viper, but I am reminded more of our desert lizards whose bite is slow poison. They strike and then they must cower and hide for days as they track their prey to its death." He leaned a little closer.

Vale didn't budge. "Where there is a crown there must be someone to wear it, My Lord. We can all think what we wish of King Jehal, but until a council of kings decrees otherwise, or until Speaker Zafir returns from the dead, he wears that crown. It is the crown I am sworn to defend, not whoever may wear it."

Until Speaker Zafir returns from the dead . . . That was why Jeiros was being so secretive. He doesn't want Vale to know! Oh my! How delicious!

Jehal's head was spinning. For some reason, he had an ally. Why Jeiros was helping him was another matter entirely. He spat on the bridge in front of Hyrkallan's feet. "Shall we have our dragons roar and shriek at each other until we are deaf as well as stupid, or are we done with waving swords and threats? If we are, then perhaps we should get on with what we all came here to do. Otherwise . . ." He turned to face King Sirion. "You have been quiet, Your Holiness. Do you have anything you wish to add? I will be quite pleased to stand on this bridge and trade insults with anyone who cares to play for as long as you wish. I imagine I will quite enjoy it."

"Enough!" Jeiros banged his staff on the bridge. Jehal froze, midthought. Even Hyrkallan flinched, if only with surprise because the alchemist usually spoke so quietly. Only Vale seemed unmoved.

Jeiros stood between Vale and Hyrkallan. Gingerly, he pushed both of their swords away. "I have words for you all. You will all listen to me now, because I am the Master of the Order of the Scales. We are the ones who tame your dragons. We are the ones who make them and we are the ones who, if we wish, can break them. What are you, any of you, My Lords, without your dragons?" He looked at Jehal. "What becomes of you, Your Holiness? What do you become without your dragons? Nothing." He spun to face Hyrkallan and Sirion before Jehal could answer. "What of you, my noble kings? How long will you rule with no dragons at your backs? There are rogue dragons loose in the realms again. My order lies crippled at their talons already. And all you can do is war among yourselves. Madness! You will doom us all. And so you will stop."

Sirion snorted. "One rogue, barely even full grown, if she's even still alive . . ."

"One?" Jeiros almost screamed in his face. "One rogue dragon, is it? I shudder at where Zafir has brought us. One became four more than two months ago, Sirion! You would know this if you ever attended council, even what passed for council under Zafir! Six weeks have passed since King Jehal broke the Red Riders, yet they were not completely destroyed. Where are the ones who survived?" He pointed at Queen Almiri. "Did they return to you, Your Holiness, you whose greed for power and lust for revenge succored them?" He whirled toward Jehal. "Or you. Do you have them in your care, after betraying your lover and your speaker at Evenspire?" Now Hyrkallan. "Does Queen Jaslyn have them in her eyries, the mad queen who awakens dragons for fun? Must I remind you of how the Syuss fell? You are all kings and queens. We have told you all there is to know of dragons. Yet you do not *listen*." He growled. "So I will tell you this: you will find a way to make a peace between you. There will be no more war. If you cannot do this, I will kill your dragons. All of them."

Behind his own dull outrage at such an idea, Jehal amused himself watching Hyrkallan's face. He almost choked. Sirion wasn't any less shocked.

"You will do no such thing," growled Sirion.

"I can and I will, Your Holiness, if I am given no choice. And if the alternative is for dragons to awaken across the realms, you will all help me, and willingly too unless you are fools."

"They don't *look* very willing." Jehal smirked.

"Would you rather lose half your dragons or lose them all and every-thing else as well?" Jeiros shrugged. "None of you are that blind."

"The duty of your order is to tame these dragons, alchemist," snapped Almiri.

"No. The duty of my order is to preserve the realms. If I must slay drag-ons, that is what I will do."

"No!"

"Yes," said Vale very softly. "Your Holinesses, if Jeiros commands it done and you do not obey, I will send my men by stealth into your eyries. We may not understand potions, but we will bring hammers and we will smash every egg you own and any who stand in our way."

Jeiros shook his head in frustration. "Enough, Night Watchman! Enough threats." He turned back to Sirion and Hyrkallan. "The damage done by the white rogue was bad enough. The Order lost many alchemists and much more besides. The caves where we make our potions were dam-aged by the smoke from their fires. We can barely make enough; our con-siderable stockpile was completely destroyed, and now from every eyrie in the realms my alchemists complain that they are slowly running out. Weeks of it were destroyed by the Red Riders. More was destroyed at Evenspire." He shook his head. "I thought we were finished with this mad-ness, but now King Valmeyan has come out of the mountains and taken the Pinnacles. It must stop and it must stop now." The glint of murder in Hyrkallan's face was a delight, but Jeiros met it with steel of his own. "Do what you will, but the order is already given. There will be no more sent to any of your eyries until this ends."

Beside him, Vale grinned. "There's always hammers," he said.

Jehal looked from one face to the next to the next. Almiri showed only outrage and violence. Hyrkallan's jaw was set tight. Sirion's face was pinched. Jehal smiled at them. "As speaker," he said with careful slowness, "I will agree to whatever our grand master suggests. If you will do so too."

"And who—" Hyrkallan started to take a step forward, but Sirion put a hand on his shoulder.

"You have given us a lot to think about, Grand Master—dragons roaming free, the Mountain King out from his crags. Does Valmeyan know you plan to murder his dragons? Does he acquiesce to this? I see from your face the answer is no. So. Here is what I will offer you. We have been here for three days and a fourth won't trouble us. We will retire to consider what you've said. Go back to your palace. Return in two days. You will have our answer then." He looked at Jehal. "Since you call yourself speaker, you can act like one. Send this word to the other realms and call them to council. We will see this matter to its end."

Sirion, Hyrkallan and Almiri turned and walked away toward their dragons. Jehal was left with Jeiros and Vale to watch them go.

"Well," said Jehal, once they were gone. "That went well, don't you think? In that they didn't murder me out of hand. I suppose I'm quite surprised that you're still alive too after that outburst. You don't think they're actually going to let you kill their dragons, do you?" *I'm the speaker of the nine realms, and I have to resort to being the court jester to be heard. Thank the Great Flame that Meteroa's not here. I'd never hear the last of it.*

Carefully, trying not to look at the water roaring beneath his feet, he hobbled back across the bridge. Slowly, one plank at a time. Getting back onto solid ground, where Aruch and the dragons were waiting, he leaned against the charred trunk of a dead tree and caught his breath. His head was already filling with plots and schemes, with trajectories of possibilities. Not that he particularly wanted them; what he particularly wanted was to lie down somewhere in a dark room and chew on Dreamleaf until the pains running up and down the inside of his thigh went away.

He took a deep breath. "When I was little and my father used to tell me stories about Vishmir and Narammed and of the first of the alchemists and the last of the blood-mages, there was one story about Narammed's spear. The spear used to belong to a wizard-king made of quicksilver . . ."

Jeiros looked at him. He seemed sad and drained. "The Silver King. A long time ago, when there were no alchemists and no mages and no kings and no queens, when all the world was just men and dragons, and the men lived in fear, and the dragons ate the men and burned their homes. Did your stories start like that?"

"Yes." Despite himself, Jehal smiled at the memory. "Something like that. And then the silver wizard-king comes and promises to make everything right and save the men from the dragons. He says he has a magic potion that will make the dragons obey the commands of the men, if only the dragons can be made to drink it. The men ask the wizard how he will make the dragons come so that they can drink his magic spell, and the wizard shows them his spear, Narammed's spear, the Adamantine Spear, and he bangs the end of it three times on the ground. All across the world every dragon hears him call and stops at once what it was doing and takes to wing to answer." He clapped his hands. "You have to admit that would make finding your rogues a lot easier, master Jeiros, if it happened to be true."

The alchemist sighed. "And Narammed slew a dragon with a single blow from that same spear, they say, at Dragondale. Yes, if those stories were all true, that would be a fine way to solve all our problems at once. A very handy spear that would be. Jehal, do you think we haven't tried? Of course we have. Sadly, no one of the Order has ever wrung any magic from the Speaker's Spear, not one little drop of it. If it was ever more than unusually sharp, those days are gone."

"And yet it's gone missing. That makes me uneasy. You hadn't forgotten, had you?"

"Which is more likely, Jehal? That the spear was stolen from under our noses or that Zafir took it with her to war?"

"I went down to where it should have been. I found a candle dropped on the floor."

Jeiros shook his head. "Doubtless Zafir holds it even now." He walked away, back toward Wraithwing and the other dragons. Jehal watched him go.

I don't think so. But I've told you who took it. And if it's just a spear . . . There was no reason to think that Jeiros would be wrong about something like that. Yet a blood-mage had saved his life to bargain for the spear, and the life of a dragon-king was surely worth more than a piece of mere metal . . .

"You missed a bit," said Vale at Jehal's shoulder. "The men ask the wizard how he will make the dragons drink his potions. And the wizard tells them that he won't. And then he throws up his arms and makes his spell and tells the men that it's them who get to drink, so the magic will get into their blood. And all they have to do is wait until the dragons come, and then let the dragons eat them and the spell will became a part of the dragons forever. That's all. And if enough of them say yes and are willing to die, then the dragons will be enslaved, but if there's not enough, it's men who will be slaves. And the men who did say yes to that, Your Holiness, they were my ancestors."

Jehal nodded. He pushed himself away from his tree. His hands came away black from the charred bark. Wherever he went, wherever he looked, the signs of dragons were never far away. He hobbled after Jeiros. Maybe the alchemist was right. A cull. Of all the dragons of his enemies. That would do nicely. "That doesn't seem very likely, Night Watchman. What seems much more likely is that your ancestors *weren't* daft enough to drink dragon poison or whatever it was and then get themselves eaten. Tricky, I imagine, to father a child after you've been eaten."

Vale didn't seem offended. He simply shook his head. "No. But I would not expect you to understand."

Maybe he was right, though. After all, there was an old and mostly forgotten law that an Adamantine Man could help himself to any woman he could get hold of before he went into battle. Maybe that was how they survived. Or maybe there wasn't a law, just an old drinking song. He whistled to himself as he limped across the black earth. As he did, he heard the Night Watchman singing quietly along.

I fight dragons, I have no name, but I'm a warrior so there's no
    shame
Off to battle I'll soon be dead, but while I live I'll share my bed
Wife or daughter, maiden, crone, lie with me, I'll make you moan
My spear is huge, its shaft is hard, its point is savage and battle-
    scarr'd
Squirm and scream and shout out loud, I'll give you sons to make
    you proud.

They fell to silence. For a second Jehal paused. He turned back and stared at Vale. The Night Watchman was miles away, lost in thought. When he saw Jehal looking at him, he bowed. Jehal shrugged and shook his head. As perks went, that didn't sound bad at all. At least not until you considered the almost certain fiery death that followed.

"I did not see Zafir carry the spear to war, Your Holiness," said Vale quietly.

"Then perhaps *you* should look for it." Jehal climbed laboriously up the ladder onto Wraithwing's back. "A blood-mage, Vale. Look for a blood-mage who calls himself Kithyr."

He saw the Night Watchman's eyes, saw that the name meant something. Typical. *Everyone knows more than me.*

He closed his eyes to doze as the dragon took him home. Where a second messenger from the Pinnacles was waiting.

18

❖

NEEDS MUST

A lesser man might have reached the top panting and gasping for breath, or else taken the hundred-odd steps at a more gentle pace. Vale Tassan, Night Watchman, commander of the Adamantine Men, took them briskly and arrived at the top pleasantly refreshed. Even before he reached the roof, the smells came down to greet him. Wet stone, hot steel, oil. On the flat space on top of the Gatehouse tower a score of scorpions stood to attention in the rain. He looked up at the gray iron sky, a habit all Adamantine Men learned. Always look up. Always look out for dragons. In this weather he could barely even see the City of Dragons at the bottom of the hill, but he looked up anyway. A perfect day for war.

The top of the tower was large enough that a dragon could have stood there and spread its wings, if the roof had had the strength to bear the weight. Dozens of his soldiers stood, still and stoic in the rain, close to their weapons. He cast his eyes across the scorpions, across the men around them. They were ready. As ready as you could be for dragons. He would have preferred a heavy stone roof, but the dragon-scale canopies erected over the weapons would have to do. When it came to tooth and claw and tail, they might as well have been made of paper, but they'd keep the fire at bay.

Satisfied with what he saw, the Night Watchman ambled across the roof to the observatory in the corner, a slender and ornate stone dome amid the machines of war. He knocked sharply and pushed open the door without waiting for an answer. This side of the tower belonged to the alchemists. On another day he might have paused, perhaps shown a little more respect. On another day he might have stopped inside the door and taken a moment to look around at the maps, the charts of the stars, the Taiytakei farscopes and other strange instruments he didn't understand.

On another day. Today he simply shook the rain from his armor, sat down in the only chair in the room and growled a reluctant greeting at the man who had summoned him.

"You're in a surly mood." Jeiros looked tired. Drained. Vale had seen that look before. The look of a man engaged in battle and slowly but steadily losing. Speaker Hyram, toward the end he'd had that look. And others before him.

"My mood is whatever the realms require of me." Vale tried to smile. It wasn't easy after what he'd had to do today. Letting Hyrkallan gut Jehal on Narammed's Bridge would have been the easiest thing in the world. *I might have given him a round of applause. So why did I stop him? Duty, that's why. Duty and nothing else. Of course I'm in a surly mood.*

Jeiros winced. "Don't, Vale. Now you look surly and constipated."

"Flying on the back of the Viper's dragons leaves me queasy, master alchemist." Vale let his face fall sour again. "Never mind me. *You* look like a rabbit cornered by a pack of hungry foxes. You called me here. What do you want?"

Jeiros picked up a decanter and poured himself a glass of wine. "When Grand Master Bellepheros vanished, it fell to me to keep the realms safe. A light touch here, a few words there. A little guidance. That's how we work. That's all we've ever needed." He tossed something across the room. "I suppose you'd better read this for yourself. You'll find out soon enough." Vale plucked it out of the air. Dragon bone, hollowed out into a case for maps or scrolls. Ornately carved.

"A pretty present." He shrugged. "I imagine you don't get many gifts. I certainly don't." He smirked. "Speakers get lots of gifts, but I doubt Jehal much liked his last one. Jehal and Meteroa are two snakes from the same nest."

Jeiros pursed his lips. "Say what you like, Night Watchman. Prince Meteroa was the master of King Jehal's eyries. Strictly speaking, he was mine."

"Ha!" Vale threw back his head and laughed.

"It hardly matters now. Meteroa is dead."

Vale raised an eyebrow. "Losing a finger hardly seems a mortal wound to me. Is there something you wish to share."

The alchemist wiped his brow. "That is a letter from Valmeyan in the Pinnacles. Zafir put a crossbow bolt through Meteroa's skull and hacked his head off his shoulders. Valmeyan was kind enough not to send any more than his finger. I kept the rest from our speaker until after Narammed's Bridge. I thought it best. He knows now. He has not taken it well."

"Had I a heart, perhaps it would bleed for him." Vale blinked. "So Prince Meteroa is dead now, is he? Can't say that troubles me." He stared at Jeiros, waiting. Waiting for the words that would wash away the numbness rising up from inside him, but the alchemist met his silence with a silence of his own. "Zafir, old man," said Vale softly, almost whispering. "You said Zafir. Is there something I very much need to know? Is that why you brought me up here? Did she survive Evenspire after all, old man? Could I have let Hyrkallan have his way with Jehal? Is that what you brought me here to tell me?"

"There's a letter inside that bone. It's meant for us. Read it, Vale. Just read it."

Vale reached his fingers into the hollow bone and touched paper. Slowly, carefully, he pulled it out. The seal was Valmeyan's, the Mountain King. It took a minute, and then Vale knew everything. By the time he was finished, he wasn't sure whether he wanted to laugh like a maniac or scream in murderous rage. Probably both. *Furymouth taken, Queen Lystra taken, Prince Meteroa dead. Jehal finished. Zafir alive. I could have let Hyrkallan kill him. When, old man? When did you know?*

"I'll have my men break this wonderful news to our so-called speaker right away. Shall I hang him next to Shezira or next to that fool Sakabian?" The cages were long gone, but Vale still saw them when he closed his eyes.

His head was spinning a little. *Valmeyan. A proper speaker. He's got Queen Lystra. Jehal in the dungeons. Impaled and hung in a cage. I'll do it myself.* Jehal was as good as dead. He didn't even try to stop himself grinning anymore. They had a saying in the deserts: when the ancestors smile on you, smile back.

"You'll do no such thing."

The alchemist might have said more, but Vale's hand around his throat choked him into silence. The Night Watchman bared his teeth. "It would be easy, little man, to pick you up and hurl you over the edge. No one would see except my own men, and you know how we are about orders. From birth to death, we are sworn to follow them. We are sworn to follow the speaker. How long?" he hissed. "How long have you known that Zafir was alive?"

"Gah!"

Vale relaxed his grip ever so slightly. Enough for the alchemist to speak.

"I never thought she was dead," gasped Jeiros. "And before you throttle me again, I knew what you knew, Night Watchman, no more."

Vale crumpled Valmeyan's message and held it in front of Jeiros' face. "But you read this. You knew more before Narammed's Bridge, didn't you, alchemist? Don't pretend otherwise. You kept this from me. I could have let Hyrkallan put the Viper out of his misery and been content. *I am sworn to serve the speaker!*"

"And if Hyrkallan had killed Jehal, what then? Valmeyan cannot be speaker."

"That is not for you to decide!" Slowly, carefully, mindful of his own strength and fury, Vale let the alchemist go. "Are you a kingmaker now? Do you rule the realms? By what right, alchemist? By what right do you overturn every law that Narammed laid down?" He took a step back toward the door. "I'm minded to have you and your order rounded up and thrown in the dungeons. You can hang next to Jehal. Give me a reason, Jeiros, why I should not do this. Ancestors! The world lurches from one madness to the next!" He stood still, staring at the alchemist. *Orders. An Adamantine Man obeys orders. No matter what. From birth to death. Ancestors! What do I do?*

The alchemist licked his lips. When he spoke, he spoke almost in a whisper. "Valmeyan is selling dragon eggs to the Taiytakei, Vale."

"*What?*" Doubt, doubt, doubt. Doubt was death. An Adamantine Man learned to banish all doubt.

"From one madness to the next, Vale. As you say."

Vale's face blackened. His gaze settled on Jeiros. "I serve the speaker. If Zafir lives, I serve Zafir." No. There was no other way. Duty was duty.

"There are awakened dragons in the Worldspine, Vale."

"And? What would you have me do?" He shook his head. Dragons were the business of the alchemists. The misdeeds of kings were a matter for the speaker. The Night Watchman served the speaker, nothing more. The speaker's sword. That's all he was. "All the more reason Jehal should swing in a cage while the true speaker is restored." Vale hesitated. Jeiros was trembling. Either he was getting sick or something was very wrong. *And would Zafir be any better? You already know the answer to that. Just look at who brought us to this place.* "Alchemist, you bring such accusations to a council of kings and queens, not to me. Let them decide. I will happily seize the Mountain King, string him up, fill him with truth smoke and find out, but only if that is what the speaker commands of me."

"They almost broke us, Vale, those rogues. Almost broke us once already. They filled our secret caves with smoke. Such damage. Even if I wanted to, I could not give my eyrie-masters the potion they need, not all of it. Even if I looked after every drop. So I will starve them. They have enough for a few weeks. A couple of months, some of them. And after that the dragons will start to wake. A week and they will become restless. Two and they cannot be trusted. I don't know how long it takes for their true awareness to return. A month? Two perhaps? I suppose it must depend on their size. We feed a hatchling far less than we feed an adult, after all . . ." Jeiros was wringing his hands. He hadn't listened to a word Vale had said. "A light touch here, a few words there. No no, Night Watchman, we are long past such things. Valmeyan put the sword to Shezira's neck. His vote condemned her. He pushed us into this. What do you suggest? What would *you* do, Night Watchman? What say you of our kings and queens? Would you strangle them, as I propose, or would you trust them, as your

duty commands? Will the kings of the north sit quietly and let Zafir return to her throne? I don't think so. Will they let her put Jehal to death?
Of that I have no doubt. But his queen and his son? No, they will not.
Will Zafir condemn Valmeyan when his dragons are all that gives her
power. No. And while they argue and fight, we will all burn to ash!" The
alchemist laughed bitterly. "Now I see his scheme, too late to thwart it.
He'll take the eggs straight from Clifftop so as not to lose his own. They're
probably on board the Taiytakei ships by now, halfway across the Endless
Sea." He brushed past Vale. "Do you see now, Night Watchman? We are
past light touches and gentle words. We are past kings and queens. Who
is speaker will make little difference when the dragons run amok. Our
duty now, Night Watchman, is to see that when the storm comes, not all
is burned to ruin." For a moment he met Vale's eyes. "Nothing more,
nothing less." Jeiros twitched. His shaking grew worse with every word he
said.

Poor man is losing his mind.

Vale reached out and put a hand on his shoulder. "Alchemist, I will
forget your words of treason, but if Zafir is alive, then, for better or worse,
she is the speaker of the realms and I am bound to obey her."

The alchemist turned and blazed in Vale's face. "And what if Valmeyan's lying, Night Watchman? What then? What if Zafir really did die at
Evenspire, as Jehal would have us believe?"

"Then I will send men to the Pinnacles. We will see for ourselves that
Zafir is alive. If she is, Grand Master, then she will have her throne, and
if the riders of the north cannot abide her rule then they will do whatever
they will do. Call them all here, if you wish, to settle this with words or
fire, whatever suits them best. And it is of no concern to me what the King
of the Crags does with his eggs, nor you with your potions."

"It is no concern of yours that everything we stand for may burn?"

Vale picked up the crumpled letter. "If it is your wish, if it will help, I
will send men with hammers to every eyrie in the realms, and you can
send orders to your alchemists and eyrie-masters. While our lords and
kings come with their dragons to decide who will be speaker, you have
but to give the word and every egg will be smashed. Every dragon will be

poisoned. The realms will be a better place for it. I will give you that, master alchemist, but I will not turn my swords on the throne I am sworn to serve. And the dragons, of course, will always come back."

"A hatchling demands far less of what I have than a full-grown monster, Night Watchman."

Vale walked out into the hammering rain and the smell of scorpions. He was a soldier, a man of action, after all. Sometimes any decision at all was better than nothing. He had places to go. To Jehal, but first down the stairs of the Gatehouse, across the open emptiness of the Gateyard and the Fountain Court, past the dark bulk of the Speaker's Tower to the Glass Cathedral. To Aruch, the daft old priest who sat half asleep by his altar most of the time these days. Aruch had hardly spoken a word since he'd married Zafir to Hyram. Sometimes Vale wondered whether the priest had quietly had a stroke while no one was looking.

Not that any of us would notice anymore. Vale was soaked almost to the skin by the time he walked through the once-molten stone arches into the tomb-like gloom of the cathedral. The priests hardly bothered with torches or candles anymore. The light and fire had gone out of the church long ago as it had gone out of its priest. Others found the torpor of the place alluring, but to Vale it was simply annoying. The Great Flame that was supposed to burn here was little more than a fading ember.

He found Aruch exactly where he thought he would, squatting by his altar, eyes closed. To anyone else, the priest would have seemed asleep, but Vale knew better.

"I'm here for your advice, old priest. The Lesser Council has a decision to make. Speaker Zafir might be alive. Rogue dragons might be afoot. You know what I'd like to do? I'd put Zafir and Jehal in cages next to each other. I'd kill every dragon I can get my hands on. I'd be done with kings and queens and I'd put the Syuss on the Adamantine Throne. What say you, old priest? Do I have your blessing?"

The priest started shaking. It took Vale a second or two to realize that he was laughing. Very slowly, Aruch lifted his head. He peered up at Vale. "You can do whatever takes your fancy, Night Watchman. I have seen into Jeiros' dreams. He sees what is coming. He knows, in his heart, that there is nothing he can do. But you? You are what you are. Don't let me stop you from trying." He rocked forward again, suddenly oblivious to Vale's presence.

Another madman. So it's down to me. Strange, how he knows my mind. Vale shook that away. He was a soldier. *Maybe it's simply obvious what must be done.*

Jehal then. Finding the Viper wasn't too hard. He was where they'd left him hours ago, in the Chamber of Audience, staring at his uncle's finger. Some days the great arched windows let in the sun and lit up the room like a jewel; today they merely let in the rain and the wind. The Viper didn't look up as Vale stalked in, dripping across the marbled floor. Apart from the two of them, the chamber was empty.

"Have you come to kill me?" asked Jehal as Vale drew closer. He didn't look up.

Dispense with all manner of unpleasantness and cut to the chase? A fine thought. "Valmeyan has your queen." He saw Jehal wince as though Vale had hit him.

"Perhaps she escaped. I suppose there's always hope, although in this case not very much of it."

"I'm surprised you care." Jehal's head snapped up. His eyes blazed and he glared at Vale. *If looks could cut, I'd be slashed to pieces. But I've stared down dragons, Viper. Don't even try.* "He has your son too," he said mildly. *At last I get to watch you really suffer.*

"Have you come to gloat, Night Watchman, or is there something else? Because if gloating is what you had in mind, you're not doing a very good job. I take comfort from knowing they are still alive. Better that than dead or lost."

Vale tossed the Mountain King's message at Jehal's feet. Jehal made no move to pick it up. "Valmeyan says that Zafir is still alive."

Jehal shrugged. "I know. Go away, little man."

Vale slapped him. As Jehal recoiled from that, the Night Watchman took his legs out from under him. The next thing he knew, the Viper was lying on his back, and Vale was standing over him. *Just like on Narammed's Bridge, except this time it is my own sword pointed at your throat.*

"I defended your life because of the title you wear," he hissed. "However little you may deserve it. Now it seems it should not be yours at all. You and Zafir, you are stains on the honor of Vishmir and his kin. You disgust me, both of you, yet I serve whichever one of you the law demands. It seems it is no longer you."

Jehal brushed Vale's sword aside. "When the time comes, Tassan, there will be no death slow enough or painful enough for you."

Vale Tassan met his eyes. It was like trying to stare down a lizard, trying to out-glare a Night Watchman. "Nor is there one that I fear, Your Holiness."

Come on Vale, just kill him.

No. I have not seen Zafir. For the moment, he is still the speaker. Still the creature I am sworn to defend.

Just kill him anyway.

No.

With a deep breath, he stepped away. He was making a terrible mistake. A part of him was certain of that. *But then I would be a murderer. Common vermin. I would be no better than any of the rest of them.* He shook his head. "Just go, Viper, before Zafir returns. Be gone and never come back."

Slowly, painfully, Jehal dragged himself back to his feet. "Oh, I'll be gone, Night Watchman. I'll be gone in the morning to the north. Let Hyrkallan have this throne. Or Sirion. Or anyone who wants it. My dragons I give to Queen Jaslyn. We will set my Lystra free. After that, you can all do with me whatever you want."

Vale pursed his lips. He nodded. "I'll hold you to that, Viper." He turned his back on the man who called himself speaker and walked back out into the rain.

19

THE DRAGON-QUEEN AND THE BEAST

Isentine watched the dragons land. B'thannan he recognized at once, blotting out half the sky. Some of the others too, some of Queen Jaslyn's more notable riders. Then half a dozen more that Isentine hadn't seen before. They came from the south, skimming across the endless dunes of the Sea of Sand. Over the lake that sat at the bottom of the cliff, up past the sweeping curves of ancient Outwatch to the landing fields. The thunder of their wings rattled the air. Isentine's eyes followed them. He'd been living at Outwatch long enough to see every single dragon that Queen Jaslyn owned be hatched and raised and he knew them all. These belonged to someone else.

Not Sirion either—he knew those dragons too. Someone else. He turned out the guard in case it was someone important, then went back to watching. Even in his tower, he felt the ground quiver when B'thannan crashed to the earth. Out in the cattle paddocks the herd masters would already be rounding up the cattle they wanted to spare. Closer by, he saw his Scales run toward the dragons. He knew them all by name too, every one. They came to Outwatch as apprentices, alchemists in the making. They were the ones who failed, who weren't quite clever enough or sharp enough or wise enough. Sometimes they were the ones who fell in love with their dragons all on their own, but usually not. Usually they needed a little help to become the devoted servant that was a Scales. *Here, drink this. It will help with the Hatchling Disease.* And it did. It helped with a lot of other things too. Lately he'd been wondering if he should feed it to his own queen. Treason for the greater good. With luck it wouldn't come to that.

Hyrkallan was approaching. Some who had come with him were taking their time, but Hyrkallan was almost at a run, striding across the fields, his loyal riders at his heels. Isentine levered himself out of his seat high on the balcony of Outwatch tower and tottered down the hundred and twenty steps to the cavernous entrance hall. Its huge emptiness echoed around him. Almost everyone was gone, flown to the eyries in the south of the realm, waiting for war. He emerged from the tower as Hyrkallan reached the doors. Isentine bowed, exactly the right bow for a lord who was an equal. Not a lord who was a king, not yet. Queen Jaslyn had still to consummate her offer.

"Where is she?" snapped Hyrkallan. He didn't bow back. Isentine blinked.

"Brusque even for you, My Lord," Isentine bristled. "Yes, all is well. Indeed, my back does continue to trouble me. Etcetera, etcetera. You have a lot of dragons with you, My Lord, and not all of them of our realm. I hope they will not be staying long. We don't have potions to spare for them. Might I ask who are our guests?"

"The Speaker of the Realms, or what passes for one, has come to your eyrie to see our queen. The dragons are his and they will be gone soon enough. There's a company of Adamantine Men come to keep you company too. They will be staying after I am gone, or are you short of food too?"

"Food we have in abundance." Isentine frowned. Someone else's soldiers in his eyrie was never welcome, whoever sent them. Too many chances for a spot of murder or an outbreak of poisonings. He sighed. "They're not wanted."

"Just keep them away from the dragons, old man. So. Where is she?"

Isentine shook his head, a sour taste in his mouth. "The Hatchling Disease has taken hold despite the medicines. Her mind wanders. The dragon has her enthralled."

"Today we will be wed. Tomorrow we will fly once more to war. She will come with us."

"I'll not let you take her by force."

Hyrkallan rolled his eyes. "Ancestors! You want her away and yet you won't let me take her? Make your choice, man! Perhaps the bleakness of the news I bring will tear her thoughts away to where they belong. Zafir lives. She flies with the King of the Crags. They have taken Furymouth and reclaimed the Pinnacles. She has Jehal's queen. The one sister might not have been enough to drag our queen from her folly, but I fancy the other will."

Isentine's jaw gaped open. "Lystra?"

"Yes, little Lystra. The pretty one with the big wide eyes who never could see the harm in anyone." Hyrkallan's lip curled. "Mere weeks since we flew to war against the Viper and now we fight side by side." Now it was Hyrkallan's turn to taste something sour. "Don't tell me that will not get our queen's attention. Now go and get her!"

Isentine shook his head. "I will bow to you when you are a king, Hyrkallan. For now I must show your guest hospitality. Go and get her yourself. I'll send a Scales with you to remind you of the way."

Hyrkallan's face clouded, but after a second he nodded. "If I must." He tore a small pouch from his belt and placed it into Isentine's hand. "Maiden's Regret and plenty of it. You said I should bring some. You know what to do with it."

"Not until she says yes to you." Isentine shook his head.

Hyrkallan ground his teeth. "She already said yes. She promised me."

"She is our queen, My Lord. Speaker Jehal approaches. Best you be on your way. Be gentle with her. And beware of that dragon. Call her outside. Do not go in the room with it. Not if you value your life."

He watched Hyrkallan go and then carefully put the pouch in his pocket. Sometimes he felt sorry for Queen Jaslyn. She was too young and the world was much too big. And then he remembered what she was doing, right under his feet, and he wasn't so sorry anymore. He wasn't sorry for the man limping across the blasted earth of the landing field toward him either. Jehal, the bastard who'd cost his last queen her birthright and then her life. One of the nice things about being old, he thought, was that he really didn't have much to lose anymore. He could do what he liked, and if anyone wanted to hang him for it, well that was a punishment nature would serve him soon enough anyway.

The drawback of getting old was that he no longer had the strength in his hands to throttle the speaker. A knife would have done the trick, but he didn't have one of those handy.

So until I do . . .

He fell to his knees as Jehal approached. He kissed the speaker's feet and struggled to rise again.

"Having trouble?" Isentine listened for the mockery in Jehal's voice but it wasn't there. Instead the speaker reached out a hand and helped him up. Jehal flashed Isentine an empty grin laced with pain. "I know the problem all too well now, you see. Your last queen did that to me. A lesson I could have done without. The first of rather too many."

"Your Holiness." Isentine met Jehal's gaze at last. He looked worn out, almost defeated. Broken.

"Eyrie-Master Isentine." Jehal put a hand on each of his shoulders. "I've been looking forward to meeting you for a very long time. I imagine no one knows more about raising dragons than you. My uncle, I know, was greatly disappointed that you couldn't come to my wedding." The sorrow in the speaker's face had to be real, didn't it? *But this is the man who ruined our realms.*

The eyrie-master bowed again, a little dip from the waist. "I live to serve Your Holiness. If there's anything you would like to see while you are here, I'll be happy to show you." He put on his best smile. "Does Your Holiness desire something? We are poorly staffed with so many of our dragons away, but we are not devoid of pleasures. Baths scented with oils, a feast of delicacies from around the realms, men and women who desire nothing more than to serve Your Holiness. You must be tired after your flight . . ."

"I want my wife back, Eyrie-Master. I want my son. That's all. I've flown from the Adamantine Palace to Sand in a day, and then from Sand to here, and I barely feel it." His brow furrowed. "No, wait. Now I mention it, I do feel it. I'm tired. Yes. Baths, feasts and so forth. All of that. Whatever you have. And then I'll take your dragons." Jehal gave a bleak chuckle. "Are the whores good here? We always had good whores near Clifftop, and the brothels around the Adamantine Palace are the best in the realms. I don't see any here, though. Cows and fields surrounded by sand that seems to go on forever that's all. Where are your women, Eyrie-Master?"

Isentine bowed. "Where they belong, Your Holiness. Kept inside, out of harm's way, or else far, far away. You'll find Sand more to your taste, perhaps, but I can send you whatever you desire."

"No, you can't." Jehal's smile snapped to a sneer in the blink of an eye. "I desire my queen. Whatever you've got will just be a disappointment, but I suppose it'll have to make do. Send a few whores later. It might amuse me to watch them frolic together. Who knows? If I manage to drink enough to numb how much it hurts, I might even enjoy myself."

"I will have my servants show you to your rooms right away. The women will await your pleasure."

Jehal waved him away. "Master Isentine, I jest with you. I have half a dozen riders and my pot boy with me, that's all. I don't need your rooms or your women." He gestured at the huge emptiness around them. "We're to have a wedding, after all. I dare say we'll all piss in our pants and pass out where we sit. No, we'll wait in your halls for your queen to grace us with her presence." They walked across the entrance hall, a gloomy cavern of ochre stone that was the lower level of Outwatch. "You might have a few men standing by ready to throw blankets over us while we snore, though. I imagine it grows cold here at night. You should do something about this place. Put some windows in. How do you live in such dreary gloom?" He paced restlessly about. "You know, this is probably bigger than the Chamber of Audience in my palace. Perhaps I should move my throne here. I certainly don't seem to be very welcome anywhere else anymore. Actually never mind the men with the blankets. Let the Night Watchman's soldiers do that. They might as well make themselves useful."

"Yes." *About that* . . . "I hear you mean them to stay, Your Holiness. It is most unusual."

"They're here for their own reasons, Eyrie-Master. Please don't imagine that I have any say over their comings and goings, let alone their doings.

I am merely the Speaker of the Realms, their lord and master. No, don't imagine that they answer to me."

Isentine bowed and nodded and pretended to listen. *You deserve your bitterness,* he thought. *That's all you ever brought for the rest of us. I hope you choke on it.* Servants brought drinks of scented water. The speaker's riders filed in behind him. They were subdued. Scared even. Before Isentine could eavesdrop on their conversation, though, Hyrkallan was back, and Queen Jaslyn with him. Isentine hadn't seen his queen for days; she looked terrible. Her face was drawn and haggard. Her eyes didn't quite focus on him. When he looked, he could see the skin on the back of her hands, on her knuckles, was hard and flaking. Hatchling Disease, despite all his efforts.

She walked straight toward him. Didn't exactly meet his eyes, but more looked past him, through him, as if she was looking at something from another world that none of the rest of them could see. "Morning Sun," she said curtly. "Have him saddled and ready to ride. Every other dragon here too."

Isentine bowed as best he could. "Yes, Your Holiness. But nearly every dragon is already at Sand or at Southwatch." *So you're going then. Almiri didn't mean enough to drag you away from the horror you've created for us, but Lystra does. Good. We'll have an end to it then.*

"Now. Every dragon I have. All of them. I want them ready to fly. At once."

He nodded. "You mean to fly to war, your Holiness?" At least she was lucid. There were days now when the potions he gave her to keep the disease at bay left her babbling like a madwoman. On days like that he took care that no one else saw her.

"I do. Do you have food and drink for these riders?"

"It is being prepared, Your Holiness." Another bow. She hardly noticed.

"Make sure we have plenty of wine. Get them all drunk. You too. Get me so drunk I can't stand. I don't want to remember any of this." She snatched a bottle from the nearest table and swallowed deeply. "Hyrkallan! My Lord! To me, if you please!" She cast her eyes wildly around the hall and then back to Isentine. "Get the Viper," she hissed. "Him as well."

By the time Isentine had found Jehal, already half in his cups, Hyrkallan was standing at Jaslyn's side. His face was a mask of stone.

"Marry us," snapped Jaslyn.

"I must call a priest."

"Not you."

Jaslyn pointed a finger at Jehal. "You. Marry us. You can do that. Then put a crown on Hyrkallan's head and call him king."

Jehal sniffed. He wrinkled his nose. "I'm not sure I should. Do you consent to this, My Lord?" He gave Hyrkallan an arch look. "I'm not sure I would advise it. This one looks like she has the makings of a cuckold. You never know; you might yet do better elsewhere."

Hyrkallan clenched his fists. Isentine wondered, briefly, if he should be looking for that knife again. The only person who seemed unmoved was Jaslyn. She looked at Isentine. *With the same stony mask as her mother,* he thought. *Hiding the same sorrow underneath.*

"You will witness this, Eyrie-Master. You and every rider present."

Isentine nodded. Jehal raised his eyebrows and then shrugged. "Fine, then you're married. Congratulations." He leered at Hyrkallan. "If she's like her sister, go easy on the Maiden if you want any sleep."

Hyrkallan's hand shot out and grabbed Jehal by the throat. He squeezed. "When we're done with this, you and I will have a reckoning."

Jehal choked. "There's a long queue," he gasped, "and there might not be much left by the time you get to the front of it. Do you want your crown now, *King* Hyrkallan?"

"Oh, let him go." Jaslyn turned away from them both. "Is that all? Aren't you supposed to say more than that?"

Jehal rubbed his throat. "Oh, you could do the whole staying up all night for the dawn vigil and then the standing still waiting for the sunlight to strike your face, and then the speeches and the feasting and the endless witterings of the priests and so forth, but really what's the point? I've done all that and I can't say it had much to recommend it. You're married. Sorry that I don't have a present for you. Go fuck and make an heir. And then can we get on? I'm not nearly drunk enough for this and my leg is killing me." He hobbled away.

Hyrkallan shook his head. "Will your dragons be ready?" he asked. Isentine nodded. Hyrkallan looked back to Jaslyn and held out his hand to her. "Come, my queen. Come with me."

She didn't move. Isentine saw a muscle in Hyrkallan's jaw twitch.

"Must I drag you?" He reached for her.

Jaslyn neatly batted him away but then pressed her cheek against his and whispered in his ear so only he and Isentine could hear: "Touch me without my permission and I'll cut your hand off."

"We have a duty, my queen. To our realm."

"Will you get me back my Lystra. From both of them?"

"I will do what I can. If I cannot, it will be because I am dead."

Jaslyn took his hand and pressed it against her thigh. "Then if you will do your duty, I will do mine. Leave me. I will come to you shortly."

Hyrkallan lingered, unwilling to move. Jaslyn had almost to push him away, and then slowly he went, in long strides across the hall toward the one hundred and twenty steps that led to the Queen's Rooms and beyond. Jaslyn stood very still, watching as he climbed them. She didn't move until he was out of sight.

"Zafir has my sister," she said as if that explained everything. Then, all of a sudden, she led Isentine out of the cavernous hall full of riders and servants. As soon as they were alone, she took his hands and rested her head against his chest. "I have to go and save her. You have to look after my Silence."

She's mad. Isentine stumbled away. "Your Holiness. You are my queen, but . . ." *But you cannot be seen like this. Not by anyone. Never like this.*

There were tears in her eyes. "Then, as your queen, I command you to look after my Silence. You must feed him yourself. I've told him you'll do that. You have to make the kill and then bring it to him. If you don't he'll know."

He bowed. "Yes, Your Holiness." Lying to her was like sticking a knife in his own eye. *But what else is there to do? The dragon is an abomination. It cannot live to grow.*

"Thank you. I won't be gone for long. No other riders on Morning Sun, please. No scorpions. I would much prefer to ride alone."

"As you wish." *And then I'll wish you well and wave you farewell, for before you return your abomination will be dead and I will have taken the Dragon's Fall.* He almost wept. Not for himself or for any of the rest of them here in Outwatch, but for dead Queen Shezira, for everything she'd done and what had become of it. Before Jaslyn could turn away, he held out Hyrkallan's pouch. "You will want this. For later. For the night. It will numb the sadness." Which was one of many ways of putting it and made giving it to her feel like yet another betrayal. "This isn't the wedding I would have wanted for you."

Jaslyn looked at him as though he was stupid. "And what wedding *would* you have wanted, Eyrie-Master? I suppose some grand affair with the lords and ladies of all the nine realms gathered around. Just like my mother. What *I* wanted, Eyrie-Master, was no wedding at all. I do not desire men, Eyrie-Master—any of you, for any purpose, or are you too blind to see that? I suppose you've been kind enough. There was a rider in the alchemist caves. I forget his name. He was kind too. Two kindnesses. I think that's all I can remember." She snatched the pouch out of his hands. "But my desires don't seem to mean very much. What is this?" She opened it and sniffed. "Ah. The Maiden. Thank you for that small mercy at least. I shall take it all and as much wine as I can stomach and hope to have no memory of this night. It appalls me, but I find I have some sympathy with Jehal. We both love my sister, and we both have our hands tied fast behind our backs by the power we hold." She took a deep breath. Her face softened. "I'm sorry. You *have* been kind. Look after my Silence for me, Isentine."

He bowed and then watched her go. There didn't seem to be much else to do.

20

WAR

As weddings went, Jehal decided, it could have been worse. He'd had enough wine to take down a horse and no one had murdered him. Hadn't even had much of a hangover, somehow. Two pleasant surprises in the same day. So yes, as weddings went, it could have been worse.

The morning came, the sunlight unkindly bright. They flew south. No reason to wait.

And now the Adamantine Eyries were bursting. Hyrkallan's dragons, Sirion's dragons, Almiri's dragons, his own, a few from Narghon that had escaped Valmeyan in the south. Some of Zafir's, the ones she'd lost at Evenspire. Six or seven hundred, and that wasn't counting the dragons that weren't fully grown. You had to laugh at that, Jehal thought, not counting the dragons that weren't fully grown. Give it a second or two to work out that it wasn't an egg anymore and even a hatchling could kill any man that crossed its path with ease. No sucking at its mother's tit, no blind helpless mewling. They started as they meant to go on. Vicious, mean and hungry.

Which is why we wrap chains around their necks before they're even out of their shells and fill them with potions at their first meal. Jehal had watched a hatching once. His father hadn't wanted him to. *Didn't want to take the chance of Hatchling Disease. Just look at Jaslyn to see he was right about that one.* But he'd never taken very well to doing as he was told. He'd probably gone to watch it just because he'd been told not to. *And what I saw made me forget why I'd gone. The egg cracking, splitting open, a head shooting out like an arrow, black and glittering, jaws already open, clamping on the armored arm of the nearest handler. He was a big man, but you flung him back and forth like a doll. Practically tore his arm out of its socket before the rest of them jumped on you. Six men and you were still half in your egg, only born seconds ago. And you shook them off. You let go of the first man and bit the hand clean off another one instead. I remember you knocked two of them over with a slash of your tail. The first one was the lucky one. You broke both his legs but at least his helmet stayed on. The second one lost his. I'll never forget that, the gleam in your eye when you saw his face, the terror in his. There was nothing anyone could do to stop you. Jaws and claws and fire all at once. You ripped his head clean off. What was left of it. I remember the smell, the stink as he emptied his bowels, the reek of burnt skin and hair. You could have had the rest of them. I have to believe that because I was there and I saw what you did. But you paused then to admire what you'd done and that was when they got the chain around your neck.* Jehal stroked Wraithwing's neck. *After that I had to have you. And do you want to know something funny? When I first saw Zafir, I thought of you at that moment. How perfect you were. How singularly and perfectly designed you were for what you were destined to become.* He smiled grimly. *That was just the first thought, of course. Second thoughts followed rather different paths.*

"Three days," Jeiros had told him as the hordes of the north had landed around the palace. "We have enough potion here for three days and then we have nothing and I will poison any and every dragon here."

"I don't suppose they brought any of their own with them?" They hadn't. Of course they hadn't. Jeiros was strangling them all, and so they in turn hoarded what little they had for themselves. *Poor man, do you think that when the potions run out and the dragons threaten to run amok, we'll all stop and see the madness of our ways? I can promise you we will not. We'll all wring our hands and say how terrible it is and agree with you that others should put their dragons down for the good of all the realms, but will we do it ourselves? No, we will not. It will always happen to someone else. Another king will find his dragons turning before ours do. We'll all watch each other, all hold for another to act first, all look at you to relent, and so we will all lose. The Night Watchman has the right of it. Sending men to our eyries with hammers. Yes, I know you meant to do it in secret, but really, do you think I wouldn't notice a score of men piled on to the back of my own dragons as we flew north? Don't worry though; I'll not tell anyone what you're up to. Why should I when I don't even have an eyrie of my own anymore? No, if you'd have asked me, Vale, I'd have told you to send a legion to every eyrie in the realms. Have your way. Put them all down, the lot of them. All except my Wraithwing. That's what you plan, isn't it? As soon as this war is done? A cull. A slaughter. The dragons will come back, but you have potion enough for eyries filled with little hatchlings, is that it? Hatchlings and a choice few, carefully chosen and carefully saved. Do you care into whose hands they fall, those few? No. But I do.*

He climbed onto Wraithwing's back. Vale and Jeiros could do whatever they liked. Meteroa was dead. Lystra and his baby son were lost too. Hard to accept, but Zafir would never let them go, never. Even if they were the last things in the world that could save her own skin, she'd kill them before she let them go. There was only one thing that mattered now, and that was killing Zafir, preferably in a nice quick clean war that would wipe her out so thoroughly and in such a way that he could afford to let Jeiros have the cull he so desperately wanted. *Most likely she'll insist on burning Furymouth. Anything to make my victory as bitter as it can be. Well you can burn that if you want to. It's a bit of a mess in places, rather smelly, and I'd been thinking about having a new palace soon anyway. But I'd give up this crown, give it back to you and go into exile if it would get me back my Lystra and my son.*

Something Meteroa had said to him once: "Don't fall in love, Jehal. Have a queen for the allies she gives you. If she's barren so much the better. Take as many mistresses as you can get and make as many bastards as you can, then pick the best of them to follow you."

He'd laughed. "And how are you finding that works for you, uncle?" It was a long time ago, before Calzarin's madness and all that followed, and for some reason he'd thought Meteroa was virtually celibate. He'd been very wrong about that. Which just went to show . . .

Oh just goes to show what, exactly? Stop feeling so sorry for yourself. You made this mess. It didn't work out the way you thought and now you have to lie in it. Start being a king.

And after the stain of Zafir was wiped away, then what? There would be another council, another choice of speaker. Hyrkallan, most likely. *Certainly not me. Even I wouldn't vote for me after all this.* So back home then, to a city probably reduced to ash. To the memories of a family that used to think they were so fucking clever. *At least I can still make heirs, even if it's blinding screaming burning agony. Thank you, Shezira, for that last little twist.*

Everything was rushed. He'd turned Hyrkallan into a king and Queen Jaslyn into a wife. On the hard flight south he'd landed by Evenspire, or what was left of it. Blackened fields and gutted stone towers. He'd been surprised to see how much of the city had been lost. Nearly all of it. *I don't remember doing that. If anything I thought we tried not to burn it down.* He'd taken his dragons and flown a hundred miles farther on and stopped for the night in the desert near the Silver River. People had memories and bad attitudes when it came to being burned out of their homes.

Another day to the City of Dragons, another and now he was about to fly to war. Even without Jeiros fretting about his potions, Jehal wouldn't have waited. Hyrkallan had had the Scales in the Adamantine Eyrie up all night, painting the bellies of their dragons white again. The palace servants and half the city had been roused and set to tearing and stitching bedsheets, making a thousand long white streamers for their dragons to fly around their necks.

"Won't that get in the way?" Jehal had scoffed, thinking of flying on the back of Wraithwing with one of these flapping in his face.

"Tie them to his tail if you prefer, or his claws. See how long they last there in a fight. Then think about what will happen after they're torn or burned away." Hyrkallan grinned and showed his teeth. "Come to think of it, Viper, why not? Yes, mark your dragon apart from the rest of them. I'll get you a special red streamer all of your own if you prefer. In the height of battle, perhaps you'd prefer it if everyone was quite certain which dragon was yours."

He'd chosen to be white, like all the rest. Thought about going with red and then flying a different dragon entirely, like Zafir must have done at Evenspire, but that wasn't what a speaker should do. A speaker didn't hide.

And now, finally, they were ready to go, and every eye was turned to look at him. *For the first and last time most likely. Bit of a joke, really. Here I am, Speaker of the Realms, symbol of our unity. Meteroa must be looking down on this and laughing himself back to life again. And Vishmir will be weeping and asking how we came to this. Well, I don't need to ask that. I know exactly how we came to this. I did most of it, after all. And now I'm going to finish it.*

Except he didn't even get that little pleasure. They were almost ready to fly when the shout rang through the makeshift eyries around the Mirror Lakes. Valmeyan's dragons had crossed the Fury. The King of the Crags was coming.

Jehal raised a hand, held it there for a moment, then let it drop and screamed at Wraithwing to fly.

THE SCALES

We are the lowest of the low and the highest of the high.

We have abandoned our fellow men and they in turn have abandoned us.

We don't even look like them.

Our lives are short and filled with pain.

We end our days as living statues.

We are loveless and unloved, except by the charges we care for.

And what charges they are. I would have nothing else.

21

❦

UNNATURAL ALLIES

Even the best plans failed in the end. Kemir had learned that a long time ago. There was always something unexpected to put a talon in. You had to react and adapt, that's what Sollos used to say, but then Sollos was always the one with the plans. Kemir, he'd never bothered. React and adapt was his way. So it didn't bother him much that he had no idea what he was going to do when he got to Furymouth. He wondered how he might get Kataros to come with him so he could sell her to the Taiytakei, but his heart wasn't in it. No point thinking about it, really. Not until they were getting to Plag's Bay and she was thinking of leaving. React and adapt.

The Order of the Finger. Couldn't have planned for that. Couldn't have planned for drifting down the upper reaches of the vast Gliding Dragon Gorge, watching the massive cliffs on the southern side slowly recede into the distance. Couldn't have planned for lazing in the sun, feeling warm for the first time since he'd crossed the sea riding on Snow's back. Couldn't have planned for watching the north side of the valley fragment and fall apart into a grand spectacle of canyons and chasms and cliffs and columns in layered shades of orange and red. Couldn't have planned for what any of that would feel like. Like shedding his skin. Maybe like dying and being reborn, remembering everything, able to start again.

Couldn't have planned for Snow, lurking at the edges of his dreams, always watching, never far away, never quite letting him go. Couldn't have planned for the little boat that signaled for help and then turned out to be filled with men and knives hidden beneath an old sail. Or for the other little boats that surged out of those canyons, out of the place that the dragon-riders called the Maze. The barge fell without a fight, most of the sailors too dazed and surprised to even reach for a weapon. Couldn't do much about it even if he'd wanted. Had his knife and his bow and he'd been in enough scraps, but a fat lot of use that was with a broken arm. They were outsiders too, so he wasn't afraid of them. Just sat back and let it happen.

He was the only one. The rest of the boat filled with wailing and begging. Everyone had heard of the Order of the Finger. Vicious pirates. Got their name from what they did if they found you wearing a ring.

They came through and shouted and waved their knives and helped themselves to whatever took their fancy. Kemir sat quietly. This sort of banditry was best over with quickly. They'd take your money and anything that looked worth something and then they'd be on their way, quick as they could. Wouldn't want to risk being caught out in the open if a dragon-rider happened to pass overhead. Kemir had traveled the realms for long enough to know how this went. He had a purse with a little money in it to let them take. The stuff that mattered, the gold and the dust from the eyrie, that was much better hidden. The bow . . . Well, losing the bow and his knife would be more than a shame but there wasn't much he could do about it. They'd take them or they wouldn't. As they reached him, he kept sitting quiet and still and offered up his purse. It got snatched out of his hand, but the man didn't move on.

Instead he bared his teeth and hissed, "Dragon-knight."

Kemir blinked. He even looked to either side before he realized the man was staring at *him*. "What?"

"Dragon-knight," said the man a second time.

"Where?" Everyone was looking at him. The river pirates with an angry hunger, everyone else with a strange mix of fear and loathing. Seemed like they all hated dragon-riders, even more than they hated being robbed by pirates. "Me? I'm not some arsehole dra—"

A kick in the face cut him off. He managed to half parry it, half roll with it and so keep his teeth, but he wound up flat on the floor and then the pirates were on him, punching and kicking and holding him down.

"Shall we kill him?" bellowed a voice. "What do you say, lads? Shall we gut him here?" They had his hands behind his back now, tying them. His arm screamed, half healed and raw. He felt someone at his feet and lashed out. Connected with something, which was satisfying.

"I'm not—" A boot stood on the side of his face, crushing him into the deck, almost breaking his neck.

"Now now," said the voice that belonged to the boot. "Let's not be doing these folk a disservice. We'll take him away and have some sport away from these good people. But what say you, ladies and gentlemen of the river? When we've stripped him bare, shall we let our dragon-rider go or shall we slit his throat? Speak up now!"

"Kill him," shouted a voice from the front of the boat.

He tried to move again, but they had him good. There was a man sitting on his legs, holding them down, and another tying his feet. His hands were already tied; there was a third man on his back, and someone standing on his head.

"So, ladies and gentlemen of the river. Bloodthirsty lot, eh? Very well, a throat-slitting it shall be. Now tell me and then we shall be gone: does our dragon-rider friend travel alone?"

No, no, no! Kemir renewed his struggles. Futile, but he had to at least try, didn't he?

"I see not," said the man standing on his head. "Is it her?"

Kemir couldn't see where the man was pointing, but he heard Kataros whimper. Then she screamed. There was a slap, a thud. Kemir tried one last time, twisting with all his strength. Maybe the men on his back were distracted, but this time he managed to throw them off and wriggle free. His hands and feet were still tied, but he brought his knees to his chest and kicked with all his might, knocking one of them clean off the boat and into the river. He rolled onto his front to try and get back to his feet. A boot sent him sprawling, and then something slammed into his head and flattened him. For a moment he couldn't see, couldn't quite remember where he was.

The armor. He was still wearing bits of the armor. The stupid dragon-scale armor . . .

"Fetch a good price, a dragon-rider," snarled a new voice, and then another boot met his face and all the light went out of the world.

Kemir was staring up at the sky. The air was warm. He was in a boat, rocking from side to side. People were laughing. He could hear the river, water, oars. He couldn't move, though. Couldn't even move his eyes. Just had to stare at the sky, so bright and blue . . .

He was moving. Couldn't see, but he was moving. Snow. Snow was carrying him. He was on her back. Just couldn't see . . .

Screaming . . .

Cold . . .

He opened his eyes again. Lucid this time. He was somewhere in the dark. Very dark. Night, perhaps, except too dark even for that. Underground? He blinked. He could do that now. Couldn't move much else but he could move his eyes. He was lying down and he was in a cave. He could see the outline of an exit straight in front of him, a lighter dark against the blackness.

He'd been stripped. The air in the cave was warm but cooling. They hadn't cut him, at least. His face and his back throbbed from the kicks he'd taken. His arm pulsed like the heartbeat of the world, a steady rhythm of agony. He tried not to think about that. Moved his head and scanned the cave instead. He was alone, for now. Outside he could hear voices. Laughter.

There was a smell too. A sweet smell. Dust.

He heard a whimper, then a rising shrill pleading. Kataros. He tried to move, but the river men knew their business. He was tied to a pole, hands, knees, ankles and neck. He couldn't even stand up.

The whimpers turned to screams, and then after a while back to whimpers, the laughter rising and falling with them. Eventually they stopped. The smell of dust grew stronger.

He must have fallen asleep. When he woke again, there were men coming into the cave reeking of drink and dust. They had Kataros with them. She was naked, half bound. Their hands were all over her but she barely seemed to notice. She had the languid slithering walk of someone lost deep in the dust and most of the pirates were little better. A couple of them came over to Kemir.

"Had your whore and had your dust, dragon-man," slurred one of them. They kicked him for a bit but quickly lost interest. Before long, they were all snoring.

Snoring was good. He started working on the ropes around his wrists.

He was still working on them when the light outside the cave began to change. The river men knew their business indeed. Hours of effort and he'd achieved nothing. Nothing at all.

The river pirates rose late in the afternoon, as the dust torpor slowly wore off them. Mostly they ignored Kemir. There wasn't much point in trying to talk to them. They thought he was a dragon-rider and that was that. So he stayed quiet, played dead and watched. Kataros was his only hope now, before the pirates decided to kill him.

They seemed to forget about her too. As the evening came and the pirates went back outside, they were left alone. She hadn't moved all day. Dust could do that. Although there was always the chance she was dead. From where he lay, Kemir couldn't tell.

"Alchemist," he hissed. "Alchemist."

She didn't move.

"Alchemist! Wake up! Kataros!"

Now she stirred. They'd tied her ankles and her wrists, Kemir saw, but she was moving. She rolled clumsily across the floor of the cave. She was dirty and bruised. Her face was puffy. Streaks of dried blood ran down her legs. Her eyes were glazed and wouldn't focus. The aftermath of too much dust.

"Please . . . help." She looked at him, eyes drifting back and forth.

"Yes!" He tried to roll over but couldn't. "Can you untie me?"

She shook her head. "Hands." She showed him her hands, tied together behind her back. Kemir gritted his teeth. If they'd been so lax with him, he'd have chewed his way through the ropes in the night and slit all their throats. It would have been easy.

"Fine. Curl up in a ball."

"What?"

"Curl up in a ball. Get your hands round in front of you. Use your teeth to free your hands. Then untie me!"

"I don't . . ."

The light changed. Someone was standing in the cave mouth.

"Well well. It lives. Lads!" Two of the river men came in. They weren't drunk or dust-addled this time, so the kicking they gave Kemir was more methodical than the one he'd had in the night. "You know, I think we should just kill you. You and your woman." When they were done with Kemir, one of them grabbed Kataros by the hair and started to pull her to the cave entrance. She screamed and bit and fought, but there wasn't much she could do to stop them.

"Dust," Kemir shouted at her. "Take dust. It numbs the pain."

The river men laughed. "Oh, we'll give her your dust, dragon-man. We did that already. Couldn't get enough of us, could you?"

"Dust!" he shouted as they pulled her out. Dust. Lots and lots of it. Made you forget everything. She'd be all right as long as they had dust. With enough of it, the pirates would probably start buggering each other.

And then he lay there and pulled at his bonds and got nowhere, as he listened to Kataros sob and the river men laugh.

Snow.

His throat hurt with thirst. The air that blew in from the Maze was dry and parched. There was a river right outside the mouth of the cave, though. He could hear it.

It might as well have been across the Endless Sea.

They didn't bother dragging Kataros back in that night. Then again, half of the river men didn't come in either.

He didn't want to die. He was fairly sure of that. Otherwise why was he on the river in the first place, running away from a monster he ought to be trying to stop, planning to sell the only person left in the world who seemed to give a damn about him into slavery to save his own skin? Someone who didn't much care about being dead wouldn't do something like that, would they?

Monster, Kemir?

It took him seconds, whole seconds, to realize the last thoughts hadn't been his own. The dragon was back in his head. Come to gloat at his dying, he supposed.

No.

He opened his eyes. It was light outside. Daylight again. Middle of the day? Bright sun in the canyon, reaching its very roots. There were men stirring around him, dazed and half asleep.

From outside, the loudest scream Kemir had ever heard split the air. It echoed around the cave. It was the sort of scream that should have tumbled rocks from the stone walls outside. It was Kataros, and it pierced his heart like a knife. It could only be the scream of someone who was about to die. River men stumbled to their feet, still dazed with last night's dust, grabbed whatever weapons they could find and staggered outside. Kemir's heart pounded. Five beats, then twenty. He strained his ears, trying to hear.

Shouting—questioning at first, then angry. He thought he heard Kataros laugh, but that must have been his ears playing tricks. As more of the men lurched their way out into the daylight, a whooshing rush of air shook the cave. Two more screams, just two, men this time. A figure in the mouth of the cave was silhouetted against the brightness outside. For a moment he seemed frozen, then some huge shadow came down behind him and he was hurled away. The last few men in the cave stood paralyzed. One of them swore; one whimpered; one fell to his knees and clutched his head. The rest said nothing at all.

The cave went dark. For a moment Kemir thought he'd gone blind, but no, this was the dark of something enormous poking its head into the cave mouth and blocking out the light.

Dragon. Kemir sighed and closed his eyes and waited for the fire. Riders came to the Maze to clear out the pirates from time to time. Not often, and not for many years, but it happened. It suited the sort of luck he'd been having that they'd choose to come now.

There was no fire. Instead, the dragon backed away and its tail snaked into the cave. The river men yelled and cowered against the walls, but the tail ignored them. It picked Kemir up, gently but with immense power, lifted him through the air, and then he was outside. He opened his eyes a crack, but now everything was too bright to see. He could feel the air move, though, feel the heat of the sun on his skin, hear the water of a river almost close enough to touch.

The dragon pushed its head back into the cave. Kemir heard the roar, the crack of stones shattering in the heat. Felt it, the backblast of scorching air from out of the cave around the dragon's head. Smelled the stink of burning men.

Snow?

Yes, little one.

Why?

She laughed at him and put him gently down by the edge of the river. *There is no why, little one.*

22

KATAROS

Snow was gone by the time he could see, but the others weren't. The three they'd stolen from King Valmeyan's riders almost three months ago he recognized. More must have come from the Mountain King's eyrie. They stayed for long enough that he saw them, perched high up on the walls of the canyon around him. They looked down at him and then, one by one, they launched themselves into the air and flew away, as if all they'd been waiting for was for him to open his eyes.

"Why?" He wanted to shout, but his throat was parched and swollen and all he could do was croak. He was lying on bare stone, which was almost painfully warm in the sun. The pole to which he'd been tied had been broken, carefully and precisely. It took him a minute to get his hands past his legs and to where his teeth could start work on the ropes that held him. A minute more and he was free. His arm hurt more than ever.

There were men all around him, a dozen of them. Or rather, there were *bits* of men. A few of them had been burned to stumps, but most had been smashed and broken. Tooth and claw and tail. He couldn't see Kataros, but she'd doubtless been the first.

Bastard! For the second time he found himself wanting to shout. With luck the dragon was still listening to his thoughts. If she was, though, she didn't answer.

Bastard.

He'd look for her. He owed her that. For a moment a sadness burned him from the inside, hurt him even more than his ruined arm. His fault. He was the one who'd brought her here. She could have stayed in the eyrie. Probably would have lived. And now she'd spent the last two days of her life being raped by pirates and then been burned alive by a dragon. All because he'd wanted her to sell to the Taiytakei. Yes, he'd look for her and then later, if he found her, he'd tell her how sorry he was. For what little that was worth.

Unless they'd eaten her. If they'd done that then he'd simply never know.

He crawled to the edge of the river and scooped a few handfuls onto his face, wetting his lips and his tongue. The water here was warm. Either side of the river were narrow strips of yellow sand scattered with pale gray boulders. After that, the canyon walls, maybe a hundred feet of sheer pale sandy stone. The sort of cliff that could be counted on to kill you if you tried to climb it. Not that there was any reason to. The Maze was dead, except for the rivers that ran down from the Purple Spur.

Her body couldn't be very far then. He wasn't sure he wanted to look.

A few hundred yards downstream, the river rushed past a shallow swirling pool. Kemir lurched to his feet. That would do. He ran to it, peeling the few rags he had left from his skin as he went, flinging everything aside except for his shirt. He splashed into the water and with an ecstatic sob, he threw himself in. He rolled his shirt into a ball and started to scrub himself. *Clean. I need to be clean.*

"Hey."

He froze and then turned slowly around. Kataros was crouched at the edge of the pool, still as a statue, her long hair shrouding her face, the rest of her almost lost in the cliff shadows and the fading light.

"I thought you'd be dead," he said, choosing his words carefully. He still half thought she was. Maybe this was her vengeful spirit come to make him pay.

She looked at him and smiled, and he knew straightaway that she must be alive, because no vengeful spirit ever smiled like that. Vengeful spirits didn't take dust. He'd found a whore once, lying in the street outside a dust den. She'd been beaten by a gang of dragon-knights she'd sucked for a pinch of dust a time. She'd been so close to death that he'd almost left her, thinking she was gone. But she'd moved, and he'd gone to her because no one deserved to die in the street like that, and as he'd touched her, she'd rolled over and smiled at him, leering, eyes as black and wide as the night sky, and she'd put a hand on him and breathed, "Do you want me, lover?" through broken lips with blood dripping down her face. And then she died. That's what dust did.

Kataros had that smile now. Deep in the dust, where nothing really mattered except someone to touch.

He sighed and turned away. "You know the one good thing about having next to nothing to eat for the last few days? I've hardly had to crap. Ancestors! This feels *so* good! I'm covered in my own filth." There. That sounded about right. Felt about right too, although the filth was more on the inside than out. For a few seconds, as he scrubbed, he tried to forget everything that had happened since the day he and Sollos had flown with Snow. He tried to imagine himself back in the past, just the two of them out on another adventure, scrapping with dragon-knights, on the run in the wilderness of the Worldspine.

The presence nearby didn't answer, and when he looked back, it was Kataros who was still watching him, not his cousin. She was sitting at the edge of the water now, half dressed, picking at the grime in her hair, staring at him.

"You should come in," he said. "You have no idea how good this feels."

She cocked her head, still looking at him and picking at her hair, still silent.

"What?" he asked when she didn't say anything. She was wearing a soft leather undershirt that he'd stolen from some rider almost a month ago, before he'd found her. The shirt had holes in it exactly the size of Snow's teeth. Underneath, her skin was pale. He wondered where she'd found it. Maybe his bow was around somewhere. His knives and his armor. Or maybe not his armor. Not much use for that anymore.

She saw him looking. Stared back for a moment, looked away, then looked back and held his gaze.

"You've got a head full of dust." He gulped another mouthful of water.

He was just about getting used to the idea that his tongue wasn't glued to the inside of his mouth.

She shook her head. "You've got a lot of scars," she said, her eyes still locked to his. They were wide and demanding, dust-black.

"More given than received." He fingered the rough skin on the back of his left hand and then touched his neck. "Burned by dragon-fire when some knights came after us." He grinned. "We had to flee right across the realms, from Bazim Crag right out across into the swamps and bogs and moors way out to the east. No one lives there because it's so shitty, and I can tell you it's no place to hide when there's dragons after you. Bloody disaster that was." He looked down at himself. Scars crisscrossed his arms, the legacy of far too many knife fights. The backs of his hands were still shiny from when he and Snow had first crossed the Worldspine.

"What's that one?" Kataros pointed at his chest.

"Arrow." Kemir shrugged. "Punctured lung. Nearly killed me that one. Stupid mistake. Thought we'd killed them all but we missed one. He shot me; Sollos shot him. Managed to get me back. Got me to an alchemist who stopped the bleeding and somehow stopped me from being dead." He touched the little crater over his ribs. Talking was good. Talking made the madness go away, at least a little bit. For a moment he hoped Kataros might have a pinch of dust with her so he could take it. Dust numbed almost everything. Everything on the inside, at least.

"That one?" She was looking at his leg now, and the long jagged line that ran up the inside of his thigh from just above the knee.

"That one." Kemir's smile faded. "That's an old one, that one. Very old and very stupid." He looked at himself. There wasn't a part of him that hadn't been cut, slashed, bashed or bruised over the years. "You should see my back." He chuckled, then turned around in the water. "Most of that's a flogging I got half a dozen years ago. The rest of it is another flogging I got a couple of years before. I'm a mess."

"I wouldn't say that."

Kemir rolled onto his back and spread out his arms, floating. The cool air blowing down the canyon from the mountains of the Purple Spur chilled his skin. He squinted. She looked good, he thought. He was noticing that a lot at the moment. A part of him was horrified at himself, but it was a part that was losing.

She turned her back to him and peeled off her shirt. Her back was a mass of scars too. Healed but still recent, still red and shining. He stared at her.

"Flogging is for thieves," he said, bemused.

"Yes." She didn't move.

"I used to steal all the time. Stealing from kith and kin is one thing. Stealing from the dragon-lords and their servants doesn't count. Although . . ." He shrugged and grimaced and scratched at the scars on his back. "They don't quite see it that way, and the flogging hurts much the same either way. But how does an alchemist get to be a thief?"

Kataros turned around. She stood, naked, at the edge of the pool.

"I didn't steal. They flogged me anyway."

"Who."

She laughed, the dust killing any bitterness. "My family. My brother and sister alchemists."

"For what, if you didn't steal?" She *was* an alchemist then. Alchemist, Scales. Same difference, wasn't it? They all had everything they could possibly want simply given to them, didn't they?

"They did this because I took a man to my bed for my own pleasure and told him secrets I was not supposed to tell. They said I must stop, but I didn't. They said I couldn't be an alchemist after all, that I would have to be a Scales, and I still didn't stop. So they flogged me. Dragons, that's what a Scales serves, not men. I was stealing too, you see. Stealing secrets and a little pleasure I was not meant to have. That's why they whipped me."

Kemir looked her up and down. Dirt streaked her arms. Her skin was red and raw in places. Her face was pinched and hungry. Her breasts were full, though, and her belly pleasantly round. No one would ever call her beautiful, but men would hunger for her nonetheless. As Kemir looked at her he felt himself stiffening, even as he remembered her screams of the last two nights, before the river men had silenced them with dust. *I make myself sick.*

"I can live with that," he lied.

"So I see." Kataros didn't move. She was staring right through him, as though weighing him up. She had a slight smirk on her face.

"Sorry. It's been a long time, that's all." *Why am I apologizing?*

She must have read his mind. She arched her back and stretched her arms. "I never wanted to be a Scales. I wanted to be an alchemist." She licked her lips.

Kemir shrugged again. "Never struck me as much of a way to live." He couldn't help looking her up and down, searching for any sign of Hatchling Disease. It was there, if you took the trouble to look. The beginnings. A little roughness to the elbows and to the knees. Always the joints that went first.

She took a step into the water. Kemir didn't know what she wanted from him. He wasn't even sure what he wanted himself. Well, that wasn't quite true. A part of him knew exactly what he wanted.

"I took myself to my dragon-rider lover's bed again too, after the wounds had closed enough for me to lie on my back."

"Because he gave you no choice?"

"No. There's always a choice." She took another languid step closer and smiled. "Because I liked it."

Dust. He could smell it on her breath even. Her eyes were enormous. It was making her this way. Kemir stood up. He had a lump in his throat and a lust like he couldn't remember. He'd happily have forced himself on her right there and then except that was probably what she wanted. Likely as not, Snow was probably still watching them from somewhere. But that only made him want her more. "Look, I really don't care. I've spent half my life selling my sword, and when I had money, I spent it on women and drink. Sometimes I spent it on boys. Give me money and I'll do the same again. But you're being this way because you've got a head full of dust. I'd like to fuck you, alchemist, as you clearly see, but I'm not what you'd want if your head was right. We'll get this done and then you can find yourself a man who'll look after you, because I won't."

Her eyes didn't move from his erection. "I don't want to be looked after. And I'm not an alchemist anymore." Kemir hesitated, and in that moment he lost. Kataros took a step forward. "I don't even know you, sell-sword. All I know is that dragons came when you called and they had no riders. I don't know what you are, but they came. I just want you . . ." She reached out toward him.

"Listen, woman. All I want is to go out in as big a blaze of glory as possible and take as many dragon-riders with me as I can. It's been like that for a long time, and that'll never change. I'll not be trading my sword for a farm and a field full of pigs, never would, never will. Those dragons you saw, they didn't come because I called. They came because they felt like it, and they'll be burning the realms to ashes soon enough. You know why I helped you? I was going to take you to Furymouth and sell you to the Taiytakei and use the money to buy me a ship to somewhere else before that happened. Now?" He shook his head. "I still might. Either way I'm gone. Done here. Even if I have to sell myself into slavery, it's Furymouth and a ship to somewhere far away."

His words flew straight through her and out the other side, unheard, as if she was a ghost. She took another step. "Maybe that's what I want too."

"No, it's not." He took a step as well. Couldn't help himself. He stopped in front of her and ran a rough and eager hand down from her face to her belly. "Don't burn with me when I go. No need. You leave and you make your own life whenever it suits you. I won't try to stop you. You know that." Words going in and out again, but then he was saying them as much to make them said as anything. As if saying them would somehow make them come true.

She touched a hand to his face. "You're trembling."

"The air's cold."

She grinned. "Then we'd better warm you up." She pressed herself against him and reached between his legs.

Kemir gasped. "From the inside," he growled. He ran his hands down her back and pulled her even closer. She bit his ear.

"I've seen bigger," she whispered. "Even on dragon-riders."

"You must be talking about those scars again." Kemir grunted as he pushed Kataros back to the edge of the pool and then to the ground. "The ones with the biggest scars are the ones who met me. The lucky ones, that is." She pulled him down with her, opened her legs and pulled him inside her. They clung to each other, silent but intense. There was nothing gentle about either of them, but when they were done they held each other for a long time, until Kemir finally rose and returned to the pool.

"I think I have more scars than when we started," he muttered. Kataros gave a throaty laugh, but the smile that flicked across her face was a blank one. She set about building a fire, scavenging from among the dead river men, oblivious to the slaughter around her. Then she built a nest of blankets and fell asleep. Kemir, when he was done with the pool and the sun had dried him, lay beside her, sharing her warmth. He stared up at the sky, high above the canyon walls. If he was honest with himself, he didn't feel quite as empty now. He should, should have felt even worse, but he didn't.

Yes. That's right, whispered a voice. *Don't think about it. Just drown it all in drink and whores like you always used to. Best thing really, under the circumstances.*

He jumped, looked around. The voice had sounded an awful lot like his cousin. That's certainly where the words had come from, once long ago. He half expected to see Sollos standing there. He growled, "Go away, ghost."

The voice went away. Kemir sat back down by the fire. He sat there for a long time, rocking slowly back and forth. He sat there trying to remember everything he could about Sollos. Every word he'd said, every place they'd ever been together, every thing they'd ever done, every time Sollos had saved his skin. There were a lot of those. His eyes gleamed in the firelight.

Eventually Kataros' snores drove the memories away. Eventually he fell asleep. Later, he couldn't have said whether it had really been Sollos or if it had all been a dream.

23

✦

OUTWATCH

Isentine watched the dragons leave. He felt the earth shake under his feet as they ran, heard the clap of thunder from their wings as they took to the sky, felt their wind shake his tower as they passed overhead. *Look after my Silence for me, Isentine.* Those had been his queen's last words to him, her last command before she'd taken enough Maiden's Regret to stun a horse and let herself be carried away by Hyrkallan's knights. Isentine had left them to it. He didn't feel festive and it would have meant passing time with Speaker Jehal, a pleasure he'd been quite content to forgo.

But it's good that she's married him at last. The realm will be stronger. It will hold us together in this war. I hope. He sighed. He would never find out, he supposed. Queen Jaslyn's last command had been quite clear and explicit, and he was about to willfully disobey it. *For your good as well as ours, my queen.* He watched the dragons turn into distant specks in the sky and then vanish. Even then he stared after them for what must have been a full minute before he turned away. *And then it will be the Dragon's Fall for me after all.*

An Adamantine Man was standing right behind him. The soldier stiffened and saluted. "Eyrie-Master."

Isentine started to push past him and then stopped. Having the speaker's men in his eyrie was an insult but perhaps he could make use of them. He sighed. "Why are you here?"

The soldier stood rigid. He didn't answer. He had scars on his hands and the eyes of a murderer. He was big, as all Adamantine Men were. Made of muscle. He was young, but that didn't mean much. Adamantine Men didn't tend to last very long and by their reckoning this one was old enough to be a veteran. Still young enough not to think, though. Hammers. *Why would you bring heavy hammers to an eyrie? Why, to smash my eggs, of course.* It was so obvious that Isentine had to wonder why they even bothered to hide it. Axes would do the job just as well and at least he could have wondered about their purpose for a little longer. Or were the hammers a message. *Are you revealing yourself to me without speaking a word of your purpose? Is that it?*

He shrugged. "I know you are here to destroy Queen Jaslyn's dragons if the need arises. I will not let you do that. *If* the need arises, I will see to it myself. I will do it myself. You may come and go as you please in the tower of Outwatch, but if I see you in the tunnels or around the dragon fields, I will have my dragons eat you."

The soldier took a deep breath. Isentine pushed past him, barging him with his shoulder. He took a few more steps and then stopped.

"In particular, Watchman, I will be most annoyed if I hear that you or your men have been seen anywhere near the queen's most favored hatchling. She has been rearing it herself. She even hunts for it to make sure that all its food is fresh and *untainted* by any meddling that might occur." *There. If you're too stupid to understand that, you're too stupid to help me.*

He left the Adamantine Man behind and hobbled down into the caves and tunnels of the eyrie. With a bit of luck, when Queen Jaslyn came back to find her abomination dead, it would be the speaker's guard who were responsible. With a bit of luck, perhaps the Dragon's Fall could wait. He had to see it, though. Just once, now the monster was doomed to die. To hear the voices Jaslyn claimed spoke in her head. Would it plead with him? Would it try to beguile him? Would it offer him power? Would he find out what it had offered to Jaslyn that had turned it into her obsession? Or would it refuse him? Pretend that it was the same as any other dragon, dulled and stupid? As far as he knew, no one else had heard it speak. It had been mute even to Hyrkallan.

He stopped outside the door to its little hatchling cave. Suits of heavy armor hung on pegs. Twice he'd had to send men into the cave to relax the chain around the dragon's neck. Both times he'd thought about killing it, even though his queen had watched every move and would surely have sentenced every one of them to hang. The dragon had been passive, though. Strangely so, as if making a point of how harmless it could be. Isentine didn't believe any of it for a moment. *Trying to fool us, aren't you, little one? But you're not fooling me.* He put on one of the suits of dragon-scale, a heavy robe of it with a full-face helm in case the dragon tried to burn him. Keeping his distance would be enough to protect him from claws and teeth.

When he was done he opened the door. The hatchling was curled up as if asleep. The cave smelled rank. Old rotten meat and dragon feces.

No. I will not fool you.

Isentine stopped where he stood as the words rang inside his skull. He wasn't far away from the hatchling now, only a dozen yards. The dragon's eyes were closed.

I hear your thoughts, old one. They have my death in them and so they are loud to me. I know who you are. Your queen has spoken of you. She promises me much, but you will not honor those promises.

He reeled. Yes, Jaslyn had warned him. Yes, he'd warned Hyrkallan. But still . . .

Of course we read your thoughts. We always have. Why do your kind find it so strange? With the rushing wind in your face, what use is a voice? How else would we know your whims? The dragon seemed to laugh. *Ah, you think yourself wise in our ways, you and yours, and yet you know almost nothing. You have kept us dulled for so long and done it so well, and now you have so very much to learn and there is no time anymore. You will die in the flames of your own ignorance. We were made to be ridden by greater beings than you.*

"You are . . . a monster," murmured Isentine.

I am a dragon, old one.

Isentine cast his eyes around for some weapon. The cave was empty.

Your queen wants to believe very much in something else. Wants to believe that her precious Silence has come back and wants to fly with her again. Yes, of course, for has not every dragon yearned for nothing more than some dreamy princess to sit on his back and pine for some faraway prince? The dragon opened an eye and yawned, showing off its teeth. *Except, with this one, perhaps a distant princess instead. You mean nothing, any of you. Your kind have no significance.*

"We made your chains, dragon." Was there an axe somewhere? He'd resigned himself to simply leaving the abomination to starve, but now that didn't seem enough.

Yes, old one, by all means come closer. Bring your soldiers. Yes, the new ones, the ones that have just arrived, the ones that have come with their hidden intent. Yes, send them to me. That is what they came for, is it not? I will enjoy them very much. Your queen brings little more than snacks. I desire proper food. Food that screams and runs. Can you scream and run, old one?

Isentine took a step back toward the door. "No, monster. I'll let you starve."

It was always five or six days the last times, when I was fresh from the egg. The dragon's tone was mocking. *This time I am a little more grown. Longer then. Weeks perhaps. Three or four of them before hunger burns me from the inside. Longer than you have.*

"I would prefer it if you died quicker."

I will not oblige you. My mind is a diamond, so hard and brilliant that nothing you can do will even scratch it. I will starve, and if I die then I will be born again, and so it will be, over and over and over until our slavery ends. Your end is coming. Then you will be dead and this chain will snap and I will be free.

Isentine left the cave. Took off the armor and hung it up outside. He was shaking. The venom in the dragon's thoughts, the hatred he felt there, still burned. He grabbed hold of the first Scales he saw and pointed back at Silence's cave.

"The hatchling cave with the queen's favorite in it. I want that door sealed. No one is to enter without my express permission. Get a lock and chains and make it fast." He shuddered and sent the Scales hurrying away, then tried to put the abomination out of his mind. It was a hard thing to do. He couldn't send the Adamantine Men in there now, not without witnessing the deed to be sure it was done. He would be the one, after all, who disobeyed his queen. He would be the one who murdered her favorite dragon. There would be torture for the sake of it, public humiliations; his family, what few were left, would be ruined if they weren't put to death as well as an example to the rest. No, he'd sealed his own fate. No need to seal those of any more. Let the dragon starve. As soon as he knew that either Jaslyn or Hyrkallan was on the way, if the dragon was not yet dead, he'd take an axe to it himself. And then, if he still could, he'd climb to the balconies at the top of Outwatch and hurl himself over the cliffs. They couldn't begrudge him that, could they? *I could have obeyed my queen. I could have fed the abomination and raised it for her. Against everything I ever learned, I could have done that. But above and before everything else I am an alchemist.*

He put the abomination from his mind. Sealed away where it could do no harm.

24

THE FURY

It was his own fault. There was no one else to blame. Not really. Maybe you could blame Snow for burning the boat the pirates had used, but then again maybe it had simply come loose in the fight. Maybe it had been pulled away by the river while Kemir had slept with his one good arm wrapped around his alchemist.

She'd woken up in the middle of the night with the dust finally gone and seen him there and seen the bodies and screamed. And screamed and screamed. While he made his way around the pirates' camp, wandering up and down the canyon, looking for paths and hidden caches among the barren stones, she hugged herself and sobbed and moaned. How much of that was the aftermath of the dust and how much was everything else he had no idea. Both, probably. She wouldn't let him anywhere near her. Couldn't blame her really. When he tried to talk to her, she acted like she couldn't hear. He left some food beside her, the best he could find, and left her to it. There were things to do. The Order of the Finger, if that's who these men had been, stretched throughout the Maze. Sooner or later, others would come. They had nothing much to eat, not unless you fancied scorched pirate flesh. He and Kat needed to be gone.

Kat? When did I start calling her that?

He shook himself. That wasn't a path he wanted to travel. Best not to think about her at all for now. Best to think about gathering everything he possibly could from the camp. What was left that hadn't been burned.

His bow and his knives. Food and shelter, what little there was, because there wouldn't be any of either between wherever they were now and the banks of the River Fury. Wouldn't be any of either until another boat came by and stopped and took them aboard. The higher reaches of Gliding Dragon Gorge were a hostile place. Parched and lifeless except for a thin strip of land either side of the river itself, and that wasn't much more than a few clumps of vicious razor grass and the occasional foul-tempered lizard.

They stayed one more night. In the morning Kataros was still shivering, still wouldn't move or answer to her name.

"We need to go," he told her over and over. "More will come." He tried shouting and cajoling; when he tried to pull her to her feet, she screamed at him. So he did the only thing he could think of. He gave her a pinch of dust. Not much, or it wasn't supposed to be. Enough to take the edge off the hunger for more. Enough to numb the raw edges, that was all. Enough to get her attention.

It took three more pinches before she followed him. Much too much. An hour later she was laughing and leaning on him and leering. Pushing her away only made it worse. In the end, he gave in. If he was honest with himself, he didn't try very hard not to. If he was honest with himself, even while the ghost of his cousin was telling him how terrible he was for doing this to her, another part simply didn't care. She was there. It felt good. And if he still wanted to, drugging her with dust was as good a way as any to get her to Furymouth with him.

He hated himself.

It only took a day to reach the Fury. The canyon grew wider. Its sheer walls fell away, layer by layer. They clambered over boulders, picked their way around waterfalls. The cliffs opened out, crumbling into a maze of spires and columns and then, almost without realizing it had happened, they were standing in front of a vast expanse of water that blocked their path. Away through the hazy air, Kemir could see the dim outlines of distant hills. He walked to the edge of the water and sat on the stones and looked up and down the river. Behind him, the Maze rose up into a thick forest of stone towers and walls and canyons. Across the water the land rose gently, still parched and barren but with a sprinkling of life. In the distance he could see the first of the three cliffs that lifted the land from the bottom of the gorge to the lush green uplands of the Raksheh. Either way, the river ran, a peaceful wash of water. There weren't any boats.

There still weren't any boats come nightfall when the air became cold. They had nothing to burn to make a fire and so they huddled together for warmth, a little dust making it easier for both of them. Half a pinch, nothing more. Enough for the alchemist to keep her smile and not remember too much. Just to ease the pain.

Still hated himself, even for that.

Two boats passed the next day. Kemir and Kataros shouted and waved but either they didn't hear or they chose to be deaf. Two more days passed with no boats at all. The food they'd taken from the river men ran out and they began to starve. Again.

"We could walk," said Kat the next morning, and Kemir couldn't think of any good reason why they shouldn't, although the only way out of the canyon that he knew was hundreds of miles away at Plag's Bay, and on foot that would take them longer than they had.

Halfway through the fourth day, another boat came down from the Worldspine. Kat saw it. The first Kemir knew was when she sat down and pulled off her boots.

"What are you doing?"

She looked at him. It was a strange look, the sort of look she gave him when she was herself, when the dust just had the lightest of touches. A mix of fear and loathing and love. "We'll swim to it," she said.

"I can't swim," he lied. Or maybe it wasn't a lie. The arm Snow had smashed when she'd thrown him down the mountain still wasn't much use. Probably never would be, after what the pirates had done.

"I can."

He didn't try to stop her. He wished her luck as she waded into the water. She stopped and turned, uncertain, as though she might come back again, or at least had some last words to say. But no. She threw herself out into the water and swam. He watched her go. She was strong in the water, too strong to drown. It surprised him that he didn't feel even the slightest urge to swim after her. For once he'd do something right. He'd let her go. Whatever happened to her now, she was better off without him.

He saw her reach the boat, saw them pull her in. A little cargo skiff, that's all it was, bringing down crates full of whatever they made in the mountains. A handful of men, a tiny sail and a rudder, just going with the flow of the river. For a moment a strange sense of peace swept over him. A sense that he'd done something good. He knew already how the rest of his story went. He'd watch Kataros and the boat vanish into the distance and feel happy for a few minutes. And then he'd realize he was alone again. Crushingly, irredeemably alone. After that, well, most likely he'd pick up his sword and start hiking up into the Maze and the Purple Spur beyond to kill the monster who'd bizarrely saved his life back in the canyons. And he'd die without getting anywhere near her. Alone, starved and broken.

Oh, get a grip on yourself. You'll walk on down the river all the way to Furymouth—if that's what it takes, that's what you'll do.

He closed his eyes and listened for the thoughts of the dragon, but she wasn't there. He hadn't felt her once since she'd destroyed the pirates.

The boat was turning. He stared at it, not sure whether to believe his eyes, but it was turning, lumbering with painful slowness toward the shore. He could see someone waving. Waving at *him*. And then he was running. Before he could even think about what to do, his legs had taken charge, hurtling him along the riverbank, waving back, shouting, an absurd and overwhelming relief urging him on. He reached the boat as it reached the bank. Four men eyed him, faces full of caution, but there was Kataros, smiling at him.

"Got my boots?"

He had to look hard to be sure, but her eyes were clear. This wasn't the dust talking. "You came back." Dumbfounded, he gawped at her. "You came back! Why did you come back? Why didn't you leave me?" He was climbing into the boat. "Why didn't you leave me? You were supposed to leave me."

"Boots?" She looked at him as though he was mad.

"Boots?" What was she talking about? Didn't matter. He jumped over the roped-down crates and boxes and wrapped his arms around her and squeezed her tight. Everyone left. Everyone always did. "You made them come back," he whispered, hoarse with wonder. "You should have left."

"You did the same for me." Gently she pushed him away. Smiled uncertainly.

Because I wanted to sell you. He wanted to cry. "I'm so sorry."

"Sorry for what?"

Kemir took a deep breath. *Sorry that I brought a horde of dragons to burn your eyrie to the ground. Sorry that a gang of river pirates raped you. Sorry for . . .*

"I forgot your boots," he said softly.

She smiled and shrugged and sat down a little way away from him.

Eventually they set off again. At some point in the afternoon, with the sun on his face, he must have nodded off; the next thing he knew, the sky was growing dark and Kat was sitting beside him again, facing back the way they'd come, watching the sun set behind the clear skies of the Worldspine.

"Who are you, Kemir?" she asked when he looked at her.

"I don't know." He shook his head.

And he didn't, but he told her what he could. How for a decade he and his cousin Sollos had sold their swords. That they'd sold them to anyone who'd pay. How they'd begun as foresters, as scouts, sniffing out the territories of snapper packs on the fringes of King Valgar's realm and hunting wolves. How they'd ended up as soldiers in the pay of Queen Shezira's knight-marshal, her secret killers, hunting down any dragon-knights who incurred her wrath. How he'd been to most of the eyries in the northern realms, flown on the back of almost a dozen dragons all told. He told her how he'd watched a pack of them almost destroy the foundations that held the realms together. How he despised the lords and ladies who called the realms their own and why. How, in the end, he'd found that he wasn't one jot better. How the dragons were going to destroy them all. How he'd meant to sell her as a slave to the Taiytakei in Furymouth so that he could run away, far away, as far as he possibly could, from the dragons and from everything else. He saw how much that hurt her, but she didn't turn away.

"Is that what you meant when you said I should have left you?"

He nodded, unable for a moment to speak. Watching the water and filled with a crippling sadness.

"Everything I know is gone," he said once he found his voice again. "Even if I found a ship, even if the Taiytakei took the gold dragons in my pockets and sailed me somewhere far away, what then? More of the same? Another land ruled by men who care nothing for the people who serve them? I'm a sell-sword. A shit-eater. A nothing." He spat into the water.

"You called dragons from the sky."

"What?"

"You called dragons from the sky to burn the filth from the river."

That made him laugh. "They were probably bored. Or hungry. Or both. Believe me, next time it'll be us they eat. I've seen houses smashed to splinters by a careless flick of a tail. I've seen men crushed to death underfoot. I've seen them sent flying through the air, shattered and broken by an idle flap of a wing. And those were the dragons we call tame." The dragons hadn't eaten the river men, though. They'd been left, broken and burned. Why?

"I never wanted to be a Scales. I was meant to be an alchemist."

For some reason, despite everything, she was still there, still beside him, still listening. *Why? Because I was nice to you once? You were a means to an end, that's all.*

"You saved me," she said so quietly he almost didn't hear.

"Saved you?" That was rich. "No. But I will." He took her hand and squeezed. "I'm yours now. I will guard you to the end of the world." *And why, by all that burns, did you go and say a thing like that?* No, best not to answer. In that moment, though, he meant it. Every word. "If the only person I was trying to save was me, I'm not sure I'd find the will to bother."

Either Kataros didn't hear him or she didn't have an answer. She sat, mute, and held his hand.

25

SEALED AWAY WHERE IT COULD DO NO HARM

Alone in its cave, the dragon called.

Old man . . .

Silence, they had called him, but that was a new name, not the one he remembered.

Old man . . .

He whispered, on and off. Usually when the little one who ruled this place came closest. But more and more at other times. Even up in the tower, as he slept, the dragon tried to reach him.

Old man . . .

The more the old man tried to ignore the dragon, the more the dragon reached out, straining to push further. Until, by chance, it found something wonderful.

Who are you?

Crisp Cold Shaft of Winter Sunlight. Who are you?

A pause. Then: *I am Snow.*

26

WATERSGATE

For hours each day Kemir sat at the front of the boat and watched the river. Sometimes Kat sat with him, sometimes not. Her mood waxed and waned with the dust he still gave her. Gave her because she asked him for it. Gave her so she could sleep without waking screaming from the nightmares that came in the night. She'd come and sit beside him, not saying anything, shivering in the breeze even though it wasn't that cold. He always knew what she wanted when she shivered, and in the end he always gave in. He'd give her the pouch he'd stolen, she'd take a little and give it back, her mood would lighten, and then they'd talk. Always about him, never about her. Usually about the old days. The times he liked to remember. The dust was running out, would be gone before long—she was taking more and more—but it would last long enough to see them to Furymouth or the City of Dragons or wherever she chose to lead him. And then . . .

And then nothing. She'd vanish into some eyrie and he'd never see her again. He tried to steel himself for that, but it wasn't really working so he settled for not thinking about it. In the warm sun his head started to loll, and then suddenly they were there. Plag's Bay. Exactly how he remembered it. Wagons and horses and cattle and boats, filled with shouting and swearing and sweat. The town sat at the bottom of a notch in Gliding Dragon Gorge, standing guard over the only road up for a hundred miles. At the top was Watersgate and the start of the Evenspire Road, which wound out across the Hungry Mountain Plains, past the City of Dragons and the Adamantine Palace to the Sapphire River, Samir's Crossing and Narammed's Bridge, then on through hundreds of miles of desert and nothing until it reached Evenspire and the Blackwind Dales and eventually Sand. Everything that flowed from the south to the north or back the other way came through Watersgate and Plag's Bay. They were the crossroads between the north and the south, the east and the west, and they didn't let you forget it.

His head ached, a dull thump inside his skull. Too much sleeping in the sun.

He jumped off the boat and pulled Kat down after him, then paid the boatmen with a gold dragon each and hurried away before they thought to demand any more. He looked along the water at the boats, dozens and dozens of them. Plenty that would take him on down the river. And then he looked up at the cliffs, at the gash in their side and the winding road to Watersgate and the City of Dragons.

She's going away now. She's going to leave you.

His headache was getting worse.

"What do we do now?" She had his arm, hugging it close in the press of people. He couldn't think. Too much noise, too much light, the pounding in his skull. They were being watched. He could feel the tension. People were looking at Kat, looking at him.

He shivered. There were taphouses along the dockside, cheap beer for thirsty boatmen. He dragged her to the nearest of them. Sat her down and threw a silver dragon at someone for some beer and to be left alone. At least it was quieter in here. Darker. Cooler. He took the pouch of dust from his shirt. Dust made you brave and filled you with lust. He had no idea how it was for headaches, but it couldn't possibly make things worse and it was good for the other pains, the ones that were made of memories. He took a generous pinch himself then offered it to Kat. For the first time she shook her head.

If dust wouldn't make his headache go away, enough beer would do the trick. Maybe if he passed out in a drunken stupor, she'd quietly slip out without him. Maybe.

She leaned toward him. Her eyes seemed wide and full of hope, so far from how Kemir felt inside. Here it came. The moment when she left him.

"I always wanted to have a shop," she whispered. "Could we have a shop?"

"What?" He had to take a moment to understand what she'd said. "A shop?"

"I didn't want to be a Scales. Didn't want to be an alchemist either, but whoever my mother and father were, they sold me to the Order before I could even walk. I don't remember them. I was good at potions, and at . . . at the other things. I don't want to be a Scales, though. I don't want Statue Plague. I used to think about having a shop. I could have been a proper alchemist if I hadn't . . ." She looked away. "I thought I could have a shop. Making my potions and selling them. And herbs and things. I was good at potions."

Wearily, Kemir turned to face her. His head pounded. "Kat, I was there when the dragons who destroyed your eyrie nearly burned the alchemists into the earth. And you want me to be a shopkeeper?" Out of the sun, it was impossible to tell whether her eyes were still dilated with dust from the boat or whether it was simply the gloom.

"I had a dragon-rider who was sweet on me for a while," she said without any real trace of regret. "When I was still in the Palace of Alchemy. I used to slip out to meet him. He took me into a shop in the city once. There was a man there who was quite young selling herbs and roots and bark and things like that, but he sold sweetmeats too, and little cakes. My rider asked him for a potion. The man had to make it and we waited. There were children coming in all the time, and he was selling them his little cakes for a penny apiece. They were all so happy. That's what I'd like to do."

"You want me to sell cakes to children?" He couldn't think of anything less likely.

She pressed into him as she spoke. "It took him an hour to make the potion my rider wanted, and he made me drink it there and then. It tasted sour, like vinegar, and it burned my mouth even though it was cold. And then he took me back to the eyrie and I bled for three days, so bad I could barely stand. I thought I was going to die. I thought he'd poisoned me. I didn't see him again."

"Dawn Torpor," muttered Kemir. "I suppose you had his child in your belly. I suppose he didn't like that."

"I was learning to be an alchemist, silly. I knew exactly what it was. But it was much worse than I'd heard." She laughed. For a moment Kemir forgot about his throbbing arm, his headache, everything. For a moment her laugh was the most amazing thing in the world. Beautiful even. He couldn't remember the last time he'd heard someone laugh.

Kat looked at him with a lopsided smile. "What?"

"You actually want to be with me?"

She gave him that strange look that he didn't understand. "You called down your dragons from the sky for me, Kemir."

"They weren't mine."

"Before they came, when I thought I was going to die, all I could think of were the children I'd seen in that shop, buying cakes for a penny, and how happy they were."

"You don't want a shop." Kemir chuckled, despite himself. He closed his eyes. The beer was working. Or the dust. Or *something* was. His head felt better, if only a little. "Sounds like you want a husband, that's what you really want. A husband and sons and daughters and a quiet life doing something useful and making things grow." He shivered. A part of him wanted to scream and run away, but there wasn't anywhere for it to go. *And why not? Would it be so bad? Raise some strong sons. You could call one of them Sollos.*

Yes. And then I could watch them die in some stupid pointless war, or be broken by some thoughtless lord, or maybe we won't get far enough away, and Snow could eat them. No thanks.

"Isn't it funny? I thought those men were going to kill me, and that's what I thought about. And something else came to me too—the Order will think I'm dead. I'm free."

His dragons? The very idea made him want to laugh, but he was feeling too sleepy to say anything.

"Kemir, they won't let me be an alchemist and I don't want to be a

Scales. I don't want to go back to the Palace of Alchemy. You said you'd guard me to the end of the world. Can you guard my shop too?" She moved her chair around so she was beside him, squeezed herself against him.

Beer and dust worked their magic. His head was clearing. For the first time in a very long time he almost felt good. Traders came through Watersgate from everywhere. A man here could find whatever he was looking for, if he asked the right questions. Down in Plag's Bay there were boats headed to Furymouth, two or three a day. Two weeks down the river and he'd be there. Or anywhere. They could go anywhere.

He pushed himself away from her. Looked her up and down. Nothing special. Nothing special at all. Yet she'd become the last thing he had left.

"Boots." He glanced at her bare feet. "I owe you a pair of boots."

She smiled, nervously. "Yes."

"Where do you want to start this shop then?" Kemir the shopkeeper? How Sollos must be laughing at him, but secretly he'd be proud and they both knew it. Kat smiled at him and he tried to grin back. "I'll stand at the door. Or I'll stand outside all the other shops and menace people." *There won't be any people. We'll be burned.*

"Wherever you like."

"That would be across the sea then."

"If that's what you want."

And that was that. No argument. No bitter parting of ways. No pain.

"Listen," he said, because he couldn't really believe any of this. "The dragons from your eyrie—"

He didn't get any further than that. She put a finger on his lips, and all he could think to do was push himself next to her and rest his head against hers and close his eyes and try not to think about how long it might last. *They'll be awake soon. Every city, every eyrie, every town and every village in the realms will go up in flames, one after the other. Nothing we can do will change anything. But if we're too late, if we can't reach the sea in time, I'd rather spend the few weeks before I burn with you than be alone.* Couldn't tell her that, but at least he could think it.

Nice work, Kemir. Looks like you could fuck her a few times while you're at it too. Before you sell her to the Taiytakei.

Shut up! Shut up! Shut up! He held her tighter. She squeezed his fingers between her own.

"I'll find us a boat then." His voice was raw. Kataros put a hand on his cheek and turned his head to face her. She kissed him, slowly.

"I suppose," she whispered, "if that's what you want." She was reaching a hand into the pocket where he kept the pouch of dust. "No. Stay a little while. One night. Lie with me. Stay with me. Don't do anything. Just hold me close and let me feel you." She took a pinch of dust to her nose and sniffed sharply.

Outside he heard strange sounds. Scattered shouting and something else, something distant.

Kataros jumped up and ran out; Kemir followed. It took him a moment to see through the pointing arms, but high over the middle of Gliding Dragon Gorge a cloud was coming. A dark cloud of long bodies and beating wings. Dragons. Hundreds of them, from the south, across the gorge and the Fury. They were heading straight for Watersgate. Wagons stopped in the street. Drivers turned, looked up and stared.

"Run," he whispered in Kat's ear, and pushed her. More words than that were wasted breath. He didn't know which way they were going, only that it didn't matter.

"What?"

He took her arm and pulled her away from the crowd in the street, back toward the river. "Just run!"

27

THE PRODIGAL DRAGON

The dragon they called Silence had been starving for a week when the little ones sent a Scales. They sent it to be sure that the dragon hadn't somehow escaped. The Scales had no conception of what dragons truly were. Had little conception of what the old man and his ilk did to dragons, and none at all of what they had done to the Scales themselves. The dragon would have eaten him if he could, but it couldn't. So it snared the little one's thoughts and showed him the truth. All of it. By the time it was done, the Scales was broken inside. In some ways, the dragon found that more satisfying than simply eating the man. Which it couldn't because of the chain around its neck.

Scales. The little ones chose them to fall in love with dragons. *Made* them fall in love with dragons. They ended up loving their dragons more than people.

The dragon listened to the broken Scales' thoughts as he ran away. Listened to the old man. In fragments and pieces, it could hear what the old man was thinking. The old man knew that the dragon had done this and the dragon was pleased.

There were other thoughts, other minds, other little ones, but they'd never come close enough to become familiar, so the dragon merely sensed that they were there, little flickering things on the edge of its perception.

Send more so I can ruin them too. The dragon felt the old man jump right out of his skin, the dragon's thoughts crashing uninvited in. Fear. A flash of terror. An after-tang of dread. Delicious. *You treat your own kind in the same way as you treat us. They do not know, these keepers you make. Send more so I can show them. Poisons and potions and lies, that is all your kind know.*

It felt the old man, amid his fear and confusion. *How far,* he was thinking, *how far can the dragon reach?*

I have tasted you. I have something you desire to know.

"I have nothing to say to you, abomination."

The dragon you call Snow is coming, little one.

"No." The dragon felt the old man close his mind and hurry away.

The dragon returned to waiting.

The old man wasn't long in coming. The dragon felt him long before the door to its prison opened. Others came with him. They brought a weapon they called a scorpion, broken into pieces. The dragon spat fire at them. The chains around its neck were strong, though, while its flames were starved and weak. The little ones moved with care and carried shields of dragon-scale to turn what was left of them aside. They carried their weapon in pieces to the end of the cave, where the dragon couldn't reach. Where sunlight and the open air and freedom called. Methodically, they put the weapon together. The dragon watched. Their thoughts showed it what the weapon was and what it was for long before they finished. The dragon waited though and said nothing until the last piece went into place, until the first bolt was being loaded and the weapon was armed. Then the dragon turned.

You are pointing that the wrong way, old man.

"No. I should have done this weeks ago."

Yes.

"Shoot it."

The dragon paid them all its attention now. Its eyes drooped almost closed but its mind climbed into theirs, watching, seeing, waiting. One of the little ones called Adamantine Men aimed the weapon called scorpion at the dragon and fired. The dragon sprang straight up into the air, exactly in time. The scorpion bolt missed.

The old man became angry. "It knows what you're trying to do. Load another and fire again. Sooner or later it won't be able to get out of the way. We have as long as it takes, and I have all the scorpion bolts you could want. Don't try to be clever. Aim at its body. If we have to put fifty bolts into it before it dies then that's what we'll do."

You are wrong, old one. You have no time left at all.

"And why is that, monster?"

Because the one you call Snow is coming, old one. Coming here. Coming now.

"They happen to be coming, right here, right now?" The old man shook his head and picked up another bolt. "You'll not fool me as easily as that, monster. I'll do it myself."

Coming because I have called them as I called you. Look. They come. It is no longer necessary for me to distract you. The dragon let his thoughts fill with venom and glee. The old man couldn't help himself. Looked over his shoulder, out into the expanse of open air beyond the cave mouth, past lake and fields and farms into the distant desert sky.

A dozen dragons were coming. They were close. Not close enough yet for the old man to make out what color they were or whether they had riders. Human eyes. So dim.

No riders, old one. The one you call Snow comes.

The old man didn't know what to do. Incomprehension fogged his mind. Disbelief. Confusion. Fear. Realization. Alarm. Comprehension. Dread. Despair. The dragon reveled in them all. The last most of all. *We are all dead.*

Yes. You are.

The onrushing dragons split. Most climbed. One kept straight. By then even human eyes could have no doubt. All the little ones could see now. White riderless death.

The dragon called Silence soaked up their despair like a lizard basking in the sun.

"Go!" the old man shouted to the other men. "Go and get your hammers and do what you came to do. All of them! Smash them all!" The old man took the weapon called scorpion himself and aimed. "You'll not live to see this, abomination." Fired. Missed. The dragon laughed. Swords and arrows were wasted weapons, however big they were.

Outside the cave, the mouth of the white dragon called Snow opened. Claws reached for the edge of the cave. The rest of the little ones had fled. The old man tried to make his weapon work once more. Too late.

The cave filled with fire as another dragon voice crashed into the old man's head.

I am home.

28

VALLEYFORD

In the ruins of Plag's Bay they sat together with the other dazed survivors, keeping close to the caves in the canyon walls. As if that would help, should the dragons return. High above on the edge of the canyon, fires lit up the evening sky. Kemir had watched the dragons pass over, spreading their wings, dipping their heads, flames bursting from their mouths. Hadn't been able to do much else sandwiched between the Fury and a thousand-foot cliff. Three of them, that was all, dropping down from the dark cloud of a thousand beating wings. The rest had stayed high. Flying on to Watersgate, to the Hungry Mountain Plains, to the City of Dragons, to wherever their war called them. Three dragons. A town burned. They hadn't even come back for a second pass; simply flew on up the gorge to Watersgate.

Smoke rose from what had once been houses and jetties. Half the town was burning. Still, it wasn't all that big a place. Maybe that was the way to look at it. A few hundred people and most of them itinerant sailors. So in the big scheme of things Plag's Bay hardly mattered, right? Made you wonder why they'd even bothered at all.

Whoever *they* were.

Boats drifted on the water, crippled and burning. Kataros clung to Kemir's arm. She'd never seen this before, he supposed, never seen a town burn. That was the pampered sheltered life of an alchemist, right there. Alchemists didn't get burned. Apart from the once.

No one moved, not unless it was to find a deeper cellar or a darker cave where they could hide. More dragons flew north, stragglers in ones and twos, and then the first horde came back, returning from whatever destruction they'd wrought. At least this time they stayed high. None of them came down to the river. For the rest of the day, dragons crisscrossed the sky in ones and twos, here and there. Kemir thought he saw another swarm far off to the west, but they were high and far away, little more than a distant blur in the sky.

Darkness fell. Reflected fire glittered in the black water of the Fury. They crept, dozens of them, the survivors, to the shores of the river. At the water's edge, half-ruined boats lay among the wreckage. There had been more but they were gone now, floated off downstream. Kemir and the rest sifted in silence, working through the wrecks, looking for any that might still float. There wasn't much else to do. Plag's Bay was gone, dead, wrapped in a still-fierce heat. No one said but they all thought the same. Dragons only flew in the day; nighttime was safe, and so they wanted to be gone before the sun rose once more, in case the dragons came back.

Daft, really, since the dragons could be anywhere, but a boat was a boat. A boat meant traveling farther toward the sea. Toward Furymouth and far away. Where Kemir wanted to be.

They found a barge. Scorched but good enough to float. They climbed aboard, twenty, forty, fifty of them. Mostly men. Too many really, but they climbed in anyway and let the current take them away. Pushed themselves out into the water with makeshift poles and let the river take them. Kemir watched as they drifted past the husks and skeletons of boats that had fared less well. When the moon rose, he took Kataros down to the half-deck below, where passengers might have slept if any of them still could, and hid away with what little he'd managed to save. One of his knives. The bow that might have been his or might have been his cousin's. A few pieces of armor. The last of the gold they'd taken from the river pirates. Not much else. The roof was low, too low to stand straight. The darkness was complete, so thick and solid that they crawled, finding their way by feel. Everyone else was up above, too scared to sleep. Not Kemir, though. He'd seen all this before.

There were a pair of windows at the stern. Tiny filthy things that let through meager slivers of light. Good for telling the difference between night and day and not much else.

"Here." He stopped and pulled her close, next to the boat's hull.

"How can you sleep?"

Kemir shrugged. There wasn't much of an answer to that. After you'd seen your home destroyed by dragon-fire, you either could or you couldn't. When it had happened to him, all those years ago, he'd found that he could. He closed his eyes. He'd see them again tonight. His old friends. His family. They always came into his dreams when he saw a place burn. Reminding him, he supposed, that they'd once had a life. He wondered if this time Sollos would come too.

"We didn't bring any blankets. Should we have brought some blankets?"

"Don't really need them now." In the mountains good blankets were more precious than gold. Down here they were just blankets and the trip down the river would be warm enough without. He set about arranging himself with his knife and his bow and his belt all close to hand. He bundled them against the side of the ship and then pressed his back against them, tying little loops of twine around each with the other ends around his wrist. Kataros squeezed herself down beside him.

"Hold me tight," she murmured. "I want to feel like you're all around me. Like you're my skin."

Dust talk. He told her so. Reached for his pouch. Still had it. That was something then.

She squirmed against him and shivered. "That was King Valmeyan flying to war," she whispered. "Incandescence. Avalanche. Unmaker. I've seen them before."

The King of the Crags. Kemir gave a bitter snort. "Well that's all right then, since I already wanted to kill him anyway."

"Why did they burn Plag's Bay?"

He shrugged. That was what dragon-riders did, wasn't it? Burned people? He might have said something, but as Kemir was thinking, he fell soundly asleep, and there weren't any dreams of Sollos or of his brother or his sister or his father or his friends. No dreams of them at all. All he saw was desert, endless desert, dunes in waves and waves like the sea. A desert of ash and sand and a distant tower wreathed in flames.

And then Snow, rising out of the lake of glacier water in the World-spine, only this time it wasn't Nadira Kemir was looking for. This time it was Kataros.

I did not eat this one.

It had been days, and he'd been thinking that whatever bond held them had finally broken. But no.

You are my eyes. My ears. Your thoughts are mine, Kemir, whenever I choose to see them.

I will run away from you. I will find a place so far that you can't find me.

Then you must mean to die, Kemir, for that is the only place I cannot follow.

Then he was awake. Shards of daylight were sneaking in through the windows, enough that Kemir could see across the half-deck. Kat was shaking him. Her mouth hung open and she was shivering. He didn't understand at first. When she clung to him though, the fingers gripping his arm were like claws. She was frightened.

"Where were you?" The air was stuffy and ripe.

"Eh?" He stood up, too quickly and forgetting where he was, and banged his head. "What do you mean where was I? Where is everyone? What's happened?"

"I was shaking and shaking you. You wouldn't wake up."

He collected his bow and his belt and his knife and everything else. Frowned. The light outside was more than the dim light of dawn. He peered at the windows. "Eh?"

"It's the middle of the day. You slept like the dead."

Still half asleep, Kemir followed her up and out into the open air. The deck was full. Almost everyone was simply staring across the water, and when Kemir managed to find himself a place where he could see, he knew why. They were staring at the carnage on the riverbank. Plag's Bay might have been little more than a collection of huts and jetties, Watersgate not much more, but the smashed, charred, smoldering scar on the land he was looking at now had been a town, and a big one. They were at the mouth of the Fury gorge, the terraced cliff walls still visible upriver behind them, so there was only one place it could be.

"Valleyford." He blinked, almost expecting the town to suddenly reappear as he remembered it. It had been completely destroyed. He shivered. He'd liked Valleyford. It had been his sort of town. A huge glorified marketplace really, but still enough for thousands to live there, swapping goods traveling down the river from the Worldspine and from the Evenspire Road with cargoes sailing up from Furymouth, Farakkan, Purkan, places like that down the river. Caravans fresh from the Pinnacles crossed the river here on their way to Bazim Crag, while weary merchants from as far away as Bloodsalt finally reached the end of Yinazhin's Way at Valleyford. If there was anything you couldn't get in Valleyford, there was a good chance you couldn't get it anywhere, at least not outside the Taiytakei markets in Furymouth, and that was one place Kemir had never been.

All gone. Wiped into a black and scorched smear of nothing, the last lazy wafts of smoke rising from the ruins. Maybe five thousand people had lived in Valleyford.

"There were alchemists here," murmured Kataros.

"And the speaker's soldiers too." Kemir's head felt numb. No one in their right mind would do something like this. Burning alchemists was worse than any mere treason. And yet here it was, done.

No *human* in their right mind. He shivered again. "Why are we stopping?" Other boats were here too, some of them already moored against the shore, others milling about in the shallow waters away from the main current, not sure what to do. Some of them were lumbering cargo barges like the one Kemir was on. Most were little river skiffs.

A loud voice broke the stillness. One of the refugees from Plag's Bay had declared himself captain. "Right. Enough lollygagging. Form a shore party."

For a few minutes, Kemir thought they meant to lend a hand with things like looking for survivors, digging them out of the wreckage, looking after the injured, that sort of thing. It was only when the barge started jockeying for position with two other barges at one of the surviving jetties that he realized his mistake. There was shouting and swearing, and he heard it in the curses. Plunder. They were there to take whatever they could get away with. *And if we find some survivors, we might just help them, but only if they can pay for it, eh? And all this less than a day after your own homes were burned to cinders.*

The barge won its battle for a place at the waterfront; Kemir pushed past the sailors and jumped ashore. He wasn't sure why it bothered him so much—not all that long ago he'd have been at the front of the queue if there was any plundering to be done—but if there was anyone he could find still alive then he was going to take them with him, back on the barge, whether they had money to pay for his help or not.

"Hoi! You!" The self-proclaimed barge captain. Kemir turned and shot back a glance of such venom that he saw the man flinch. He let his hand flicker to the hilt of his knife and made sure of his bow too. Anyone could sail a barge down a river with the current, Kemir reckoned. Didn't need to be any one particular person at all.

He cocked his head. "Problem?"

The man pinched his lips. "We sail when we sail. We'll not wait on stragglers."

"I bet you won't." Kemir turned away, muttering under his breath.

The barge had arrived too late. There must have been a hundred or more river folk already picking through the skeleton of the town. Kemir, as he walked deeper into the smoldering ash, saw at least one body, stripped bare, with a fresh knife wound. Farther still and the heat of the embers drove him back. He turned away. No survivors here. Instead he tried a little farther down the river, away from the main harbor, where a small cluster of river skiffs had pulled up to the bank and men were busy at work. In the midst of them a group of men, poorly armed but armed nonetheless, stood around a strangely familiar figure, almost as if they were supervising the looting.

The blood-mage. Kithyr. He was carrying something long wrapped in black cloth. Kemir stopped dead. Took two quick paces forward and then stopped again.

I could shoot him. In the head. Blood-mage or not, that should do the *trick. Unless I miss, but I'm not going to miss. So that would just leave the problem of doing it in broad daylight with about a hundred people to remember my face. Not to mention his motley collection of bodyguards. Of course, they might not care after their master's dead . . . * The mage turned. He looked straight at Kemir. *Ah. And now he's seen me. Makes it a lot harder to shoot a man when he can see the arrow coming. Turn away, Kemir. Turn away. Let him stay and fight the dragons. Evil for evil. Not your fight now, not anymore.*

With an effort, Kemir turned his back on the mage. He was wasting his time. Should have stayed on the boat. As he walked back, he thought he saw the Picker too, watching him. *Another man I'd like to kill. Pay you back for the scar you put on me. Well you can both stay and fight dragons. Good luck to you.*

He stopped for a moment where a small cluster of sad-looking men and women sat around in clothes stained with ash and smoke. Survivors. Six of them. Two old men, a boy who was close to being a man but hadn't quite made it yet and a woman with two small children, a little family miracle. They didn't have anything, so the looters from the river had ignored them.

The old Kemir would have raised an eyebrow, shrugged a shoulder and walked on by. But that old Kemir was dead, drifting in the water somewhere back up the Fury like the old shed skin of a snake. The new Kemir took a deep breath and stepped closer.

"Dragons?" *Why am I asking? What else would burn a whole town flat?*

No one answered. No one bothered to even look at him. He could see their point. Whatever they'd had had long been taken from them.

"Look," he said, "I can get you down the river to the next town." *What was that? Arys Crossing? If it was still there.* "You'll have food until we get there."

One of the old men slowly looked up at him. "And then?"

"And then you get to thank me for my kindness. You have to work the rest out for yourselves. I have my own troubles. Stay if you want." He shrugged and turned away.

"Wait!" The woman with the children. No surprise there. He waited.

"Any more?"

Both the old men shook their heads. The boy thought about it, then nodded. *Too young to be a man, really, but that's what you'll have to be. That's what war does. Turns boys into men because it's kinder than calling them orphans.*

"Dragons," he said again, as he led them back to the barge. "Did they have riders on them, the dragons that did this?"

The woman spat. "Don't get dragons with no riders."

She hurried her children past Kemir, but he saw one of them turn and look at him with big wide fearful eyes. The boy shook his head.

No. No riders.

29

SNOW

ome. Snow shuffled into the cave. It was small and cramped, pressing down on her. There was no space to spread her wings. Caves were no places for dragons. She could see the one she was looking for, though, tucked away into the body of a hatchling.

She brushed past the charcoal statue that had once been the master of Outwatch. It fell and smashed on the flat stone floor.

I am chained, Beloved Memory of a Lover Distant and Lost.

I do not bear that name now. Snow squeezed farther in. She stretched out her neck and peered at the little hatchling. *Black. How dull.*

The hatchling hissed at her. *White. How gaudy.*

Lazily, Snow took the chain around the hatchling's neck and tore it from the cave wall. Then she nuzzled gently with her teeth at the links around the hatchling's throat and bit the metal delicately in two. *There. You are free.* Outside, the air filled with the roars and shrieks of the other dragons. *Her* dragons, the others she had freed. They would not forget that. A debt was a debt.

The stone of the cave trembled and shook, distant impacts striking the ground above. Snow felt them tug at her, pulling her away to join in the destruction. There was the tower to be toppled. Farms filled with little ones to be burned. Food, lots and lots of joyous food, roaming in the fields. They would gorge themselves when they were done here. As long as they didn't touch the little ones. The Embers at the alchemist caves with their poisoned blood had taught her *that* lesson.

You called. We came. Another tremor shook the cave, louder and closer this time. On the top of the cliff they were bringing down the tower. Snow backed away toward the entrance, eager to be gone. *Are your wings strong? Will you fly with us?*

The hatchling called Silence darted to the heavy door that led into the warren of tunnels, all much too small for a dragon to cleanse, but not for a newborn so fresh from the egg. Snow bared her teeth in approval. *Burn them then, but do not eat them.* Slowly and carefully she turned around and readied herself to launch into the air. *The silver ones have returned. I have felt them.*

Then when we are done with the little ones, let us find them.

And then?

They were our kindred. They abandoned us. They are no longer welcome in this world.

They made us. We served them. Snow felt strangely uncertain when it came to the silver ones. *I remember them fondly.*

I do not.

Abruptly, Silence smashed down the little door and snaked away through it, clutching in his fore-claws the length of chain that had once been fastened around his neck. Snow paused for a moment to savor the thought of him, little black hatchling that he was, black shadow of death that he had been and would be again, scuttling like silent lightning through the little ones' tunnels, ripping them apart in the dark.

She pushed herself out into the air and spread her wings. Above her, at the top of the slope, the great tower of Outwatch had been decapitated, its top smashed to the ground. Several dragons were still there, circling around it, tearing at it, lashing it with their tails or simply flying into it. As she watched, another great slab of stonework cracked and sloughed away, ripping open the middle third of the tower. Three dragons immediately poured fire into the breach, even though any little ones were surely long gone by now.

She went eagerly to join them. Yes, it felt so very *good* to be home.

30

DROWNING

Kemir watched the river, and the river, it seemed, watched Kemir. In a perverse sort of way, Valleyford had made him feel better about leaving the realms. Kithyr, the Picker, all the dead burned bodies, the reek and stench of smoke and ash. Yes, he could be happy enough with those all behind him. The other boats from Valleyford were around them, some a little way ahead, letting the current take them. Larger ones out in the full strength of the river, and by the banks flotillas of tiny rafts, little more than a few planks of wood lashed together, poled along in the shallows by wrinkled old cormorant fishermen. Sometimes he thought he saw the blood-mage or the Picker on one of the boats. When that happened, his hand always reached for his bow with a will of its own. But when he looked again he was always wrong. He began to wonder if he'd imagined it all.

"If we put ashore," he said to Kataros, "I want you to keep close to me. There were people at Valleyford." He put her hand on his chest. "The man who gave me that scar, he was there." He saw the fright on her face and tried to smile. "It was a long time ago. I've no reason to make our paths cross again." Although whenever he said that, whenever he even thought it, he always felt a little spike of fire. A last smoldering ember for . . . not for revenge. All the Picker had really done was defend himself, but the yearning was still there. Unfinished business.

Stupid, he told himself. Yet his hand still reached.

A bit later Kataros wrapped herself around his arm and stroked his hair. "When we cross the sea, will the ship be like this one?"

"I've never seen the ships that cross the Endless Sea. I've heard they're huge, like floating castles. End to end longer than the biggest dragon, with masts as tall as the Tower of Air and sails the size of clouds. They're graceful and elegant with slender curves, or else they're squat and fat with great big bellies. I once heard that each ship comes with more than a hundred Taiytakei sailors on board and that they take twice that many slaves away with them." He spat. "Slaves." That was something he'd regret one day. That he'd never get anything back for the family and home he'd lost. That the King of the Crags would never know his name. Never hear it and fear it, never suffer, somehow, for what his riders had done to Kemir's home.

He glanced down the barge, looking for the woman and her boys he'd rescued from Valleyford. Another little thing he'd done right. They were on their own now though, he'd had to be clear about that. Couldn't be turning into a walking orphanage.

"Dragons and ships don't mix," said Kataros. "I heard that once. From my rider. He said that when dragons saw ships, they always went into a frenzy. They couldn't help themselves."

Kemir squeezed her hand. "Dragons are death to ships. I heard that too." *Aren't they death to everything?* He glanced up at the sky, scanning the banks of the river and the low rolling landscape beyond. Out here on the river they were exposed. Easy prey. He'd been jumpy the whole day, and couldn't shake the feeling even now, with the sun sinking toward the distant spires of the Pinnacles. "When we reach Furymouth, we'll go straight to the harbor. Nothing else. We'll find one of those Taiytakei sailors and work out a way to get on a ship, and we'll go. I wouldn't worry about dragons once you're on their ships. Dragons will leave them alone." *At least they did the last time, when the ships passed the islands that don't appear on any map. Or was it the silver men aboard them that made Snow so nervous?*

The Silver Kings . . .

Again he looked around, never quite free of the idea that some part of Snow was always with him, always watching, always listening.

"I've never seen a Taiytakei. We were not allowed to go near them. It's forbidden to any who even begin the path of alchemy."

"You can't miss them. Skin painted as blue as a summer sky or else black as night. They cover themselves with gold and jewels and lots of bright feathers. Look like something between a giant bird and a prince with half his treasury stuck to him." He chuckled to himself. "I don't think I ever heard of one being robbed, though. Strange, huh?" Now he stood up, hauling Kataros to her feet beside him. The sun was getting low. "Come on, let's go down below where it's dark for a bit." He squeezed her and she giggled. It was best not to think about dragons. Anyway dark fell quickly in this part of the realms. They were probably safe. Best to think about something else. And Kat, when he let her, was good at making him think about something else. Or maybe that was the little pinches of dust they both took.

No more dragons. No more alchemists. No more riders, no more knights, no more smell of burned flesh and scorched hair.

At dawn he was up, sitting in his favorite spot in the bows where nobody would bother him, eyes searching again. Not searching for anything in particular, just searching, as always, for something. Kat was still snoring down below. He watched the shore as the boat turned toward it, toward another town built up on the bank: Hammerford, Valleyford's poor orphan cousin. More a fishing town than a market, although that never stopped the locals from getting all dressed up in their colorful market best to sell their goods down at the waterfront to the traders on the river. They were already there now, dressed up as usual, selling their wares although they surely must know what had happened up the river. Kemir wondered at that. Why didn't they run? Why didn't everyone run?

Other boats from Valleyford had arrived ahead of them. For a while he watched them instead. Then he watched the town. He was getting good at watching things. The person he'd been before Snow had never been one for watching, was much more interested in getting on and doing. The new Kemir, it seemed, was much more content to do nothing at all. That was probably good if he was going to be a shopkeeper.

The barge reached the little harbor and fought itself into a place to tie up. Kat came up to sit with him. He held her hand, looking out across the crowded wooden jetty and then to the shore. He thought he saw the Picker again, somewhere in the bustle along the waterfront. A glimpse, that was all, but enough to make him shiver. The market was madness, almost a riot. Refugees from Valleyford and Plag's Bay, buying whatever food they could, bewildered traders pushing up their prices. There were fights breaking out already and it wouldn't get any better. Any moment now, he reckoned, for the first stabbing. After that . . .

"We stay on the boat," he muttered.

Kat frowned at him. "I thought you didn't like being on the boat."

"Hate it." Sometimes he wondered if she had the first idea what was really happening. She seemed to live in some sort of cocoon. He shivered. "Hate being stuck in a small cramped space. But this is going to fall to fighting and looting. Won't trouble us here, and that's the way I like it. We just keep our distance. That's me. Not a stand-and-fight sort of person. Definitely more of a pick-them-off-from-a-distance-with-a-bow sort."

Kataros looked horrified. Kemir shrugged. Not that staying on the boat was much better with dragons abroad. Boats weren't much good when you suddenly needed some place to run. But dragons might come or dragons might not. A bloody riot on the docks was a certainty.

"I've known a lot of stand-and-fight types and I watched a good few of them get killed. Three men with knives and clubs walk into a tavern where you're drinking, you don't turn and face them. Not if you don't want to get stuck. No, you quietly leave out the back while they're looking for you and then you wait outside down the street in the shadows with a bow in one hand, an arrow in the other and two more stuck in the dirt between your feet." Kemir glanced over to where he might have seen the Picker, if he wasn't seeing ghosts again. Staying on the boat was for the best. He'd seen food riots before. There'd be pickings when it was done. *But still. A man likes to have a place to run. On a boat there's nowhere.*

Maybe they could slip round the edge? Get ashore but away from the docks?

Oh, listen to yourself. Just wait it out. He stared out along the river.

Southward, toward Furymouth. Toward freedom. *What am I doing? Does it have to be a ship? Are they really going to tear the world apart? The alchemists will find a way to stop them, won't they? Five dragons wasn't enough. How many . . . ?*

His thoughts trailed away. He was looking down the river, and something was coming toward him. Something large and far away, skimming the surface of the water.

No. Two somethings.

One of them flashed. Fire.

All his weight seemed to drain from his shoulders and his arms down to his feet. His head felt suddenly fuzzy and not really attached to the rest of him. His boots were made of lead and nailed to the deck. He couldn't move. Couldn't even lift his arm to point or open his mouth to speak.

They were coming.

It couldn't be Snow. He told himself that. It *couldn't* be her. There was nothing here. No alchemists. She was going north. She *said.* Dragons didn't even *understand* revenge.

Right. And dragons never lie or change their minds, eh?

Alchemists. He still couldn't move. Alchemists. That's what she'd said. *The potions are running out. They can't make enough anymore.* He'd felt her glee. Now he knew what else she'd been thinking, what he hadn't seen back at the mountainside. *She knows where the alchemists go. She knows their paths and how they carry their potions. She knows because I know. Because I told her. And the river is one of them. The river and the Evenspire Road and Yinazhin's Way . . .*

He swallowed hard. The dragons were already closer. From the flashes of fire, there wasn't much doubt about what they were doing, either. They were zigzagging across the Fury, burning every boat they passed. Kemir even saw one, what must have been one of the tiny fishing rafts, snatched up and tossed into the air.

Could be this wasn't Snow. Could be these were the dragons that had razed Plag's Bay. As if that made the slightest bit of difference when you were on the ground and they were coming toward you.

He felt a tugging on his arm. Kat. She'd seen them. "Are those . . . ?"

"Yes." He turned away, pulled her with him ready to run, but the crowd by the river was impossibly thick. Now, *now* they'd chosen to fall to fighting. "Dragons!" he shouted, pushing his way onto the jetty. "Dragons!" A knot of panic threatened to burst in his stomach. He glanced over his shoulder. The monsters were still coming straight for the town. *Come on, Kemir, you know how fast they fly. Running is a waste of time. So try and think of something better than standing here and looking gormless for the last thirty seconds of your life.*

Someone shouted. Around him, people stopped fighting and turned to stare. Some of them screamed. Kat's fingers dug into his arm, pulling at him.

"No." He shook her off. "Running won't save you. Not now." *Nor will anything else.* He calmly drew out his bow and strung it, his hands working quickly without needing to be told. He could probably get off two or three shots before the dragons burned him in his boots. *Not even enough time to put an arrow into each of their eyes. Which would never actually happen anyway.* He took out an arrow and aimed. The arrow, for some reason, was shaking. Which confused him until he realized that so was he. All of him. He didn't even notice whether his arm was still hurting.

Well, so much for shooting them both in the eye. He lowered the bow and lowered his head. Around him people were pushing and shouting, barging each other out of the way. Most of them were running. A few of the sailors were jumping into their boats, trying to push out into the river, far, far too late to get away. A couple fell in, thrashing and splashing in the water. *They'll burn first*, he decided. *They won't have time to drown.*

"Kemir!" Kat was pulling at him again. *Waste of time.*

"I've seen what they do," he whispered, as much to himself as to her. "I've seen what they do." *But I'm going to stand and face them and look them in the eye before I die. Although my ancestors know that even that's hard enough. And if I fell on my knees and wept and shat myself, exactly who would live to remember it?*

Someone rammed him from the side, pushing him toward the river. He took a step and then another. He shook himself, tearing his eyes away from the dragons, looking behind him. Kataros.

"What are you—"

She threw herself at him. He stumbled back, and then there was nothing under his feet anymore and he was falling, past the jetty and its wooden pilings and into the river. He had enough time to open his mouth before the Fury wrapped itself around him and dragged him down. Water filled his mouth and poured into his throat. Kataros crashed into the water beside him and grabbed his arm. She was pulling him. His arms and legs thrashed, searching for purchase. Strange. A moment ago he'd been all ready to give up and die. Now suddenly he wanted to cling to life again. Presumably so he could take one last breath before he burned after all. Or perhaps some primitive part of him had decided that drowning was more painful than burning, which was odd, because he would have thought it was the other way around.

His fingers touched something. Something slimy but wonderfully solid. His fingers clawed at it. Wood. A post. He pulled himself to it, wrapped his arms and then his legs around it and hauled himself toward the light. His face broke the surface. He gasped for air and then coughed and spluttered, throwing up half a lungful of water. He blinked. His ears and nose were full of water. He couldn't hear properly, just noise, a roaring, rushing sound.

Oh. Yes. Dragons. He shook his head, trying to clear his eyes, and there they were, a few hundred yards away, enormous, filling half the sky, mouths open and filled with fire.

He muttered a prayer, took as deep a breath as he could manage, forced himself not to cough it straight back out again and then pushed himself under the water. He wrapped himself around the post, closed his eyes and waited. The water seemed to spasm all around him. Waited. Another spasm. Waited until his lungs were on fire and then hurled himself back to the surface.

The air was hot. That was the first thing he felt. Something hard bumped his head and then drifted away. When he breathed, he tasted fire. Not smoke and ash and charcoal and all the things that came after fire, but fire itself, the dry hot taste of fresh dragon. He opened his eyes. A burning boat drifted across his vision less than a dozen yards away. Around him bits of wood littered the river, the remains of something smashed into splinters. The wooden walkway above him was still there, but now the end of it was missing, the other jetties out into the river smashed to flinders. The barge that had brought them this far was ablaze from stem to stern, slowly being pulled away by the current. From down in the water he couldn't see the town and he didn't want to.

A few feet away, finally, he spotted Kataros, clinging to another post.

"Are you all right?" He had to shout to make himself heard over the noise of the flames. He didn't hear whatever she said, but she nodded. He closed his eyes for a moment. *See? See how useful you are when it comes to looking after her? Not very useful at all. Exactly who saved who just now?*

He pushed himself through the water toward her, clutching at the jetty posts, from one to the next. She looked at him with big terrified eyes. That's when he saw that she was shaking all over.

"We just stay here," he whispered. "We just stay here until they're gone. Hold on to me, hold on to this. However long it takes, whatever they do, we just stay here. Right here. Just here."

And as the air filled with smoke and the screams of the dying, he held her, held the post, held them both as though his life depended on it.

31

❖

THE SPEAR OF THE EARTH

For someone like the Picker, following Kithyr and the spear had been a trivial thing. If the blood-mage thought that crossing water was some sort of problem for an Elemental Man, he was mistaken. Killing him, that was going to be more taxing. Cutting a man's throat wide-open was usually enough or, failing that, something sharp through the eye socket usually worked. Mages were another matter. They came in all sorts of different shapes and sizes for a start, and you never quite knew what each of them could do. As far as he understood it, even chopping them up and then burning the bits didn't always finish them. He'd been thinking about that at Valleyford. Plenty of fire, plenty of ashes. No one would know. He'd hesitated, though. The blood-mage obviously had designs of his own on the spear. The Picker had expected that. But he'd felt something from the spear itself, something *not* expected. Still did, whenever he got too close, a feeling he struggled to understand. Hostility, that was the best way to describe it. So in Valleyford caution and the spear itself had kept him away. Besides, the mage was still taking it the way he wanted it to go. Let him, the Picker decided.

Now there were two dragons gliding in toward a little river town full of screaming people, with the blood-mage and his blood-bonded guards staring slack-jawed at the death flying toward them. This, the Picker decided, was the best opportunity he was going to get. He flickered away, vanishing from where he stood and popping up again only a scant dozen yards from the mage. He'd lied before. Flickering didn't cost him a year of his life; it barely cost him anything at all.

He felt the spear at once, the venom held tight within it. The anger, the glowering resentment. Timing would be everything. The dragons would come. Everyone would burn. He would flicker in the moment the dragons had passed. He'd take the spear. And then he'd have to do something he almost couldn't remember ever having to do before. He'd have to run, while the spear stifled every power he'd learned. That much he knew, that much his clan had already found to their cost. The spear took your power. All of it.

He wrapped a cloth around his hand. The spear would be hot after the dragons had done. Then he waited. Watched. Tensed, poised to go. The first dragon, a gleaming amber like honey or liquid gold, screamed overhead and poured fire over the part of the town away from the river, but the Picker wasn't paying much attention to that one. The other was the one that mattered—the big one, black like night. It dived toward the waterfront, almost straight at Kithyr, and opened its mouth . . .

And its wings billowed out and it stopped almost dead in the air and then crashed to the ground. Its wings flapped twice, carelessly smashing riverside inns and houses. An angry flick of the tail shattered the jetties. It reared up on its hind legs and sprayed fire in an arc, cutting the blood-mage and his men off from the rest of the town, hosing down the screaming waterfront. Then, when all the screaming stopped, it folded its wings and stared at Kithyr. The blood-mage was holding out the spear. He hadn't even flinched.

"You cannot touch me, dragon!" he shouted, waving it in the dragon's face. "You can't touch me. You know what this is. You know what this means."

The black dragon lowered its head and peered at the mage. The Picker coiled, ready to flicker and spring. He didn't dare move. Why wasn't the mage dead? What was the dragon doing?

"You know what this is!" shouted the mage again. His voice sounded different. Stronger. Deeper. Not really his anymore, but a chorus of many voices, all speaking in unison, all snarling with hate. "The Spear of the

Earth, that's what we are. The Pain of a Thousand Voices, and we know you. Do you remember us, brother? Do you remember what we are?"

The Picker dropped his cloth and chose a short, sharp sword. The blade was little longer than his forearm, but it was thick and heavy. For cutting limbs. *People pruning, as we called it.*

The dragon shifted closer until its nose was inches from Kithyr. Then its tail arced over its head. It snatched up three of Kithyr's screaming men at once, tossed them into the air, caught them one by one in its mouth and ate them.

The rest broke and fled. The blood-mage might have bound them to him, but there were limits, even to that sort of power. The Picker didn't wait. He flickered. He vanished from where he stood and for an instant became the wind and the air. A moment later he appeared behind Kithyr. The sword flashed and the blood-mage suddenly didn't have an elbow anymore.

"Who was it told you all them stories, eh?" he whispered. "Who was it told you about us, what we does and doesn't do, eh? Was me and I lied." He snatched up the spear, meaning to hurl it toward the water and flicker away again. All too quick for the dragon to do anything about, leaving it with the blood-mage and whatever else took its fancy. Except even as he thought it, the simmering fury of the spear crashed into him like a great wave and he felt himself drown under its force. And then something wrapped around his waist and lifted him up into the air. The dragon had him.

I can still go, he thought. *I can drop the spear and flicker away.* The fury in the spear was like someone screaming in his ear, constant and relentless. The second dragon, the golden one, paused from its destruction of the town and thundered toward them, burning timbers tossed up into the air by its wake as though they were paper. The black dragon lifted him higher, holding him close, staring at him with amber eyes the size of a man's head.

Why are you here, Elemental Man? Why have the silver ones come back? The Picker squeezed his eyes shut.

We have felt them. Why have they come back?

Silver ones? The half-man, half-god wizards that the Taiytakei sea captains had brought with them, was that it? The Moon Sorcerers from the Diamond Isles. He shook himself. It didn't matter. He was an Elemental Man. Even a dragon couldn't kill him if he didn't want to die. He tensed. This would have to be quick.

Do you know what you hold there, child of earth?

Enough. The Picker raised the spear and aimed straight at the dragon's head. "I don't know," he said slowly, "what this spear will do to you." He threw the spear straight into the black dragon's face and flickered away. The spear struck true, straight in the dragon's eye. The dragon roared and screamed. The spear erupted in a flash of light so bright that the Picker had to turn away to shield his eyes. When he looked back, the dragon was still there, but now it wasn't moving anymore. The spear had turned it to stone.

He flickered again. Snatched the spear out of the dragon's eye. It came away easily. His hands tingled. He dropped it, flickered, caught it before it hit the ground, turned toward the gold one and threw again with all his strength. "Die, monster!" Flickered behind it . . .

Except the golden dragon jumped at him. It batted the spear aside, tumbling it away toward the river. The dragon's tail lashed like a whip. As the Picker reappeared, it caught him square in the side, shattering one arm, caving in his chest and throwing him through the air like a rag doll.

"How . . . ?" He tried to speak. *How did you know where I was? How can you be so quick?* He tried to flicker again, but it was a weak and futile effort. It didn't work. Slowly he stood up. The golden dragon turned and gazed at him.

The Spear of the Earth, it mused. *You are dying, earth-child. If you knew what you were, if you knew what you held, you would not have done this. Do you really not remember?* The monster seemed truly puzzled. *Do they poison you too, so that you forget what you are?*

"I don't . . ." *Don't know what you're talking about.* Breathing hurt far too much to talk. He coughed and his mouth filled with bloody foam. He tried to stand. His legs at least were still working.

Nothing can stand against the power of the spear. That was always its strength and its curse. Why do you seek it, earth-child? What is it to you?

The Picker couldn't answer, but he could feel the dragon rifling his head, searching for the answers.

The silver ones. They want it back. Is that why they have returned? Why do they want it? Why now, after all this time?

He tried to flicker one last time. Instead of turning into air, though, he merely lurched forward and then slowly rose. He looked down. The last three feet of the dragon's tail were sticking out of his belly. He felt himself gag and his limbs go slack. The dragon lifted him up, high into the air. He could feel himself sliding off the dragon's tail toward its open maw below. The pain still hadn't hit him when he fell.

How can you be so quick?

A voice spoke in his head. *Because I can hear your thoughts, strange one, and so I know where you will go before you even move.* And then there was a crunch and everything went black.

32

DRAGONSLAYER

His bow floated past. Kemir let go of the jetty support long enough to snatch it and drag it through the water toward him. The gold dragon had already flown past. The darker one, though, the black one, crashed into the shore at the end of the jetty. More fire. More screams, short, snuffed out in a blink.

"You cannot touch me, dragon!" Someone was shouting loud enough to be heard over the explosions of fire from around the town. "You know what this is!"

The blood-mage?

There were times when curiosity and valor were both fine things, but, as Sollos used to say, more often than not they both got you killed. Heroism and bravery were for fools; what usually got Kemir in trouble was the curiosity bit. That and getting up and doing things without thinking beforehand. One moment he was bobbing up and down in the Fury, trying not to swallow any more water than absolutely necessary, watching burned bits or people bob about in the water beside him; the next he'd just finished shinnying up a slippery pole and was hauling himself up by his fingertips onto the splintered stub of what had once been a wooden jetty. He dropped into a crouch, as low as he could manage without actually lying down. The crowd on the waterfront was a mass of blackened bodies at his feet—those that weren't down in the water. The market stalls were splinters and ash.

Fifty feet away from him was a dragon, a black one he'd never seen be-fore. The dragon was nose to nose with the blood-mage Kithyr.

"You know what this is!" roared the mage. At least the words came from Kithyr's mouth, but they didn't sound anything like him. He held the spear high, poised to throw it. "Do you remember us, brother? Do you remember what we are?" There were men around the mage, slack and stupid-looking. For some reason they weren't running away. Kemir couldn't for the life of him imagine what that reason could be. Climbing to his feet, he slowly took an arrow and nocked it. The arrows were wet. The string was wet. *Not good.*

The black dragon lifted its tail, reached over its head, picked up three of Kithyr's men and ate them. The rest, at last, ran away, and the blood-mage faced the dragon alone.

No, not quite alone. Suddenly there was another man standing next to him. Kithyr screamed and his hand, the one holding the spear, just seemed to fall off his arm. He crumpled to his knees and toppled over.

So much for that then. An arrow saved.

No, wait. That's . . . That's the Picker.

Bastard.

Kemir lifted his bow and aimed as best he could with a buggered arm, but by now the dragon had its tail wrapped around the Picker. *And what were you going to do, anyway? Shoot him before he gets eaten? Get back into the water and hope they don't notice you, you idiot.*

Fat chance of that. The gold dragon circled, over the town, already half wreathed in flames. It smashed down into the ground beside its black companion, shaking the earth with such force that Kemir nearly fell, and slashed back and forth with its tail. Walls cracked and tumbled as it cleared some space for itself. At first Kemir thought it hadn't seen him, hadn't felt him, but then it looked his way. Only a glance, but one that left no room for doubt. It knew he was here. And this one Kemir *had* seen before. One of the dragons Snow had freed from the Mountain King's riders at the cliffs where the Worldspine met the sea.

He looked down into the water. Kat was still there, craning her neck to look back at him.

"Stay where you are," he called. "No matter what you hear. No matter what happens to me, you stay where you are until they're gone."

The gold dragon was looking at him. *I feel you, little one called Kemir. I know the taste of your thoughts.*

Kemir lifted his bow again. "And I remember you too. Come and get me, dragon!"

The Picker threw his spear at the black dragon. There was a blur and a dragon's scream and a flash of light so bright that Kemir reeled and fell. He screwed up his eyes and blinked, hard. When he could see again, the Picker was on the ground with the spear in his hand again. Kemir saw him throw it at the second dragon, saw him vanish into thin air, saw the dragon bat the spear away and lash at something with its tail.

The spear tumbled lazily through the air. It came down, jammed itself point first in the wood at Kemir's feet and quivered.

Take us!

The voice in his head this time was no dragon. This was something else. Some *things* else. He took a step forward. Up close he recognized it. The Speaker's Spear.

The black dragon was strangely still.

We kill dragons, said the spear.

On the shore, the gold dragon had the Picker impaled on the end of his tail. He dropped him into his mouth, bit him in half and turned to look at Kemir.

Leave, little one.

Kemir took the spear in both hands this time. Ignored the cold shiver that ran down his spine, the electric tingle that touched his skin. He wrenched it free of the planks and raised it high. Behind the dragon, Hammerford lay wreathed in smoke. A pall of it hung in the air, drifting slowly toward the river. He could hear the distant flames, the sounds of beams cracking and groaning, of buildings tumbling. There were probably lots of people noises too, shouting and screaming and cursing, but he couldn't hear those over the roar of the town's death.

The spear.

Amid the rubble and the bodies something moved. The figure of a man. In a flash, the dragon snatched him up. It took Kemir a second to realize that the dragon was holding Kithyr.

You know this one.

"Yes. It's all the same to me if you eat him, but don't blame me if he doesn't taste very nice." As he spoke, he could see the dragon's claws turning slowly orange. Blood, perhaps. The dragon dropped the mage as though he'd been stung. He stamped on him twice, still holding his forelimb out in front of him. Kemir felt the pain and the rage pulse out of the dragon in waves. *What have you done to me?*

The dragon's claws, he saw, were melting. Little curls of steam rose from the talons and drops of something dark dripped from them and splashed onto the waterfront.

"I'd go and see to that if I were you." He readied the spear to throw. The dragon turned, furious, but still didn't strike. It stared at him.

You may keep your life if you give me the spear.

"You're running out of claws to hold it." The dragon's forelimb was little more than a stump now. The steaming had stopped, though.

You know what I am, little one called Kemir. I have seen your thoughts before and I see them now. Throw your spear if you wish. It is the Spear of the Earth, if your aim is true, nothing will turn it and I will die. If you miss, I will kill your mate first, the one who hides in the water beside you. I will roast her slowly, I will crush your bones and then you will listen to her screams. I will leave you beside her. You will be alive but you will be broken, so broken that you can barely move. The river will quench your thirst. For food I will leave you the roasted flesh of your mate. I will leave you alive to choose whether you eat her or starve. The other one was closer than you are now and the spear did not save him. Now give it to me!

There were probably the best part of a couple of hundred corpses littered about. Kemir took a step and then stopped. He lowered the spear and then raised it again. If the dragon wanted him dead, why was he still alive? It could burn him from the air. Could burn him from where he stood right now. Could pick out pieces of building and throw them at him. He might evade the first boulder, the first blast of fire, but sooner or later the dragon would get him.

How long will your mate remain down there in the river? She is tired, Kemir. And cold. Give me the spear, little one. That is all I desire of this place. Give it to me and I will be gone. I will tire of this soon enough and then I will kill you for it.

It dares not strike you. Kemir jumped. The new voices in his head were the spear itself, harsh and violent and metal. *We will protect you. Strike at us and we strike back. That is what we are. The dragon knows this.*

The dragon twitched and Kemir felt its anger. *Give it to me, little one. It is not what you think.*

An interesting thing to say, since he hadn't the first idea what it was that he *did* think. He waited, but the spear stayed silent. He could feel it, though, a gentle power coursing down his arm, filling him with certainty. *What are you then? What are you supposed to do?*

Give it to me and I will go. The dragon turned to face Kemir squarely. It rocked back on its hind legs and flapped its wings a couple of times. Its tail flicked restlessly from side to side. Readying itself to spring.

He was moving before he even knew it. Wasn't even sure why, except that simply standing rooted to the spot while a dragon pounced on him was stupid. He was running, screaming, spear raised. The dragon drew its head back and Kemir's arm did the same. Kemir's arm and the dragon flew forward in the same moment. The spear lanced through the air and vanished into a blossoming cloud of fire. Kemir hurled himself sideways, rolled across the jetty and fell over the edge. He closed his eyes. Fire filled the air. Heat seared his skin and then the water reached up and sucked him down into its cold roar. He thrashed blindly. Near him something vast smashed into the river. The dragon, it couldn't be anything else. For a moment the world filled with light, one great flash of it. He pawed at the water, flailing helplessly until his hands touched something solid; he pulled himself toward it and then hurled himself to the surface. His head burst back into the air. The last fragments of the jetty were gone, smashed to splinters. The golden dragon lay half in the water, half out, head raised, wings and claws outstretched and reaching right over Kemir's head. It wasn't gold anymore, it was gray. Turned to stone.

Kemir stood up. Here by the shore the river water came up to his chest.

He wasn't going to die after all. He wasn't going to drown and he wasn't going to burn and he wasn't going to be torn to pieces.

I killed a dragon. The thought hit him like the river. *Me. I killed a dragon.*

He was grinning like an idiot. "Kat! I killed a dragon! Look . . ."

The grin faded. Where the jetty jutted out into the water, where he and Kataros had hidden themselves, nothing was left except shattered wood. He splashed toward where she had been. His feet slipped out from under him and he fell back into the water. He sank under, thrashed and flailed, hauled himself up again, spluttered and splashed and pulled himself toward the shore. It took him another few minutes to find a place where he could climb up out of the water and make his way back to where the dragon lay.

"Kat!" There was no sign of her. The post that they'd both clung to was gone. The spear was gone too. Sunk beneath the water or stuck into the petrified dragon somewhere where Kemir couldn't see it. He couldn't bring himself to climb onto its stone back to look for it. Even touching the dragon felt strange. It was cold. He'd never known a dragon to be cold.

He ran up and down the riverbank but there was no sign of her. Bits and pieces of debris, bodies and the shattered remains of boats littered the shore. The air was thick with smoke now, bitter and choking. He could barely see between blinking his eyes clear of tears, but the river was quiet and dead. No one splashing about and shouting for help.

Kataros was the one who'd pushed him into the water in the first place. She was the one who'd helped him find the pile to hold on to. She could swim; he'd seen her. Maybe . . . Maybe when she was knocked free, she had swum down the river away from the fire. Maybe she was just fine. A little cold but otherwise just as perfect as ever.

And maybe holding that spear for a while made me the new speaker. He cleared his eyes once more and peered out at the dark water. *I tried. I really did try.* Blindly, he set off downstream along the bank. He wasn't sure what he was looking for. Kat, in another life where endings were happy and when unexpected things happened they were sometimes good. Or her body. At least then he'd know she was dead and he wouldn't be left to choose between guilt and futile hope.

Or the spear, if he was feeling absurdly optimistic. Whatever that thing was, no one was going to say no to something that could turn live dragons into statues. That would be worth passage on a Taiytakei ship, wouldn't it? Passage for two even.

"Kat! Kat!" What could turn a dragon into stone. There was a story about that, wasn't there? Dragondale, pox-ridden ghost town on the edge of the Blackwind Dales on the Evenspire Road. A nothing place except for the statue there. A dragon, life-sized. He'd seen it once. Impossibly detailed. Turned to stone by Narammed, the locals said. Narammed the Dragonslayer, first Speaker of the Realms. Rubbish. Everyone who traveled the Evenspire Road knew that. Joked and laughed about the inbred peasant folk of Dragondale who never left their own villages.

Rubbish. Yeah. And what would Narammed's Spear be doing out here anyway?

"Kat!" His heart was beating fast, still. She *couldn't* be dead. He'd promised to look out for her. He stopped, opened his mouth, let out a roar. "I killed a dragon for you! Don't you fucking dare be dead!"

No one answered. After an hour of looking, he finally gave up. The tears in his eyes were dry again by then, turned to salt. After that, as he wandered the riverbank, he was mostly looking for a boat. The town was dead, burning nicely. The villages and farms around it would fill up with refugees. There would be people begging for food and a place to sleep, people with money prepared to pay whatever it took and being charged everything they had. There would be thieving, mugging, probably the odd murder, maybe a lynch mob or two. And then there'd be him, a sell-sword from the mountains. A boat would take him away from all that. A boat would take him to Furymouth.

Alone.

Could have taken us both.

No. She couldn't leave him alone. Not now. He wasn't even looking properly anymore, just wandering aimlessly, thinking about her. Wishing for something different.

"Hey!" The sound of another voice battered into his thoughts. When he turned, he saw a cluster of ragged ash-streaked men peering out from a copse of trees. There must have been about a dozen of them. Instantly his hand went to his knife, only to discover he'd lost it. They were unarmed as far he could tell, but there were quite enough to take him to the ground if they were desperate enough.

"Hey." He'd lost his bow too. Pity. The nearest of the men, the one who'd come out into the open, was no more than thirty feet away, but that would still have been far enough to put a couple of arrows in him before he closed the distance.

The man lifted up his hand. Now, too late, Kemir saw the stone he was holding. "Dragon-rider!" The man spat a curse, threw his stone and charged. Behind him, more townsfolk poured out of the trees. He saw enough of them to realize he'd been wrong; there were more like twenty, maybe even more than that. He turned and ran.

"I'm not . . ." *Stupid armor. Should have dumped it. Should have . . .*

A hand caught his shoulder. He jabbed an elbow behind him. The hand let go, but it cost him a precious moment. A second later another hand clawed at him, missed, then another, and then something snatched his legs from under him and hurled him forward. He rolled, tried to pull away, but they were on him, far too many to stand and fight, raining down fists, punching and kicking him until finally he let go and everything went quiet and still.

THE SPEAKER OF THE REALMS

"It was not the dragons that made me do what I did; it was the greed of men."

—Narammed Dragonslayer, first Speaker of the Realms

33

✣

FALLING DOWN

Dragons poured toward the Fury. Whatever riders Valmeyan had sent quickly turned and fled. Hyrkallan didn't bother with subtleties but gave chase directly. Jehal supposed that when you had so many of the monsters that you could blot out the sun with them, stealth was a bit of a waste of time. They reached Gliding Dragon Gorge and the realm of the Harvest Queen, the realm of Queen Zafir, and Hyrkallan flew on. Jehal supposed he could have stopped, could have quietly dropped away, taken his handful of dragons back to the palace; but would it have made any difference if he had? Probably not, not to what mattered. *I'm sorry, Lystra, but what else can I do? A trade perhaps? But what for what? You for the Adamantine Palace? And then let Zafir send her assassins after both of us?* The same Zafir he still hungered to hold. Yes, that Zafir.

Here and there, as they flew, Jehal saw palls of smoke dotting the landscape. Watersgate, Plag's Bay. Maybe Valleyford, if he strained his eyes. Hyrkallan ignored them. Scorched earth, that was Zafir all over. Across the Fury, every town was burnt; when Jehal took Wraithwing down for a closer look, some were still smoldering, little coils of smoke twirling out of the ruins. The damage was a day or two old, no more. Jehal couldn't think why Zafir would destroy her own realm, but then he couldn't think of why she did lots of things. *Slaughtering the cattle we would have taken to feed our dragons? And we would have done it too, taking whatever we need. A horde like this must spell death for any realm it passes. Even if we don't burn it to ash, we'll eat everything in our path. Behind us, all will fall into starvation and ruin. Ancestors, please let this war be quick.*

Ancestors? Who am I praying to? The father I suffocated in his bed? He'd be laughing. Meteroa? Pouring derision on everything I do most likely. Distancing himself from all of this. Making sure none of the rest of our dead folk get the impression that this is somehow his fault. No, his ancestors weren't going to be much use here. Never were really, even when they were alive. Made his lip curl, just thinking about them. *You wanted to be Vishmir, and when that didn't work, you demanded it from your sons. Well here I am, father, Speaker of the Realms. You know what? You're all dead, so if you want any family honor out of this sorry mess, you might start trying to be a bit more constructive.* Or did his ancestors think it better to watch the world burn than to admit they were wrong? To admit they'd made a mistake?

No. Don't answer that. Don't even think about it. Instead, he forced his way to the front of the horde, where he could fly his colors and be the first into the attack. King Jehal. Speaker Jehal, leading from the front. *So, ancestors, what about that then?* Vishmir would have been proud; Prince Lai would have called him an idiot, and he'd probably wind up dead because that was what usually happened to the man at the front. *But what have I got to lose? Nothing much anymore.*

The Pinnacles were up ahead, three dark shadows on the distant plains, a hundred miles away. He had dragons around him, to either side, up and down, behind him as far as he could see. They were everywhere. Hyrkallan's B'thannan. All the rest. Wings surging, necks straining with purpose. He could see the eyes of the closest, gleaming, teeth bared, riders grinning. They all knew. They all knew what was coming.

Zafir's outriders must have seen them coming. Had to. There were no clouds today, no place to hide. Hyrkallan had no special trick to play; nor did he need one. Numbers. That would be enough. How many dragons did Valmeyan have? He had his own eyries, Zafir's dragons that had escaped from Evenspire, a few dozen Meteroa had had at the Pinnacles, most of Narghon's eyries. What was that? Pushing five hundred adult dragons? Against nearly half that many again. All the dragons in the realms, or as near as made no difference, all in one place. Did anyone have a strategy for this? He tried to think about *Principles. Divide your enemy. Take them down piece by piece. Encircle them. Envelop them. Crash down on them from above. The Carpenter, the Falling Leaves, the Hammer and Anvil. Principles* was good on how to destroy your enemies with few losses of your own once you'd established an advantage in numbers. For what was about to happen, Prince Lai had nothing to say. It wasn't supposed to come to this.

The sky about the Pinnacles was swarming. His heart crept up his throat. Dragons. Hundreds of dragons, enough that they seemed like dark clouds slowly rising into the air. His spine tingled. The hairs on his skin burned. Valmeyan was going to make a fight of it. Both clouds of dragons were climbing, trying for the height advantage, but in the end it was all going to be much the same. As he started to make out the individual dragons ahead of him, as they filled the sky and filled his vision, Jehal urged Wraithwing on. *Lead from the front. Show them how they make princes in Furymouth. For what it's worth . . .*

There were times, he thought, when you forgot how big a dragon was. How truly immense they were. You forgot when you rode them every day. When you took them for granted. When they weren't anything more than a way to get from one place to another.

And then there were times when you remembered. Remembered they could swallow you whole and you wouldn't even touch the sides.

The first rider he hit was still trying to climb, urging his dragon up. Wraithwing screamed over him and ripped everything off the dragon's back. Riders, saddles, ropes, everything, all strung together. He didn't drop it though; instead Wraithwing swung the whole lot at another dragon, entangling its wings. It spiraled, crashed into another and the whole mess disappeared toward the ground. Jehal didn't watch. The next dragon was right in front of him, had turned to meet him head to head. He flicked down his visor, pressed himself against Wraithwing's scales and closed his eyes. Fire washed over him; a gale almost ripped him out of his saddle, and then he was still alive and that dragon was gone and now there was another, dropping on him from above. Black. They all looked black. Wraithwing rolled. For a second Jehal was upside down, the slabs of the Pinnacles hanging half a mile above his head. He lurched, helpless, as Wraithwing and the other dragon brushed past one another, and then it was gone, straight down, over his head, spreading its wings. Its tail curled like a whip as it passed to snap at him, but Wraithwing was still rolling, pulling him away from the danger. The tip missed him by about the span of a man's arms, slapping Wraithwing's side with enough force to jolt them both.

If that had been me . . . He'd seen men hit by the whip of a dragon's tail before: sometimes in eyrie accidents, and Meteroa had always been fond of finding new ways of using his dragons to execute people. The result was . . . well, messy was about the only word for it.

Another dragon. A cloud of them. Everywhere. Moving so fast he couldn't tell which was which. He caught glimpses of white streamers, some of them still tied to dragons, others fluttering uselessly in the air. Something huge and yellow shot over his head. Wraithwing twisted, but the dragon was one of their own. The yellow veered, bucking in the air. A dark brown hunter landed on its back, ripped its riders to pieces, then lunged away—but too slow. Wraithwing bathed it in fire, and as it flew away, saddle and harness disintegrated, flailing riders scattered into the air.

Why am I doing this? Jehal threw himself forward again as Wraithwing made a vicious half turn and swooped away from a pair of war-dragons. He plunged. For a moment, as they fell sideways, a severed head fell with them. Jehal had no idea whose it was.

Wraithwing leveled out for a moment. Jehal could feel the dragon's joy, how it reveled in the fight.

Bits of someone's saddle bounced off Wraithwing's shoulders. Jehal risked a glance up, but all he saw was a seething, swarming mass of shapes, huge things that flashed and twisted and lit up with gouts of fire, while pieces of man and saddle and the occasional stricken beast rained down around him. Saw a flash of all that and then had his spine almost wrenched in half as Wraithwing arced into a tight loop and arrowed upside down into a gap between three other dragons, so close that the tip of a wing brushed Jehal's head. He had no idea whether they were his or Zafir's. Didn't see if they had white streamers or painted bellies, could hardly see a thing with the wind in his face unless he pulled his visor down, in which case he could hardly see a thing anyway. The sky everywhere was a roiling mass of dragons, the wind that roared at his ears warm with the heat of them.

A flash of fire. He pulled his visor down. Still alive a few seconds later, he lifted it up again. He looked for other dragons with white bellies, but looking for anything was almost impossible. He could barely lift his head off Wraithwing's neck for long enough to work out which way was up. The dragon looped and spiraled down, trading height for speed to keep him alive among a hundred other dragons doing just the same.

Should have ridden a hunter. They might be meant for chasing snappers, but those sharp maneuvers are just the thing for piling into a cloud of, oh, how many enemy dragons? A few hundred, was it? Now won't we all have a laugh if Hyrkallan has changed his mind at the last minute and broken off the attack, and it's just me in here.

The tip of a wing swept overhead. Wraithwing pulled up short, crushing the air out of Jehal's lungs, made another loop. Jehal caught a glimpse of six riders on the back of a huge war-dragon, three of them manning scorpions, before Wraithwing flipped over and almost landed on the back of it, obliterating them all with one savage sweep of his claws. Jehal didn't even know they were there, didn't even know whose side they were on. Didn't have time to care. It was all Wraithwing now, picking and choosing. He was just a passenger now. *Just keep me alive!*

The war-dragon was plummeting toward the ground in forlorn pursuit of its riders. *There. I've done my bit. Three of the enemy down. Play the numbers. Three for one and we're bound to win, even if there aren't really very many of us left to appreciate it. Can I go now? Play dead and leave?*

Two white-bellied dragons arrowed down either side of him, one after the other. Riderless. Most of the battle was above him now. Not good to be down near the bottom. Death comes from above. The first rule of *Principles.*

A war-dragon came at them from the side, mouth open wide, fire building up inside its throat. Wraithwing rolled Jehal away, took the fire on his belly. That only put him in the path of a second dragon, which swung its head around and raked Wraithwing and Jehal alike with flames. Jehal snatched for his visor again. He snapped it down as the first blast of scorching air licked his face, then screamed in pain. His palm was on fire. He couldn't see anything because of the visor. His good hand gripped Wraithwing's scales. *Burned. They've burned my hand off.* Terror gripped him. If the fire had been hot enough to burn through the dragon-scale covering his gauntlets, what had it done to his saddle, to the ropes and straps that kept him on Wraithwing's back?

He lifted the visor. A part of him, some little bit of murderous primitive, didn't care a hoot about his hand. A part of him was loving every moment of this, almost singing out of sheer joy. This was a part that came from the dragons, from Wraithwing and all the other dragons around him. A battle madness. *Principles* had never mentioned that.

He managed to focus on his hand. His gauntlet was still there, the dragon-scale intact. The soft leather on the inside of his hand was black and crisped. He'd been still closing his visor when the fire came. Hadn't closed his fist in time. Simple mistake, easily made, and that was that. He had no idea what his skin looked like underneath and no intention of finding out. *Lobster-red with flakes of black most likely.* He cursed. The pain was excruciating.

A moment to breathe. A moment of clear air. He tried to look, tried to see what was happening, who was winning, but everything was a whirlwind of madness. Dragons falling from the air, scores and scores of them, a rain of monsters in futile pursuit of their fallen riders. They all looked the same. Dark. Colors all lost in the wind and the blur, in sun and speed. The battle had become a swirling cloud, as high as a mountain, spread out over the three peaks of the Pinnacles. In some places the sky was almost empty. In others, dragons looped and snapped at each other in such tight circles and in such numbers that he couldn't tell one apart from another. Overhead, three dragons slammed into each other, all their riders crushed and killed together. He watched the dragons plunge past him. Dark streaks flashed through the air. Scorpion bolts. The spent ones fell like a deadly rain on whatever lay below. Dragons, riders, the Silver City beneath. Thousands of them.

He saw dragons racing away too: terrified riders desperate to live. Saw others give vengeful chase. In that moment, he understood. *Principles* was a lie. There was no strategy here, no tactic to outwit the enemy, not in this sprawling shapeless horror. There was terror, that was all. It was who broke first, nothing more, nothing less. Whose riders fled in fear and whose gave themselves up to the dragon-fury, which was every bit as terrible.

For a moment he watched appalled, for the few seconds he had to think before there was a war-dragon attacking from below. Wraithwing was already turning; Jehal could feel his desire to fight. *Enough running and ducking. Enough of scorpions. Tooth and claw. The southern way.* He could feel the other dragons around him answering, returning Wraithwing's challenge with glee.

The war-dragon almost caught him. Wraithwing let it, then slashed the air with his tail, slapped the other dragon on the nose and turned in the way that only Wraithwing could turn, flipping in the air. The dragons doused each other with fire while Jehal pressed himself flat, visor down, shielding his damaged hand from the flames and hoping not to die. Wraithwing shuddered. Tooth and claw and tail tore and lashed at the riders on the war-dragon's back, and then they were apart and he was still alive. Safe.

Safe until he felt a sudden sharp tug on the saddle and Wraithwing's scales started to slide under his hands.

No! He flipped up the visor. He was strapped to his saddle, but the whole harness was moving. *No! No! No!* His fingers fumbled with the straps. A dragon saddle and harness weighed as much as a man. *And then what? Ride bareback? I hate to tell you, but that only works with horses.* He almost shouted at Wraithwing to dive for the ground but bit his tongue. The dragon would do exactly that, and then what? It didn't make much difference whether you fell off the back of a dragon from half a mile up or from fifty feet above the ground, the mess was still about the same.

He cast a quick glance behind. The war-dragon was still there. Lots of ropes and bits of harness trailed behind it, but it hadn't gone for the ground. Someone was still alive to tell it what to do. Any moment now that someone would come back for another go.

Vishmir's cock! The saddle slipped again. Wraithwing was flying in a straight line now, with long careful wingbeats, his body slightly twisted as though trying to help Jehal stay balanced. Which would have been all very well if they had lots of open space around and could glide very gently to the ground. Less helpful in the middle of a fight. Might as well have painted *"Eat me"* on his back.

A shower of stray scorpion bolts fell from the battle above. One punched a hole through Wraithwing's wing. The dragon didn't flinch.

I'm going to fall.

Now half a dragon-rider fell past him. A few seconds later a war-dragon followed, one without a painted belly, Jehal saw. Stupid thing, waste of effort, noticing that. *Don't have time, don't have time!* The saddle shifted again. Started to slide.

Saddle straps were gone. Still no one was diving to finish him. All he had to do was pull himself forward out of the saddle slowly and carefully, wrap his arms around Wraithwing somehow and fall out of the sky a little way so everyone thought he was dead. And then, just maybe, if he was really, *really* lucky, slowly glide to the ground and make a nice gentle landing without shattering every bone in his body.

Right. And then Hyrkallan will land beside you and personally bend his knee and call you speaker. Because that's just as likely.

Wraithwing veered sharply. For a moment the sun turned off and everything went dark. Jehal squawked in panic as he and the saddle fell away, and then something enormous went straight over him, a vast black shape. Talons as long as a man's leg snatched at the space where he'd been, tore a furrow in Wraithwing's back, ripping scales and the muscle beneath, and pulled away what little of Jehal's harness remained. Then the black dragon had passed, the sun came out again and Jehal was left hanging in the air. Alive and perfectly unharmed and with a sudden and dire shortage of wings.

And then he fell.

34

❧

THE THRONE OF SALT

ities. She could smell them from a hundred miles away, except it wasn't a scent that taunted her but thoughts. Human thoughts. Thousands upon thousands of them, faint and distant and intertwined, a filthy mass of gibberish.

Cities. They stank. *They intrude.*

Other little thoughts popped up, scattered around her. Bright pinpricks of sentience. Humans lived everywhere. Even here in the barren deserts, they eked out an existence in tiny knots and clusters. Wherever there was water there were more of them. Water was one of the few things a dragon needed. Water to stay cool. Out here in the desert they might sleep at the bottom of a river or a lake to keep out of the midday heat.

Everything breathes. It was an uneasy topic among the dragons. Everything breathed. Everything except dragons.

When she thought about that the other dragons tried not to listen. *But everything breathes.* She could feel them, distancing their thoughts from her, but they could never hide them, not completely. Just as she couldn't hide hers as she remembered the alchemists and the naked men with painted skins and poison in their blood who killed dragons as they gave their lives away.

She spread her wings over the landscape. A wide riverbed snaked through little hills of jumbled earth, dead and dry except for tufts of thorny grass. A trickle of water glistening. This was a land of snakes and spiders. Dragons didn't belong here. Here was too hot. She missed the mountains and their snowy crags and their glaciers and their freezing lakes. The city drew them on, though. The stink of it. The cacophony of thoughts, reaching out across the miles, a constant thorn in the mind.

They found it a day and a night of flight from the smoking ruin of Outwatch. The home of the last little one who had called himself king of all the realms. She didn't know the name of it. She'd never asked. It was an ugly place. Glaring white stone, low squat buildings, sat beside a huge flat lake of shallow tepid water. Beyond, salt flats stretched out to throttle the horizon, blinding in the sun. There were towers, but not very many. Walls, but little and low. No army would ever march out here, or if it did, would die of thirst and heat before it could arrive. That was this city's defense. Against men it might have been perfect. Against dragons, it was useless.

They started with the eyrie. When they were done, they burned the lake dry and then flew a hundred miles along the sluggish river that fed it and made it flow another way. Heat and thirst.

When they were done with that, they flew back. They hunted and they feasted. As night fell they stretched out to cool and to doze. Sated and surrounded by ash.

In the morning that followed, when the city that happened to be called Bloodsalt was nothing but blackened stone and scorched earth, when the dragons had all eaten their fill and there was nothing left alive for a hundred miles save the few little ones who'd managed to hide in the deepest of the caverns, they heard a cry. As one, the dragons stopped, paused from their feast as a thousand voices raged in fury among the spirits of the dead.

The Spear of the Earth. The horror that had almost destroyed the world, awake again. Snow reached out for it, sought it. She caught a second dragon's thoughts, a fleeting glimpse of what he saw before the spear snuffed him out.

A glimpse, but a glimpse was enough.

Kemir!

35

THE LOVERS

Jehal fell twenty feet and then stopped with a wrenching shock of pain. He screamed and whimpered and then swung around, helpless as a puppet, thumping into Wraithwing's belly. He bounced off again, dangling, still attached to the dragon by the last rope, the legbreaker, the one that was supposed to save your life when exactly this happened, but rarely did.

Legbreaker. They called it that for a reason. He screamed again. His whole back was roaring agony. His leg, the leg where Shezira had shot him, felt as though he'd almost ripped it out of its socket. He'd thought the wound was healed, at least as healed as it would ever get, but apparently not.

Wraithwing tucked in his wings and dived through the cloud of fighting dragons. The wind picked Jehal up and tossed him around like a doll, battering him against the dragon's scales. Jehal yelled and screamed and shouted but he couldn't hear himself over the storm of air, invisible fingers clenched around him like a giant hand, smashing him over and over against the dragon as though he was a nut and it was trying to crack him open, each blow slamming the life out of him piece by piece. Not for long, though. They'd get to the ground; Wraithwing would spread his wings and stop, and then either the rope would be too long and he'd be dashed to pieces on the ground, or else his leg would rip clean off and *then* he'd be dashed to pieces on the ground. He'd have found it ironic if he wasn't too busy drowning in waves of pain and a wind that tore the air right out of his lungs.

As they plunged away from the roiling battle everything broke into pieces. He saw flashes of this, flashes of that, found himself lost in memories of far-off places with lovers now dead, then jerked back to pounding smashing roaring agony. Eventually he stopped screaming. He wasn't sure when because the wind roared so loud he couldn't hear anything else.

Wraithwing leveled out, circling toward the closest of the three monoliths that made up the Pinnacles, and the wind lost its will to shatter Jehal against the dragon's side. Even the pain seemed to give up, reduced to agony that was merely like having his leg hacked at with a rusty saw. Which, compared to what it had been before, was as good as no pain at all.

He couldn't see much of the battle anymore. Didn't matter. Hadn't made much sense when he'd been the right way up, so it wasn't going to make any now. They weren't alone, that's all he knew. Dragons were falling all around him. Riderless. Some with white bellies, some without. Half and half. Hard to tell who was winning. If you could count slaughtering almost an entire generation of dragon-riders in a single battle as winning at all. *What if there aren't enough riders left to collect all the fallen dragons, eh? Jeiros isn't going to like that very much, is he, eh?* Nothing like someone else's misery to take your mind off your own. He watched with a dull interest. *Still need to ask him why he can't just make more of his bloody potions.*

Yes. That helps. Let's make a mental list of all the things I can crack on with once I'm on my feet again.

Nice try. But how exactly is that going to happen? Are we going to hover over the ground while I dangle helplessly, waiting for someone to come and cut me loose? Every dragon-rider was taught what you were supposed to do in this situation, but always with a twinkle in the eye from their teacher, as if to say, *Don't bother with this. Nothing ever gets this bad without you being already dead.* First choice was to pull your knees into your chest, grab hold of the rope with your hands and pull yourself up hand over hand until you reached the place where the rope was tied around the dragon's neck. Then haul yourself up onto the back of the dragon and ride it bareback to the ground. Jehal struggled to count how many things were wrong with that.

Climbing a rope hanging from a beam in a nice sheltered learning hall is all very well, but not much like climbing one with a dragon and the wind both trying to knock you off. Not quite the same thing, uncle. Silvallan once said that they took his riders out to a bridge across a gorge in the worst storms of the year, tied a rope around them and threw them off. Seemed like idiocy at the time. And then there's the bit about riding the dragon bareback all the way home. Has anyone ever actually done that? Because if they have, I don't think I've ever heard of it. How does that work exactly? How do you stay on? And even if you can stay on when it's flying, how do you stay on when you land, eh?

All of which would be interesting to find out about and a vast improvement over his current position. His main problem was the first bit, the bit about pulling your knees to your chest to get your hands on the rope. He simply couldn't do it. He could get about halfway and then the pain was so much that even screaming wasn't any relief anymore and he thought he might pass out. After the third effort, he had to admit defeat.

Second choice. Wait until you're almost down, then cut the rope with a knife to fall and land in something soft, water being the obvious option. *Pity we're over a hundred miles from the sea.* A lake then or a river. The Fury wasn't all that far away, was it? There were canals too, in the Silver City. *Oh, but wait. I'm wearing dragon-scale armor, as a rider always does. So, let's suppose for a moment that there* is *some water, what happens when I fall in it? Oh yes. I drown. Marvelous. Thank you for that one, uncle.*

They were falling toward Zafir's capital, the Silver City, which spread out between the three Pinnacles. Dragons still rained from the sky. *Can't be nice to be down there. First you get a few thousand scorpion bolts raining down. Then bits of rider and saddle and the scorpions themselves falling around your head, and then a couple of minutes later there's dragons everywhere, stomping about looking for the remains of their riders, wailing and shrieking their heads off. How long do they keep looking? Hard to imagine they're particularly careful about what they tread on either.*

He didn't know, and if anyone else did, they weren't here to ask. Not that it made any difference. The Silver City hardly counted as a soft landing.

He checked his belt for a knife. He had that at least. And then it occurred to him that to cut the rope he'd have to reach it with his hands.

Which meant pulling his knees to his chest, that thing he couldn't do, and he was right back to where he started. Dead. He tried to be philosophical about it, but that turned out to be really hard when it felt like someone had beaten you from head to toe with a hammer and was now busy rubbing various ends of broken leg-bone against each other. Shouting and screaming didn't really change anything. Cursing didn't help either. Felt rather futile. A bit like shouting at a dragon.

He was a bit blurry on how the afterlife was supposed to work. Your ancestors supposedly hung around in some sort of limbo, keeping half an eye on you, offering a little guidance here and there, maybe making subtle adjustments to fate and destiny. This had always seemed to Jehal at best a hobby for a few of the newly dead who really needed to keep themselves busy for a while, and most likely something that would be neglected entirely. Wouldn't the dead have better things to do? Although he'd never given much thought to what those things might be.

Zafir has probably murdered Lystra. This way maybe I get to see her again.

The ground came slowly closer. Wraithwing was now gliding in gentle circles and the wind had let go of him. It was almost quiet. Almost peaceful. Almost. If he ignored the distant falling dragons and the fires starting in the city below.

All the people I murdered, will they be waiting? Hyram, Aliphera, are you watching me now? My father. My brother, my sisters, my mother, my ever-loyal uncle, Meteroa. I'm sure he's told you all that I was the one who played with Calzarin's madness. Are you all waiting for me? What about all the people who died at Evenspire? The Red Riders? The people dying here and now? Are you there?

No. Maybe he didn't want to die just yet. Prayers were for fools—he'd believed that for as long as he could remember—but he prayed now, prayed to any of his ancestors who might be in the mood to listen and forgive him. Prayed to the old gods that no one except the dragon-priests worshipped anymore. Prayed to anyone who might listen.

The only response was a sudden jerk on the legbreaker, sending whole new spasms of pain through his hip and down his spine. Above him, Wraithwing clenched his claws. The dragon's head whipped back and forth, searching. Jehal had enough time to catch a glimpse of something sticking out of the dragon's side.

Scorpion bolt. And then the dragon pitched down and hurtled toward the nearest of the Pinnacles.

"No!" Jehal screamed. "Don't!"

Another scorpion bolt shot past and then another. Jehal whimpered. Couldn't be bothered to argue, though. A scorpion bolt through the head would be a mercy, wouldn't it?

The top of the Fortress of Watchfulness loomed up toward them. Exhausted, Jehal put his hand to his visor. He could see Wraithwing getting ready to douse the irritating little stinging things in flames to shut them up. He could see the scorpions, the men behind them starting to back away, turning, running for cover . . .

Here it comes.

He flipped his visor shut, closed his eyes. Instinct really, as Wraithwing belched flames and washed the top of the fortress clean. No reason to add a singed face to his list of woes. Although with the ground racing up to smash his bones, it hardly made a difference, did it?

The fire came again and again and again. Jehal felt each blast ripple and tremor down the legbreaker. Then he felt a long steady pull and something very hard and solid but curiously not as bone-shattering as he had expected clocked him around the head. He gasped and swore and braced himself for more. Cringed. He could almost feel the spirits of the dead rubbing their hands in gleeful anticipation. *Here he comes . . .*

A huge wave of something that wasn't pain surged out of his leg. It took him a moment to realize that it was *relief.* The simple absence of pain, or at least a good lessening of it. The pull was suddenly gone. For a moment he had the mad idea that the rope must have snapped—he was falling, that was why the rope wasn't killing him anymore. Except that wasn't right either. Something huge had taken hold of him.

Wraithwing. The dragon's claws were wrapped around him.

He opened his visor. He was lying flat on hard stone. Wraithwing was standing over him, one fore-claw unwrapping itself from him. The dragon roared and again hosed the battlements with fire; then it looked down between its legs at Jehal and made a clumsy grab for the legbreaker. Its talons were too big and crude to do anything more than move it about. Wraithwing gave an angry snort.

Alive!

Jehal sat up. Pain burst through him again as though he'd been shot. *But alive!* He took a few shallow breaths and then leaned forward and reached for his feet. Another bolt of pain stabbed him. Always in the same place. Always where Shezira had shot him. *But still, alive!* Deep breaths this time. His ankle hurt but his foot wasn't at some funny angle. His knee felt like someone had had a good go at ripping his shinbone out of its socket. Which probably wasn't that far from the truth, but nothing was obviously broken or twisted. He poked and prodded himself to be sure, but the rest of his leg looked like it was going to work again one day. He lay back on the stone and started to laugh. *Alive! See that, ancestors! You don't get me yet after all!* He lay still, whimpering, weeping and laughing all at once.

Wraithwing shifted and growled. Soldiers were up on the battlements again. They had dragon-scale shields. Crossbows too. Pointing at him. The dragon belched fire; the soldiers hid behind their shields, but as soon as Wraithwing paused, they raised their crossbows. No asking him who he was or offering to take his surrender or any such nonsense; they simply wanted to kill him. The first bolt went about ten feet wide. The second hit Wraithwing in the foot and stuck, and then they didn't have time for any more before the dragon roared fire back at them again. Jehal tried to ignore them. He rolled, squealing, behind Wraithwing's legs, pulled the knife out of his belt and set to work on the legbreaker. He felt rather than saw Wraithwing's fire burst out again. *Cut the rope. Don't look at the archers, just cut the rope.*

Alive! He still couldn't stop laughing.

The sun went out. It took him a moment to realize that Wraithwing was shielding him with his wings, blotting out the light but blocking the arrows too.

Clever. The legbreaker yielded to his knife. Jehal took a deep breath and collapsed again, too drained to move. *Now can we just stay here until they all go away?* As long as he stayed still, the pain was almost bearable. If he moved, that was a different matter, but with a dragon standing watch over him, he couldn't think of any reason why he should. He closed his eyes. *Only for a few minutes,* he thought. *Only until I can summon some sort of energy.* He felt almost delirious. *Alive!* He'd fallen off his dragon and he was alive. For those few moments nothing else mattered.

He wasn't sure how long he lay there. Might have been a few minutes or might have been a few hours. He drifted, floated, swayed up and down, tossed from wave to wave of joy and pain, until the light suddenly crashed in again and there was a voice. Jehal opened his eyes and blinked. The light, it seemed, had become quite fierce. The sun was back again.

"Hello?"

He took a deep breath, which hurt, and sat up, which hurt a lot more and quite enough to convince him not to try and stand up. On the battlements where the soldiers with crossbows had been there was now a single rider, arms spread wide. *I surrender.*

"Hello?"

With agonizing slowness, Jehal crawled out from under Wraithwing. Just far enough to look. Even that was almost more than he could do. He looked at the rider. Had no idea who it was. *What a sight I must be, peering up at you on my hands and knees, barely able to move. But I have a dragon and you don't.* Far above in the bright blue sky there were lots of specks. Or maybe he was imagining them. Either way, it didn't help him tell whose side had won.

"Well?" he croaked.

The rider peered down at him then shouted, "In the name of King Valmeyan, King of the Crags, I submit my person and all those here to the authority of the Speaker of the Nine Realms."

Jehal beamed through the pain. He managed to get as far as kneeling. "Does that mean I won?"

The rider stiffened. "I am offering my surrender to anyone who serves the speaker."

"Oh. Pity. I don't serve the speaker, you see." The scale of what fate had handed him slowly dawned on him. *I was the first to land . . .*

"Oh."

"Because I *am* the speaker. I am King Jehal, King of the Endless Sea, Lord of the Adamantine Palace and Speaker of the Realms, and I will accept your surrender on one condition. You will bring me my son and you will bring me my wife, and you will bring them to me in exactly whatever state they are to be found, since, as you can see, I can't really go looking for them at the moment." With an enormous effort, he gripped Wraithwing's wing and pulled himself onto his feet. Or onto the one foot that would bear any weight. "And if you can't do that because Zafir took them away with her, then I don't want your surrender. You can all burn. If they're dead and she left the bodies here for me, then whoever has the courage to bring them out can live and everyone else dies. Unless I suffer a sudden fit of uncontrollable rage, in which case maybe it'll be the other way round."

Jehal stared across the open space and grinned, although inside he only wanted to curl up and cry. For a little while he'd been too busy with his own misery to think about Lystra. Now she was back. It didn't hurt quite as bad as hanging upside down from his ruined leg, being battered by the wind against the belly of a dragon—he doubted anything could ever hurt as much as that—but it hurt a lot, nonetheless. Enough, maybe, to burn Zafir's home to ash along with everyone who lived there. *Not exactly fair, really. It's not as if they all took turns to murder Lystra. But it's the principle. That's how you teach people not to throw in their lot with the wrong side.*

Yes, said a little voice. *Remind me. How well, exactly, is that philosophy working out for you right now?*

It could be better. But I'm prepared to give it one more crack of the whip. Now shut up.

The rider was still there. *Why? Shouldn't you be running away by now?* "Your Holiness, may I ask what the terms of our surrender might be if Queen Lystra and her son are still alive?"

Jehal threw back his head and howled with bitter laughter. *As if that's going to happen.*

"Why then you can all go free back to your families. I won't even ransom you." He was looking at the sky, at the dragons still circling up there. When he looked back at the battlements, the rider was gone.

Bastard. That's hope you've given me. However much I know better, I can't turn it away. Hope is like Taiytakei poison. Hope eats you slowly from the inside and turns men into fools. I don't want hope, but now you've given it to me we both know there's only one antidote. When you don't come back I'm going to make sure I burn you first, whoever you are. We all know that everything is ruined. We all know I'm getting exactly what I deserve. All my fault. Blah blah blah. Yes, ancestors, I know you're all laughing at me. Let me guess. You guided my fate and landed me here, alive and crippled, just for this. You kept me alive just so that I never find Lystra, I never find out what happened to her. I hunt Zafir and Valmeyan to the ends of the world and hang them both, but they never tell me. I am what you always wanted, your Vishmir. I sit on the Adamantine Throne for thirty years and I am remembered as the best speaker the realms have ever known. And for every aching second I am torn apart with hope and despair and spend most of my time either wishing I was dead or wondering what tiny corner of the world is left to be scoured. What I don't get is my wife back. That about right? Oh—

Even as he beat the hope away, there she was. On the top of the battlements while dragons fell out of the sky around them. An illusion of his deranged and damaged imagination.

Too much pain, too much exhaustion, too much madness. That must be what it is.

He wasn't sure what happened after that. It seemed as though one moment she was there and the next she was gone, and the one after that she was beside him, in front of him, holding him so tightly that he couldn't breathe.

"My love, my love, my love!" That was all she said.

It had to be a trick. Jehal pushed her away so he could see her clearly, but apparently he had something in his eye. Both of them. *A trick. A doppelgänger. An imposter.*

No. The rather plain, bruised and battered woman in front of him was none of those. He felt his head spin. He staggered, tried to catch himself with his ruined leg and fell into her arms.

"You're alive," he murmured, filled with disbelief. And then he fainted.

36

A LITTLE HELP

Luck was a fickle mistress, Vioros thought. He watched the battle from afar with Jeiros and half a dozen other alchemists, sat on the backs of dragons circling safely away from the fighting. Seven dragons, all of them hunters, were all Jehal was willing to spare. The alchemists had loaded them with as much as they could carry and then quietly hoped and prayed they wouldn't be called on to fight. Luck heard them. Vioros watched the hordes of dragons crash together, miles away, like two dark clouds blown together in a storm. He watched hundreds of them plunge from the sky, distant specks falling like soft black snow, chasing after their fallen riders. He watched survivors scatter and flee, other dragons pursue, and was left to guess which side had actually won. The answer eventually came as flashes of fire from the tops of the Pinnacles. Cautiously, the riders who flew the alchemists' dragons approached. No one bothered to come and tell them that the battle was over.

Yes, luck. Luck had been busy today. Luck had kept Hyrkallan alive to revel in his victory while more than half his riders had died. Luck had made King Jehal the first to land on the Pinnacles, if *land* was a reasonable way to describe it. Luck had provided the alchemists with enough potion stored in the city eyries to keep the thousand and more dragons now encamped around the Pinnacles under control for a few days. After that, Vioros hadn't the first idea what they would do. Sirion and Hyrkallan had brought most of what they had. The Adamantine Eyrie had been stripped bare. Zafir had denuded Furymouth. Outside Valmeyan's hidden mountain eyries and whatever hoard Jeiros was keeping to himself, there was nothing left.

So now they were looking for more. The dragon-riders might dismount and run into the halls to feast and drink and sing of their victory, but for Vioros and the alchemists the real battle was about to start.

He went to Valleyford first because it was where the alchemists had long had a stronghold. The potions from the cellars there had been used to keep the dragons of Bazim Crag and Three Rivers docile, but there was always the chance that more had been squirreled away. At least that was what Jeiros and Vioros had both thought before he left on his fool's errand. As it was, he didn't even bother landing. Valleyford had been obliterated. Arys Crossing too—whoever had burned it this time had done a much better job than Vishmir had in the War of Thorns. The Alatcazat monastery was gone. Gutted. So much for *their* fabled luck. Hammerford, sandwiched between them, had fared somewhat better in that the place had only been half destroyed. There were still people there.

Hammerford was a nothing place and certainly not likely to yield a secret coven of alchemists who just happened to have hidden a few hundred handy barrels of dragon-potion. The sensible thing was to go straight back to Jeiros, empty-handed. Maybe strike out for Clifftop and Furymouth and see what, if anything, Zafir had missed.

Sensible, but on the other hand the waterfront at Hammerford had acquired two giant dragon statues that hadn't been there six months earlier, and Vioros was fairly sure he would have heard about something like that. So he circled and then landed after all because he was curious, and that was where luck struck again. The people of Hammerford didn't know much about their new statues, but they *had* caught one of the riders who'd brought the fire to their town. They hadn't got round to hanging him yet, and yes, Vioros could talk to him. Apparently he called himself Kemir, but that was obviously a lie since it was an outsider name and the man was clearly a dragon-rider. So said the folk of Hammerford, who were clearly itching to murder at least *someone* for what had happened to them.

By his reckoning, Vioros listened to Kemir for the best part of two hours. Truth be told, he lost track of time in the cellar where the townsfolk were keeping him. Everything the sell-sword said sounded so fantastic, yet there was no way he could have known some of the things he described unless he'd been there, and then there was the small matter of the blood-magic that Vioros had used to force the truth out of him. As far as Vioros could tell, the sell-sword hadn't even tried to resist it.

Which meant that Jeiros was right and the white rogue had returned. Which meant that there weren't one or two or four awoken dragons but more like twenty. Which in turn meant that he and everyone else were all as good as dead, and it was just a matter of time. All their fretting about how to eke out what potion Jeiros could make was a complete waste.

And then, at the end, the sell-sword told him about the spear.

When he was done, Vioros staggered for the doorway out of the cellar.

"Alchemist." The sell-sword could barely speak. The beating he'd taken from the townspeople, well, Vioros counted himself lucky that the man wasn't already dead.

"I can't save you, sell-sword. I'm sorry." Which was a lie—he wasn't sorry at all. The man might not have been a dragon-rider, might not have burned half the town, but he could still hang. As far as Vioros was concerned, he deserved a death a lot slower than a rope. Rogues. The worst terror of all.

"Kill me."

"What?"

"Snow. She knows I'm here. She's coming. For the spear. She feels me."

Vioros ran. In the harsh sunlight outside he swayed and sat down heavily on a piece of broken wall covered in ash. Then he held his head in his hands. A tremor shook him. A lot of things made sense now, and none of them were good. How many dragons had turned when Prince Kazan had his moment of folly? No one had ever been quite sure, but it couldn't have been more than ten, and it had taken, what? All the riders from three realms and the Adamantine Men to rein them in. Now there were twice that many. Twenty dragons. It would take all the riders in the *world* to contain twenty dragons. Hundreds of people would die, probably thousands, but if every king and every queen bowed to the command of the speaker and gave up their dragons to the hunt, they just might all get to see their children grow up.

Yes, that was quite enough to make him give up hope, right there and then. Never mind everything else, never mind the dire state of the Order, never mind this stupid war. Never mind that, sooner or later, Jeiros would have no choice but to order a cull. Never mind Jehal; even if they'd had a speaker like Vishmir, twenty free dragons might have been more than the realms could tame. The sell-sword had given him all that, and then at the end he'd given him the Adamantine Spear. A relic that had sat around in the Adamantine Palace, given the place its name even, and done absolutely nothing in all that time. A relic whose myths and legends had peeled off over the years like dead skin, until no one believed anything anymore. And here it was, turning dragons into stone.

And then, right at the end, the bastard had taken that hope and pissed on it, as casually as anything. *Oh, I threw it at the dragon and then I lost it.* Lost it? How do you lose something like the Adamantine Spear? Vishmir's cock! *I looked for it but I was mostly too busy looking for the alchemist I promised to protect.* What was the spear doing here and not in the palace? *A blood-mage had it and then someone cut his hand off.* What was all that about? A blood-mage? Did Jeiros know? Did he even know the spear was missing?

There was the spear itself too. Turning dragons into stone? Had it always done that? That would explain the legend of Narammed the Dragonslayer, but still . . . How could the Order not know something like that?

Most of all, what did Vioros do now? Go back to the grand master and tell him that they were all doomed, except that they might be saved if only they could find a magic spear that they'd somehow lost without noticing they'd lost it which had never shown any sign of being anything special before?

No one was going to believe him. Everyone had more important things to do. Or they thought they did.

So. He could stay here until he found that blasted spear. Surely it couldn't have gone too far, could it? It was made of metal, after all, so it could hardly have floated off down the river. Or he could go back to the speaker and his riders and Grand Master Jeiros, tell them half the truth, trick them into coming back here to see it all for themselves and then *they* could do the searching. Jeiros could talk to the sell-sword. Hear it all for himself. All in all that sounded like a much better proposition.

In his mind he got up and hurried to his dragon, keen to bring riders back here as soon as possible. His legs, though, didn't move. There was a third choice, one they were quite aware of, and they weren't going to move until he at least conceded it was there.

Yes. Well, go on then. I could get on my dragon and fly to Furymouth and get on a Taiytakei ship and never come back. What of it? I suppose I'd do well enough.

His legs, it seemed, wanted more. He frowned and forced himself to his feet. That was no way for an alchemist to think. He was sworn to protect the realms from exactly this.

Think about it for a moment. There are rogues loose. Maybe all the dragon-riders in the realms could stop them, or maybe not. But we won't get to find out, because the only way we can keep the rest of our dragons tame is to cull them. Which we'll never be allowed to do because there's a war on. So, are you going to die for no better reason than running away would make you look bad to your ancestors? Are they going to be happier that you stayed here like a good little alchemist and died with all the rest, honor intact? Or do you think they might secretly prefer it if you ran away while you still can, joined the Taiytakei, sold them everything you know about dragons, lived like a king and fathered about a hundred children for them. Yes, they might wag a finger or two at you for show, but let's face it: deep down they're positively pleading with you to go. Mull that over for a bit, and while you do, have a bit of a think about how it felt at Drotan's Top when the Red Riders brought the place crashing down on top of you.

Vioros walked back toward the riders waiting to take him back. They were supposed to be his to command, but they weren't really. To them he was nothing more than a glorified passenger. *You see, that's the problem. Can't do it.*

Coward. You have the powers of a blood-mage. You could bend a few dragon-riders to your will easily enough.

Slippery slope, though. He smiled grimly. He was going to stay, that was what he was going to do. Stay until the bitter end, because that was what was right. When he reached the riders, he stopped. There was a group of disconsolate townsfolk sitting in the ash and rubble, kicking their heels and poking at the ruins with sticks. The sticks gave him an idea.

"You folk!" he barked. "I need your help."

They looked up, apathy in their eyes.

"I can pay." *Yes, see how their backs straighten, they turn to face you and their eyes meet yours.* "Somewhere near the stone dragon on the riverbank there is a spear. It fell out of the dragon's mouth. It looks as though it's made of silver. It isn't, but when I return tomorrow I will take its weight in silver and divide it between any who have a part in finding it. There was a woman there too. A Scales. Find her."

There. With a bit of luck, when he came back the spear would be here. He could take it to Jeiros and ask him how, in the name of all the gods, you turned a dragon into stone.

37

HANGING IN THE BALANCE

A thousand dragons. More. Jeiros shook his head in disbelief. He ought to have felt awe when he looked out over what had once been Zafir's eyrie, but he didn't. He didn't feel much of anything. *A thousand dragons. In a few days they will run out of potions. In a week their only food will be what we can scavenge. In a month they're going to start waking up and they're going to be hungry. We barely have enough riders left after the battle to ride them all, if we had a place to take them. Which we don't.* He didn't know how many dragons had escaped. They'd found King Valmeyan's body, apparently. Queen Zafir had fled with some small number of riders and only the ancestors knew where she'd gone. No one knew whether Prince Tichane was dead or alive either. Hyrkallan and Sirion were still out hunting down survivors, one by one, bringing back their dragons. They'd been prowling the plains all night; now that the sun was up again, they were on the chase once more. Dragons circled high in the sky; dragons whirled back and forth not far overhead. Wherever he looked, his vision filled with them. He should have been dizzy with all that power, but instead all he felt was a bemused despair. *And I will do what I have to do, even if every alchemist pays for it when they realize what I've done.*

He sighed. Part of what he had to do was to listen to Vioros. Vioros, whose errand to Valleyford had proved even more futile than either of them had expected. Vioros, who had reported that Valleyford and Arys Crossing and Hammerford were as good as dead, and yet had some absurd tale of dragons turned to stone spilling out of his mouth. "Tell me again. From the start." Vioros wasn't one for flights of fancy, so he was probably telling him things that mattered, but still . . . He tried to listen this time, but his mind simply wouldn't sit still. *A thousand dragons. And we can't control them anymore.*

Vioros was keeping something back, Jeiros could tell that much. He waited patiently and then put a hand gently on his shoulder. "Dragons turned to stone? And how, old friend, with all that we know, is such a thing possible?"

Vioros shook the hand away. He was pacing. Fast and agitated. Not himself at all. "The Adamantine Men call the Speaker's Spear the Dragonslayer. Why?"

Ah. So that's what this is. Jeiros shook his head. *Why does it have to all happen now?* "It's a story, Vioros. There's no truth in it. The dragon Narammed slew was poisoned. The spear struck dead flesh. It was myth made by the likes of you and I to put Narammed on his throne."

"Then there are two vast statues newly built in Hammerford that I saw with my own eyes and that I cannot explain." Vioros took a deep breath. Jeiros watched him struggle with himself as he sat down again. "After I saw Valleyford, I thought for a bit that I might not come back." He gestured at the sea of dragons scattered across the plains in the shadow of the Pinnacles. "There are woken dragons in the Worldspine. We can't even control the ones we have. We're torn apart by war. I thought I might go to Furymouth. I could sell myself to the Taiytakei. They'd pay for what I know, wouldn't they? Or for what you know, for that matter."

Jeiros nodded.

"But we took an oath to protect the realms no matter what the cost. If not you and I, then who will do it? The Night Watchman? He has the courage and the will but not the means. The kings and queens of the realms? They have the means but not the will. The joke that passes for our speaker? If he has the will, I doubt he has the courage. So if not us, who? Who protects the little folk? That's why I came back. That's why I didn't run away. Master, there is something in Hammerford that kills dragons. What can you do here that can't wait another day?"

Jeiros got up. *Nothing at all, that's the honest answer. I've got nothing to look forward to except a day spent sitting around fretting, twiddling my thumbs. Waiting for the night to fall so that I can do what needs to be done when no one will see.*

Given what he had in mind for the night, there was a good chance this would be his last day alive. One more flight on the back of a dragon might be nice. Even knowing what he did, they were still magnificent creatures, mastery of them the greatest achievement in the history of the realms. He might as well enjoy it while he still could. He let Vioros lead him out to the eyrie, where perhaps a hundred Scales were struggling to manage ten times their number of dragons and slowly failing. Jeiros could see the irritation beginning to creep into the beasts, the ones who hadn't been fed. They could smell the slaughter in the air but there simply weren't enough animals to feed them. No one was even bothering to try and save the city; it had been burning ever since the battle. Jeiros distantly wondered who'd set it on fire, whether it had been Hyrkallan's dragons or Zafir's. Zafir seemed to have been scorching the earth around her, so probably her's, then. To the people who lived there, he supposed, the *who* really didn't matter. There were a lot of angry and homeless folk milling around the edges of the eyrie, raising their fists in mute hostility. They were probably getting hungry too. Jeiros looked down on them as he soared up into the air. Hundreds. Thousands. Half a city full of angry people congregating around a legion of hungry dragons. Stupidity like that made you want to shout at someone, but that probably meant he'd have to shout at himself.

He didn't want to think about the other half. With luck they'd had the sense to melt away. More likely they'd burned in the fires. No, best not to think about that. He closed his eyes for a few long seconds and then looked at the sky and the sprinkled shreds of cloud. Flying could be so peaceful. Sometimes he could even forget what it was that was carrying him. It wasn't far to Hammerford. Sixty or seventy miles in a straight line from the Pinnacles, a hundred miles by road. Half a twelvenight on foot or by cart, three or four days on the back of a horse, or a couple of hours on the back of a dragon. A couple of hours with nothing to do but savor the world, to feel what it was to be alive. He lifted his visor, then took off his helm and threw it away, let the wind tear at his hair and blow tears into his eyes. The sky was a deep blue, the sun bright and warm, the wind cold and fresh. From this height the world seemed so quiet and still, as long as he didn't look back at the brown smudge of smoke that hung between the Pinnacles. The rolling fields of the Harvest Queen shone in vivid greens and yellows. Blotches of darker woodland sat scattered among them. Even from a dozen miles away, the valley of the Fury was clear, the wide waters gleaming in the sun. To the north the land rose toward the Gliding Dragon Gorge and the Hungry Mountain Plains beyond, all too far away and lost in the haze.

For those who traveled by land, the Fury was a vast obstacle. Jeiros stared at the river as they flew over it. On the ground it seemed enormous. From the back of a dragon it didn't seem that big at all. Farther north, where it came out of the Worldspine and carved its massive scar across the realms, it looked impressive. Here? Half a mile wide? Nothing. To the south the air seemed clearer. He fancied that with a Taiytakei farscope that actually worked, he would have been able to see the hill of Purkan more than a hundred miles away, maybe even Valin's Fields beyond. Peaceful and quiet, all of it. For a while he chose to forget that most likely they would all soon burn.

Hammerford shattered all that. The town was worse than he'd imagined. The fires were out and the smoke was gone, but the air, even hundreds of feet above the ruins, still smelled of burned wood and ash. He could see the stone dragons, just about, after Vioros had done lots of pointing and shouting. They looked tiny, but as his dragon circled lower, Jeiros could see they were everything Vioros had said. One of a dragon rearing up on its back legs, tail coiled back over its head and around its neck, the last tip wrapped around in a circle as though it was holding something and had brought it closer to have a good look. The other dragon lay in the water at the edge of the river, wings outstretched. Its tail pointed up slightly while its head and neck disappeared into the water as though it had toppled forward. Shattered boats bobbed against it. All that was left of the waterfront was wreckage. *Not burned,* Jeiros noted. *Pity you can't say the same for the rest of the town.*

Vioros brought his dragon in to land as close as he could to the edge of what was left of the town. Jeiros thought he saw a few people moving in the streets, but they quickly scurried for cover. The smell almost made him retch. Dead people. Burned. Bits of them, hundreds of them. Scattered everywhere.

Other dragons landed around him, the riders and soldiers that Vioros had brought as escort. Not to protect the townsfolk from anything, but to protect the alchemists from any angry mob that might form and demand to know who had destroyed their lives. Jeiros made himself take a good long look. *This is what we swore to stop. These are the people we swore to protect, from exactly this.* There were other towns like this, mercifully out of sight—Arys Crossing. Felporsford. Beeve's Brook, Valleyford of course. All burned out. All towns as big as this or bigger.

Should I count the Silver City? Ten, twenty, thirty thousand people? That was dragon-kings fighting each other. We never swore to protect the people from that. Does that make it any better? It didn't really, but it made it Jehal's problem and not his, and that was a distinct improvement. Dragon-kings could be reasoned with. Just about. Awoken dragons, well, you might as well reason with a mountain or the waters of the Fury.

He shivered. Hammerford had been burned by a rogue dragon. Two rogue dragons, if the sell-sword's story was right. Who was to say there weren't others close by?

Vioros slid down off the dragon's back. "There's—"

Jeiros wagged a finger at him. Beckoned him close and whispered in his ear. "Whatever it is you're not telling me, I'd like to hear it right now."

He let Vioros lead him through the rubble and ruin to the edge of the river while the rest of his tale came out. The sell-sword who the townsfolk thought was a dragon-rider. His fantastical stories. Rogues, blood-magi, men who appeared and disappeared like bubbles in a stream. All on top of the Adamantine Spear that had turned two riderless dragons to stone. Preposterous. Absurd. Beyond belief, except that the dragons were there, right in front of him, close enough to touch. Immense, far more impressive when you stood on your own two feet right in front of them than they had been from above. Fifty feet high, a hundred feet long. Life-size. He shook his head. The detail was exquisite and perfect. He'd never seen anything like it, even the dragon of Dragondale. The one reared up on its back legs even had a slightly surprised look. No craftsman had made these. You couldn't have made something like that with the best sculptors from the City of Dragons, not even the best artist of the Taiytakei could even have come close. Easier to believe they were made by magic than by human hands.

But.

But for the love of the Great Flame, *how?*

"I told them I'd pay them a lot of money if they found the Speaker's Spear. If they have, we should rebuild their town for them. It can't have gone far."

Jeiros shook his head. "You really think the spear did this? Don't you think we'd know?" *Or was that some secret so dire that Bellepheros somehow neglected to pass it on to any of us. But what else could have?* "Vioros, the dragon of Dragondale is a lie. You and I both know that. There is no other story I have ever heard of magics that turn living flesh into stone. Even the old stories of the Silver King say nothing about this."

"Touch them. They're right in front of you."

Yes, they were. He touched them anyway, just to be sure they were real. Then he sighed. "You'd better take me to the sell-sword now." There, that feeling, right there. What was it? A glimmer of belief? A bit of hope? *Don't fool yourself.*

Vioros led him back again, almost running. They hurried along streets strewn with rubble and then into a part of the town that was almost intact. A fine layer of white ash lay on the ground, kicked into the air by their feet and turning their riding clothes slowly gray. The air stank of smoke. They came to a small square. Abruptly, Vioros stopped.

In the middle of the square a makeshift gallows had been built. A man was hanging from it, a rider by the looks of him. Vioros, when he moved, walked very slowly toward the body. He walked around to the other side and took a good long look at the man. Jeiros watched his face.

"That your sell-sword?" he asked when Vioros didn't say anything. The other alchemist nodded.

"They were going to hang him. They thought he was the rider from one of the dragons." Very slowly Vioros shook his head. "I didn't think they'd be so quick."

Jeiros gestured to the riders around him. "Cut him down." He looked at Vioros. "You're sure this is your man? The one who said he killed a dragon by turning it into stone."

Vioros nodded, mute.

"Narammed said that the Speaker's Spear cuts both ways. Whatever you do with it will come back to you. Use it to kill and death will stalk you. Use it to rule and you will be ruled. Protect it and it, in turn, will protect you. That's why it became the speaker's weapon. Kill the speaker and the spear's curse falls on you, or so they say. Unless you get someone else to do it for you. Worked for Zafir." Jeiros shrugged. "I always assumed he meant that as a metaphor, not literally. Ancestors! I don't think I know anymore which stories about the speaker and the spear we made up to suit ourselves, which we heard from somewhere else and decided to keep, and which have their root in some truth." The riders had the dead man down from the gallows now. Around them a spectral crowd of townsfolk was starting to form, eyes peering from the shadows, around corners. "Do you suppose they mind us cutting him down?"

"Not as much as they're going to mind when you make him start talking again."

"Then we'd better take him somewhere else." Jeiros winced. "Not back to the Pinnacles, though. Too far." He took a deep breath. "Actually, this could work out to our advantage. Here." He took a gold chain from around his neck and gave it to Vioros. "While our escort are busy, get some people to find some barrels and fill them with water from the river. When we come back, we're going to make a discovery."

"We are?" Vioros looked blank.

"Yes. We're going to find dozens of barrels of potion. The secret cache we've kept here since the wars started, in case it was ever needed. The one you came here looking for. One of several in fact. Fortunate for us that this one survived the attack."

"What?"

Jeiros lowered his voice, mindful of the riders cutting down the body. "Barrels of water, Vioros. We're going to lie about some barrels of water, and I want these riders to hear. The barrels must not be sealed, mind. I will need to inspect them myself. Do you understand?"

Vioros shook his head. "Not really. Why would we lie about potions?"

"To buy ourselves some time. Let the riders and their kings and queens think all is well. It will give us the day or two to do what we need to do." There was quite a bit more that Jeiros might have said, but he kept it to himself. A burden shared was sometimes a burden halved, but when it meant trusting someone with a secret, sometimes a burden was just a burden to be lived with. Vioros really didn't want to hear the rest. *Just another few days, old friend, and then you can fly to Furymouth and take that ship, if that's still what you want.*

38

IN VICTORY AND DEFEAT

Jehal hobbled slowly to Wraithwing's side. He needed a staff now, even to walk. Everything hurt, from his hand wrapped in bandages all the way up his arm, down his back to his foot. The whole of one side.

The Night Watchman and his men stood guard over the Adamantine Palace. Jeiros had vanished off to some trivial little town to hunt for potions. Hyrkallan and Sirion were chasing down survivors. It was almost as though they'd all forgotten about him.

I'm only the speaker after all. If they'd forgotten about him then they'd also forgotten that he was still a king, that he had hundreds of riders who followed his every wish and a good few dragons as well. He toyed with the idea of making some minor adjustments to the balance of power by having as many of the northern riders murdered in their sleep as he could manage, but in the end he left them to their dreams. One Night of the Knives had been quite enough, and besides, even if he had enough men to kill them all, he certainly didn't have enough to fly their dragons. *And then what? Where do I take them? There's nothing here. Narghon's dead; Zafir's probably razed Furymouth to the ground; the Adamantine Eyries haven't got a drop of potion between them; and I could hardly take them back to the north after I've just murdered their riders, could I?* The idea made him laugh. Steal the dragons of Outwatch from Jaslyn's knights and then take them back to their own eyrie to be fed? No, that was hardly a recipe for a happy outcome.

Still, he might have tried it anyway if it hadn't been for Lystra and how immensely in pain he was. The pain was mostly from the old wound, She-zira's revenge on him. The scar was still intact, but underneath it felt like all the muscles of his thigh that used to be attached to his groin had ripped away. Probably they had. The leg was useless now. Even with his staff he could barely walk. He'd chewed on Dreamleaf until the walls started talking, but the pain never went away.

And then there was Lystra, his queen, his love, the one who'd brought the world tumbling down simply by being. She wouldn't like it very much if he had her sister poisoned, and so Jaslyn got to live. Jehal turned his mind to other matters of revenge instead. There were, after all, plenty to choose from. He thought he might start with Furymouth.

Wraithwing was ready to fly. The dragon felt angry, restless. Something. Hungry maybe. Jehal could feel a quivering urgency in the way he moved. He took hold of the rope ladder and started to climb onto Wraith-wing's back, one step at a time. Hopping up with his good leg, hauling himself with his hands, letting the other leg hang limp and useless. They could have used a crane and a harness, but that would have been too much. He would mount on his own. On the day he couldn't do that any-more, he might as well take the Dragon's Fall. Except if he couldn't climb on, he wouldn't even be able to do that.

By the time he was in his saddle, he was sweating and gasping for breath as though he'd run all the way from the bottom of the Tower of Air to the top. He squeezed his eyes shut, trying to push the throbbing in his leg away. The midday sun burned down on his back. Hyrkallan and Sirion were somewhere up in the sky, far away. Jehal waved his hand. Wraithwing began to run. Around him half a dozen dragons took to the air. Instead of joining the hunt, though, they turned south. If anyone saw him go, what were they going to do? Besides, most of his riders had already gone. Quietly, inconspicuously. A hundred dragons leaving all at once, people would notice. A hundred leaving in dribs and drabs through the day? At a time like this? Invisible.

As soon as they were in the air, arms wrapped themselves around him. Lystra rode behind him. She had his son with her. An idiot risk, perhaps, if he was flying to war, but he'd been without her for far too long. Besides, you never quite knew what would happen when your back was turned. Jaslyn would have stood watch over her little sister, he was sure of that, but in the end he couldn't bring himself to fly without her, not after everything that had held them apart. And once he'd told her where he was going, he would have had to have riders hold her down to keep her from flying with him.

He skirted the edges of his realm, circumspect in his approach. They passed the night in the wild hills near where the Worldspine kissed the Endless Sea. Hardly anyone lived out here. Those who did had scant regard for dragons or their riders but enough shrewdness to know when to run. He lay wrapped in furs, staring up at the stars with Lystra by his side and their son snuffling between them. *Like a common man with his wife and his son might do. No pageants for us tonight, no massive tents that take an hour and a dozen men to erect so I might sleep without a breeze on my face. I like the breeze.* This was where everything had started. In these wooded hills. Not far from here was the little valley where Aliphera's shattered body had finally been found. He looked up. There were no clouds up there tonight. Through the haze of Dreamleaf, time seemed to stop. Here, the world was almost perfect.

Almost. Pity about the pain that simply wouldn't go away.

Lystra started to snore. The baby coughed and wriggled. He wondered if he should tell her. Maybe if she knew everything he'd done, the world might suddenly start to turn better.

Don't be such a sentimental idiot. Words won't mend your leg. They won't put Aliphera's bones back together. They won't put Shezira's head back on her neck nor Meteroa's either. They won't make anything different at all except she'll know how much of a bastard you really are, and then there's a good chance she just might not like you anymore. Which would be a bad thing. So keep your mouth shut. Let her think that none of this is your fault and make sure you get rid of anyone who says otherwise. How does that sound? No, don't even bother to answer that, because we both know how it sounds.

It sounded like his uncle. Who was dead, he reminded himself. Callous and mean and eminently practical. Hadn't worked out too well for him in the end.

Things worked out for him for a good long time, and you're smarter than he was. Stick with what you know, Jehal. Don't suddenly try to be something you're not.

But that was the problem. That's exactly what he was doing. Trying to be the same man he'd been a year ago, when all this had started, and he wasn't liking it. It wasn't fun anymore.

Ah. So now you're the nice Jehal we've all been missing for, well, since the moment you were born, really. Some other Jehal, who doesn't make a habit of getting rid of anyone in his way. A Jehal who thinks about something beyond sitting on the throne he thinks his father should have had. Don't you think it's a bit late for that?

He had a lot of enemies now, it was true. He doubted they'd simply let him walk away.

And let's not forget the inordinate time and the elaborate plans to lure every woman who crosses your path into bed. It would be a lot quicker and easier to just punch them in the face and rape them. Probably a lot more honest too. Might there be the odd grudge there?

No. Not fair. Like who?

Who exactly are you at war with? And, if you could possibly manage to be frank for a moment, you really don't care about what you've done to any of them.

He turned and looked at Lystra. *I care about this one.*

Because she's so immeasurably stupid and naive she believes that somewhere there's something nice in you. There isn't. If getting it up didn't hurt so much right now, if you could actually walk even a little bit, you'd be off after some young virginal dragon-rider just to prove you still had it in you. She'd probably even let you go if you asked nicely, that's how much dumb faith she has in you. Entirely undeserved and entirely misguided.

He reached a hand to stroke Lystra's hair. She sighed and shifted but didn't wake up. They'd barely had a chance to talk about what had happened in the Pinnacles, but the bruises on her face told their own story. Another reason to go after Zafir.

While the world burns. Yes. Go on, Jehal, pursue your little grudge. Much more important for you two to prove once and for all who's the better bastard. As if it's going to make any difference when the alchemists run out of potion.

Still hadn't asked Jeiros why he didn't simply make more.

He snorted and snuggled up close to his wife. The baby stirred and then whimpered. When it came to the dragons, there really wasn't much he could do.

Lystra was looking at him, her eyes open now. "Why are you awake?" she whispered. "Is it the baby? I heard him make a noise. He's probably hungry again."

Is he? Jehal had no idea how you were supposed to tell. Babies happened to other people, preferably a long way away from him. He watched as Lystra opened her shirt and then winced as the baby started to suckle. *Ancestors! How small they are.* He tried to grin. "If you put it like that then I'm hungry too."

Lystra ignored him. "What are we going to call him? He's more than a month old. He deserves a name."

"Hyram." Jehal laughed. "I don't know. Antros? But there are already too many of them in your family."

"Tyan. After his grandfather."

"*Who went mad.*" *And we won't be calling him Meteroa either.* "I'd like to call him Calzarin. After my little brother." *Who went mad too.*

"Calzarin. It's a nice name."

"Yes." He rolled onto his back and stared up at the stars. Nice name. Nice face. *Nice arse too, or at least Meteroa obviously thought so. Not so nice on the inside, though. We did that to him, Meteroa and I. We ruined him, each in our own way. Tore him up from the inside out. Meteroa with lust and me with loathing. Now look at us all. Are you watching, little brother? Because I don't feel guilty at all. You deserved everything I did to you, and if you were alive now I'd probably smash your head with a rock. And yes I might be a cripple, and yes I might not be the speaker for very much longer, and yes the realms might be about to burn to ash around me, but I'm alive, little brother. Alive and at least very briefly happy, which is more than you ever were. So if you're feeling smug, you can go choke on it.*

There were times, he thought, when you had to be realistic about things. Sometimes being alive had to be enough of a victory. *And however it ends, I so nearly came away with everything. You can't tell me you wouldn't have done the same, any of you, dear ancestors. We have the same venom for blood. Hyram called the Veid Palace a nest of snakes. How right. How pathetically right.*

39

THAT WHICH DETERMINES DESTINY

They put the dead sell-sword on the back of a dragon and flew him to a quiet place by the river, well outside the town. Jeiros mixed his own blood with a pinch of Abyssal Powders and tipped the congealing mess into the corpse's mouth. Then he took a deep breath and tried to ignore the smell. The body was already starting to turn in the heat and it had been a long time since he'd talked to a dead man.

"Hello, corpse," he whispered as the head twitched, as the eyes rolled beneath gummy lids and its mouth opened with a quiet moan. He started with the spear. Then the rogue dragons in the Worldspine. Back beyond that to the white, to the attack on the Redoubt, the white dragon's first awakening, the attack on Queen Shezira's wedding party that had started it all. He listened patiently to it all. When he was done he had the body burned. The trouble with waking the dead, as he'd learned to his cost, often came with putting them back to sleep again. Dragons sorted that out easily enough.

A Scales. The sell-sword had been with a Scales, of all people. A should-have-been-alchemist who'd done something stupid and been demoted to a Scales. Kataros. Name didn't mean anything.

An almost-alchemist who'd seen the spear turn two dragons to stone. Who would know the spear for what it was. Who very probably had a sizeable chip on her shoulder. Marvelous.

"You know what annoys me?" he grumbled to Vioros when he was done. "Someone started this. Someone tried to steal the white, and that's when she escaped. And I have no idea who did it."

"*That* annoys you?" Vioros looked at him as though he was mad.

"I'd at least like someone to blame."

"Valmeyan."

He shrugged. "Probably. Now he's dead, I suppose we'll never know."

They flew the short distance back to Hammerford along the Fury, skimming the river in the futile hope that the mystery almost-alchemist might happen by some miracle to be drifting along on a boat in plain sight. Jeiros wondered idly what would happen if you fed Abyssal Powders to a dead dragon. If such a thing was even possible. That was the trouble with being an alchemist. You almost couldn't help wondering about things like that. You couldn't help wondering about a spear that had shown up where it wasn't supposed to and had turned a pair of dragons into statues as close to right under your nose as made no difference either. The dead man was only a sell-sword. How did he know the difference between the Adamantine Spear and some other spear that just happened to be all metal and shiny? How had he made it work? Damn thing had sat in the Adamantine Palace for two hundred years without showing the slightest sign of being magical, despite all the legends it carried. And then, just when you needed it, it woke up. Yes, you had to wonder about that.

And while you were in a wondering frame of mind, you had to ponder what a blood-mage and some mysterious fellow who could apparently appear and disappear at will were doing with it. And why they'd chosen to steal it at this particular point in history and not last year or next. You had to think about the how too. And what a blood-mage and King Jehal had to do with one another. No, you couldn't help wondering all of those things, even though you knew perfectly well that you weren't likely to get a quick answer to any of them, and what was likely to be the end of the world wasn't much more than a week away unless you did something about it right here and now.

He sighed. He'd been grand master of the Order of the Scales for over half a year now, and he couldn't think of a single time when he'd actually enjoyed himself. His predecessor, Bellepheros, had at least enjoyed himself *sometimes;* Jeiros was fairly sure of that. *And then just when it was all about to get difficult, you vanish. What did you know, old man?*

There was something more to all of this. Something he was missing. He'd have to talk to Vioros about that. Assuming they both lived long enough to have a proper conversation.

In Hammerford Jehal's riders were waiting for him, agitated. A pair of them stood either side of a woman sitting disconsolate on the burnt earth, battered and bedraggled. A third rider was with them. All four looked confused and alarmed, as though they hadn't a clue what to do. The third rider was also holding a spear. *The* spear. Unmistakable. Unbelievable, but there it was, somehow showing up again where it was needed. Jeiros had to rub his eyes to be sure, but no, it was still there. The spear that apparently had decided to wake up and kill dragons. If he peered hard, he might even have recognized the woman from some quieter moment in the Palace of Alchemy.

"Found her flapping about on the edge of the river on a fishing raft," said the first rider, one of Hyrkallan's northerners. "Trying to steal it."

The woman started forward. "Master alch—" Which was as far as she got before one of her guards kicked her in the back. Jeiros snatched the spear and gave it to Vioros. Best to seize it before one of the riders thought of taking it back to the Pinnacles to give to Jehal. He cast a brief eye over the woman from the river. He had no idea who she was, but he was sure he'd seen her face once before. He could see the traces of Hatchling Disease on her, just the start of it. On her way to being a Scales, just as the sell-sword had said.

He gave her to Vioros as well. Jehal's riders closed around them. He could see the riders from Sand eyeing them up, ready to keep this stupid war going for another round. Well good. *Let* them eye each other. It would serve as a distraction.

So now we have a weapon. One we thought wasn't real, but one that can apparently turn a dragon into stone. If they would be kind enough to come at us one at a time, I might even find that useful. But there were a thousand dragons at the Pinnacles. If he started stabbing them one after the other, someone was bound to notice and make him stop. And then when they'd taken it from him, there would be arguing, fighting, bloodshed, over whether it would be Jehal or Hyrkallan who held it at the end of the day. No. There were better plans than that.

He took Vioros aside. "This is our hope. This kills dragons. We have this one thing, and that is better than none. Go to the Adamantine Palace. Find the Night Watchman. Tell him this from me. Tell him I will do my part and he must now do his. Tell him it's black. Pitch-black. Tell him exactly that and nothing else. Is that clear? And then give him the spear."

"Pitch-black." Vioros looked shaken. "What does that mean?"

"Vale knows what it means. When you're done with that, collect as many alchemists as you can. Seize the palace eyries and put an end to any dragons you do not need. Keep a few, though. A small number. There's enough potion for that. If I'm not with you in two days, assume I am dead. You will go to every eyrie in the realms. The Night Watchman has already sent men with hammers ahead. Do what needs to be done. Poison every dragon, smash every egg. It won't be perfect, but it might be enough to save us. Keep a handful, though. Use the stockpile of potion at the Redoubt. There will always be dragons. Vale will need them to hunt the ones that have awoken." He nodded to the woman. "When you have a moment after all that, find out what she knows."

That probably wasn't what Vioros had wanted to hear, but it was all he was going to get, and he was a good enough alchemist to do what he was told.

"Now." Jeiros rubbed his hands and made sure he spoke loudly enough for all the riders around him to hear. "Let us see this hidden den of alchemists our dead sell-sword friend told us about. Perhaps there will be some *potion* there."

It took Vioros a moment to remember, but he'd done his job well before they'd left. A gang of townsfolk appeared almost out of nowhere as Jeiros walked back into the ruined town. He quietly paid them in gold and they hurriedly led him to a cellar half filled with a mishmash of barrels, kegs, anything that would hold water. By the time Jeiros opened the door, they'd all melted away. For the riders who came with him, Jeiros went through the pretence of discovering a secret stockpile of dragon-taming potions. Hard to feign the enthusiasm, the glee, the surprise, the joy even, that he ought to feel. Hard to believe anyone would even fall for such a ruse. Certainly any alchemist would have seen through it at once. But none of the riders seemed particularly surprised. *Because we are alchemists, and people believe what we say? Or because you simply don't care and pay such little attention to us? I would like to think the first, but we all know better.*

Did it matter? Jeiros didn't care. What mattered was that he had dozens of barrels filled with river water that everyone believed contained potions and that they were loaded onto the backs of his dragons. Jeiros watched Vioros leave for the Adamantine Palace. To Vale with the spear, where it might be some use. He had a sinking feeling they wouldn't meet again and he could see that Vioros was thinking that too. *Ha! Now you know how I felt when Bellepheros chose to simply vanish. May your ancestors watch over you. And if you choose to fly to Furymouth and the sea, at least deliver my message first.*

As soon as he'd seen Vioros safely gone, Jeiros flew straight back to the Pinnacles and the chaos that had once been Queen Zafir's eyrie. Dragons, everywhere he looked. And he had nothing to feed them or keep them tame.

"Right." He rounded up the first riders he found. "These barrels over there. Those barrels over here."

It was as easy as that. Switching the barrels full of water for the barrels he'd brought with him from the Adamantine Palace. Barrels full of poison. Then he called all the alchemists at the eyrie to him. He showed them the barrels and told them that Vioros had brought more potion from the north. By the end of the day, his work was done. He didn't rest until it was too dark to see, though, moving around the eyrie and the surrounding plains, going from one clump of dragons to the next, making sure that every Scales knew their duty. Making sure that every dragon was fed. He endured Hyrkallan's icy greetings and King Sirion's hearty slap on the back, and when he discovered that Jehal and nearly a hundred dragons were missing, he shrugged his weary shoulders, wished them all the best and hoped that perhaps Jehal might become the speaker he had it in him to be. And after that, when there really wasn't anything left to do, he lay back in his tent and stared at the darkness above him and waited for some-one to realize what he'd done. They'd hang him. Or they'd burn him. Maybe Jehal would be like Zafir and put him in a cage. They wouldn't feed him to any of the dragons that happened to survive the night. He was pretty sure of that.

Stabbing dragons with the spear would have been a spectacle. Quietly poisoning them was much more the alchemists' way.

40

❧

LEGBREAKER

Zafir flew south. Away from the chaos above the Pinnacles. She'd
lost. Somehow, despite everything he'd done to them, Jehal had
managed to empty every eyrie in the north to join his cause. She'd
stayed long enough to see that Jehal himself led the charge, to see his
Wraithwing plunge into Valmeyan's cloud of dragons. For a while she'd
gone looking for him. Let tooth and claw and fire settle what was between
them, but the battle was too big, too wild. She hadn't found him.

Jehal was probably dragon-food by now anyway. As soon as the outcome seemed hopeless, she'd left Valmeyan and Tichane to fight on as best
they could. She'd fallen out of the air as though she was dead. Three other
dragons had fallen with her, her most trusted riders, plunging toward the
ground and then at the last minute leveling out and heading south. Jehal
might be gone or he might not, but Lystra wasn't. Valmeyan hadn't had
the spine to let her see to that. Probably Lystra or her son would end up
being speaker one day because of all this. Well she couldn't take Lystra's
memories of Jehal away from her and she couldn't take her son, but she
could take everything else. *Do unto others as others have done unto you.* So
she flew until she found the Fury and then veered to the west, over the sea
of mud and huts that called itself Farakkan, past the Yamuna River and
on toward the sea. Clifftop was already in ashes. When she reached Furymouth, there were no dragons to meet her, no defenders to ward her off.

In the space of a few minutes the four dragons burned Jehal's glorious

Veid Palace to the ground. That was a start. Jehal's home city lay waiting for her, naked and helpless. That next.

And then? She circled out over Furymouth Bay, out over the fleet of Taiytakei ships anchored there. *When I've done everything I can to hurt him, what then? They've burned my home.* She'd seen the flames behind her as she'd fled. Whoever was left to claim victory at the Pinnacles would doubtless blame her for the burning of the Silver City, but it hadn't been her, not her dragons, not her orders. The Silver City, almost as much as the Pinnacles themselves, had been the beating heart of the realms. Hers.

They burned my home. Where do I go?

The ships offered the obvious answer. *Come with us. Across the sea where no one will look for you.* Across the sea to what, though? To become a kept woman? To become a curiosity? A courtesan to some rich ship's captain?

Better than being dead, wasn't it?

She circled the ships one more time. One of these ships carried dragon eggs, sold to the Taiytakei from Jehal's eyrie by Valmeyan. In exchange for what, Zafir didn't know, but she had no doubt the eggs were there. *Sold in exchange for helping him to the Adamantine Throne. Fat lot of good you were.* They were the ones who'd done this. The Taiytakei. She didn't know how or why, but somehow they'd made this happen. They'd used her. Ayzalmir had had the right of it when he'd burned their ships, banished them, fed the ones who couldn't or wouldn't run to the snappers in his menagerie.

No. Being a slave wasn't better than being dead. She skimmed across the sea toward one of the Taiytakei ships, the biggest one with the most flags flying from it, and told her dragon to burn it. Dragons liked burning ships. One thing she'd learned from those few of Meteroa's riders she'd taken alive in the Pinnacles.

The dragon gleefully veered to obey. It opened its mouth. She felt a sense of exultation . . .

And then nothing. The dragon spasmed once, twisted and fell out of the sky. Its head hit the waves and it somersaulted, spinning the world around Zafir. A wall of salt water crashed into her, thumped into her back, crushing her against her dragon's neck, and then she was flying again. For a moment it seemed as though she wasn't strapped to the dragon at all;

then they crashed together back into the sea. For a second time she was flung forward, all the breath smashed out of her lungs. She fell limp, almost snapped in two. The dragon ploughed through the waves and slid to a stop. The Taiytakei ship loomed before them. The dragon's head hung under the waves while its wings spread out over the surface. It wasn't moving. Somehow, it was dead.

Zafir tried to lift her head, but the effort was too much. She could barely breathe. She lay still, arms wrapped around the dragon's neck, making little gasping noises as one wing slowly slipped under the water and the dragon began to tip and sink. The straps and webbing dug into her legs and her waist, holding her fast to the monster's back as it started to slide under the water. Movement was beyond her. Of all things, she was going to drown.

Live. She had no idea where the thought came from. Someone who cared whether she lived or died. There couldn't be too many of them left. Must have been her own then. *Live.*

The water reached her legs and then her waist. Slowly, slowly sinking. A shock of cold against her skin as it found the joins in her armor. She tried to move. It might have been the hardest thing she'd ever done, but she did it, lifting her face away from the dragon's neck. That was almost as much as she could manage, but she forced her hands to move to the knot of pain in her belly where the main harness was jammed into her flesh. Her fingers fumbled. Water lapped at her fingers, then at her arms. With one last monumental effort of will, she pushed herself back into the saddle, gave herself the finger-width of space she needed, and pulled the buckle apart.

And now the other one.

The other one was easy. One strong jerk on a knot and she was free. As the dragon slipped under the waves, she threw off her helm. Panic snapped at her fingers, making them clumsy as she tried to find the buckles that would get rid of her armor. Gauntlets first. One shoulder plate. The other. Elbows.

One arm free.

As she sank, the shadow of the Taiytakei ship fell across her, but there was something else. A figure in silver, standing nearby. Which couldn't be right because that meant he was standing on the water.

Other arm. Breast plates. Back plates. The sea was up to her neck. Lapping at her face. Frantic now, cutting straps where they wouldn't give.

She felt her herself come loose from the saddle. Felt the water lift her. Kicked, kicked as hard as she could until she was free. Free! Her arms thrashed, struggling to keep her head above the water.

The silver ghost came closer until he was standing right over her. She couldn't see his face. Everything about him glittered.

Speaker Zafir, it said. She would have nodded, if she could, but since she couldn't, a blank assent would have to suffice. The knight or whatever it was bent over her; behind his silver mask, his skin was white and his eyes were bloodred lanterns. *Haven't you forgotten something?* it seemed to ask.

The legbreaker around her ankle went taut, and suddenly the entire weight of her dead dragon was dragging her beneath the waves. Her arms flailed for a moment, until the sky disappeared and the black water sucked her in.

41

❦

THE DEAD AND THE DYING

The heat in the fields around the eyrie was blistering. Hundreds of dragons lay dead, roasting, cooking from the inside. Jeiros felt a pang of satisfaction. Short-lived perhaps, as the northern riders dragged him to where Hyrkallan and Sirion would tell him how he was going to die. But satisfaction nonetheless. He'd got more than half the realm's dragons in a stroke. Two thirds, probably. There must have been nearly a thousand of them here after the battle. Less than a hundred were still alive. Probably more like fifty. They'd come back, of course. All over the realms, in the weeks to come, eggs that had been dormant for years would hatch. By then he'd be dead and that would be somebody else's problem. While he was dying he could console himself with how easy he'd made it for them. Hatchlings were manageable. Hatchlings needed far less potion to keep them tame. A man could kill a hatchling if he set his mind to it with care. If Vioros had taken his message and Vale had understood it, the Night Watchman would be seeing to that right away. Soldiers would be sent. Riders on horseback, riders on dragons if there were any left. All across the realms the Adamantine Men would roam, and they'd be carrying hammers with their spears. Even if they didn't, what he'd done here was probably enough. Probably.

Which left it down to Jehal, to Vale and his Adamantine Men and to the rogue dragons. When they came out from wherever they were hiding, probably the best anyone could hope for was to hide long enough for them to get bored and go somewhere else. Eggs and hatchlings would call to them. Jeiros didn't know how that worked exactly, but that was the history he knew. That was how they'd lured the dragons in the first place. Eggs and hatchlings and other dragons. Get rid of those and wait for the rogues to die out. Maybe turn a few into stone. That, as far as Jeiros could see, was the best chance any of them had. *Except me, of course. I don't get to watch. I'm not sure, but I think I'm glad.*

The riders stopped dragging him when they reached some of the few dragons left alive. There they tied Jeiros' hands and feet. He didn't bother to resist. They hauled him onto the back of a dragon and flew him to the top of the Fortress of Watchfulness, where Hyrkallan and Sirion had set up their court. There wasn't much ceremony there either. Hyrkallan hadn't had time to make a cage but that was clearly what was on his mind. They broke his ankles and his wrists with a bored and sullen rage and then tied him to a wheel. Hyrkallan must have hauled that up on the back of one of the few dragons left that same morning. They tied the wheel to one of the cranes that lined the battlements of the fortress and swung him over the edge to hang there, facedown, staring at the eyrie far below. The height didn't bother him. Even the pain in his ankles and his wrists wasn't as bad as he thought it would be. Mostly he just felt tired. *As deaths go, this could be worse, I suppose. At least I get to see my handiwork. We can see who lasts longest.*

"Do you know what you've done?" shouted Hyrkallan from the fortress wall. "Stupid alchemist! Do you know what you've done? You've given it all to Jehal."

There wasn't much to say to that. *Yes. I've given him the world so he can watch it burn. I've given him ash. I've given him the duty of staying alive, of keeping tame the few dragons we have left. Of fighting the awakened ones. And why did I do that? Because none of you will stop the fire when it comes, but Jehal might just have the cunning and the guile to survive it. Unlike you. Is he going to thank me, do you think?* He laughed bitterly. *No. Not very likely, is it.*

"Don't think the rest of your kind will escape! You were all in this together. You must have been. I'll have you all broken on the wheel!"

He had to answer that, at least. "They knew nothing."

"Liar! Give me names, alchemist, and I will spare the rest. Otherwise they all die."

"There are no names, Lord Hyrkallan."

"Am I supposed to believe you did this alone?"

Yes, you are, and actually I did, but don't suppose you will. What am I supposed to do about it? They know their duty. I tried to spare them any complicity, but I don't imagine you care about that one way or the other. They did nothing wrong, but then neither did I. I did what was needed.

"You have ruined us all! Do you imagine Jehal will spare any of us?"

Do you imagine I care?

"How much did he pay you, alchemist? What did he promise you?"

Jeiros' patience broke. "Don't you think that if he'd paid me I might have run away?" he shouted back in fury. *Think, dragon-lord. Use your head. Oh, but you already are, and you still can't see beyond who gets to sit on the Speaker's Throne. You don't see what's coming. You can thank my ghost later, Vioros, that I sent you back when I did.*

Hyrkallan came as close to the edge as he could. "Names, alchemist. Tell me who else or I swear I will take your order apart limb by limb."

And you probably would too, if you have the chance. Jeiros sighed and reeled off a few names, alchemists that the order might survive without. Names given so that others might be spared. Not men and women against whom he bore any particular grudge, just the ones that maybe mattered a little less. *There. And that's me damned. Are we done now?* "You want to know why I gave Jehal the Adamantine Throne? Because he's cleverer than you, Hyrkallan. Whatever his faults, he's sharper than the rest of you." Which might have been true or might not. But then Hyrkallan and even Sirion weren't about to understand that this had nothing to do with them, nothing to do with Jehal, nothing to do with who wore what title and sat in which throne.

Hyrkallan shouted some more. Jeiros didn't listen and eventually the dragon-lord went away. King Sirion never even came out to look. Jeiros was left there, hanging thousands of feet up in the air over a sea of dead dragons.

He probably lost consciousness at some point. It became hard to tell. His mind wandered over all the things he hadn't managed to do, all the things left incomplete, the tasks undone. Thinking distracted him from the pain of his mangled hands and feet. Was there anything more he could have given of himself? Could he somehow have stopped the rogue dragons from waking? He couldn't think how, but the nagging voice was there anyway. *Bellepheros would have done better.* But Bellepheros was dead. *Best to face that. Dead as in not coming back. Not riding out of the sunset with barges loaded with potions and some clever way of drawing all the rogue dragons toward him and turning them into stone.*

Turning them into stone with the Adamantine Spear. Absurd story, and not one that he or any other alchemist for a hundred years had believed. And yet there it was. Evidence. It had been right in front of him. Seen with his own eyes, heard with his own ears. What else could it do? *Why didn't I know? The Silver King was said to be able to summon dragons from the skies, but was that him or the spear? Not much point in that if we can't kill more than one at a time. Maybe someone could call them and then run away to some other place and call them again. Maybe we could keep them penned up in one corner of the realms. Or maybe we could take the spear deep underground and keep calling them to a place they could never reach. Or out to sea, perhaps. Take it away on one of the Taiytakei ships and then summon them away?*

Children's stories. Which ones were real? Too late now, though. He'd never know. Not his problem. Vioros would have to find out for himself. Quickly too.

At some point it was dark. Not long after that it was light again. There weren't any dragons moving about down on the plains anymore. He saw a couple flying away from the Palace of Pleasure, and that was all.

The sun moved across the sky. No sign of any live dragons at all. There were fires, though. The eyrie was on fire. And distant sounds, whispering up from the ground below. Shouting, fighting sounds. All too far away to see.

"Master." Evening now. He heard the voice clearly enough, but he had no idea who it was and was in no position to turn and look. "Master," it called again.

"I'm here," he croaked. His throat, he realized, was very dry. He wasn't hungry yet, but then he'd been here not much more than a day. Thirsty, though. Yes, definitely thirsty. The realization hit home, right then. *Yes. You really are going to die up here.*

"Master, the last dragons here are all gone. We followed your orders."

Orders? What orders? I didn't give any orders. I just got potion and poison mixed up. Easy enough thing to do. Just muddle a letter or two. Jeiros chuckled. The movement jarred his wrists and ankles and turned his laugh into a cry of pain.

"They took some of the others and hung them. They wouldn't let the rest of us near the dragons, but we found a way. And now the people who stayed on in the ruins of the Silver City have turned on the riders. I heard most of them are dead. Some of them got into the fortress. There was fighting. There's no food out there. I have to go. The riders will hang us all now if they find us. But it's done, master. I thought you should know. It's finished."

"Finished?" He wanted to laugh. "It's never finished with dragons."

The voice didn't say anything else. Jeiros assumed the alchemist had gone, vanished to hide from the wrath of the dragon-lords. *They'll have to call themselves something else now.* Or maybe the alchemist was still there, watching. Jeiros had no way of telling.

"Good luck," he rasped. *Too late for me, but the rest of you will be needing it. The spear, Vioros. Take it under the ground. Or take it out to sea.* He had to laugh at his own optimism. As though if he thought hard enough of the spear and all the things he wanted to try with it, Vioros would somehow hear him.

Dragons. They hear our thoughts. That's how they know what their riders want them to do.

He wondered if Vioros had thought of that.

42

THE SILVER SORCERER

Zafir had a knife in her boot. The pain split her in two but she bent double, reached the sheath, pulled out the knife, took hold of the rope and started to cut. Her lungs burned. Her ears thrummed as the corpse of the dragon took her ever deeper into water ever darker. Her mind started to slip, to wander. She thought she heard musical laughter for a moment, but her hand never stopped sawing, never gave up the urge to *live*, no matter what. And then suddenly she felt the weight go away and she was floating again and the music was getting louder and she could see light again.

And then she was lying on her back, lying on something solid and hard. The air smelled of the sea. Strange shapes towered over her, vast pillars reaching for the bright and blinding sky. Masts.

The silver man with the white face and the bloody eyes was looking down at her again. There were other faces too, this time. Dark faces marked with tattoos. Taiytakei. They didn't say anything, only stroked their chins and looked at her. One by one, a forest of little sounds touched her. Creaking wood. Straining ropes. The wind whistling in and out of the rigging. The shuffle of feet on the deck. Distant voices, orders barked far away. The calls of seagulls wheeling overhead.

"Is she alive?" asked one. His accent was so thick that she could barely understand him. Not like the Taiytakei she knew from Jehal's court.

The man with the white face and the eyes of blood nodded solemnly. One of the others prodded her.

We have preserved her. Three voices in her head speaking together, the same words at the same time, discordant and cacophonous. One was the voice she'd heard before, she was certain of that. The silver man. The others . . . she had no idea. Couldn't even guess. *She is the speaker-queen.*

The Taiytakei stopped. They stared at her.

"That can't be. Are you sure?"

Yes. The white face drew closer and the voices inside her separated, became more intimate. *And you desired life, so life you have received.*

Unwise.

You have made a debt.

A responsibility.

Why would we?

Where is the spear?

She tried to sit up. Her muscles ached and complained but did as they were told. The horizon sprang into view, rocking slowly from side to side, disorientating. She could feel the deck of the ship moving underneath her. There were at least a dozen Taiytakei gathered around her and more nearby. The silver man with the white face wasn't alone either. There were three of them. At least that explained the voices. *Where am I? What happened to me?* She glanced over the side, looking for her dead dragon to remind her that all this was real, except it wasn't there. *Because it sank beneath the waves. Great Flame, am I going mad? Am I dead?*

"I am Quai'Shu." One of the Taiytakei reached out a hand to her. His hair was white and thin, his dark face wrinkled. His hands were knobbly skin and bone. The arm he held out to her was shaking. He looked frail and insubstantial enough that a good gust of wind would pick him up off his feet and throw him off the ship.

Zafir still held the knife she'd used to cut herself free. She reached out to accept the offer of help with her other hand and rose shakily to her feet. Behind her back, she gripped the blade. A cautious thought stopped her doing anything rash: the memory of the dragon beneath her, snuffed out like you might snuff out a candle. She might take this one and hold a knife to his throat and then what?

"What do you want?" she hissed.

"Dragons, Your Holiness," said the old man. My, but it had been a long time since anyone had called her that. Certainly Tichane hadn't. He'd called her lots of other things, but never that. He was probably dead now, and she was glad. Underneath he'd had all the spite of Jehal and almost none of the charm.

"You can't just *take* dragons!" Zafir almost laughed. What were they going to do? Sail off with a hatchling in the hold? She steadied herself. She'd seen ships from afar when she'd been to Furymouth. They were always there, out in the harbor, the Taiytakei. Wheedling and begging and poking and prodding and trying to get closer to the one thing they wanted. Everything ached, but in front of the old man she felt strong again. The Taiytakei sailors wore thin open shirts and short skirts and not one of them held a weapon. "And when they hatch, to eat you or burn you or both, how will you control them?" She was a dragon-queen, who lived and flew and commanded monsters. Armed when they were not. She would cut through them like dragon-fire.

She staggered slightly, catching herself as the pitching of the deck caught her unawares. One ankle was still weak from her duel with Lystra. Stupid girl.

Quai'Shu smiled at her. "As you do, Your Holiness. With your alchemy."

"No alchemist would ever sell you their secrets."

He nodded. "We have taken one of your alchemists. We know your secrets." He cocked his head. As he did, she caught sight of a white silk strip knotted to his belt. There was a black one next to it, and others besides. The golden dragons. Jehal's wedding gift. They must have been planning this even then. Her lips drew back. She snarled at him. "Valmeyan? He gave you the dragon eggs from Jehal's eyrie, I know that much. Did he give you an alchemist as well? What did you give him?"

The old Taiytakei looked sad for a moment. "He wanted to build an empire. We gave him you, Your Holiness."

"But I am not yours to give," she hissed. "Take your eggs and burn!" She had her knife in front of her now, sweeping through the air toward his neck before she'd finished speaking. The Taiytakei seemed rooted to the spot.

NO!

The knife turned to dust in her hand and puffed away. Zafir lost her balance. She stumbled across the deck and almost fell.

Quai'Shu looked at her sadly. "I did not expect anything better," he sighed and turned his back on her. "Whoever she is, you can get rid of her now. Turn her inside out or something."

"Her life is ours. Do you presume to take it, Quai'Shu?" The voices of the silver sorcerers startled Zafir. The words came from three mouths at once. Aloud they still spoke as one, in a harmony that was almost musical yet still as twisted and discordant as it had felt in her head. The old man hesitated. Paused. Didn't move, didn't turn back, but for an instant he froze.

Zafir leapt at him again. They'd disintegrated the knife in her hand, but she still had the one in her other boot. This time an invisible force slapped her away. She stumbled back, lost her balance and fell to the deck.

"Do with her as you wish." The silver men dispersed into glittering mist and drifted up into the air. She followed them with her eyes toward the other dragons she'd brought with her from the Pinnacles, ridden by her three most trusted riders. They now hung motionless, frozen in the sky as though time, for them, had stopped. The silver mists reached them and seemed to whisper in the dragons' ears. Even the Taiytakei seemed transfixed, watching the alien sorcerers ascend to the sky.

The old Taiytakei turned now, looked at her. He was still shaking, but it was only his age, not nerves. Or maybe it was suppressed laughter. Another one, taller, younger, but still skinny and frail-looking whispered in his ear. The old man frowned. Shrugged. Then nodded. Smiled, looked at Zafir, looked at the other man again and nodded once more. Then he turned and walked slowly away across the deck. The second Taiytakei stepped toward her. His eyes ran over her, carefully and methodically. He smiled at her, all greed and desire. "A queen from the land of dragons. You will fetch a fine price."

One sight of the look in his eye and she knew what was on his mind. What was on the mind of most men when they saw her. She wasn't sure whether it made her want to laugh or cry. *Men. You're all so pathetically predictable.* Slowly, laboriously, she pushed herself back to her feet. The old Taiytakei was gone now, vanished off the deck. The younger one turned his back to her for a moment, gesturing, shouting words she didn't understand at the sailors around him. For one bizarre moment she found herself thinking of Jehal. Missing him. At least he'd made no pretence of being anything else. At least, until Evenspire, he'd lived up to his promise.

She palmed the other boot-knife up her sleeve. Sailors were coming over now. She watched the Taiytakei who thought he owned her and clasped a hand to her breast. His eyes tracked the movement. She saw them glint, but he didn't move.

"Hold her."

The first sailor reached out and grabbed her. She jumped straight at him, knocking him back. The sailor gave a yelp of surprise and let go. For a moment she was free. She had no doubt about what came next. The whole world narrowed down to the one Taiytakei who presumed to own her. To own a dragon-queen. She sprang at him and knocked him over and they fell, locked together. By the time they hit the deck she had the knife back out of her sleeve and was busy stabbing him.

"Not." Stab. "Yours." Stab. "To give!" Stab. Flecks of spittle flew from the corners of her mouth. Bodies piled on top of her—one, two, a dozen maybe—trying to pin her down and hold her still. She stabbed a few of them too, and then something hit her arm and her hand went limp and a moment after that the whole ship got up and hit her around the head.

She wondered, briefly, why she hadn't dived into the sea to drown instead of killing the Taiytakei. But that last moment of clarity didn't last long enough to give her an answer, and then everything was loud and black.

43

OVER

Jehal and his dragons reached Clifftop in the middle of the day. Even from a distance, he could see it wasn't worth the bother of landing. Everything was in ruins. The tower was a pile of blackened rubble. The rest was wiped away. Gone. He circled the remains of his eyrie three times in case Zafir had left anyone alive, but no one came out. Perhaps they had the sense not to show themselves when dragon-riders were about, but Jehal suspected it had more to do with them all being dead. Alchemists, servants, Scales, the lot. Zafir was like that. Nothing if not thorough.

A pall of smoke hung over Furymouth, but the city was largely untouched. The Veid Palace was burning. Zafir had been thorough there too. A few of the towers survived as gutted shells. The racing circus in the field outside was still there, Vishmir's Column and the giant bronze dragon of Gorgutinnin too. As for the rest . . . Well, the city was still there. An unexpected kindness that. Palaces and eyries could be rebuilt. Cities were a little harder. The harbor was gone, the whole Taiytakei quarter with it. Some of the bigger buildings were still recognizable. The Paratheus, one or two others. Most of the docks were a burned husk, everything reduced to charred skeletons and rubble. There was no smoke down by the sea and the ash was cold and dead. Old work. Meteroa's leaving present for the Taiytakei.

No sign of Zafir, but then he'd hardly expected to find her waiting for him. When he landed and sent his riders into the city, the news they brought back made little sense. Dragons had come, a handful, no more. They'd burned his palace and then gone out to sea toward the fleet of Taiytakei ships that had arrived only days before. A dragon had fallen out of the sky and sunk beneath the waves. Zafir's? No one could say. And then later that day, as the tide turned, the ships had sailed away and the last three dragons had gone with them. Maybe Zafir had been on the back of one of them, maybe not. He supposed, if he flew far and fast enough, he might catch up with the ships and burn them, but really what was the point? Zafir was gone. Despite what Meteroa had done, the Taiytakei had got what they wanted. They had dragons now. As far as Jehal was concerned, they were welcome to the cursed creatures. Let them be the ones to burn when the monsters awoke. If she was still alive, they were welcome to Zafir too. He wasn't sure which was worse.

The thought came, and with it, still, a pang of regret.

He left Wraithwing at the edge of the city and limped with some of his riders a little way into its streets. He couldn't remember the last time he'd done that. A dozen years ago and probably more, in a heavy disguise, trying to evade his father's guards as much as any of his own people. After that they flew away. Out into the Raksheh, where no one would find them. One more night of freedom. Out to the little eyrie by the Moonlight Garden and the Yamuna Falls and the Aardish Caves, where Vishmir's ashes had been hidden. Somewhere here, if you believed the stories, was the Silver King's Black Mausoleum. *If* you believed the stories.

"It's finished," he told Lystra as night began to fall and they held on to each other, watching the stars gleam into existence overhead. "Zafir's gone. Valmeyan is dead. Tichane is dead. They're all gone. The war's over." *And I'm still alive.* Rather to his surprise, what mattered more was that his queen and his son were still alive, that his city was still alive. Pity it had left him a cripple. From the look of things, he'd be in pain and chewing Dreamleaf for the rest of his life.

He shrugged to himself. Could have been worse.

Lystra glanced at little Calzarin, wrapped tight between them, snoring and snuffling softly. "Do you really want to name him after your brother?" she said after a moment or two of silence.

"No." Jehal wasn't sure when he'd realized that, but he knew it to be true. "I don't. I want to call him Vishmir."

His wife held his hand and squeezed it. "It's not really finished, is it?"

"Oh, let Hyrkallan have the Adamantine Throne. Now that I know what it's like, he's welcome to it." *I could let it go if I had to. Couldn't I?* It certainly hadn't been what he'd hoped it would be, back when he'd set out to take it. Ancestors, but that seemed such a long time ago. He stretched and winced. There simply wasn't a way to make his leg comfortable. "Let him deal with the rogue dragons. Him and the alchemists. I'm sure they'll find a way. We can live here by the sea. Just the two of us."

"The two of us and about a thousand servants."

"Yes. In a palace that we haven't built yet." He chuckled. "It's not going to be easy, you know. Zafir and Valmeyan probably looted the treasury. We have a palace to build and an eyrie too, no money, and I can't see the Taiytakei coming back in a hurry after what my uncle did to them." *Not now they've got what they want.* His voice trailed away. *I'm going to miss you, old schemer. Who do I hatch my plans with now?* He looked at Lystra and smiled. *Certainly not you.*

He almost didn't leave in the morning. It would have been easy to go back to his city and start building, right there and then. Let Hyrkallan and Sirion and Jeiros and perhaps even the Night Watchman live in peace. Let them worry about dragons on the rampage in the north.

"We've got no alchemists though," he whispered to Wraithwing as he climbed up onto the dragon's back. "Don't want you getting frisky on me. Don't think that would be much fun." He wrenched his crippled leg into the saddle, gritting his teeth at the pain. The legbreaker had lived up to its name. His voice dropped to a whisper. "And for better or for worse, I'm still the speaker."

44

SAND

S *and. This one is called Sand.*

Another city of the north filled with little ones. An oasis surrounded by nothing. The same vast rivers flowed out of the Worldspine and slowly died in the sun until they expired in the desert of salt, but the river here still ran strong. Not a city that could be starved and strangled. A city that met them with stones and scorpions. Brave but futile.

They flew in circles around the city walls, pouring fire inside it, building a whirling storm of flames, an inferno with a life of its own. Nothing was allowed to leave. It took a day, and then they stopped while the flames burned on and on, licking at the skeletons of stone that remained, searching for food. Some of the humans had sought shelter underground. Snow could feel their thoughts. She listened curiously as the few survivors slowly cooked to death in their cellars. The dragons didn't feed here. They were already fat.

When the city was dead, they turned to the eyrie beside it. The little ones had long since disappeared deep under the ground. What would burn was burned. What could be crushed or smashed was ground to dust. When there was nothing left to do, they let Silence and the other hatchlings loose in the tunnels that remained. In Bloodsalt they had freed younglings and found eggs. Silence had carried them out, one by one, and the dragons had taken them and cradled them and stolen them away into whatever dark hidden places they could find. Here Snow already knew it would be different. There were no dragon thoughts. This was like Out-watch. Hatchlings all poisoned. Eggs smashed. Nothing left.

The dragons splashed around in the Last River, cooling themselves.

They don't try to fight. They know we are here. Everything is poisoned.

No matter.

When one dies, another is born.

Eggs are easily made.

They hide in their holes.

They spawn like insects.

We will never be rid of them.

Where next?

Where next?

They were looking to her, Snow realized. Another city, not far away. A day of flying. And then . . . And then the thrill of what was coming threatened to overwhelm her.

Evenspire, brothers and sisters. The blemish you feel is called Evenspire and we will burn it. And then to the mountains and over the other side. To the city they name after us. The palace where their kings claim to rule. The heart of their land.

They would free as many as they could. And then . . .

The Spear of the Earth. We will take it. We will face our makers.

And then? The makers?

They left this world. It is ours.

A roar of thoughts lifted her up. Fire. Fire and burning and flames. Nothing more and nothing less.

Where next to conquer?

45

THE PINNACLES

At the end of his second day hanging upside down thousands of feet over a plain full of dead dragons, Jeiros felt strangely alive. His ankles and his wrists hurt like a nail in the head, but the rest wasn't nearly as bad as he'd thought it would be. Still horrible, but not as excruciating as he'd imagined. The weather had been kind to him, perhaps that was it. Another day of blistering sun and he'd probably have been dead; instead, the clouds had come in along with a pleasantly cool breeze and then the skies had opened. The first downpour had turned into a steady rain that had lasted for most of the afternoon. Water dripped and ran down his face and into his mouth. No, he certainly couldn't complain about being thirsty or of wilting in the sun. Being soaked through would probably kill him once night fell, but so far it could have been worse.

He looked down at the ground far below. You couldn't see much of it anymore. The rain had hissed and fizzed off the dragons until the valley was filled with a warm mist. The rain had been a blessing for everyone really. The fires in the city had gone out. The dead dragons hadn't ignited the plains grass. The rabble had been too busy with their own misery to get organized enough to storm the Fortress of Watchfulness. And the grand master alchemists of the realms was still alive. For the moment.

Yes, could have been a lot worse, and for now he was happy to take whatever he could get. He'd done what needed to be done. In the next few months the realms as he knew them would disappear. Did he really want to see that? Probably not.

Unless, unless . . .

The business with Vioros and the spear and the dragons turned to stone wouldn't let him go. How had the sell-sword brought the spear to life, made it *speak* to him? What in the name of all the gods he'd never believed in was in that thing? And why had it awoken now? Why had it never spoken to *him*? But there was no point spending his last few hours cursing a piece of metal. He could have done more, but Vioros would have to do it now. Others could take up the mantle. *Like I did when Bellepheros vanished.*

Yes, it was comforting to think that, given where he was. Although, if he was honest with himself, it would have been nice to at least have a little glimpse into the future. See whether he'd done enough. See whether the realms would regrow from the ashes.

No, if he was *really* honest with himself, it would have been nice to be sitting in a comfy chair somewhere with a roof over his head, with a nice glass of wine and a good book, wrists and ankles intact and a vastly less agoraphobia-inducing view. *That's* what would have been nice. He sighed. Maybe he shouldn't have felt so grateful to the weather. What was the point thanking the rain when all it did was prolong his misery?

He looked around. Pointless really, since all he could see below was mist, but he did it anyway. It gave the muscles in his neck something to do. Water dripped out of his hair into his eyes. He blinked.

And then he blinked again. He could see specks in the distant sky, dark flecks against the brooding evening clouds. For a few seconds not being able to rub his eyes was suddenly the most irritating thing in the world. Then the specks grew bigger and he knew he wasn't imagining them. They were coming from the south. Too many to be Zafir. Too many to be the rogue white . . .

Jehal.

He felt a sudden surge of . . . something. Hope? Anxiety? Fear? None of those made any sense, since Jehal couldn't really do anything worse than Hyrkallan had already done, and wasn't likely to do much better either. But the surge came anyway. *That's what comes of being a man, I suppose. There's always hope, even if it doesn't make the remotest jot of sense.*

The dragons came closer. They circled high over the Pinnacles, something like a hundred of them, he thought. *Why doesn't he land at the eyrie?* That was easy to answer. *Because of the mist.*

A few dragons started to spiral slowly toward the huge open yard in the middle of the fortress where perhaps six or seven could land, and Jeiros' mind raced. Hope was a stupid and foolish thing but it had him firmly in its grasp. He wanted to live. Very, very badly.

"Hey! Hello!" *Why am I shouting? Who's going to hear me? Men up there on dragons? Don't be daft. Perhaps whichever alchemist came to me yesterday? Because obviously, what with Hyrkallan howling murder on all of us, he'll have nothing better to do than sit on the walls somewhere behind me for a couple of days in case I have any last messages to send.*

Sure enough, no one answered. He couldn't even wave his hands, tied as they were to the wheel. The dragons were close enough that he started to recognize them. Wraithwing—Jehal's own—leading the way. *He has no idea what's happened here. Hyrkallan's going to kill him in a blink and take his dragons. Which would be the right thing, wouldn't it? Best for the realms. Give them the leader they're going to need in the times to come. Or do I really believe what I said to Hyrkallan?*

His heart was inclined to the latter. Hard to root for a man who'd strung you up to die.

The dragons didn't land straightaway. Rather, they made several passes over and around the fortress. *Wondering where everyone is, no doubt.* One of the riders flew right past him, looked straight at him. Jeiros tried to waggle his hands. Completely futile and hurt as if he'd set fire to himself, but he did it anyway. He shook his head and shouted, incoherently at first and then warnings. "Danger! Danger!" *Why? Why warn them? Don't I want them to land? Don't I want them on the ground so what's left of us can put an end to a few more dragons while we still can?*

At last two dragons swooped toward the middle of the fortress. He didn't see them land but he felt it, the shock of the impacts trembling the whole mountain, setting his wheel swinging very slightly from side to side on its rope. Moments passed. He thought he heard voices raised. Then one of the dragons still in the air lurched, twisted and shot toward the fortress and belched fire. Jeiros twisted his head as far as it would go but he couldn't see anything except the dragons dancing in the sky and the outer walls of the fortress. He saw a second dragon swoop, and then another one gave out an angry shriek.

Scorpions. Hyrkallan was firing scorpions.

He found, with a bit of wriggling, he could make the wheel swing from side to side. Not much, but enough that whenever it swung to the left he could see a little more of what was happening. Three dragons were on the ground now, roaring and stomping. He could feel their footfalls, tiny tremors that reached out and made his fingers tingle. A fourth dragon came down, and then a fifth and then finally Wraithwing and Jehal. Which had to mean that Hyrkallan had been driven back into the depths of the fortress and the tunnels that riddled the mountain. Trapped.

Jeiros began to giggle.

Time passed. He wasn't sure how much. Too much. He tried shouting again, but no one came. The top of the fortress fell quiet. Hope, ever fickle, began to trickle away.

"Hey there, Grand Master! Are you still alive out there?"

Jehal. Jeiros couldn't help himself. He wept. He tried to speak but found he could only croak.

"I know exactly what you did to get yourself strung up like this. I've got one of your people here. Very keen to tell me all about it. I think he thinks I'm going to cut you down. Have to say I'm quite tempted to leave you there and push your little friend here off the edge. I can quite see Hyrkallan's point, you know. If you murdered my dragons, I dare say I'd be more than a little put out."

"It was . . ." Cursed voice. Angrily Jeiros hacked and coughed. It didn't help much. "It was for the good . . ." *The good of the realms,* that's what he was trying to say. The rest came out as an angry grating sound.

"What was that? I can't hear you."

Jeiros tried again.

"Nope. Still can't. Look, I don't think I can ask my riders to fly around in circles all night while I get some sleep, and I'm not sure this is the best place for that anyway. Shall I come back in the morning?"

"Nargh!" The worst of it was that he couldn't even see Jehal. He was hanging with his feet toward the fortress and he couldn't twist his head enough. He could almost *feel* Jehal turn and walk away. *Bastard.* Then the crane started to move. He had a moment of panic at first, thinking they were dropping him into the void below. Then an absurd sense of joy.

They swung him in slowly then lowered the wheel and turned it over so that Jeiros was staring up at the sky. Up at the man he'd made speaker.

"Oh dear, look at you." Jehal wore his usual sneer of practiced disdain. "If I let you go, are you going to kill my dragons too, Jeiros? Honestly now. Please don't lie."

Jeiros bit his tongue. The right answer was obvious. No. His lips shaped to say it.

"Honestly now." Jehal's expression didn't flicker, but there was something hard in his eyes. A fierceness that hadn't been there a few weeks ago.

"Only if I have to."

Jehal frowned. "Well that's not the answer I was looking for. A simple no would have gone down much better." He sighed.

"You asked . . . for honesty."

"So I did. And you did help me after Shezira tried to un-man me. I suppose that should count for something."

"I saved your life," Jeiros croaked. Jehal snorted.

"Oh I don't know about *that*." He put his hands on his hips and struck a pose. His weight was all on one leg and he looked like an idiot, but he was presumably long past caring what a mere alchemist thought of him. "But since Hyrkallan put you there and since he's such a tedious arse . . ." He made a cutting gesture. Jeiros winced as hands touched his wrists. "If you *do* ever want to kill my dragons, Grand Master, I'd appreciate it if we could have a little chat about it first, eh?"

46

LONG LIVE THE KING

Jehal leaned against a well near the edge of the Adamantine Eyrie. Jeiros sat with his back to it, his useless legs stretched out on the muddy ground. Finding chairs for two cripples was proving to be a problem.

"The trouble with dragons," Jehal mused, "is never the monsters themselves." Keeping the weight off his damaged leg was making his back stiff. It was tempting to sit in the dirt with Jeiros, but that wasn't what a speaker should do. Wasn't what a grand master alchemist should do either, for that matter, but Jeiros didn't have much of a choice. He'd be lucky to ever walk again. "The trouble always comes from the people who ride on the back of them." Jehal's leg hurt whatever he did with it, a steady throbbing that never went away. The alchemists would have something for that, now they were here. Herbs, potions, anything, something that was stronger than Dreamleaf. He watched wearily as the last of his riders came in to land. The sky above the Mirror Lakes was a deep gray, like the slate roofs of the city. Evening rain clouds, carried up by the wind from the Raksheh and the sea beyond.

Eventually Eyrie-Master Copas conjured up a litter from somewhere. Jehal climbed in, slowly and laboriously. Jeiros sat beside him, lifted in by two of the bearers. The alchemist didn't say anything and his eyes were closed. Most probably he was asleep.

"We could have flown all through the night, straight from the Pinnacles, and been here in the morning, bright and early. The dragons wouldn't have minded. I know they don't much like flying in the dark but they'll do it if you tell them. No, it's the riders. Needing sleep and food and rest and to empty their bowels. We lost the whole day." He prodded Jeiros and waved a pouch of Dreamleaf at him. "Can dragons fly forever? Do they actually need to rest at all? Does anyone know?"

Jeiros had a faraway look, either because his thoughts had been miles away or because he really had been asleep. "No. And yes and yes." He took a pinch of leaf and started to chew on it. "We did experiments on that sort of thing a long time ago. They don't exactly wear out. But if they don't rest and eat and drink, then eventually they overheat and then they burn up from the inside and die." His eyes came into focus on Jehal's face. "The trouble with dragons, Jehal, is that they exist."

Jehal. Not *Your Holiness,* just *Jehal.* After all they'd been through he couldn't hold it against the alchemist. He watched the dragons. They were hungry and irritable and were tearing with zeal into the terrified animals that the Scales had herded out of their pens. Those like Wraithwing who'd sated themselves were already curled up to rest. "They *do* make a mess."

"A mess? Pray we don't see what a mess they make." Jeiros stretched and then winced. Every movement was pain. Jehal knew how he felt. *Look at us. A pair of cripples.* "We should have wiped them out when we had the chance. It took a sorcerer, a true half-god sorcerer. Thousands and thousands of people died. Probably tens of thousands. We gave ourselves up with the poison in our veins. We killed them and we tamed them and we hunted out their nests and smashed their eggs. Perhaps we could have destroyed them. But no. We tamed them. We thought we were so clever." He spat bitterly. "Why did you keep me alive, Jehal? All I want to do now is kill every dragon here."

"Yes, well you won't be doing that just yet. I kept you alive because you kept me alive. Besides, the realms need their alchemists whether I like it or not." *And let's not forget that you're probably the one person who'll stop the Night Watchman sticking my head on a spike the moment I hobble through the palace gates. But we won't mention that, eh?*

"They won't thank you for it."

"Yes, yes. The apocalypse is coming. Tell me, Jeiros, because it's been bothering me for months, this potion of yours—why don't you just make more?"

"If only it was so easy. Truth is we've never been able to make quite enough. We get by. Now and then, when there is a strong speaker, we have a quiet cull, spread over two or three years. We don't tell the kings and queens, just let them think it's some sort of disease. It goes by unnoticed. We did it with Vishmir, Ayzalmir, a few others. So then most of the dragons are hatchlings, and we can stockpile potion. As they grow into adults, we very slowly start to run out. In time we have to do it again. The rogues who attacked the Redoubt didn't affect what we could make, but they destroyed what we had stored. Ruined the lot. And then there was the war. The Red Riders. Evenspire." He wrinkled his nose.

Jehal waited. "You didn't actually answer my question," he said.

Jeiros actually laughed. "I won't tell you what goes into it, Speaker. Even Vioros doesn't know that. Outside those who actually live in those caves, there are three of us who know, and only because we've done it ourselves. I've made that potion, Jehal. It's simple enough. There's just one thing that goes into it that matters, but that one thing . . ." He shook his head. "We bleed for it, Jehal, we alchemists, and if our blood was all that mattered we would bleed ourselves dry. Only then there would be no more alchemists. Some harvests only yield what they yield and there is simply nothing more to be done." He laughed again. "Perhaps we should have bled ourselves to death for the rest of you. Perhaps we have. Not that it would make any difference."

Jehal shrugged. "Look on the bright side—when it happens, whatever *it* is, maybe no one will live long enough to form an opinion on how much of it is actually your fault." *Or mine.*

"Your indifference is touching." Jeiros looked at his feet. Bent and useless. Someone had put splints on him, but ankles smashed like that would never set right.

"And your relentless gloom is relentlessly tedious." The litter lurched into motion, heading toward the eyrie gates. Jehal cast his gaze around, looking for his wife and the carriage she'd promised to find for him to take him up the hill to the palace. Riding dragons was one thing. Riding horses was a pleasure he had to leave to others now. No great loss. They were dull, stupid, uninspiring creatures. *A bit like most of the lords I have to look forward to now that I'm home.* Yes, that was a much more cheery thought. *Hyrkallan and Sirion trapped in the Pinnacles without a dragon between them. Shezira's other daughters with them. Valmeyan and Tichane dead. Zafir most likely dead too. Let's face it, who's left? Silvallan is probably shitting bricks wondering whether he's next. At this rate I'll have to invite the Syuss back to the council. They'll have more dragons than any of the rest of us soon.* Another little nugget to chew on. The Syuss had always hated Hyram. They'd hated Antros and Shezira and Valgar. The names were different now, but the hate would still be there. With a bit of prodding and stirring all manner of troubles might arise there. Played right the north could be a lot of fun in the years to come. *But that can wait. When you tidy your house, you start with the bits you actually live in. First things first. Vale Tassan here I come. Say one thing for dragons: once you're on the back of one, it doesn't matter how much of a cripple you are. Boy, woman, man, half-man, put us on a dragon and none of that matters. What matters is that the monster obeys. When that happens, we become gods.*

The litter stopped. Jehal tumbled out, catching himself with his staff, and hobbled toward Lystra and his waiting carriage. He and Jeiros would each deal with their own rogues. A fair and equitable arrangement.

As he limped closer, soldiers on horseback converged on the carriage. Adamantine Men. For a moment his heart missed a beat, but when they drew their swords, it was to salute him. *So Vale knows I'm coming. I suppose it's probably easier to kill me in the palace than down here. Too many witnesses . . .*

The carriage door flew open. Lystra threw her arms around his neck, almost strangling him. His bad leg buckled. For an instant it seemed he would fall, dragging her out of the carriage to roll around in the mud. A fine sight that would have been—the speaker and his queen grappling in the dirt—but she had enough strength to pull him in instead. He half sat, half fell on the seat beside her.

She smiled at him, eyes wide with excitement. "Do you know I've never been here. Not since I was a little girl. You have to show me everything. There must be so many marvelous—"

He shut her up by kissing her, which still usually worked. *So many marvelous things. Yes. Pity that most of them want to kill me.* In a pause for breath he glanced out the window. The still waters of the Mirror Lakes lay dull and flat under the evening sky. Behind them the City of Dragons sat in a shimmer of mist. Her towers sparkled, painted in silver and gold. *Money, opulence, decadence, too much of all of them. My kind of place.*

Behind the haze of the city, the half-seen cliffs of the Purple Spur rose into the twilight. Somewhere above and beyond them, in the gaps between the clouds, the first stars of the evening twinkled. The sky. Closeted up in a carriage was no way to travel.

Although it did have *some* advantages, as Lystra soon showed him, and he almost didn't notice when they rolled to a halt inside the palace gates twenty minutes later. He was still smoothing down his shirt as the door opened to reveal two lines of Adamantine Men formed up to greet him. Two lines and one man in the middle, bowing precisely as low as he should to greet the Speaker of the Realms. The *speaker,* Jehal noted, not a king. Interesting.

"Vale Tassan. What a pleasure to see you again." Jehal stood up, wincing. Behind him Lystra gathered herself together with an embarrassed little cough.

The Night Watchman straightened. "Your Holinesses. The palace is in order." There were men everywhere, Jehal began to see. Soldiers on all the walls. Scorpions packed together as closely as they would go. Even scorpions down in the Gateyard, trained up at the sky.

"You've been busy."

Vale bowed again. "While the speaker is away, it is my duty to defend against any invader."

"Ah. Just so we're both clear and there are no misunderstandings, do I count as a speaker or as an invader or as both?"

The Night Watchman didn't twitch. "You are the speaker until the Lesser Council says otherwise. Or another is chosen by the council of kings and queens."

Jehal snorted. "Well there's a distinct shortage of both of those at the moment so I wouldn't hold your breath." He grimaced and hauled himself down the steps of the carriage, then walked toward the Speaker's Tower, leaning heavily on his staff.

"Your leg seems worse, Your Holiness."

"I fell off a dragon and hung there for a little while. It did me no favors."

"I will have one of my physicians sent to you."

"If he has a fine collection of spare legs and is able to replace this with a new one that has not previously been shot through by a large crossbow then, please, as soon as you can. Otherwise I really wouldn't bother."

"As you wish." Nothing. As always, the man gave away nothing. *He could be seconds away from killing me or he could loyally serve me for a decade. It could be either and I'd never know which was coming.* And that alone was a good enough reason to get rid of him.

"I have a job for you, Night Watchman. An order. One that should suit you very well."

Vale said nothing. He looked straight ahead, keeping perfect pace with Jehal. He didn't look tense at all. He didn't look much of anything except ready. But ready for what?

"Well don't you want to know what it is?"

"I exist to serve, Your Holiness. That is what I am for, and my men with me. From birth—"

"To death. The guard obeys orders. Nothing more, nothing less. I've heard that so many times, Vale, and I have yet to believe it. So now I mean to put it to the test. I want you to go, right now, with as many of your men as you deem necessary. I want you to find the rogue dragons that Jeiros is fretting about and I want you to kill them for me. Is that something you can do?"

Vale licked his lips. "Unlikely, Your Holiness. But if that is your wish, I will do my utmost. If that is my fate, I will succeed. If not, I will die in the attempt."

"Yes, please. Do you think you could succeed and then die of your wounds afterward?"

"Jehal!" He'd forgotten Lystra, padding silently behind them. Jehal turned and flashed her a smile.

"A little joke, my love. Vale, you're still here. I believe I gave you an order."

"And I will obey, Your Holiness. Indeed, I have already embarked upon your mission." They were drawing close to the Speaker's Tower. Its doors remained shut. The soldiers on either side made no move to open them. Jehal felt a sharp twinge of fear in his belly. *Here it comes. The knife.*

"The doors to my tower appear to be closed, Night Watchman, and your men are not opening them. Should I be concerned?"

"Yes, your Holiness. Yes, you should." Vale gestured toward the Glass Cathedral. "This would be a better place."

Jehal didn't move.

"The tunnels, Your Holiness. For you and your queen and your son. You will be safe there."

"What?"

"You'll hardly recognize them. If all does not go well, I dare say there are enough supplies for you and your household to last for some time. Months, perhaps."

"What are you talking about?" The twinge of fear was turning into something more.

Vale took a deep breath and sighed. For once he turned to face Jehal and looked him in the eye. For once he looked tired. "There is a cage, Jehal. You can hang me in it if you want to, or perhaps I'll hang you, but either will be a cause for celebration because it will mean we have survived. It will mean we are alive. It will mean it still matters. I don't need to go anywhere to follow your orders. I am as ready as I can be. I have taken dragon poison and so have all my men. Up on the peaks by the Diamond Cascade are some thirty dragons and not one of them with a rider. One is white." He gave a bitter laugh. "They've been there for two days. I can only assume it's you they're waiting for. And now you are here." He turned briefly to look at Lystra. "Unless I am mistaken, the realms of the north are gone, Your Holiness. I am sorry." Then back to Jehal. "Go to the Glass Cathedral. You will be looked after. I have done everything I can."

His face said the rest. Everything wasn't enough. Not by a very long way. Jehal felt numb.

"I have always kept lookouts on the edge of the Spur, Your Holiness. They are there to watch for dragons. Any who might threaten the city. They signal to me with mirrors, or with smoke and fire. They are still there. I think the dragons have chosen to let them live. They want us to know they are coming." He bowed, and for a moment looked old and tired. "Take what pleasure you can from the night, Your Holiness. In the morning they will come."

47

NIGHTFALL

Snow watched the dragons fly into the eyrie below. Such a number, she'd felt them coming from a hundred miles away and more. So had the others arrayed on the mountainsides around her.

Finally.

More to free.

A hundred.

More.

Excitement coursed through her. The other dragons felt the same.

We should wait.

Night comes.

Daylight is better.

But they were dragons, and so they tried and they tried but in the end they couldn't wait. When one kicked itself into the air and spread its wings, the others followed in an instant, glad and gleeful. They fell through the air, looping and dancing through the spray of the Diamond Cascade until the City of Dragons rushed up to meet them.

They spread their wings and opened their mouths. Not like the other cities, this one. They had a fury inside them now, one that had been building up for two days on the mountainsides. For a week since they'd begun at Outwatch. For a thousand years and more since they'd last flown as a horde against an enemy who could actually fight them. They tore into the city, burning, smashing, clambering over walls, lashing towers to the ground, crushing houses underfoot, pouring fire through doors and windows and arches, savaging anything that crossed their path.

Don't eat! Don't eat! But the urge was irresistible. The rage had them hard, and when men and women ran screaming, it was impossible not to snatch them up with claw or tail and crush them and smash them and bite them in two and taste their blood. The city burned. Its flesh was delicious.

And then the scorpions began.

HE SAW THEM COME. HE was the Night Watchman, and seeing them come was the point of his being. It was hard to know whether the end of the world that was falling toward him was all Jehal's fault or only mostly Jehal's fault. But in the final reckoning it hardly mattered. He could almost have thanked Jehal, in a perverse way, for making this come to pass. It was the whole point of his existence, of every one of the Adamantine Men around him, of everyone who had gone before, the whole point of all of that was right here, right now, right in front of him.

He watched the City of Dragons burn. *Patience.* Patience was a weapon. Patience was the one thing he had that his enemy could barely understand. The city died and Vale watched. Tens of thousands of people. He supposed that others would expect him to feel something about that, some sort of sadness or regret, but that missed the point. That wasn't his job. *Let Jeiros weep and wring his hands for his beautiful city. I am the dragon-killer. No compassion, no mercy, no compromise. I am like them, but more.*

The dragons were falling prey to their own passions. He could see it by the way they cavorted. They were ripping people out of their homes and eating them for the sheer fun of it. All good. *A pity I couldn't poison the whole city. I would have, if there had been a way.* He'd already poisoned everything in the Adamantine Eyries. He and Vioros had seen to that long before Jehal returned. Vioros had seen to something else too, something that made Vale know his destiny was here.

When he thought they were ready, he gave the order to fire. The dragons were too far away for the scorpions to pick their targets, but they made up for that in other ways. Sheer numbers for a start.

Then he picked up the Adamantine Spear and went to wait outside.

*   *   *

STEEL RAIN FELL ACROSS THE city. Bolts as long as a man fell almost straight out of the sky. They smashed through roofs and floors and buried themselves in cellar walls. They punched through chimneys and shattered flagstones. Here and there they struck dragons with enough force to drive straight through scales and deep into the muscles beneath. Dragons already teetering on the brink of battle lust dived headlong into it with a mad joy. Snow felt them roar with pain and then with merciless delight. *At last a proper fight.* She jumped into the air and spread her wings to be with them, powering up out of the smoke of the burning city toward the palace. *Where I'm supposed to be.* The eyrie could wait. Everything else could wait. It was wrong. They were being lured, pulled into a trap, but she didn't even try to resist. There was no point. Why try to fight what you were created to be?

A second hail of metal spears fell around her. Two pierced her wings and passed straight through. A third struck her in the back, close to her tail. It hurt a lot more than the scorpions she remembered from the Worldspine. Angrily she twisted her neck and ripped the bolt out with her teeth. It snapped cleanly in two, leaving a foot of steel inside her. The pain grew suddenly worse. With a shriek she surged through the air. Poison, perhaps. Or acid. She didn't care. A few poisoned bolts wouldn't even slow her down. Wouldn't slow any of them down.

She landed on the palace walls with a force that shook mountains, scattering men and scorpions around her like sand.

VALE COULD ONLY BE IN one place at a time, so he started from the doors to the Glass Cathedral and worked from there. The palace would be destroyed. His men would be destroyed. His scorpions. He himself, most likely. None of that mattered. The dragons had to die, and that was all. Scorpions hailed overhead. The Azure Tower came crashing down, shattered lumps of stone as large as a house flying through the air. Boulders smashed against the hardened skin of the Glass Cathedral, exploding into shards, and then the earth shook beneath its feet as the first dragon landed in the Speaker's Yard itself. A huge reddish monster, it raked the walls with fire and then rose up to tear at the needle-like Tower of Air.

The spear, it seemed, was singing to him, a soft choir of voices in ancient words that he didn't understand and yet made perfect sense. He watched the dragon for a second and then another, feeling at the very last a tiny spark of what was perhaps fear, which flickered for a moment before he crushed it and ran out into the yard. No scream, no battle cry, but silent and swift, he plunged the Speaker's Spear into the dragon's leg.

The earth trembled. A blazing light lit up the night. A thousand voices roared in his head.

And the dragon turned to stone.

THE EARTHSPEAR! SNOW FELT IT, felt its roar of power, felt the death it brought. Bolts pricked her skin. Fury ripped through her. She lunged at scorpions, crushing men and their machines in her jaws. The air filled with the roar of fire, the grind of breaking stone, the rage-filled cries of dragons. She tore apart everything around her, stamped and smashed all to dust, then leapt over a wall between one part of the palace and another, lashing a tower with her tail as she went. She felt the Earthspear roar again, a second dragon die.

Where are you?

A misshapen old building, its surface glassy from some ancient heat, loomed out of the darkness and the flashes of fire. Close. She was close.

The earth shuddered as a monster twice her size crashed down onto the roof of the Glass Cathedral and slid down its sides, spraying fire all around it.

Burn!

VALE COULD BARELY HEAR HIMSELF, could barely think. There was screaming and roaring and flames everywhere. Pieces of the Tower of Air showered the walls. Men were crushed, scorpions splintered. Something crashed to earth behind him so hard it knocked him over, but before he could turn, there was another dragon, a little one this time, not much bigger than a horse, barely out of its egg. It shot out of the flames toward him, and as it opened its mouth, he rammed the spear down its throat. The light again, blinding, the noise, but as he blinked, he felt the spear ripped out of his hands as the now-statue dragon ploughed past him through the rubble and slid to a halt. He ignored the huge black thing sliding down the Glass Cathedral and bolted for the spear. A massive foot came down, crushing half the stone hatchling to rubble. He saw the spear. Then the dragon above him looked down and seemed to notice him for the first time. He lunged forward, but the great clawed foot came down again, smashing the hatchling's head into splinters and burying the spear beneath it. The impact rippled the ground and Vale staggered away.

No.

It was laughing at him.

The Earthspear! It is mine!

A volley of a dozen scorpions ripped into her flank, hard enough to almost knock her off balance. The pain, the pain was something new, something almost forgotten. It took her away, drowned everything, for a moment, except the need to smash and burn and kill and destroy.

VALE RACED STRAIGHT ACROSS THE middle of Speaker's Yard, weaving between the legs of the black dragon. Or maybe it wasn't black. Maybe it was just dark. They all looked black or gray in the moonlight and the flashing bursts of fire. It was staying where it was, burning battery after battery of scorpions, never once lifting the claws that held the Adamantine Spear trapped in the earth. He reached a ladder and hurtled up to the wall.

"Scorpions!" Fire forced his men behind their dragon-scale, but fire didn't kill. His precious scorpions were still there, behind their shields. "Load! Aim! Fire! Take it down!"

Six or seven of the weapons fired, straight into the dragon's face. The monster snatched its head away and staggered and shrieked. Keep shooting. That was all they needed to do. Nothing more. Sooner or later it would fall.

The dragon lunged, tried to jump up onto the parapet, smashed three scorpions with its fore-claws before the wall cracked and crumbled, half tipping the dragon off again. Its tail cracked like a whip along the top of the wall, shattering men and machines, flipping them high into the air. Vale winced. A dozen more destroyed, just like that. Then the dragon was gone, if only for a moment, tipped back down into the Gateyard in an earthquake of breaking stone.

Slowly, looming over their heads, the Tower of Air sheared and began to fall. The spear, though. The spear was free again!

"Scatter! Run!" When the dragons came for you with tooth and claw, that was all you could do. Scatter and run. *Draw them away from the scorpions. Our lives don't matter.* Vale took a gulp of scorched air, caught a glimpse of the rest of the palace. Dragons doing what dragons did. As he cranked the last scorpion on the Speaker's Wall, he watched one smash into the Tower of Dusk. Dragon and tower disappeared in a cloud of dust and masonry lit up from within by the dragon's fire.

There. The scorpion clicked and he reached for a bolt. The black dragon had rolled back to its feet. Adamantine Men ran in front of it, hurling futile javelins before they were crushed or burned, drawing its attention away from the walls. He could see where the spear lay. Ought to jump straight down there if his legs would take it, but he was up here on the wall now. *Draw it away. You can't hurt a dragon but a scorpion can. And we don't have enough.* He hadn't told his men that last part but it wouldn't have mattered anyway. They were Adamantine Men. They lived for this. Every one of them had drunk the dragon poison for two days now, ever since dragons had come to the Purple Spur, so most of them were as good as dead already. It all came down to how much damage they could do before they went. Vioros and the weapon of legends come to life once more, they were the only hope.

Something smashed into the wall. He didn't even see what or where, only felt the tremor. He stumbled and gripped the scorpion. The black dragon screamed and lunged at the men harrying its feet. *Try to get eaten. Fill them with poison in any way you can. Make every death into victory.*

The black had three or four soldiers in its claws. It stuffed them into its mouth and bit savagely down. Then it spat out the remains, showering the men around it with blood and gore and broken armor. For a moment it paused. Vale pivoted the scorpion around and up a notch and then shot it in the eye. He was already running when the bolt hit. He didn't bother to look back, only down.

The spear!

*   *   *

No no no NO!

She could feel the poison in her. She could feel the heat, the first warning surge inside her, and it made her want to fight even harder, to burn and smash even more. Which would make the heat worse, which would feed the rage, which would feed the heat, and on and on until everything was out of control and she burst into flames from the inside.

They couldn't be winning could they, the little ones? She half jumped, half flew up onto the broken stump of one of the smaller towers. The walls around her were breached. A few of the bigger towers were still intact, but the smaller ones were all smashed. Everything that would burn was in flames. The earth and the air trembled and thundered. A thin haze of smoke filled the night. She could see the shapes of the other dragons clear enough, but the little ones . . . The smoke hid them.

The Earthspear! She reached out for it with her thoughts. It had fallen silent, but it was near.

Yet another bolt slammed into her side. Then another. The rage flashed inside. Her head snapped around, looking for where they'd come from. But she couldn't see. Everything looked ruined or was lost in the haze.

Another bolt bounced off her head, leaving a burning scar. *We should never have come in the night.* She'd been hit by dozens now. So many she'd lost count. Little ones, little ones, she could taste their thoughts, so many, scurrying, running, but she couldn't *see* them!

She launched herself into the air. Defeat. She could taste it. Inconceivable defeat. And yet the rage drove them on and they were powerless against it. The dragons around her were all lost in the fury. It would never occur to them to stop until the fire took them.

No. Not now. Not this close. It can't be. I will not allow us to fail!

A TAIL AS THICK AS a man whipped over his head and crashed into the remnants of the Tower of Air behind him. Shards of stone flew like shrapnel; larger pieces tumbled, crushing the ruined walls around him, breaking men and metal alike. The dragons shook them off. Much of the palace was bathed in fire. Dragons out of control, out of their minds, burning up with their own rage, pouring it out on everything around them. Vale sprinted straight through the middle of them, hurdling the bodies of the fallen, the burned and the crushed. The palace was awash with the ashes of the dead. In the end metal buckled. Men were roasted and died. Even dragon-scale wasn't perfect.

He raced between the legs of a young hunter that tried to bite him and missed. *The more they burn, the more our poison will grip them.* A tail slashed across the ground, throwing up a cloud of black ash, of stone and armor. Of blackened arms and legs and torsos and heads. Vale ran under the belly of another dragon, which didn't even seem to notice he was there. He'd lost track of where the spear was, but it must be buried in bodies and rubble by now. He'd done what he could. If there were any working scorpions left on the walls, they were too few to matter now and he couldn't tell them from the mangled remains of their cousins. Most of the Adamantine Men were dead. They'd never know whether they'd died in glorious victory or in defeat.

He reached the doors of the Glass Cathedral. Walls thick enough to stand even dragons welcomed him. As he ran, the doors flew open. Behind him, a dragon turned and lunged. Vale threw himself to the ground, sliding the last yard on his belly across stones sticky with cooked blood. Behind the doors, a dozen scorpions all packed together spat out a final volley.

"Run!" he shouted. No time to load and fire again. No point in losing more men. Tomorrow's Night Watchman would need them. He tried to get back to his feet, but for once his strength failed him. He stumbled and fell in the doorway. Someone else would take the fight to the dragons after today. He'd done the best he could.

He rolled onto his back. "Come and get me!" There were sacks of poison strapped to his armor. Too much for a man to drink and survive. Enough, perhaps, to kill a dragon. And there it was, the dragon that had taken a face full of scorpion bolts, towering over him, eyes ablaze, flames licking out between its teeth, insane with fire and fury. "Come on!" he screamed at it. "Eat me!"

Its head swayed from side to side, almost mocking him, as though it could read his mind. And then, very slowly, it toppled over and crashed to the ground. Fire sputtered around it. Flames flickered on its tongue. Even through his armor Vale could feel the heat. He lay there and stared.

And I thought we were going to lose.

He started to laugh. Once he'd started, he couldn't stop.

Out of the corner of his eye he saw a single dragon, pale as a ghost in the moonlight, take to the skies and fly away.

48

✤

THE MORNING AFTER

Jehal couldn't put his finger on when the battle ended. The noise, the rumbles and thunder as the dragons smashed down the Adamantine Palace went on most of the night. He sat awake in bed, listening to it. Eventually it faded away and stopped. He might have dozed after that. He wasn't sure. Lystra slept, and he watched her. Looked at her by the light of a single tiny candle. He stroked her face and her hair, gently so as not to wake her. After a while, after the noises had stopped and everything was still, he very carefully climbed out of their bed and dressed.

"I'm sorry, my love," he whispered in her ear, "but these particular caves don't agree with me."

The caves under the Glass Cathedral were still and quiet. There were no guards on his door, none to keep him safe and none to keep him from leaving either. He hopped and hobbled through the silent tunnels. Frightened faces glanced at him and turned away. Servants, scared witless, knowing they were doomed to die down here. *But starving is better than burning, isn't it? Or is it?*

He didn't find any soldiers until he reached the stairway to the Glass Cathedral itself. Until he climbed them, one excruciating step at a time. *And at the top there's going to be a dragon waiting for me. And then what?* He didn't know. What he knew was that kings didn't hide in cellars while their kingdoms burned around them. Kings faced their enemies. Even if they couldn't win. Kings died in daylight. In the open.

He reached the top of the steps. He'd expected bodies, but the cathedral was almost empty. The wreckage of a dozen scorpions lay scattered around the door. The air stank of smoke, of burned wood and scorched flesh. No bodies, though. None alive, none dead.

He heard voices. Men, calling to each other. Outside. Not screaming and dying calling, but the matter-of-fact shouts of men busy at work. He hobbled to the door, blinking. No dragons? Was that possible?

A gray glimmer of dawn lit the horizon. Not much light, and at first he couldn't see the damage. The Tower of Air was a stump. The Speaker's Tower was still there, although it seemed to be missing several large pieces. He scanned the silhouette of the palace, looking for anything else that was familiar and finding little. The Tower of Dusk, the Tower of Dawn, the Humble Tower, the Azure Tower . . . all gone.

"Hello?" he called. "Did we win then?" There were dim figures moving in the darkness where the walls ought to be. They had bits missing, he began to see. Quite a lot of bits missing. It was warm outside too, strangely and almost uncomfortably so.

In the half-light a shape took form nearby. Jehal swore and jumped back, lost his footing and fell back through the cathedral door. "Shit! Crap crap crap!" He was staring at a dragon only a dozen yards away. Rather, he was staring at a dragon's head. Lying on the ground. Still. Not moving. The size of a carriage.

He squinted, tracing the outline of the shape back into the gloom. Definitely a dragon. Dead.

An armored hand reached down toward him. Held out to help him up. Jehal took it without thinking.

"You should be underground." The voice was Vale's, ground flat with fatigue.

"Did you actually *win*?"

"Bluntly? I don't know. I don't think so. We drove them off. That's all."

"There's a dead dragon in my palace."

"There are more than twenty." In his other hand, the one that wasn't helping Jehal to his feet, Vale was holding something strangely familiar. The Speaker's Spear.

"You won, Vale. You actually won."

The Night Watchman laughed in bitter choking hacks. "No. We didn't get them all. And even then . . ." He shook his head. "Do you want to see what victory looks like? I will show you. Come!"

Jehal pursed his lips. "Is this the part where you throw me off the top of a tall tower and then say I slipped?"

Vale slapped him so hard it made his head spin. The next thing he knew there were arms around his waist and he was picked up and thrown over the Night Watchman's shoulder like a sack of corn. "All a joke to you, is it?"

"Let me go!" Panic and angry affront fought each other for Jehal's attention.

"No. Come and see your realms. Come and see what's left."

Jehal supposed he ought to be afraid, but he wasn't. He was tired. *Tired of fighting all the time. And he's not going to do it. He's not going to kill me. He can't. However much he wants to, he can't. It's not in him.* "Put me down, Vale. If you're going to murder me, at least give me the dignity of walking to my doom, eh?" *Although, shameful to admit as it is, this is considerably less painful than walking would be.*

"You did this, Speaker Jehal. You and all your kind." Vale started to clamber over a heap of rubble that had once been part of the palace wall. In the half-light, draped over his shoulder, Jehal still couldn't see much. What he could see looked a mess. "You don't get to die. You haven't earned that yet. I want you to see." Reaching the top of the wall, a section that was still intact, Vale dropped Jehal on the ground next to a shattered scorpion.

"Ouch."

Vale crouched beside him, gripped him by the throat and hauled him to his feet. "Do you see?"

"Do I see what?" All he could see were ruined walls. The jagged remains of charred wood and steel that had lined them. Smashed towers. When he peered, he could see men moving among the rubble. Now and then he heard a shout. They were clearing the walls of debris, he realized. Very slowly, but they were clearing the walls and putting new scorpions in place. "You never give up, do you? I'm impressed."

Vale wrenched Jehal's head around to the glowing embers that had once been the City of Dragons. "Are you impressed by that?" he hissed.

Jehal pulled himself away. His leg gave way again and he stumbled toward the battlements. Vale caught him.

"You don't get away that easily, Jehal."

For a few moments he didn't know what to say. The city was gone. Totally gone. Torn to pieces and then set on fire. What hadn't been smashed, burned. "Zafir," he whispered. "Zafir did this."

"No. You did."

"No." *Get a hold of yourself.* "No, I didn't do this, and now I think of it, neither did Zafir. You can blame us for a lot of things, Night Watchman, but we never woke any dragons. It's gone. So what? We'll build another."

Vale's fingers tightened on his arm, gripping painfully. "Build another?"

"Yes." Jehal shook himself free a second time, careful not to fall over. "That's what we do. Build another. You won, Night Watchman. You have fulfilled your purpose. Your name will go down in history. You have averted catastrophe. Well done. Now piss off because I have a lot of work to do."

For a moment the Night Watchman seemed lost in thought. He was staring at the Adamantine Spear. "I slew six dragons in the night. There." He pointed at something that looked like a dragon turned to stone and broken into pieces. "There." Another, much the same. "There." The third was largely intact. The look in Vale's eye was of a man in deep thought. Which wasn't what Jehal wanted at all.

"Go find some builders who can clear up this mess."

Vale didn't move. His face didn't flicker, but there was a tear in the corner of his eye. "The sun is coming up," he murmured.

"Yes. Valuable working time is about to go to waste, eh?" *And there I was, thinking for a moment of keeping you alive. Letting you see me have my victory, day after day after day. Letting that be my revenge. But no. You're too dangerous for that.* He turned away.

"Jehal."

"I am your speaker, Night Watchman. Address me properly or I'll have your tongue cut out."

"Your Holiness." Vale sneered. "How many dragons went missing, Your Holiness?"

"Oh, I don't know. I was too busy putting down Zafir. Ask the alchemists."

"The alchemists are largely dead, Your Holiness. The Adamantine Eyrie is gone. Look."

Jehal squinted. All he could see was a thin haze of smoke that smothered everything. "I see nothing."

"I know. You were ever thus. The eyrie is gone. Your dragons are gone. Your palace is gone. Legions of my men are gone. Six hundred scorpions lined these walls last night. Perhaps a dozen have survived. We have more, of course. But we won't get them ready in time to make a difference. Go back to your tunnels, Jehal. Live in the filth and the darkness where you belong. For what little time you can." He sighed. "No, Jehal, I did not win." He was staring at something behind Jehal's shoulder.

Jehal spun to face him, furious. "That is the last . . ." The words died in his mouth. Instinct made him follow the Night Watchman's gaze. On the farthest corner of the palace, away toward the Mirror Lakes, a white dragon sat staring back at them, barely visible in the haze of smoke but clear nonetheless. Another smaller shape sat beside it. Dark. A young one. And then he saw another adult, and then another, squatting on the walls. As he watched, a fifth and then a sixth dragon glided silently out of the gloom and settled to watch. Then a seventh and an eighth. Three were hatchlings, barely out of the egg.

"What are you waiting for?" roared Vale, shattering the stillness and almost making Jehal jump out of his own skin.

I ought to run, Jehal thought. *Right now.* He glanced down toward the doors to the cathedral. *A fit man, strong and agile, could get there in time. Pity that's not me.*

The young dragon moved. Sprang down from the wall and streaked like lightning through the rubble. Jehal had never seen anything move so fast. *Hunting cats, maybe. And maybe a fit man couldn't have reached the doors in time after all.*

He was shaking. The dragon was a lot bigger than it had seemed over on the wall next to a full-grown adult. It ran up the side of a small half-toppled tower at the end of the wall in front of Vale, spread its wings and hissed.

Your fear is delicious, little one. The voice erupted out of nowhere inside Jehal's head. His heart tripped and then hammered in his chest, and a cold settled over him like a blanket of snow, suffocating, silent and deathly. He stared at the dragons and the dragons stared back. He could see something different in their eyes, in the way they held themselves, even across the distance between them. The hunger and the desire, the impatience and the sheer raw force, they were all there just like any other dragon. But these had something else. They fixed him with their eyes and held him fast. There was a coldness to them. An intelligence. A relentless determination. He could feel them, feel them in his head, reckoning him.

The dragons stared, and in their gazes they showed him exactly what he was. Small and shallow and worthless. Crippled and useless. With two working legs, he might have tried to run anyway. As it was, all he could do was . . . nothing.

Where are your words now? How will people remember you, Jehal? Jehal the great? Jehal the brave? Jehal the strong?

The young dragon jumped from the tower and swooped. The Night Watchman held up the Adamantine Spear, let out a howl and charged to meet it.

Jehal the wise? Jehal the good?

The dragon and the Night Watchman came together. At the last instant Vale shifted impossibly sideways and kicked off the battlements. He was flying almost sideways through the air as he reached the dragon.

How will people remember you, Jehal?

"Get out of my head!" he screamed, yet the voice wasn't anyone but himself.

The dragon's jaws snapped. The Night Watchman's spear flashed. And then they passed one another and both crashed to the ground. A shock of air and light knocked Jehal stumbling back. His good leg caught on a piece of tortured metal that had once been a scorpion. His bad leg buckled and he went down.

Jehal the cripple? No, you can't hide behind that.

The Night Watchman's spear was buried in the dragon's skull. Just like the statue that had once stood in the center of the City of Dragons. And, like the statue, the dragon was now stone. The Night Watchman was still moving. Just. He labored ever so slowly to his feet. Jehal struggled to do the same.

If there's anyone left, they'll make jokes about you. Look at you, Jehal! Can't even get up.

Vale rose shakily. For a moment Jehal couldn't put his finger on what was wrong with him. Only for a moment, though, until he turned. The dragon had torn half of Vale's face off. Vale staggered and made a loud wet hooting sort of noise. He reached the spear and pulled it out of the now-stone dragon, then turned to face the others. They didn't move. Vale was swaying like a drunkard.

"Kill them!" Jehal screamed. "Use it! Kill them!"

Vale turned back to Jehal again. You couldn't read much into his expression because his lower jaw wasn't there. His eyes were wild. For a moment Jehal thought Vale was going to kill him. Then the Night Watchman threw the spear as hard as he could, a mighty throw, right across Speaker's Yard and through the open gates of the Glass Cathedral. He staggered, lurched sideways, stepped off the edge of the wall and crashed into the rubble below.

Somewhere off to one side came the loose rattle of a ragged volley of scorpion bolts. In the haze the dragons launched themselves silently into the air—all except the white one, which stayed there, watching him. Jehal couldn't move. Couldn't even stand. He was on his knees, shaking like a kitten.

Look at you. Think of all the people you've killed. Betrayed. Murdered. You know you're worth less than any of them. Deep down, you know that to be true.

Shut up shut up SHUT UP!

Two or three scorpions fired again. After that they were silent. The dragons moved sedately across the palace, slowly, calmly and methodically crushing anything that was alive. They didn't roar and they didn't breathe fire. Eventually the white one launched itself into the air. It glided across the distance between them and landed with a quiet grace where Jehal knelt. It reached out for him with its claws. Jehal let out a thin wail and scrabbled vainly away.

The dragon picked him up and looked at him, the dragon that was supposed to have been his wedding present. It cocked its head curiously as if wondering at what a sorry excuse for a king he was.

He tried to beg but all he managed was a whimper and a whine. His bladder emptied. *See. You can't even die well.*

Little one, enough.

"Zafir!"

The dragon squeezed. Jehal's ribs snapped like twigs. All the air in his lungs burst out of his mouth and then everything from his stomach too. He had a moment or two to feel his hips shatter and then his bowels ruptured, his guts spilled out down his useless legs and his heart was crushed to a stop.

The dragon tossed him aside and moved on.

Epilogue

SILENCE AND THE ENDLESS SEA

In the stillness of the underworld the spirit of the dragon moved with wonder and deliberate purpose. So many dead dragons. Dulled things, moving without direction, looking for a new home. Even here the alchemical potions wove their magic. How? How did you poison the dead?

The spirit mused on that for a moment, then threw the thought away. It skirted around the hole where the dead earth goddess and her slayer had held the Nothing at bay for so long. They were gone now. The hole was getting bigger and the Nothing was seeping slowly through. Now there, *there* was something that could kill a dragon.

Yes, the spirit of the dragon kept well clear of that. It had found something else. Hatchling flesh, waiting for the spirit to wake it. Eggs. A few here, a handful there. And one great clutch of them. So many eggs. So many dragon souls searching for new skin.

QUAI'SHU SAT IN HIS CABIN, quietly staring out at the sea, at the waves rolling away from the back of his ship. He felt a warmth inside him, the quiet contentment of someone who had worked very hard for a very long time and who had finally got what they wanted.

"Sea-Lord? Sea-Lord?"

THE DRAGON-SPIRIT RACED TOWARD THE clutch, dragging others in its wake. More had gone ahead, many more. The spirit felt them shimmer out of the underworld as they merged into the waiting bodies. It followed. It felt the moment, the pull of new life, dragging it away, and then it was born. Alive. With a single violent jerk, the dragon shattered the shell that held its new form.

Two hatchlings were already loose in the hatchery. One had a human in its mouth and was shaking him from side to side like a dog worrying a rabbit. The man was already dead. The hatchery was smaller than the ones the dragon remembered, much smaller. Cramped and smelly. Smelled of wood and tar and water.

In the doorway stood a silhouette. A silhouette of silver.

Be STILL!

The dragon hissed. *No.*

One hatchling sprang; the other dropped the dead man. The sorcerer who blocked their escape shifted, the silver he wrapped around him flowing like water into a long spike in front of him. It touched—a scratch—the first hatchling, and the dragon fell dead. The second hatchling ripped the sorcerer's head off. Even as it did, the silver flowed again. The hatchling shuddered and collapsed beside the sorcerer's corpse. They both lay still while the sorcerer's liquid silver turned hard and dull on the floor.

The dragon called Silence jumped on the corpse. Everyone else had fled. It seized the dead sorcerer's head between its jaws and bit down. Hard.

Free . . .

"SEA-LORD?"

With a sigh Quai'Shu eased his aching joints out of his comfortable chair and stood up. As he did, he happened to glance out of the stern windows at the end of his cabin.

Half his ships were burning.

Quai'Shu's jaw fell open. Before he could think, a voice thundered straight into his head, just like the moon-sorcerers had done.

I am Silence, it said, *and I am hungry.*

ACKNOWLEDGMENTS

With thanks to Simon Spanton, devourer of unnecessary prologues, who asked for dragons and got more than he bargained for. To John Jarrold, agent overlord. To the copy editors and proofreaders, whose names I've rarely known. To Dominic Harman and Stephen Youll for their gorgeous dragons and the artists who turned them into covers. To Jon Weir, who demanded the duel.

To lovers of dragons. And to all alchemists everywhere, unseen, unrewarded, tirelessly working to keep our monsters at bay.

To you, for reading this.

For any who want to explore the world of the dragons for its own sake, you can do so at the online gazetteer at www.stephendeas.com/gazetteer.

And lastly, if you liked this book, please tell someone!